The Fool

Taylor K Scott

This is a work of fiction. Names, characters, places and incidents are either the product of the author's imagination or are used fictitiously. Any resemblance to actual persons, living or dead, business establishments, events, or locales is entirely coincidental.

Copyright ©2023 Taylor K. Scott

All rights reserved. No part of this publication may be reproduced, stored in or introduced into a retrieval system, or transmitted, in any form, or by any means (electronic, mechanical, photocopying, recording, or otherwise) without prior written permission of the author.

Warning: The following work of fiction describes content of a sexual nature. It also discusses sensitive themes including violence and mental health issues. See Author's Note for more information.

DEDICATION

To my fellow cygnet inkers, a special group of authors, readers and reviewers, set up by the amazing TL Swan, whose books got me hooked on this wonderful journey.

MUSICAL INFLUENCES

No Air – Jordin Sparks

Kissing You – Des'ree

Iris – Goo Goo Dolls

Say Something – A Great Big World and Christina Aquilera

I Wanna Dance With Somebody – Marian Hill

Numb – Linkin Park

Dangerous Woman – Ariana Grande

Breathin – Ariana Grande

Stronger – Sugababes

I Fell in Love with the Devil – Avril Lavigne (The Devil-Book 3)

Into Your Arms – Witt Lowry

Apologize – Timbaland (feat. One Republic)

Here With Me - Dido

Keeping Your Head Up - Birdy

ACKNOWLEDGMENTS

Thank you to the community of writers and readers out there who have answered questions, read my work, given me advice, and shared my work. Thank you to all of you!

To my beta readers, Liz Rogers, Freya Martin, Charlotte Mieu, Phoebe Black, and Mama Sue, who all took the time to read this book during the early stages. Just to have someone read my work and offer their opinion is always so empowering for me. I sincerely appreciate you offering me your time, support, and advice.

I must also thank my poor, suffering husband for supporting me through my obsession with writing. Not only has he had to live with my reading habit, which is becoming more and more consuming, but also has the added bonus of losing me to my own works of fiction. Know that I love you dearly, as well as our two beautiful girls, and appreciate all the encouragement you have given me.

Finally, but most importantly, thanks to everyone who has taken a chance on my novel. I hope it hasn't disappointed, and that you might take a chance to read some of my upcoming releases. Thank you so much again.

Author's Note
(Trigger Warnings)

I write fictional books that encompass more than a central romance plot. Experience with mental health, living with PTSD, and working with people from different backgrounds have all helped me to shape my characters and their storylines. A lot of what I've included in my books is based on real people and real situations, or at least, a version of them. This includes my own experiences. I write stories that are sometimes hard to read; I don't shy away from trauma. I also don't write flawless characters because real people are never without fault. My characters might act irrationally or choose an option that an objective person might question, but they do, based on what I've seen and lived, behave realistically.

This series contains scenes that may be hard to read and may trigger some people. They include sexual, physical, and emotional abuse. This series has a major theme of mental health running through it, including attempted suicide, depression, abuse, bullying, anxiety, and PTSD. There are also references to early miscarriage.

"The fool doth think he is wise,
But the wise man knows himself to be a fool."

-William Shakespeare

Prologue

Let us begin with a party.

An innocent night of care-free fun amongst teenagers.

Nate Carter, the popular boy with a heart, was throwing one of his infamous bashes that aimed to let the kids of Westlake Prep let down their hair and give into their urges within the safe confines of the Carter household. Everyone knew who the Carters were, the girls in particular. There were few who hadn't had a crush on at least one of them. The fact that they were known for their charming and respectful personalities as well as their mother's Italian good looks, caused many a girl to daydream about being their girlfriend. Whereas the boys all wanted to be on first-name terms with them. Nate never discriminated against anyone who wanted to come, so long as they respected both his house and his rules.

However, with the number of people who were sure to attend, it was impossible for him to know each and everyone there. The odd guy with a pocketful of LSD; maybe a girl with itchy fingers for Mrs Carter's jewelry; a man looking to take advantage of a naïve teenage girl, or perhaps a girl who had just been betrayed in the worst possible way and was looking for somewhere to escape from the pain. It would have been so easy for them to slip in undetected. Everyone knew Nate Carter; Nate Carter didn't know everyone.

For one of those people, this night could have potentially been her last. Perhaps if she had met someone like the boy himself, he might have been able to change despair into hope. But she didn't meet him on this night, she met someone who sought to take advantage of her vulnerability. Somebody who pushed her over the edge.

She only just managed to survive that night and what was to follow, but she didn't begin living again for a long time. She didn't begin to believe in a '*happy ever after*' or forgiveness until she finally met the youngest Carter brother.

And on that note, I shall begin with my story. The story of how I fell for ***The Fool***, otherwise known as Nathaniel Carter.

Chapter 1

Past

Bea, 18

Have you ever asked yourself, what's the worst thing you've ever done?

What would your answer be?

Ran away from home?

Slept with another woman's husband?

Caused someone to lose their life?

Called your brother in the middle of the night after taking a potent concoction of vodka and painkillers? And you did it right; you took those pills over time, hoping that when someone finally found you, you would have already slipped away.

I managed to tick off each of these transgressions before I'd even turned nineteen. My run of bad decisions began early in life, and I take responsibility for all of them. I could list off my excuses, and blame others for what I did, but ultimately, it was me who took my brother's car without permission. It was my body that gave itself to a man who wasn't free to take it. It was my actions that caused another to die, regardless of what they said. It was my finger that shakily managed to dial Ben's number when I thought I was on my way out of this world. It was me; all me.

My admission has got you thinking now, got you questioning what the hell happened to turn this girl into a monster. It all began when my high school began an innocent online platform so students could talk to each other. A safe place, a private place, an unpoliced place. While they thought it would be a secure cyberspace for us to communicate about school projects, missed notes, or perhaps college choices, it turned into a place where you could let loose your ugly without anyone knowing who you really are. The wholesome jock and the homecoming queen who smile and hold the door open for everyone, the head of the school council, even the kid who donates his time to charity, they could all become villainous.

If you ever had the chance to read some of the comments that appeared online, you might believe the seven deadly sins had come up from the pits of hell to wreak havoc.

Envy frequently appeared in the form of gossiping about the girl who got the boy; did you hear? She opened her legs on the first date because she's a slut with enough STDs to land you in the hospital if you so much as look at her.

Greed came in the form of the popular kids who wanted even more people to look up to them. The more likes and followers you had, the more you could tell yourself you were better than all the rest.

Vanity was for all those kids who masked what they really

looked like with too many filters to count, people like my sister.

Lust is something we could all be accused of, the wanting someone from behind closed doors, even those who we already thought we had. I'll openly admit, I lusted after my boyfriend, even after he hurt me in the worst possible way.

Sloth was for those kids who spent hours in front of this platform when they should have been working, spending time with their families, being at school, or even getting fresh air. It became an obsession for most, a time waster, something to help you avoid having to face real life.

Wrath frequently gave into itself on this platform, for where else could you vent your kind of hate without comeback, or revealing your true identity?

Pride came to all of us. No one wanted to admit it was getting just a little too much on there; to ruin it for everybody else.

And finally, gluttony. This was on all those people like me, the ones who kept on returning. You knew it was bad for you, and yet, you kept on going back for more – *a glutton for punishment.*

It didn't destroy me straight away. Like any vice, it crept up on me, prayed on my weaknesses, my fears, as well as my bad days. Just when my senior year was coming to an end, and I naively thought I had survived it all, the bad days came at me like a series of tidal waves. I fought them at first, dove straight beneath the break, but pretty soon, they came at me without any pause for breath. I could no longer duck below the torrent of crushing water.

It was easy to spot the passive-aggressive messages that turned up on Western High's webchat, the sly digs from people who you thought were your friends. However, I would usually let it slide off my back. I was the tomboy who had managed to bag one of the pretty boys; I was positively an urban legend. But this is exactly how Dean and I got together. I was one of the boys until my body morphed into something that could no longer hide the fact that I was a girl. A flirtation ensued before he finally leaned in and kissed me. It was so out of the blue, it was like a fairy tale. I kissed him right back and that was how we became Western High's odd couple. I never paid it much attention, not even when I was told outright that I was extremely lucky to have him.

But then, shortly after me, my sister also morphed into something that made her look more woman than child. Whereas I had kept being who I was, she embraced the world of social media, the vanity, the make-up, and handbags. She seemed happy, even if I didn't understand how she had come to change so much in such a short period of time. I didn't question it, but that didn't mean I didn't worry about her.

Bea, 18

"What the hell are you doing?"

I have to try hard to stop myself from laughing at the scene playing out before me because from where I'm standing, it looks pretty ridiculous. Full on pout with makeup troweled on to perfection, my baby sister, Emma, is extending her favorite life support, her mobile, at arm's length. Several clicks later, she studies her art for several intense moments before finally responding to the actual human being in the room.

"I'm taking a selfie for my profile page," she says as though I'm pathetically stupid for not having come to that conclusion myself. Being only a year younger than me, she pities the fact that I don't choose to make myself up in the middle of a Saturday afternoon, only to stare at my phone with a pose that any

Kardashian would be proud of.

"You should try it sometime. You might get yourself more friends if you did."

"Oh, because befriending people who take an interest in me based on how many likes I get on social media is clearly the way forward. Trust me, I know what people say about me and I'd rather not see it in black and white."

I scoff over her ridiculous outlook on life, shake my head with an eye roll, and wander off to answer the door.

Don't ask me why my boyfriend of two years insists on knocking when he could just walk in. Maybe he's being polite, maybe he's being respectful, or maybe it's because he always looks like he's about to piss his pants every time he sees my big brother, Ben. Either way, he's here that often, I've told him he should just come in.

Dean's shaggy blond hair greets me as he continues staring down at his phone when I open the front door. He manages to kiss me on the cheek without even taking his eyes away from the screen.

"Hi?" I exclaim, seeking acknowledgment from the guy who once told me he could stare at me all day. Granted, it was leading up to a rather intimate moment, but still, it kind of bums me out that he's so easily distracted. "I could have been Emma for all you know," I huff.

Taking his sweet time to look up at me, he smirks cheekily and with an air of confidence any life coach would be proud of, before sauntering over to kiss me properly.

"Nah, I saw your shoes," he says as Emma sashays into the kitchen, face plastered in makeup and wearing a low-cut top that shows off her very sizeable bust. "She wouldn't be caught dead in trainers, would you, Em? Nice pic, by the way, you already have at least a dozen likes."

She gasps over the very idea of being seen in my raggedy old trainers, then proceeds to pour herself a glass of OJ.

"I don't do scruffy shoes, that's Bea's signature style."

Feigning insult, I mouth the word 'bitch' to her before sinking back against Dean's lean frame with a casual grin. He wraps his arms around my waist before resting his chin on top of my head because I'm that small.

"Maybe she has a point, babe," he says to me, "you could sex it up a bit. The guys are always telling me what a tomboy you are. I'm sure Emma would help you out."

"Damn straight!" Emma's eyes bulge with renewed enthusiasm. "Please let me make you over, pretty please!"

She dramatically sinks to the floor, hands poised in a begging position, making both Dean and I laugh, just as Mom walks in with two heavy bags of shopping.

"Gee, thanks, you guys, I think I'm actually offended," I say half-heartedly as I rush over to relieve Mom of the bags, which have left red indents inside of her small fingers. She blows onto her mangled hands before offering a smile in thanks. Neither Dean nor Emma have noticed the exchange, being that they are currently engaged in a non-verbal affair with their phones.

"Mom, do you think I need a makeover?"

"What? No, you are beautiful; don't mess with perfection!" she says with her mom goggles on, but I love her for it. A pang of hurt hits my chest without warning. Why doesn't Dean see me in this rose-tinted light? I thought he loved me, but if he did, surely, he'd want me to be who I am, not an Emma wannabe.

"Yesss! One hundred likes in only five minutes. That's how it's done, bitches!"

She begins jumping up and down like an idiot. She manages to gain Dean's attention with her jiggling chest, hypnotizing his primitive urges with their rhythmic movements.

"What?" Mom gasps when she finally looks up from sorting items around in the fridge. "Oh, where are you going, Emma? Out on a date?"

"No, why?"

Emma looks positively confused, not realizing it's a perfectly valid question given the fact she looks ready to hit the local nightlife at three in the afternoon. Mom simply gestures to her outfit with a quirk of her brow.

"Oh, no," she says as she flaps her hand in front of her perfectly coiffed head, laughing at Mom condescendingly because she's clueless to social media. "This is just for my profile pic."

Mom makes an 'oh' shape with her mouth but still looks just as oblivious. I shake my head and smile, silently telling her it's not something to worry about, just another first-world issue.

"Right, then," Emma finally says to me before grabbing a hold of my hand, "time to get this party started. Dean, come back in a couple of hours, and I'll have her ready for you."

She blows him a kiss as he walks over to peck me on the cheek.

"Can't wait," he says with a suggestive waggle of his eyebrows.

This was the beginning of the end; the moment I began to

realize that being just me was never going to be enough.

———

Bea

"Is this really necessary?" I huff at the mirror as Emma vigorously straightens my hair; I wouldn't be surprised if she's slowly killing off my hair follicles.

"I've seen your profile and yes, it is necessary," she sighs. "After all, you can't expect to hold on to a major catch like Dean and not put some effort into it."

"Hey, I do," I argue, "I spend every weekend with him, and last month, I paid for us to go paintballing. I then acted the submissive girlfriend in front of the guys who, once upon a time, I would have been laughing and joking with. Guys who I could beat any one of them when challenged to an arm wrestle…well, before they developed muscles, that is. I kept a smile up all evening and even engaged in useless chit-chat with their sinfully boring girlfriends. I put on such a show, even Dean thought I liked them. Not to mention I gave him my…"

I fall silent and look away embarrassed, feeling annoyed that I let my verbal diarrhea run away with me.

"Virginity?" She smirks at me through the mirror. "And how long did you make him wait for that one? Two years, was it?" She almost laughs but the look I give instantly stops her. "Do you know how much shit he got for that? It was all over his profile page last year. Even the kids in my year were jibing him for not popping your cherry sooner. One person even suggested that maybe you were a guy, especially with the way you dress and all."

"Seriously?!" I cry with outrage. "How the hell did people know? Surely that's between Dean and me."

"God, don't you ever look on there?" she says in an almost disgusted tone of voice. "People just know, especially when you're in high school. I lost mine ages ago."

With those words, I spin the chair around and drop my mouth open in shock, looking akin to a gaping fish out of water. I didn't even know she had a boyfriend.

"Emma," I finally manage to say, though still sounding utterly flabbergasted, "why didn't you tell me? Who with?"

For a moment or two, I think she's going to break down in tears, she looks that sad, but then she shakes it off and grins back at me with one of her online fake smiles.

"Oh, some guy I went on a date with a few times; a college guy," she announces like it's something to be proud of. "Losing your virginity isn't a big deal anymore. Men expect you to go that bit further, you know? Look at Love Island; you need to be beach body ready and looking like a porn star twenty-four-seven."

"I'm going to ignore that whole pile of S-H-I-T you just said and focus on the important bit here," I reply, suddenly standing up to match my baby sister's stance. As her big sister and best friend, I have to show her that I'm here for her, that I will protect her if she needs me to. "What happened? After you slept with the college guy?"

"Well, he had to go back to college," she shrugs like it's no big deal. "I wasn't expecting a marriage proposal or anything."

She can't fool me though, I can see the tears threatening to fall, as well as behind the mask she's trying to wear, so I take her into my arms and let her give me the truth. With relief, she takes it and eventually sobs against my shoulder for what feels like a long time. Closing my eyes to her muffled cries, I weep with her.

"It's fine, I'm fine," she eventually says with plenty of sniffing, desperately wiping underneath her eyes so her mascara won't run.

"Listen, Emma," I begin, feeling frustrated at her trying to brush over her pain, like it's an everyday occurrence to lose your virginity to a complete stranger who blanks you afterward. I grip both of her shoulders with a look of authority before telling her that it is not 'fine' at all. "Promise me, you will save the next time for someone you really care about, and who really cares about you. He took advantage of an underage girl, that is not 'fine'."

"Oh, Bea," she smiles, "you are so blissfully naïve to the real world."

I look at her with a furrowed brow, only now realizing this is truly what she believes. This is how she has been schooled to think, through peer pressure and the damn media blasting out mindless crap twenty-four-seven. She's a smart girl with amazing grades, but when it comes down to it, she believes in all this reality TV, social media, barbie doll beauty bullshit. How has it come to this?

I couldn't sleep that night; I was too busy worrying about Emma and how everything is beginning to affect her. My little sister, my best friend, lost to what society expects teenage girls to aspire to. She was like me before the hormones hit, so how did we end up so different? How can I help her if I don't understand any of it? How can I keep her ***my*** Emma without losing myself in the process?

I never expected to find the answers to those questions; not in one sleepless night anyway.

I never expected to have her betray me in the worst possible way, shortly before Nathaniel Carter's party.

I never expected a lot of things to happen that night or the days that were to follow.

I never expected my heart to stop beating. But it did. In more ways than one.

Chapter 2

Present

Bea 27

"I swear my boss fucking hates me," I cry to Leah after another hideous day at work.

"What the hell did the jerk do this time?" she asks, having heard this declaration nearly every day for the last eighteen months. She's way feistier than I am and would have happily kicked his ass by now. Not only that, but she would also have done so with a huge smile on her face. Believe me, I've been tempted to let her more than once over the past year and a half of working under my bully of a boss; he certainly deserves it.

"Nothing new, really, it's just the way he belittles me in front of everyone who comes into the office. I hate him…with a passion!"

My boss is none other than Nathaniel Carter, or 'Nate' as he is known to those he likes, which is pretty much everyone else but me. Who would have thought the popular boy with a heart from school would end up being such an asshole to work for?

Alas, when I took the job working for the infamous Cameron Carter of Westlake Prep, I was desperate. Besides, he had always seemed nice, and his employees all raved about what an awesome boss he was. And I'll admit, he is. His brother, however, is the complete opposite.

I began working for him after I was offered extra training to become a personal assistant. I was originally a receptionist, far away from the top floor and all the bosses. However, when Cameron forced his lay-about brother to come and actually work for a living, I was 'promoted' to being his assistant. Having known who he was throughout high school, being that he was the town's golden boy, I was a little excited to meet him. Alas, the reality didn't exactly live up to the legend of Nate, high-school-dream-boy, Carter. In fact, I have absolutely no idea who everyone had been creaming their panties over, but it surely can't have been the guy who I have to work for every day of the week.

"Why don't you just leave, hun?" Leah asks the obvious. "But kick his balls on the way out."

We laugh over the delicious thought of kicking him in the crotch with steel-capped boots, possibly encrusted with metal spikes on the toe. Seriously though, if I don't laugh, I'll end up crying. Lord knows he's made me do enough of that over the last year or so.

"Because the big boss, Cameron Carter, has been so good to me over the years," I explain, "he took me on with virtually no experience, kept me going even when his bitchy girlfriends insisted that he fire me, and then paid for me to train up as a PA. He even promoted me to Nathaniel's PA because he was so impressed with my professionalism. I can't just take the company's money to train me and then fuck off."

"People do that all the time, Bea," she says as she begins rubbing my leg soothingly. "No one would look down on you if you did."

"Perhaps, but before I was promoted to Nathaniel, I loved it at Medina Technologies. It has a real family feel and they reward their employees well. Like, really well! I'd be hard pushed to find the same benefits package anywhere else."

"Hmm, well couldn't you ask to be someone else's PA?" she suggests.

"I don't know, it would be like taking a step down. The only other way to go is to be promoted to Cameron's PA, but I know Jack isn't leaving anytime soon. Face it, I'm stuck."

"Well, you might have to reconsider that step down if this continues, Bea. I've already had to hold your brother off from going down there to beat the shit out of him," she says matter of factly. I believe her too. Living with Ben means he's witnessed what Nate Carter has put me through. Ben is just a tad overprotective of me; though, I only have myself to blame for that one.

"I hope it's not affecting you guys?" I ask, feeling suddenly panicked. Leah is Ben's girlfriend so I would hate for them to be arguing over his attempts to march in and save the day, so to speak.

"Nah, I have your big brother wrapped around my little finger," she giggles at the same time as holding up her right pinky.

"Well, I know that, but he can be a right sulky, stubborn bastard when he wants to be," I reply.

"True," she nods with a smirk.

"Is someone talking about me?" Ben shouts out as he walks through the door. "I heard the words 'stubborn' and 'bastard' being thrown around."

Ben walks into the room, all six foot something of him, filling it like a basketball player hooked on steroids. His messy, dark blonde hair pointing this way and that in an effortless, Abercrombie and Fitch model kind of style. His unapologetic grin spreads over his chiseled features the moment his eyes feast on Leah's naked legs and low-cut top. The boy is always thinking with his penis and feels zero shame in displaying this fact openly and proudly.

Ben, the easiest lay in his high school days, chased, caught, and pretty much fucked the entire cheerleading squad in true cliché jock fashion. Even though he's my big brother, I know he's a good-looking guy with a body that is the envy of most gym junkies. However, he chose to pursue the one girl who didn't drop her panties within the first five seconds of meeting him. Like a true player, this only made the hunt that much more exhilarating for him. The poor guy never saw that it was Leah who was trapping his little heart until it was too late. She definitely won the initial round of cat and mouse.

Smitten as he is, Ben has undeniably turned the figurative tables, refusing to move out with her until he deems me fit enough to live without his brotherly protection. I can protest as much as I like, but Ben takes stubbornness to an all-new, sky-soaring level, arguing black is white if it suits him. Leah may as well live here, but I know, deep down, she wants them to make that next step together, in their own space, without his kid sister cramping their style with her history of fucked up mental health.

"Your sister's boss is being a grade-A asshole again," Leah says to him with a wink for me.

"Beatrice Summers, for the love of God, give me the word and I will be down there so fast, you won't even see me pass through your office to get to him," he says through gritted, frustrated teeth.

"No!" I gasp, sloshing my wine as I reach out to flap at him. "As subtle as your form of payback would be, it would completely ruin my career. I can handle it, I promise."

Perhaps I need to stop telling them everything, but what can I say? Ben's always been my go-to port of call; my safety net; my big brother in every way.

"Fine, but then we need to stop talking about it because it's going to wind me up. Leah, baby, are we still on tonight?" he asks.

"Yep, I'll nip home to get ready and then you can pick me up, like a proper date."

Ben rolls his eyes, knowing he'll have to face her roommate, Saffy, who drives him up the wall with her political rants and feminist rhetoric. I've never met her before, but I sure as hell have had to hear him going on about how much she annoys him. Whenever I suggest moving out might be the answer to this problem, he usually tuts and musses with my hair before skulking off to his man pit.

"Ok but that means we're coming back here tonight," he declares when she gets up to go.

"Oh, God, please don't come back here having loud, cringe-worthy sex," I groan.

"Sorry, little sis, but we're always loud!" He smiles smugly at the same time as I put my finger in my mouth to feign sickness. Leah's no better, grinning as she kisses him on the cheek to say goodbye.

"See you later, Bea," she says with a wave, "we'll talk strategies later."

When the door bangs shut, Ben puts his hand on my shoulder and smiles sympathetically. He's an overprotective pain in the ass sometimes, but he has always had my back. No one could ask for a better guy to be their brother.

"Seriously, Bea," he says softly, "I hate seeing that guy upset you like this. Don't let him bring you down. You must be good if that Cameron whatever-his-name-is thinks you are, he is the CEO after all."

I'm so exhausted and crestfallen over it all, I simply offer him a fake smile and a nod. I think he knows I'm pretending but chooses to let it go. After a moment of contemplative thought next to one another, he eventually gets up to go and get ready for his date. Meanwhile, I release a long sigh and take a healthy swig of wine. Another night alone with a good book and solitary drinking. I would call my best friend, Finn, but I know he's working at his top-notch restaurant. Sometimes, Finn is the only one who can bring me out of my funk, but I guess that's not going to happen tonight. At least it's Thursday already, which means only one more day to get through with Satan in a suit.

Bea

"Good morning, Mr Carter," I beam with a big fake smile for him as he walks through my office. My grin is stretched across on my face to the point whereby my cheeks hurt from how horrifically wide it is. Of course, Nathaniel completely ignores me and walks past with a familiar frown, all the way up to his own office. I shrug the whole thing off for it's no different from his usual response to me. Robotically, I turn to face my desk and switch on my computer for the day, however, out of the corner of my eye, I notice he has stopped. My whole body freezes in nervous anticipation of what he is about to complain about.

Truthfully, it could be absolutely anything. He once chastised me in front of the whole office for wearing a blouse he considered to be too bright. He also, rather embarrassingly, called it an abomination to fashion and an insult to anyone who had the misfortune to look directly at it. That was a particularly bad day, one that led straight to a bottle of wine in the fridge as soon as I got home and cried for the entire evening. I'm ashamed to say, I threw the shirt away.

"Some of us have been here since seven, Miss Summers," he says dryly, "the least you can do is be here on time."

"Oh, I decided to pick up your mail early. I know how much you hate waiting for it, so I thought I'd have it here waiting for you," I try to explain. *Actually, I was here ten minutes early, asshole!*

"Be that as it may, I expect you to be at your desk by eight thirty, sharp!" he demands.

"Yes, Mr Carter, sorry, Mr Carter," I reply in a fluster.

"And it would be nice to have a coffee waiting for me when I come in," he bellows over his shoulder as he walks into his office, slamming the door behind him for good measure.

And so, it begins!

Bea

At ten o'clock, I bring Nathaniel his cup of coffee, ensuring it is to his exact liking. He once spat it out because I had taken too long which meant it wasn't hot enough. By now, I think you can understand why I wince every time I knock on his door. I want to interact with Nathaniel Carter as much as I want to listen to my brother's sexual antics all night. Alas, I have little choice with either.

"Come in!" he summons, sounding like he's the king of the world.

Taking in a deep breath, I eventually brave it to walk inside, only to find Cameron Carter, the CEO, sitting in the chair opposite to him. His laid-back stance inside the office chair, together with his beaming smile that always appears to be genuine, puts me a little more at ease. Usually, a man this attractive, especially in a position of authority, would have me feeling like jelly, however, I know he is completely besotted with his fiancée. I doubt he even sees me as a woman. The way he looks at Lily whenever she comes to visit is something I aspire to one day have with a man of my own. If only I would allow myself to let anyone come near me, I might be in with a chance. Even after all these years, I still don't trust anyone enough to let them get close. Only my parents, Ben, Finn, and Leah.

Looking at them both in such close proximity to one other is like looking at twins. They both have a dark complexion with black hair and olive skin. Nathaniel is slightly fairer than Cameron but only marginally so. Cameron is also taller and broader than his younger brother but again, not by much. Nate's also taken to growing a short beard, as is the fashion at the moment, whereas Cameron remains clean-shaven. I am forever noticing the attention they receive from the opposite sex; it can be quite comical to see women swooning at their feet. Not that I can blame them, it's just a pity one of them is a complete dick.

"Morning, Bea!" Cameron beams at me with his kilowatt smile. "How's my favorite PA this morning?"

"Oh, I'm so sorry, Mr Carter, I would have gotten you a drink too if I had known you'd be here," I apologize, knowing his younger brother still would have reprimanded me if I had unintentionally missed him. "But I'm fine, thank you, Sir."

"Oh, don't even worry about it, and none of this 'Sir' crap," he says in a friendly tone of voice, "call me Cam."

I laugh nervously, knowing I could never comfortably refer to any of the management by their Christian names. I immediately look over at Nathaniel whose expression is currently pulled into the polar opposite to that of his brother. He's sitting back in his chair, looking stiff and stern, the whole time clicking his pen in and out while he waits for me to finish putting his coffee on a coaster.

"So, I hope you're all ready to attend next week's meetings in London, Bea," Cameron says with another breathtaking smile. "And I hope it doesn't inconvenience you too much being away for the week. We will, of course, compensate you for your travel."

My first reaction is to frown, most likely looking as though I'm trying to work out some inexplicable equation. In truth, I'm simply trying to find the words with which to answer him.

"Sorry, but I'm afraid I have no idea what you are talking about," I finally reply.

Nathaniel sighs over my confession, dropping the pen to the desk with a loud clunk on his perfectly ordered workspace. For all the rumors I hear about his party-boy ways, the guy is a complete control freak. I bet he requests his tighty whiteys ironed, along with his designer socks, the cost of which are probably the same as my monthly rent.

"Didn't Nate tell you about the meetings that are taking place with several companies in London next week?"

From the look of cluelessness on my face, he immediately turns toward his brother with a confused frown to rival my own.

"I'm sure I mentioned it to Miss Summers," Nate says with a bored sigh. "You and Sam will be accompanying me and Nick to London next week. It's only for three nights. I'm sure you can take the time out of your 'busy' schedule. It is expected of PAs to attend business trips away."

I continue to stare at him, probably looking completely dumbfounded. He damn well knows he didn't bother to tell me about this rather inconvenient trip. I had plans with my best friend, Finn, for next week. What with his busy life at the restaurant, it means I won't get to see him for a few weeks now.

"I can send Jack if you're busy, Bea," Cameron offers, obviously sensing the tension. "I can see my brother has failed to mention this rather important piece of information to you."

He turns to glare at Nathaniel, but he simply shrugs his shoulders and takes a sip of his coffee. I'm shocked he doesn't spit it out and begin complaining about it. I take in a noisy breath through my nose and put on one of my perfected smiles. I refuse to let him get the better of me by making me look emotional and unprofessional in front of the big boss.

"No, that won't be necessary," I reply politely, "I can handle it."

"Excellent!" Cameron replies, looking relieved. "And don't worry, I've had accommodation fixed up for you in a rented house with two self-contained apartments, so no living in a stuffy little hotel room. Nate and Nick will take the top floor, while you and Sam can take the bottom floor…are you ok staying with a guy for a few nights?"

Nathaniel scoffs with a smug grin on his face and I can't help but give some evil eye his way.

"It's fine," I answer, "I live with my brother actually, so I'm used to guys and their living habits."

"Ah, yes, we can be a little much to live with at times, can't we, Nate?" he asks with a laugh, sounding jovial even though I can tell his brother has pissed him off. Nate, however, just rolls his eyes with a disinterested look on his face.

"Is there anything else I can do before I get back to it?" I ask, gesturing to the safety of my office.

"Oh, yeah," Cameron says, "Lils said she'd pop by at lunchtime, she's keen to see you. Take some extra time and go out for lunch with her, will you? She gets so bored during the long summer break."

"Sure, but don't you and she have a wedding to plan? It's not long now, is it?" I ask, smiling genuinely for the first time.

"Yes, just a few weeks away, but everything is done, so she's all yours," he says, and I can tell from the look on his face that he's excited about it. Apparently, it's been a long engagement.

"Ok, well, thank you, Cameron," I reply with a nervous laugh, wincing over calling him that. "Mr Carter," I say formally to Nathaniel, to which he moodily nods.

Having survived another interaction with Nathaniel Carter, I return to my office, close the door, and release a deep breath of relief. After all, that could have been a lot worse. In fact, for Nathaniel, that went fairly well.

———

Nate

"Could you not?" I snap at Cam with a sigh.

"What?" he laughs, throwing up his hands in the air.

"Be so pathetically over-the-top nice. And why the fuck are you letting my PA have extra-long lunch breaks?" I scowl at him.

"Because I own the company," he replies smugly. "Fuck, you are a miserable bastard to her, aren't you? What's your fucking problem?"

"Nothing, I just don't want my PA taking advantage," I snap, getting more and more frustrated by the second. "I'm her boss, not her friend."

"God, I remember you being less of a dick before you started working here. I'm not asking you to be her friend but treating her with dignity is mandatory. So, please, could you make a little bit more of an effort to be nice? I don't want her going to HR because you've pushed her over the edge. Besides, she's excellent at what she does, you ungrateful asshole."

"Well, maybe she should work with one of the other bosses," I suggest, hoping he considers it. Beatrice Summers and I just clash, which is saying something; I don't recall clashing with anyone other than our brother-in-law, Evan. I can admit it's partly my issue, she hasn't said or done anything to warrant my attitude, it's just an off-vibe I get from her.

"No, that would be a step down for her and you know that"

Cam snaps me out of my thoughts with his irritating truth. "Just because something crawled up your ass and died doesn't mean she should suffer."

"There's nothing wrong with me," I argue, becoming irritated with his insults. "Some people just aren't meant to get along. Miss Summers and I are two of those people. Can't explain it, but that doesn't change the fact that I don't get on with her."

"Nate, you are one of the most fun-loving, approachable, and friendly guys I know. It's why I wanted you here, to schmooze with new clients, but for some reason, you are a total shit when it comes to her. There's not liking someone, and there's blatant nastiness. What's the deal?"

"I don't know, she just…I don't fucking know! She's unnaturally polite all the goddam time, like she's pretending to be someone she's not. I tried being friendly in the beginning, but all I got was nervous laughter. It felt like she was looking down on me, as though I wasn't worth the effort of her making any kind of conversation with. She's closed off and snooty, probably only thinks I'm here because we're related. So, I'm showing her otherwise, that she has no place judging me."

"You sure those aren't your own doubts? I've known her for a few years now, and I've only ever found her to be the opposite of everything you've just said."

"As I said, some people aren't meant to get along," I argue, fast getting bored of this conversation. In fact, I turn away to begin answering an email on my computer, effectively shutting it down.

"Well, sort your shit out, I mean it!" he says and gets up to leave. "And next week you'd better be nice. She's going to another country with three dudes so just remember that when you aren't 'getting along'. You're right, you are her boss, and with that comes a responsibility to look after her."

"Are we done? Ok then, get lost," I huff, still with my eyes on the screen.

For fuck's sake, I'm looking forward to this trip like a hole in the head!

Chapter 3

Bea

"Hey, Bea!" Lily beams as she walks in with her friend, Callie, both dressed in their jeans and t-shirts, completely contrasting with the corporate world all around us. For a moment, I envy them for being the sort of girl I once was – happy, relaxed, able to ignore everyone else's drama. I used to love who I was, and even prided myself on staying well away from girly fights and high school gossip. That is until ***I*** became high school gossip.

Slut deserved it.

She was never good enough for Dean.

No wonder he did what he did.

Bea, you should just go ahead and die.

I flinch as I recall reading those comments for the first time, already having been broken by those who I loved more than anything in the world. I feel momentarily sick and have to take a gulp of water before smiling back at them.

"Hi," I reply shyly, "I'm just sending off an email; can you give me a moment?"

"Oh, sure, go ahead," Lily replies with a flap of her hand, "this is the one time of the year when I have bags of time."

She really is lovely, and I'm pleased for her and Cameron, they are such a beautiful couple, both inside and out. It really makes me consider how the hell someone as nice as Cameron can be related to someone as vile as Nathaniel. I mean, sure, they look practically the same, but as far as personalities go, they couldn't be more different. Mind you, I think sadly, I suppose he is charming and lovely to everyone else, it's just me who he hates.

"You ready?" Callie asks as I hit the send button, and I nod before grabbing my bag to leave. I then take a moment to brace myself before pressing the intercom button into my boss's office. "Mr Carter, I'm off to lunch."

"I will see you in one hour, Miss Summers," he growls through the intercom.

Lily and Callie burst out laughing while looking completely flabbergasted at the same time, just more evidence of how differently he treats me compared to everyone else. I have no idea why, but I am literally part of the office supplies to this guy, an old broom to stuff inside the cupboard until needed.

"She'll be back in two," Lily calls out, then giggles.

A few moments later, Nathaniel opens the door and gives both girls a stern eyeballing before embracing them with kisses and cuddles. He instantly becomes the charming man in an Armani suit that all the other people see.

"Hello, darling, how are you?" he says to his future sister-in-law in such a way, I can't help but roll my eyes over his complete personality change.

"Nathaniel," she greets him back. "What's this about being

back in an hour? Cam told me she can have longer," Lily questions as she stares him down, complete with crossed arms and a cluck of her tongue. I have to bite my lip just to hide my smile, for it is quite delicious to watch someone giving him a hard time for once.

"I have to leave for a meeting at three, so I need her back to make sure the phones are covered, Lily," he argues, though still smiling… for them.

"Oh, fuck off," Callie chimes in, "I'm sure you can leave the phones unattended for half an hour."

"Ok, an hour and a half then?" Lily bargains.

"Fine," he says with reluctance, then turns to face me with his usual stern expression. "But bring me back a chicken mayo salad and a coffee."

"You're kind of an asshole boss," Callie says with a grimace. "Where's the Nate who used to drink shots with the waitresses back at Mick's place?"

"Yeah, and the Nate who tried dirty dancing with Mick to piss him off when he was working?" Lily adds.

My eyes bulge over the thought of seeing a fun-loving and carefree Nathaniel Carter. However, I soon feel the heat of him glaring in my direction, as if to warn me to never mention what I've just been privy to again. Trust me, I wouldn't risk having to engage with him any more than I have to. When it comes to Nathaniel Carter, I stick to professional talk, and even then, I keep it to the bare minimum.

"Good afternoon, ladies," he utters as he turns his back and waves, returning to his office with a bounce in his step.

"I know I'm going to pay for that later," I mumble to myself, only to see that Callie and Lily must have heard me, given the confused expressions on their faces. I offer nothing more than a fake smile and quickly shuffle out the door to avoid any questions about it. They only know the Nathaniel Carter who is loved by all, who am I to give them the other version of him?

She's a nobody who thought she could do better; what a bitch. Dean deserves so much better. She should go and crawl under a rock and die somewhere. Slut!

No one, that's who. I'm nobody.

Bea

After a short walk away from the *Medina Technologies* building, we reach a small café and take a seat in one of the booths to have our lunch. It's a beautiful day so everyone has decided to sit on the veranda out front, which means the café itself is quiet. It's a place I usually come to when I get to have a rare lunch with Finn. In fact, it was the very first place we came to after our first group therapy meeting; we often argue over who introduced who to it. It sells all the normal lunch stuff - sandwiches, salads, baked potatoes, fries, plus a huge selection of ridiculously delicious cakes and cookies. Alas, I settle for ordering a salad today, only because I feel under pressure to at least look like I give a shit about what I eat.

"Green salad, please," I tell the waiter.

To my surprise, Callie and Lily look at me like I just ordered grilled roadkill, which to be fair, would probably be far tastier. I can't say I'm looking forward to stomach rumbles all afternoon, but perhaps Nathaniel will allow me five minutes to go and raid the vending machines.

"Chicken and avocado baguette, please, with sweet potato fries," Callie orders, not giving two shits about calories or fat content.

Girl could lose some weight too. Have you seen how much she eats at lunch? She might hang with the boys, but it doesn't mean she can eat like one.

"Ooh, sounds good," Lily says, "I'll have what she said but with sweet potato *chips*." She grins smugly while Callie rolls her eyes. Lily is from England but moved over here when she was a teenager. Her accent can be a little strange sometimes, but ultimately, she sounds British.

"Can I scrap my order, please?" I quickly ask the waiter, trying to block out the negativity of my past. Finn is constantly reminding me to be in the present; to not listen to my history. "I'll have the ham and cheese toasted sandwich and regular fries, please."

The waiter gives me a quick nod and a wink before taking the order through to the kitchen. I bet he's laughing at me, but at least I can't see it.

"Good girl!" Callie laughs before taking a sip of her soda.

"So, Cameron says you're both ready for your wedding, Lily, you must be so excited." I give her a beaming smile, which is beginning to feel real instead of one made from anxiety.

"Yeah, most of it is done," she says casually, and with a wave of her hand.

"Are you nervous?" I ask. Getting married must be exciting, not that I'll ever know. I won't let a man near me; I would say that's a pretty big barrier to my getting married.

"Nope," she replies with a shrug of her shoulders. "But, since you asked, we were wondering if you would like to be Callie's guest. If you're not busy, that is."

"I'm a totally fun wedding guest; I'll look after you," Callie adds with a grin. Knowing what little I do know about Callie, I don't doubt her.

"Really?" I can't help smiling, probably with too many teeth on show. In fact, I suddenly feel overcome with emotion. "I don't know what to say, that's really sweet of you. I've never been to a wedding before."

"Oh, you'll love it," Callie says with a smile written all over her face. "Two words - free bar!" She then winks at me, and I can't help but laugh. Her fun and happy attitude is incredibly infectious.

"So, is that a yes?" Lily asks, looking genuinely excited by the prospect. I can't remember the last time I had girlfriends, except Leah, but I've always considered her friendship mandatory because of Ben. As much as I love her, I don't believe she would choose to be friends if it wasn't for my relationship with him.

"I'd love to, thank you," I finally reply, but then my heart drops and I feel the smile slip from my face. It must be obvious too, for their confused expressions are now staring at me for some sort of explanation.

"What's wrong? Do you have other plans?" Lily asks with concern written all over her face.

"No, nothing like that, but..." How do I put my worries into words that won't paint her future brother-in-law and friend into the cold bastard he usually is to me? "Well, it's just that...I'm not so sure Nathaniel will be pleased to see me there."

"Oh, screw Mr Moody Pants," Callie says, swatting her hand out in front of her. "Plus, we won't tell him. It's not like it's a work thing, is it?"

I nod my head, even though I'm totally unconvinced by her words.

"What is it with you two anyway?" Lily asks before slurping on her drink, looking thoroughly perplexed by whatever it is between Nathaniel and me. At first, all I can do is shrug my shoulders, because, in all honesty, I don't really know what his damn problem is.

"I have no idea, but he doesn't seem to like me very much. Maybe it's just a personality clash or something."

"I can't understand it because you're a sweetheart and he's…well, he's Nate," she blurts out. "Nate is well known for loving everybody, especially women."

She looks at Callie with a knowing expression, to which Callie nods her head slowly and with a smile on her face. This is no surprise, I've more than heard about his reputation with women; I've even had to send flowers to some of them.

"Well, this is one woman he certainly doesn't love!" I reply, smiling at the waiter when he begins serving us our food. "Can I have a chicken salad to go when we're finished, please?"

"Sure thing," he says, then winks again before walking away. I look at the girls to see if they saw. Apparently, they did.

"Ooh, he likes you," Callie grins, "you should totally come next Saturday if that's how waiters respond to you; we might get free drinks!"

"What's next Saturday?" I ask.

"A little impromptu night out before Lily hands her freedom over to Cam," Callie explains, "could get very messy."

"Oh, yeah, please come. It's only me, Callie, Ellie, Helena, and James going. You have to come!"

They look at me as though I have no choice in the matter, but to be honest, I'm kind of excited. My youth died on that fateful night, so perhaps this is what I need to kick-start myself into living again.

"Ok, sure," I reply, smiling with growing confidence, "I'd love to."

Lily and Callie high-five each other before we finally tuck into our much-more-exciting-than-a-green-salad lunch.

Chapter 4

Bea

Ten minutes earlier than agreed, Callie, Lily, and I walk back into my office, complete with his lordship's chicken mayo salad. Hopefully, this should keep his wrath at bay. That and the fact there are only a few hours left until the weekend. Then I get to have two whole Nathaniel Carter free days.

"I can't believe that guy wrote his number on your receipt," Lily laughs as we enter the office, where Nathaniel is already waiting for me with an even bigger scowl than usual.

"You should totally call him," Callie says, but I simply giggle and shake my head over the idea. An idea that fills me full of gut-wrenching fear more than heart-fluttering excitement. I wonder if I'll ever feel comfortable enough to date a man again.

"Excuse me, ladies," Nathaniel says with about as much politeness as he can muster, none of which is for my benefit. "I need to talk to my assistant…alone!"

Oh, shit, what did I do wrong now?

While I internalize my abject fear, Callie gifts him a smile, then kisses me on the cheek to say goodbye. Lily teases him by giving him a mock salute, but he even ignores her playfulness. She blows him a kiss, then whispers behind her hand, "be nice!"

"Right, I'm off to see my hu…honey! I'll see you next Saturday," she says before kissing my cheek and walking out the door with Callie. "Good luck in London next week both of you!"

They're soon walking past the glass windows that close my office in, all the while waving goodbye. I return the farewell even though I'm silently screaming, "Help!". This ball of anxiety stuck inside of my chest is in no way helped when I see Nathaniel's fuming face glaring at me.

"Is there a problem, Mr Carter?" I ask timidly, wishing I had a fraction of Callie's confidence to shut him down.

"Yes, there's a problem! Why haven't you booked *Silantro's* tonight, like I asked you to last week?"

The volume at which he's barking at me causes a few heads to pop up and begin staring at us through the office windows, which is now doubling as a wide-screen television to my humiliation. This is classic Nathaniel Carter behavior when it comes to me; the reason why I probably drink too much during the week. He enjoys growling just loud enough so others can hear him destroying me with just his words, making me look like a bigger waste of space than I already do on a daily basis. It's not only humiliating and degrading, but it also takes me right back to being a frightened schoolgirl. I absolutely hate it.

"You told me to book it for last night," I try to argue.

I'm gifted with a long sigh and a shake of his head, the type a parent gives their child when they've majorly screwed up.

"No, I asked you to book it for Friday; that is today!"

"I don't wish to argue with you, Mr Carter, but you told me to do it for Thursday because you would be seeing your parents tonight," I assert, though quietly so. I swear he did but now he's caused me to doubt myself.

"Who am I, Miss Summers?" he asks in an arrogant tone of voice. His jaw is ticking away all the while he glares at me with unforgiving eyes. His usual emerald, green irises have turned a violent shade darker and have me quivering. This is the sort of thing I should go to HR about like Ben has nagged me to do countless times before. If it wasn't for the fact Cameron Carter has been so good to me, and how much I want to work for this company, perhaps I would. Or perhaps if I had a backbone, I might. My backbone was stolen from me a long time ago,, back when the world I thought I knew came crashing down all around me.

"Er…Nathaniel Carter?"

Damn it, I don't know what he wants me to answer with, but I can already guess that whatever I say, it will be wrong.

"And who is that?"

He leans in close, and I feel the hairs on the back of my neck stand on end. Then the smell of his masculine aftershave attacks my nostrils and I begin to feel nauseated.

"My boss?" I barely manage to voice.

"That's right, I'm your boss so when you decide to try and contradict me again, just remember that!"

He keeps his glare on me until I have to look away first, and with my cheeks heating under the embarrassment of being spoken down to like a child in front of a whole office full of my colleagues. The same people I have to face every day, feeling and looking like a complete imbecile.

"I apologize, Mr Carter," I murmur, looking down at the floor with unwarranted shame. But I'm not fucking sorry, this was his mistake, all of it.

My apology goes unanswered. Instead, Nathaniel storms out of the office muttering obscenities under his breath, probably loud enough for everyone else to hear but me. A few of the employees on the other side of the glass watch him pace off before looking at me with pity in their eyes. This is so demeaning, to the point where I want to run home and hide under the duvet.

I wipe a sweaty palm over my face and clench my lips together tightly in anger. Someone mouths "Are you ok?" to me, but all I can manage is a shy nod and my usual fake smile.

Pretending to look as though I care very little about my boss shouting me down in the middle of the afternoon, I tentatively sit in my chair and turn the computer toward me, only so no one can see my face. Once I am safely hidden, I finally let the tears fall silently down my cheeks, lifting my hand every now and then to wipe them away. Their presence only frustrates me further; I always cry when I'm angry. God, I wish I could go psycho bitch on him, just like old me would have done. Perhaps I should go downtown this weekend and buy a voodoo doll with extra pins and miniature clamps for his testicles.

Nate

Standing on Mom and Dad's front porch feels more nostalgic than usual. We're summoned here at least once or twice a month, a get-together of the family Carter, but I usually feel quite pleased to see my folks. Mom will have made a dinner that tastes like real, homecooked food, and Dad will pat me on the back for making it yet another week in proper work, usually with a teasing comment about my brother being the CEO. I'll laugh it off with a self-derogatory comment to pretend he hasn't pissed me off, and we'll settle into sipping back expensive liquor. Cameron will ask Lily if she's seen some childhood piece of crap so he can take her upstairs and bang her in his old room, which some may say is a kink of his. And Helena...? Well, Helena might be there physically, but mentally, she checked out of this house when she married Evan. I wish I could get her to open up, but I'm not even sure she is capable of doing so.

However, this time isn't going to be like that; this time, I'm going to be given shit for being an asshole to Beatrice earlier on. And I'll admit, I was an asshole. The girl brings out the worst in me, but I know her type well. The quiet type, the I'm-better-than-you type. Believe me, I wasn't always this frosty toward her. When I was first introduced, I was charming, polite, and friendly; the girl gave me nothing but silence. Not like Helena silence, a silence that said I wasn't worthy of being where I was, that I was living off my brother's coattails.

"And this is Beatrice Summers, your new Personal Assistant," Cam announces, acting every bit the smug CEO, so much so, I have to bite my lip to stifle my laughter. I turn to face the timid-looking girl in front of me and offer her my hand.

"Nice to meet you, I'm Na-"

"Nathaniel Carter," she says for me, eyeing my hand like it's infected, then steps back and offers the briefest of smiles before breathing out a long, steady stream of air. "I'm sorry, I've got chili on my hands from lunch; I'd hate to get it on you."

"Oh, sure, ok," I reply, putting my hands up in defeat, but

keep smiling to try and put her at ease.

"Right, well, I'll leave you two to get better acquainted," Cameron says with a theatrical clap of his hands. "I've got a zoom meeting in about…" he pauses, and checks his Rolex before finishing, "…eight minutes. Catch you later, brother."

He marches out of the office, leaving Beatrice and me to feel awkward; something you could never accuse me of being with a woman. It's unnerving but probably for the best seeing as she's my PA.

"I've heard a lot about you," she utters quietly, not even bothering to look me in the eye.

"Oh, really? What have you heard?" I ask, beginning to get a weird vibe from her, enough to make me act standoffish.

"J-just that you like to…er…that is to say…you like to party?" she asks with a wince, like the idea of partying is something to feel ashamed of.

"I see," I murmur, trying to make sense of what she is trying to suggest here.

"And now you have come to work for your brother, how lovely," she says with what sounds like condescension. It would seem she cannot even bear to voice what I suspect too; I am here because of him, not my own merits.

"Well, we all have to grow up some time," I tell her with a fake smile, the one I often use when trying to schmooze potential clients.

"I suppose," she says with a sad tone to her voice, then looks down at her fidgeting fingers, thus avoiding my gaze altogether. She coughs to clear her throat before stepping back

and looking at me with a professional stance. "I'll start on your calendar; do you need anything else?"

"A coffee, perhaps?"

"Of course, I'll go right now," she says and turns almost immediately to begin walking away.

"Milk, no…" I trail off for she's already turned the corner.

"Great first impression, Nate," I mutter to myself.

Things did not improve after that first meeting, in fact, she only seemed to recoil from me more and more. She often had a vacant stare whenever I spoke to her, as if it wasn't worth her time to listen to me. And she never, ever, got my coffee the way I like it.

Then, after months of this treatment, I remembered something – I'm the fucking boss here. I shouldn't be trying to impress my PA; she should be making that effort for me. If she wants to treat me like an asshole with no manners, then that is what she'll get. Alas, I can be a lot better at playing the evil boss, so word soon got to Cam and Ellie, my cousin who works a few floors down, about poor Beatrice Summers, and now I never hear the end of it. I guess hating her comes naturally to me.

With Beatrice Summers playing the victim in mind, I brace myself and open the front door, ready to receive the fallout for being Nate Carter, the baby of the family. The guy who is forever living in his perfect big brother's shadow.

Bea

On Sunday, I finally begin the arduous task of packing for

my trip to London, a job I've been putting off in the hopes that it might get canceled. Don't get me wrong, I've never been to London before, and part of me is excited to be going, but an even bigger part wants to avoid having to spend a whole week away with my boss. Nathaniel Carter plus two other guys I hardly know sounds like a recipe for a migraine all week. Admittedly, Sam, Nick Clayton's PA, had at least come to introduce himself to me on Friday afternoon. He's fairly new, and although he seems nice, I still don't fancy having to share an apartment with him. Nick Clayton, on the other hand, is the Head of Technical Support. He is much like Nathaniel in that he seems to have no problem with getting plenty of female attention. He's pale and has lighter brown hair than Nathaniel, but he's just as tall and has that same panty-melting smile. Also, just like Nathaniel, he's got a cocky way about him that lets you know he loves himself. I half wonder if he and Nathaniel get together to share tips on how to bag women. That being said, I do find him a lot more likable than Nathaniel, mainly because he doesn't belittle me on a daily basis.

"Mom, what should I take to London?" I ask her on the speakerphone while I pack.

"Well, it's summer over there so I guess similar sorts of stuff to what you would wear here," she suggests. "Though, you might want to check their weather because I think they can have good summers and bad summers."

"Good call," I reply and begin to google the weather forecast. "High seventies and sunshine, good, good."

"How's Ben doing? Him and Leah still ok?" she asks casually.

"As far as I know. Judging by their ability to keep me up most nights, I would say they're very much still in lust," I mutter.

"Bea, a mother doesn't really want to know that sort of information about her son…or daughters," she says, sounding thoroughly unimpressed.

"Well neither does a sister but it appears I have no choice in the matter so suck it up. I'm taking you down with me."

"Bea, sweetie?" Oh, I know that tone, it means she has something to say that will either require me to do something or piss me off. "Your sister's here," she says softly, "would you like to say hello?"

Yep, it's the latter.

"No, thank you," I reply without pausing for thought.

"Oh, Bea, come on," my mother pleads, "she's desperate to talk to you. It's been years!"

"Well, it's been years since I had a sister so that would be why," I huff.

"Bea, it's Emma, please talk to me," says the voice of a girl who I used to be so close to, I thought we'd one day live together. Perhaps even end up at the same nursing home where we'd earn a reputation for behaving badly. But now, when I hear her voice, I immediately hang up the phone and continue packing as though what just happened, hadn't. I feel guilty for hanging up on Mom, but she should respect my wishes. I refuse to be railroaded into talking to a woman who I used to call my sister.

"She's not going to take the hint, is she?" Ben's soft voice travels through my room from where he's leaning against the door frame. I turn to face him with a sad smile, looking at his crossed arms and sympathetic expression.

"Nope, but I can't blame Mom for trying," I reply. Ben's

always been on my side.

"Listen, Leah says she can take you to the airport if you like," he says, perking up and walking in to help me fold my scattered clothes. I simply nod with a renewed happy smile on my face, pleased to have ended the previous conversation. "I would take you myself, but if I see your boss there, I might end up jeopardizing your career, as you so often tell me."

"I love you for wanting to though," I tell him at the same time as throwing my arms around his huge shoulders. He merely pushes me away in a jovial, brotherly kind of way, making the both of us laugh over our sibling theatrics.

———

Bea

That evening, I eat at home, trying to feel ok about everything at work. It works about as well as trying to convince Finn that McDonalds is real food. The thought has me longing to see my best friend, even if he's working and can only spare me two minutes of conversation every now and then. It's close to finish so he won't mind me hanging around at his fancy pants restaurant bar; I might even score a free drink or two. Lord knows I need one right about now, especially as Ben and Leah finished the last bottle of white wine.

After a lot of guilting, which then turned into whining, which then turned into me trying very badly to feed his already over-inflated ego, Ben agreed to drive me down to Finn's place. When I get there, only one or two tables are left. Even better, they look like they've already eaten and are now drowning their gourmet meal with tumblers of liquor. Finn is perched on one of the bar stools with a waiter, chatting and laughing while knocking back a bottle of beer. His carefree smile and slouched figure have me smiling to myself; I haven't seen him in ages. I suddenly remember how much I've missed him, how much he soothes my frazzled nerves, and how much he makes me laugh, even when I don't want to. I watch him talking away to the other guy before glancing over to catch me staring. He offers me a wave and a huge smile.

"There's my girl," he calls out while getting up to slap his arms around my back. "I'd forgotten what you look like!"

I beam at him, comforted by the fact that no matter how bad things are at the time, he instantly puts me at ease with myself. If only there was more between us than friendship, he might have been the man to break me out of my abstinence from all things relationships.

"You say that like it's down to me!" I pout at the same time as I chuck my coat on the stool next door to his. The waiter from before knocks back his shot, looks me up and down, then grins unashamedly. His unsubtle approach isn't missed by my best friend who simply shakes his head at him.

"No way, brother, this girl is all mine, and you are so not good enough for her," Finn teases. His waiter friend merely smirks, gives him the finger before taking my hand and kissing the back of it.

"Another time, beautiful," he whispers, then saunters into the kitchen and out of sight.

"Jerk!" Finn scoffs before turning back to face me.

Finn and I have known each other for a good few years now, but honestly, it feels like a lifetime. If only he had been at high school with me when I truly needed his kind of loyal friendship. Instead, we met at a support group that Ben had railroaded me into. We took turns sharing our sad little stories, consolidated one another with words of reassurance, then felt the immediate need for something cold and alcoholic. We've been as thick as thieves ever since.

About a year into our friendship, I went as his plus one to a work event. His friends jibed him about why he hadn't yet snapped me up, to which we laughed and brushed it off. But come the end of the night, when he was dropping me home, he admitted he kind of liked me, so we agreed to try and kiss, to see what would happen. After all, he was the only unrelated man with whom I felt safe. Alas, it felt like I was kissing Ben. As soon as it was over, he sort of grimaced, and we both burst out laughing. Funnily enough, the first thing he said was, "I feel like I've just committed incest!" We agreed to stick with the friendship, which to me, after everything I had been through, was worth so much more than having a boyfriend.

A swell of guilt whirls around inside my stomach because part of the reason for coming tonight is to cancel our long-awaited plans for next week. From the look on his face, he's already guessed, but there's nothing I can do about it.

"Go on, say it," he says with a strange concoction of a smirk and a wearisome sigh. "You're about to cancel on me aren't you." I offer him no words, just wince, and slump on top of the stool. His smirk morphs into disappointment which has me feeling shitty all over again. "You're kidding me, Bea!"

"I'm sorry," I tell him as I slap a hand over his dropped shoulders. "My boss screwed me over and now I have to go to London." He peers through his fingers, looking thoroughly pissed off, but when he sees my pathetic attempt at a smile, he ends up laughing at me. "If it makes you feel any better, I'm just as annoyed as you are."

"It doesn't," he sulks, so I wrap my arms around his shoulders to try and soothe his sad expression.

"Finn, that was another excellent meal! I…Oh, Miss Summers? I'm sorry, I didn't realize you were here. What a coincidence to find you in a restaurant like this; we're obviously paying you too much. No offense, Finn, but this place is ridiculously priced."

Finn and I both shoot our faces up to look at the man who has just interrupted us. Finn smiles with what looks like a genuinely happy expression, whereas my mouth drops open in horrified shock. Why the hell is my asshole boss looking at my best friend like they're old buddies?

"I hope I'm not interrupting a personal moment?" He grins with his million-dollar kilowatt smile that makes most women swoon at his Italian leather-encased feet.

"No, no," Finn says rather too quickly for my liking, "Bea and I are just friends." He says it like he can't get the words out fast enough, as though to admit to us being anything more would be beyond embarrassing. This isn't the Finn I know and love; has Nathaniel Carter got magical powers whereby he can infect others with his utter dislike for me?

"How do you know Bea, Mr Carter?"

"Please, I've told you before, Finn, call me Nate." My frown of curiosity only deepens the longer I watch this vomit-worthy display between my ass-kissing friend and my mean girl of a boss. Nathaniel, however, ignores my confusion and slaps a large hand over Finn's right shoulder, smiling like they're long-lost frat brothers. "Miss Summers is my personal assistant," he replies, grinning at me like he's the nicest boss in the world. "We've been together for, what? Eighteen months now, is it?"

"Mm-hmm," is about all I can muster, with a fake smile and a quick gulp of Finn's drink.

"I was just coming to see if you would like to join us, Finn?" Nathaniel asks as he waves back at his table of beautiful people, including three busty females, all scantily dressed and full of lip enhancers and fake tits. While I silently judge them for fawning over men like Mr Big-Bank-Balance Carter and his modelesque features, Finn's eyes are practically falling out of his head. "We're heading over to that new place that's just opened a few blocks from here."

"Put your tongue away, Finn," I mutter, sounding completely unimpressed by how unsubtle he's being. "Drool isn't a very attractive trait, even in a strip club where you can pay for flesh."

"I would invite you too, Miss Summers, but we do have that early flight tomorrow. Besides, I don't think it is quite your scene," he says, looking me up and down in my casual outfit; and by 'outfit', I mean something I threw on quickly so I could catch my best friend before I have to leave for a trip my asshole boss didn't even think to mention until it was too late.

"That's very considerate of you, Mr Carter," I reply with a strong hint of sarcasm in my voice. Being as arrogant as he is, he doesn't take the hint and merely smiles back at me.

"Well, Finn, are you game?" he asks, turning his back on me so I may as well not even be here. "Only if I'm not interrupting something here," he says, still with his back to me. I want to scream, but then I notice Finn looking completely torn, so I decide to take myself out of the equation and make it easy on him, even if the whole thing has pissed me off.

"Go on, you go," I tell him with a sigh. "Besides, Mr Carter is right; I've got that flight in the morning."

"You sure?" he asks, at least pretending to look guilty. But as soon as I nod my confirmation, he almost fist bumps the air. He only stopped himself because he knew that if he had done, I most likely would have kicked him in the balls. Instead, he kisses my temple before whispering, "Call me as soon as you land in London."

"Mmm," I just about reply.

I turn away to purposefully ignore him jumping off his stool to go and get his stuff from out back, all with a gleeful bounce in his step. Conceding defeat, I tap out a text to Ben to come and get me, only to realize Nathaniel is still here, watching me with keen interest. I tentatively look up at him, with my furrowed brow back in place.

"Is there anything else I can do for you, Mr Carter?"

"No, not right now, Miss Summers," he says without expression, "but make sure you're on time tomorrow."

I sneer at his retreating back, eyeing him with disdain as he saunters back to his table, acting the life and soul for his friends, which now includes *my* friend. He smiles, laughs, and charms them all without effort, and yet, I only ever get the straight-laced miserable son of a bitch boss who has just whipped my friend away from right under my nose. I thought I'd left high school behind years ago, but here I am, sitting all alone, with my best friend having been commandeered by the cool kids, while the mean bully continues to make my life hell.

Thankfully, it's not long before Ben walks in wearing his biker gear and with his helmet perched firmly underneath his arm. As he begins marching up to me, together with a gruff look on his face, Nathaniel and his cronies begin walking out. Ben doesn't notice, except to acknowledge them when they pass by one another. Though, Nathaniel definitely seems to notice my brother. In fact, he hovers by the door for a few moments, taking in the scene of Ben coming up to ruffle my hair with brotherly affection, aka, siblings trying to annoy the hell out of one another. Unlike me, Ben is super tall, so people often assume we're a couple. The look on Nathaniel's face is peculiar, to say the least, but it somewhat pleases me to know that whatever it is, he's clearly not impressed. *Good, fuck you, Nathaniel Carter!*

Nate

I am not often left speechless, but Beatrice Summers has indeed rendered me lost for words. Of course, I never expected to see her in a pretentious place like the one I just left, for you have to be earning a heck of a lot more than she is paid to afford an entrée, let alone a full-blown dinner. That might well sound arrogant, but it's true. My family certainly wouldn't have dined here before Cameron made it big. But her talking to Finn soon cleared up that conundrum. No, the thing that made me question my usual assessment of her character is the way she was dressed. I seriously expected her to always dress in her prim and proper cardigan sets, with a set of pearls and a tight updo to match. Instead, she was sporting a pair of ripped jeans and a leather jacket that looked like it'd been well worn. Her hair was down and flowing almost to her ass, which, though it pains me to say, was quite a delectable sight.

Then there was her boyfriend who looked like a blond Viking, dressed to pillage the local village and ride off with the damsel in distress. I would not have put them together in a million years; surely, she should be with a preppy guy named Chad or Wilson who likes to go glamping or attend murder mystery weekends.

"Nate, you coming?" Lucia asks me from outside. I can't even tear my eyes away for long enough to answer her, I'm too fixated on this strange turn of events.

"Yeah, you go ahead," I tell her over my shoulder, "I'm just…"

I trail off, mesmerized by the Viking who is now messing with Bea's hair. I wouldn't say I feel mad about the scene, but not exactly happy about it either. A hand soon slides over my shoulder while I try to work out what this weird feeling is; it's unsettling that I'm feeling anything at all about it. Why should I care about some mountain of a man putting his hands all over my PA? She's smiling about it, even nudging him back. I should only feel indifferent about it, shouldn't I?

"She's very pretty, do you know her?" Lucia purrs inside my ear, then giggles when I shake, then nod my head.

"She's my PA, that's all," I murmur, still staring at Bea.

"And, of course, you are simply making sure she is ok," she says, though her voice sounds teasing. "After all, as a member of staff, you are somewhat responsible for her, no?"

"No, I…" I turn to face Lucia, a stunning ex-model from Paris. We've dabbled, but she's like me, keeps it wild and friendly, nothing more. She's grinning at me like she knows something I don't. I shake my head with my own laugh this time, silently telling her not to even think that my watching Bea could be anything more than simple curiosity.

"You are absolutely right, Lucia, I am merely looking out for her wellbeing," I tell her as I begin walking out, though it feels uncomfortable to do so, as though I've left my phone or wallet behind.

"Of course, I am always right," she says smugly as she links her arm through mine. "It's a good thing she has a handsome man with her to keep her safe, otherwise you might have to do the unthinkable and escort her back home, maybe even tuck her up in bed."

"You are too naughty for your own good, Lucia," I laugh. "Put that woman to bed?" I theatrically shiver with a fake grimace to make her laugh even harder. "Thank God that doesn't have to happen."

Chapter 5

Bea

At six am, the morning after Nathaniel had so easily convinced my best friend to ditch me, I shuffle down to the parking lot where Leah helps me to put on the spare helmet to her Suzuki V-Strom, otherwise known as her pride and joy. Motorbikes and grime were how she and Ben bonded, back when they were at college. After everything happened, when I was eighteen, I moved into this apartment with Ben. It took a lot of convincing to get me to go outside, so Ben said I could go anywhere I wanted and promised not to leave my side. I immediately thought of a huge bike store where Ben liked to go and spend his hard-earned cash. The smell of leather, motorbike parts, and various oils was nostalgic and put me at ease. Afterward, we went to a vintage, second-hand shop where Ben pulled out an old leather jacket that he'd had his eye on for me. He promised to teach me how to ride. I always wanted to be like him, to be a motorbike nut, but I guess driving one wasn't as easy as I thought it would be. I quickly decided it wasn't for me and given how I had very nearly written off Ben's bike, he agreed. Instead, I always wear the jacket whenever I ride on the back with either him or Leah firmly in the driving seat.

I'd shoved on a pair of old jeans and some flat, ankle books, making sure I was casual and comfortable. I knew we'd be traveling all day, so comfort was a priority. Besides, the email from Cameron Carter said to not bother wearing workwear for we weren't going to be meeting with anyone today.

So, why do I feel so out of place and nervous about Nathaniel and the other guys from work seeing me like this? Why do I feel so naked in this outfit? Where is my usual mask?

I begin worrying about it all while Leah and I ride along the straight monotonous roads that are virtually empty. It's early and the sun is still rising in the clear blue sky; it's going to be another hot, still day. As we approach the airport, I focus my attention on the planes that are taking off and landing, their thunderous engines roaring through the air. I haven't traveled much by plane, but air crafts do fascinate me, from the outside anyway. They remind me of escaping and leaving all my troubles behind. Inside, however, they're little metal tubes full of recycled air and hours of boredom, trapping you in with strangers – lovers, siblings, families, cheaters, bullies, possibly homicidal maniacs – the possibilities are endless.

We pull up outside of the 'Departures' building where I can already see the oh, so happy, smiling face of my employer, Nathaniel Carter. He's standing next to a genuinely cheerful Sam and the handsome Nick Clayton, who is looking the epitome of suave and trendy. All three of them are wearing sunglasses to shield their eyes from the punishing rays of the rising sun. They soon glance over at the sound of Leah's bike with its impressive roar amongst the early morning silence. They quickly look away again, not for one second suspecting it would be me riding on the back of a beautiful machine like this one. Leah brings her love to a stop and switches the engine off before raising her visor.

"You ok, Bea? Or do you need help?" she calls out. I'm

already dismounting, getting ready to pull off my helmet, so shake my head with a reassuring, 'I'm fine' slipping through my lips.

"Are they your colleagues?" she asks, jutting her chin out toward the three of them, who are now taking more note of us. I guess biker chicks can have a bit of a reputation, one they seem more than interested to explore.

"Yep," I reply through my helmet.

"Which one is dick face?" she asks, making me smile.

"The one with the black shirt on, in the middle," I reply as quietly as I can.

"Well, at least he's pretty to look at," she giggles. "Do me a favor and flip your hair when you remove your helmet."

"What?! I'm not flipping my damn hair!" I huff as I fumble around in my bag, trying to retrieve my passport so I can just hand it over. The last thing I want to do is keep his royal highness waiting, he'd probably make an example of me right in front of an airport full of people.

"Just do it, I want to see his reaction. Call it payment for the lift." I groan before giving in and pulling the helmet off, only to end up doing less of a flip and more of an anxious shake. I feel completely ridiculous and self-conscious, especially knowing that he's watching me.

"Ah-ha," she says.

"What?"

"Well, I think all three of them would bang you right now," she laughs, "but none more so than your asshole of a boss. This is why I love being a biker chick, you get to look as sexy as hell but can flip them the bird before riding off into the sunset…or rise."

"Whatever, I'm done. You ok to get me on Friday morning?" I ask with a frustrated sigh, to which she simply nods. "Cool, I'll text you with the flight number. Thanks, Leah."

As soon as she rides off, I start my anxious walk over to the three men waiting for me. Nick and Sam are smiling, whereas the boss who was apparently so interested in me, looks aghast over my choice of clothing today.

"Fuck me, is that you, Beatrice Summers?" Nick calls over at the same time as removing his designer sunglasses. He looks me up and down while emitting a wolf whistle, consequently making me want to go and jump in a hole somewhere. I've had more than my fill of being the center of attention in this lifetime.

"Wow, Bea," Sam says while smiling, "you look so…so different."

"It's just a jacket and a pair of jeans," I mutter with embarrassment, "I wear less when I'm at work. I thought we were expected to dress casually today."

"Correct, Miss Summers, though I do hope you have packed something more appropriate to wear," Nathaniel growls at me. "We have a lot of important meetings this coming week, and 'rough biker chick' doesn't really say professional, does it?"

Sam's mouth drops open at the same time as Nick rolls his eyes and begins wheeling his bag toward the entrance. At least their reaction confirms I'm not reading too much into his attitude; they can see it too.

"Don't worry, Mr Carter," I reply with my fake smile in place, "I have packed accordingly."

"Good," is all he can answer me with. "Let's go and check in; we're running behind now," he says while looking at me accusingly. Sam's eyes glare at me with a '*what-the-fuck-is-his-problem?*' expression, but I ignore it and fall into step. We're soon trailing behind Nathaniel and Nick like little children following their parents.

Bea

I was shocked when I heard Cameron had spent out on first-class tickets for Sam and me, but now that I'm here, I am beyond grateful. There's space to stretch out all your limbs, as well as complimentary champagne. Nathaniel and Nick seem to take it all in their stride, but Sam and I can't help but grin with giddy excitement. Let's face it, I'm never going to experience this ever again, so I might as well make the most of it.

"Beatrice, darling, do you mind sitting with me?" Nick asks with a seductive grin plastered on his face.

"Er…"

"No!" Nathaniel snaps. "I need to talk to you about strategies, Nick. Miss Summers can sit with Sam."

I frown over the fact that I am always called 'Miss Summers', but the men are referred to by their Christian names.

However, I'm secretly relieved that I get to sit next to Sam, so I let it go. I think I would have felt uncomfortably intimidated sitting next to either Nathaniel or Nick during a long-haul flight to London. Without further ado, Sam and I take the opportunity to leave our bosses behind and take our seats on the other side of the cabin.

"Thank God," Sam says what I'm thinking, "we can talk freely over here. No watching what we are saying in front of the managers!" I bulge my eyes in complete agreement with him. "Plus, your boss is a real jerk when he's around you."

"Is it that noticeable?"

"Oh yeah, everyone on our floor knows he's a real piece of work with you," he says matter of factly. "Lucky you!"

"Yeah, lucky me indeed!" I reply with a long, sad sigh.

As soon as I sit down in my luxury plane seat, I take out my phone to switch it onto flight mode. Before I do so, I notice an unread message from Finn and scowl at it. I'm still peeved at him for ditching me last night, especially after I had told him about Nathaniel being such a dick of a boss. Leah had wound me up even further by ranting on about friends needing to have your back. Ben tried to defend Finn, but only because he's secretly hoping that I'll end up with him. He knows he can trust him. However, after I told them what Nathaniel had said to me afterward, not even he could defend Finn's actions.

I feel like a dick for leaving you last night. I can't believe you're talking about the same person when you tell me about Nate. He's such a cool person. I'm sorry though, I was a crap friend. Forgive me? X

I'm not ready to forgive him yet, especially when I see Nathaniel rabbiting away to Nick with his smug face and over-the-top hand gesturing. Instead, I sneer at his message and feel even more pissed with him.

No!

Halfway through the flight, Sam has gone to sleep, and I've taken out one of my favorite books if only to calm my nerves after reading Finn's text message. A seventeenth-century play might not be everyone's choice of literature, especially when trying to ease your stress, but it's always been my source of comfort. It had been one of the last plays I had studied before my life went downhill, back when I had hopes and dreams. I scored one of my best marks for an essay I had written about its dark humor and how it compares to that of Shakespeare. I'm so deeply engrossed, I don't immediately notice Nick standing over me, smiling in his usual charming way.

"There she is," he grins with his white, straight teeth. He really is quite handsome, but far too flirtatious for my preference. "Apologies, but would you mind switching seats for ten minutes? Nate wants to run through what he needs you to do during our trip."

"Oh, sure, sorry, yeah," I fluster, feeling a creeping blush all over my face and neck, most likely due to my inability to speak at all coherently in front of him and that wicked grin of his. He laughs knowingly; I guess he has this effect on many women.

Still blushing, I shuffle out of my seat and begin walking over with my book in hand. I'm not entirely sure why I didn't put it away but I'm sure Nick's disarming presence had something to do with it. *Cool, Bea, as always, really cool.*

Nathaniel doesn't even bother to look up at me when I arrive, so I just slide in and sit next to him without any words. He continues to tap away on his keyboard while sipping at his glass of something amber and alcoholic. No acknowledgment whatsoever. I'm obviously not worthy of his time or his manners.

Eventually, I cough to clear my throat, and to also let him know that I'm here, waiting, and ready to do his bidding.

"Mr Clayton said you wanted to run through some things

with me," I murmur when I realize he's not going to relieve me of my awkwardness and speak to me.

"Yes, ready?"

Great, no small talk or polite greeting of any kind, just more Nathaniel Carter rudeness.

"Ready," I reply, clutching my phone, ready to type.

"We'll be meeting with various companies; the schedule has been emailed to you. Double-check the times and make sure you are there at least fifteen minutes beforehand. You are to take minutes, have relevant details at the ready, and make sure you personally know information about the attendees. As soon as we arrive in London, I need you to arrange to have some flowers sent to Miss Vivian Spencer, along with an invitation to have dinner with me on Wednesday night. You need to arrange the restaurant, somewhere impressive, somewhere…romantic."

He pauses for a moment and smiles to himself, as if in deep thought over what he is going to do to Miss Vivian Spencer after their romantic dinner.

"Time?" I ask robotically.

"About eight should be fine. Please arrange for some food to be brought to the apartments so we have breakfast and other essentials available. Also, email the office to let them know we have arrived and make sure you keep them posted on all details surrounding our meetings and developments."

"Is that all, Mr Carter?" I finally ask when he offers nothing other than a slurp of his drink. "I take it you won't be needing my services in the evenings?"

"That's all for now," he says, but watches me as I switch

my phone back to its home page. "And no, I do not foresee me needing your services in the evenings. You will be free to do as you wish. Who is that?"

He juts his chin out, pointing it toward the screensaver on my phone. At first, I frown over his sudden interest in my phone, along with the rather impromptu question, but eventually, look down to see a picture of Ben and me. We're actually smiling together; Mom must have taken it.

"Oh, that's my big brother," I reply, smiling affectionately at the picture for a moment or two.

"The one you live with?"

"Yes," I reply slowly, having no idea as to where this is going. "He's the only one I have."

"He was the guy who picked you up last night," he states, and I nod. "And the girl on the bike?" he asks, which only adds to the weirdness of this conversation.

"She's my brother's girlfriend, Leah," I answer, hoping this is the end of the strange conversation. But then he looks at the book in my hand and raises his brow with what appears to be curiosity.

"Ben Jonson?" he asks while pointing at the book. "He's a play-write, isn't he?"

I offer nothing other than a slow nod of my head, still too stunned to answer him with anything more intellectual.

"I'm not familiar with his work, but I've heard of him, mainly through Lily" he explains. "She studied him at college and raves on about him and Shakespeare all the time. Do you often read old English plays?"

"I read a range of things, but I do like Jonson and Shakespeare, yes," I reply, relieved at finally being able to communicate something beyond a nod and a frown. However, from the look on his face, I sense he's waiting for me to elaborate. "I'm named after one of Shakespeare's characters from *Much Ado About Nothing*. Beatrice is a strong female role model, and my mother was a fan of his comedies, so she named me after her. She used to watch the film adaptations with me, then took me to see a few plays in the theatre. I didn't read them properly until I turned into a teen and began studying them at school. My English teacher introduced Jonson to me when I was a junior. I've always wanted to see this live in the theatre, but I am yet to find anywhere that shows it. As far as dark comedy goes, this is by far my favorite. Though, Beatrice will always have a special place in my heart; how could she not?"

"How very…*romantic* of you," he says with a smug smirk on his face, one that tells me he will never take me seriously, even when discussing the merits of seventeenth-century literature.

"I wouldn't call *Volpone* romantic; it's about the lust and greed of already wealthy and powerful men. Volpone seeks to spend the night with another man's young and beautiful wife, which her husband agrees to in the hopes that he will be made the sole heir to Volpone's vast fortune. However, their plans inevitably fail, and they all get their just desserts in the end. You should read it if you can, I think you'd learn a lot from it."

Feeling a little smug, I give him a wide, fake, innocent grin. All I need to do is bat my eyelashes and he'd totally be able to guess I was just mocking him.

Nathaniel looks at me in wonder, as though I have surprised him, both in my reading choice and my open insult. For a moment or two, he sips his drink, all the while looking pensive.

"Is that what ***you*** think should happen?" he eventually asks. "That all 'baddies' should get their 'just desserts'?"

"I'm not naïve, Mr Carter," I reply, "I do not believe in baddies and goodies, for everyone has the potential to be both. I also know that those who do bad things do not necessarily get what's coming to them. However, it would be nice to believe that no crime goes unpunished."

He runs a finger over his bottom lip while he silently assesses me. This time, I stare right back at him, refusing to back away from the intensity of his eyes on mine. This is a silent battle of wills, one I refuse to back down from, and he knows it.

"That will be all, Miss Summers," he says blankly before effectively dismissing me by turning away to work on his laptop.

Taking that as my cue to go, I ungraciously shuffle out of the seat and walk slowly back to my original place. That was, without a doubt, one of the strangest conversations I've ever had with him. It's also one of the longest conversations that didn't involve some sort of insult or chastisement. I'm sure we still hate each other though.

Chapter 6

Bea

It's Tuesday night, two days into our trip to one of the most fascinating cities in the world, steeped in history, fashion, and architecture, and all I can tell you is how thoroughly boring it's been. Admittedly, we have been fortunate enough to pass by various famous landmarks, including Big Ben and Oxford Street, but only when on our way to business meetings. Other than that, there has been zero excitement.

The meetings themselves have been long and arduous, filled with nothing but facts and figures that would have most people falling asleep. I'm sure if it wasn't for the fact that I've been taking minutes, as well as trying to figure out why Nathaniel Carter has been looking at me strangely (somewhere between sneering and curiosity), I'm sure I wouldn't have survived them. We've risen early and finished late, with only cafeteria food in between. Bar the odd eyeballing, Nathaniel treats me no better than back at home. In fact, I'd go so far as to say he's stepped his charming personality up a gear. Yesterday was perhaps the worst day of being Nathaniel's PA to date. The bastard had a nice willing audience to perform for, and I was an active participant whether I wanted to be or not.

Let me set the scene; the first meeting had gone well as far as I could tell. The prospective buyer was impressed with what we had to offer and wanted to invest in one of our top packages. The second meeting of the day, however, reminded me just how little Nathaniel thinks of me. I had been typing up minutes while everything was, again, going sweetly for Nathaniel. He oozed charm and had people wrapped around his finger within minutes of meeting them.

The CEO of the company was a kindly, older gentleman, who could easily double up as Father Christmas if he really wanted to. He chuckled at each of Nathaniel's office-appropriate jokes, winked at me with reassurance, and spoke to everyone with warmth and friendliness. It was actually one of the better meetings, purely because of this gentleman who was respectful to all who he came across. I could imagine him stopping off to feed the birds on his way home from work, tipping his hat to all who he came across, then quietly reading a battered copy of 'Great Expectations' by the fire with his evening glass of tipple.

The finance director, however, was more of a Nathaniel type, just in female form. She was stunningly beautiful and filthy rich from both the look and smell of her. If her fragrance wasn't enough of a clue, then the fact she was covered in designer labels and spoke in a cliché, posh English accent, was certainly a big enough giveaway. It was far more prominent than Lily's accent, as in it was most likely fake. This woman obviously attended a private school and only associated with like-minded people, i.e., those who think they are better and more deserving of their position in life. I accepted her completely ignoring my existence from the second we walked into the room. To be fair, after meeting her, I didn't expect anything more. She openly gushed at Nathaniel and constantly flicked her hair, pursed her lips, and laughed far too enthusiastically at all of his semi-funny work jokes. It goes without saying that I instantly disliked her.

Halfway through the meeting, my laptop switched off by itself. Several expletives had whizzed though my mind all the while I pressed on the power button, only to have nothing happen. I then began looking around for a power cable, but when I did find it, and plugged it in, nothing changed. By this point, the attendees had noticed something was up and were looking at me for some sort of explanation.

"Is there a problem, Miss Summers?" Nathaniel asked curtly.

"The laptop seems to have stopped working," I said, looking at him blankly. "The power cable isn't doing anything; there must be something wrong with it."

Miss Snooty Pants had laughed with condescension before looking at Nathaniel with a smug expression, her eyes bulging and her head subtly shaking, as if goading him to lose his shit with me. Nathaniel smiled a smile that didn't reach his eyes. Instead, it told me I was about to feel his wrath in a chilling and humiliating way.

"What can I say? You just can't get the staff these days." He faked laughed, which only prompted bitch face to do the same. If I was brave enough, I would have loved to have slapped both of them around their smug faces.

"***I*** would say you can't get the technology," the older gentleman laughed sympathetically, then gifted me with a reassuring wink.

"May I borrow some paper and a pen?" I asked with a shy

smile toward the old man. "I can take minutes the old-fashioned way."

"No point, Miss Summers," Nathaniel said with a smell under his nose, "we have nearly finished the meeting, so you are excused."

He stared at me until I packed up my things and left the room. Miss Up-Her-Own-Ass had smirked the entire time, just like the girls at school used to do whenever I happened to breathe the same air as them. This is when I finally went straight to the toilets and screamed at my reflection, along with a few choice words.

Luckily, I woke up today with a whole new outlook. I decided that this was his issue, not mine. I gave myself a stern pep talk in the bathroom mirror, put on a little more war paint than usual, and marched out with renewed determination.

By the time lunchtime approached, all had gone ok, even with Nathaniel and the snooty bitch from yesterday flirting up a storm. They were doing that annoying and rude habit of whispering to one another, followed by smug laughter, and winking.

We all sat for lunch together, the peasants and the big bosses, pretending that we all liked one another and weren't feeling at all awkward. Fortunately, the kindly old CEO from yesterday, Mr Paul Chambers, was sitting next to me. Although he was our big target, and the one we needed to really impress to seal the contract, he put me at ease. I guess he felt like a parental figure to me - calm, reassuring, and caring. Not only that, but he spotted my well-read copy of 'Volpone' and began discussing Shakespeare with me, something I could actually talk about with enthusiasm.

"I especially like to watch such plays in the summer, when

you can find performances in outside arenas, like old abbeys and castles. My wife and I enjoy taking a picnic and watching them in outdoor theatres. Beaulieu Abbey is one of our favorites."

"Sounds amazing," I reply, feeling genuinely enchanted by the picture he paints. "I would love to go and see a play while being surrounded by history."

Alas, our conversation is cut short by the sound of loud, obnoxious laughter which is coming from the other end of our table.

"It is so very rare to find a good PA, isn't it?" Bitch Face says, completely ignoring the fact that Sam and I are both within earshot. Actually, she's probably saying it ***because*** we're within earshot, especially me. I can't help but glance at Mr Chambers, feeling incredibly embarrassed and suddenly beneath him… beneath everyone. I remember this feeling well; I had hoped to never feel this way again.

"I disagree," Nathaniel pipes in with a smirk, one that contradicts what he just said. "My previous PA was outstanding, he really was. Jack was punctual, efficient and knew every detail about my likes and dislikes. I was sad to see him go, to be honest, but I can hardly argue with my big brother if he decides he wants what I have. I suppose it was payback for my antics during childhood. I always wanted what he had, and I usually got it."

"Oh, poor baby," Bitch Face teases and laughs over his cutesy story, which only made him sound like a complete brat in my opinion. I notice both Nick and Sam looking uncomfortable, with Nick choosing not to engage.

"I also have to disagree with you," Mr Chambers suddenly announces from my right. "I have a fantastic PA, couldn't ask for anyone better." He then turns to face me, giving me his full attention and looking so serious and respectful, I'm in danger of letting my mounting tears escape. "You remind me a lot of her. From what I've seen, Miss Summers, if you ever wish to relocate to London, please look me up and I will gladly give you a position. If there's one thing I've learned over many years of experience in this profession, it's to never let a good PA go. You are never as good without your PA."

I have to smile at the old man for giving Nathaniel his polite version of the finger. Not only that, but as soon as he's seen that I've been reassured, he turns back to face Nathaniel with a quirk of his eyebrow.

"Thank you, Mr Chambers, you are very kind, and that really means a lot," I politely reply. "If you'll excuse me though, I suddenly feel unwell. I think I will make my way back to the apartment. Sam," I begin, and he turns to look up at me, "would you mind walking me back? I think I might get lost if I try and walk on my own."

"Of course, gladly," Sam replies, then stands to join me.

"Thank you again, Mr Chambers, it's been a real pleasure to meet you."

Once the fresh air hits me, I feel the sting of tears running down my cheeks, and the need to have a good cry becomes so overwhelming, I can only hope the apartment isn't too far from here. Embarrassingly, Sam sees the effect that lunch has had on me, so quietly turns in to hold me. He doesn't say anything, but I'm relieved for his silence.

"Let's get out of here," I eventually mutter with a noisy sniff.

"Sure thing, Bea," he says soothingly, and we walk back to

our little home away from home.

Bea

Night is upon us, and it's the first one that we've finished at a decent hour. In fact, after our hideous lunch, Sam and I were told to take the entire afternoon off. I could have taken offense at this, but I honestly didn't have the energy to question it that deeply. Instead, we picked up some takeout pizza, grabbed some chocolate and cheap booze, and headed back to the apartment to watch whatever movie we could find on the television. We probably should have taken advantage of the free time by going on a tourist tour, or perhaps wandered down to Harrods for a bit of window shopping, but I think Nathaniel managed to zap me of all my energy when he practically accused me of being a shit PA. As for Sam, I just think he's plain lazy. It took very little to convince him to stay in for the night.

Nick and Nathaniel came home a few hours after lunch, both silent, both heading straight up to their top-floor apartment. Nick took precisely twenty-eight minutes to get suited and booted, after which, he flew out the door with a quick wave goodbye. Nathaniel took a little longer, but pretty much followed in his footsteps, minus the wave or any kind of acknowledgment of our existence. *Good riddance* was all I could think of saying once he had exited the building.

With the bosses gone, Sam and I change into our slob gear before setting up our provisions, mainly in the form of junk food and syrupy homemade cocktails. We then choose a nice gory horror flick that's more cheesy than scary and sit with our feet perched on the small coffee table.

"Are we really sad for not going out to experience the

nightlife of London?" I giggle to Sam.

"Yeah," he laughs with me, "but I'm shattered after two boring days of meetings, and I also have a very, *very*, limited budget."

"Hmm, well, we can't all be mega-rich management types, can we?" I agree, flicking through the TV again because the movie was *too* cheesy, even for me. After a couple of rounds with the remote, I finally stop when I find *The Breakfast Club*.

"I'm really into this film at the moment," I tell him, "I'm so attracted to the bad boy."

"I bet you are, Miss Summers," Sam smirks wickedly. "Speaking of which, you have anyone back home who you're seeing at the moment?"

"Oh, God, no," I reply, looking at him as though he's crazy for even thinking such a thing. "You?"

He shakes his head with a sad sigh, putting his bottle down so he can turn to face me.

"That means we're free to have wild sex if we get really bored," he says with a half-serious, half-amused expression. I cannot help but look a little stunned, but when he breaks into a wide grin, I throw an ice cube at him for teasing me.

"The last girl I dated said I was too full on for her, so she ditched me," he explains, wincing over the memory of it. "What a bitch."

"Were you though?" I ask with the alcohol obliterating my brain-to-mouth filter.

"I don't know," he says contemplatively. "Let me show

you; set the scene, as it were. Come on, I need you to stand up and pretend to be her."

"Er…you're not going to do anything weird or creepy are you?"

"God, no, just stand woman!" he orders, so we both stand up in the middle of the living room, feeling a little tipsy. Once we are standing face-to-face, he reaches out and takes hold of my hands in his, then looks deep into my eyes. I can tell by the way his pupils are dilated that he's a bit farther gone than I am. My body suddenly tenses, knowing just how far drunk people can go.

"Have another one, beautiful, I'll look after you…"

"I said to her, I said 'Chelsea, Chelsea…'" he slurs, the alcohol suddenly smelling potent on his breath. "I think you are the most beautiful, most perfect woman I have ever met. I want to kiss you now and I hope you will kiss me back because if you don't, I shall die," he laughs in a high-pitched way, only to then turn serious. He looks at me with his eyes rolling around, before pulling me against his chest and beginning to lean down with his lips pursed, getting ready to attack my own.

"That's it, beautiful, drink all of it, then we can have some fun…"

"Sam," I gasp, trying to back out of his grip, "Sam, stop it!"

"What the fuck is going on here?!" a voice cries out from the doorway, the same one that I am certain was closed a minute ago. However, Nathaniel Carter is now standing where the door was with his tall, broad frame looking both tense and intimidating. His brow is furrowed, his eyes dark, and his jaw tightly clenched. I don't think I've ever seen him looking so furious before, and I've seen him mad…a lot!

"Get the fuck away from her!"

It's almost comical, as well as a welcome relief when Sam leaps back sheepishly and begins scratching at the back of his neck. Conversely, I remain frozen solid on the spot, probably looking as though my father has just caught me with a boy in my room.

"Need I remind the both of you that office relationships are forbidden and will not be tolerated?! Now get your fucking hands off one another before I fire you both on the spot!"

"It's not what it looks like, Mr Carter," Sam says in a fluster. "We were just messing –"

"I don't give a shit! You have no right to use a business trip as an excuse to fuck each other, do I make myself clear?"

The way he's barking at us, together with everything else that's come to pass over the last few days, causes something to snap inside of me. My shock and humiliation turn to rage and the angry bull inside has me refusing to back down, so I cross my arms and narrow my eyes in challenge. He looks back at me with a cross between fury and mild confusion over my defiant stance, quirking an eyebrow in question over my refusal to look meek and mild before him. I simply tip my head to the side, as if daring him to take one more step closer. I daren't open my mouth to say something for I think I really would lose my job if I allowed the running roll of expletives to fall from my lips. Still, he looks on at me, trying to work out if the usual mouse of a woman is really going to challenge him. *Hold your ground, Beatrice Summers.*

"Y-yes, Mr Carter," Sam stutters, looking to the floor like a good little employee. Nathaniel continues to glare at me before finally slamming the door and stomping up the stairs.

"Oh, my fuck, I thought I was going to piss my pants," Sam laughs. "What a dick! Hey, are you ok?"

"No, Sam, I'm not ok," I tell him before directing my anger toward him. After all, the little stunt he just tried to pull ended in me being crapped on by my boss once again. "And yes, you did come across too strong."

Before he can say anything, I about turn and walk into my bedroom. I'm so over this trip.

Chapter 7

Bea

An overnight flight back home has me begging to fall asleep. Alas, I am unable to. Truthfully, I haven't slept properly since Nathaniel shouted at Sam and me on Wednesday night. I'm beginning to think Leah and my brother are right; this can't go on. Something needs to give or else one of us is most likely going to end up murdering the other.

As soon as we step outside the 'Arrivals' building, with the early morning sun looking exactly the same as when we were leaving, nearly a week ago, I let out a sigh of relief. I then plaster on a smile for Leah, who is already sitting on top of her bike, waiting for me to come and hop on behind her. Seeing her brings up a lot of emotions I didn't expect to feel, but I do know I am beyond thankful to be going home. Without so much as a goodbye to the others, I begin marching in her direction. I don't even know if I am expected to work today; there are still a whole load of business hours left.

"Beatrice?" I recognize Nick's voice shouting out to me before I can escape completely. I could pretend not to hear him and tell Leah to drive on regardless, however, guilt stops me in my quest to get the hell away from my boss. After all, Nick has been the only one of them to not treat me like crap.

"Sorry, Mr Clayton, I forgot…I'm…"

I realize I have no idea how to even form a coherent sentence after my lack of sleep, or the shed load of stress from the last few days. In the end, I blow air through my lips and simply shake my head.

"Don't worry, I'm pretty jet-lagged too," he says with his charming smile, "and please, call me Nick."

"Sorry…Nick, what time should I come in today?" I fake smile, praying I'll be given a reprieve from work today.

"Don't worry about coming in until next week. I'll square it with Cameron, as well as your idiot of a boss," he says with a serious expression I don't often see him wearing. "Trust me when I say, we don't all feel that way about PAs. You guys do a stellar job and if he can't see that, then that's his flaw, not yours."

I offer him a nervous smile, suddenly aware of his hand resting on my arm and its heat spreading out over my otherwise numb limb, for I'm that tired. Before I can even thank him, Nathaniel and Sam walk up from behind. Nathaniel is frowning over our exchange, but I'll take what Nick's offering and let him deal with it. I cannot imagine for one minute that Cameron will care, so I nod my thanks to Nick, then race over to Leah before Nathaniel can get involved and force me to go in. I'll let Monday me worry about having to deal with him.

Nate

"When did you tell her to be in today?" I ask Nick as we watch Bea ride away on her friend's bike.

"She's not coming in today, Nate," he says with a sigh laced with disappointment. "Perhaps you shouldn't either."

"What's that supposed to mean?" I snap, already knowing what it means. I lost my cool yet again.

"Mr Clayton, if it's ok with you, I'm going to head home and get changed," Sam says, avoiding all eye contact with me. Good, he should after what I saw the other night.

"Sure, Sam, I'll see you on Monday," Nick says with a warm smile for his PA, something I haven't given mine since that first meeting. A pang of guilt hits me and I begin to wonder if what Cameron had said is right; have I been projecting my own doubts onto her?

"Are you sure? I'm happy to still come in today," he says, showing genuine willingness to come in and put in the extra mile for Nick. Beatrice couldn't wait to get away from me.

"No, you take the day," he replies, "couldn't have done London without you, Sam, I really appreciate it. Go and enjoy a long weekend; work can always wait."

"Thank you," Sam says with an embarrassed smile, though he is clearly reveling in his boss' words. He then turns to face me, and I step back, shocked that he would acknowledge me, particularly with such a serious expression. There's not a hint of intimidation or, dare I say it, respect.

"Mr Carter," he says, sounding as confident as he can, "what you saw the other evening was completely innocent. Yes, we had been drinking, but I was telling Bea about an ex who…Look, never mind, the point is, it was nothing. I respect her too much to try and get with her under the influence of alcohol. I know you don't think a lot of her, but you should. Even I can see she's only living half a life, and every time you chip away at her, she lives it even less. From someone who grew up in extreme poverty, who never knew when he'd get his next real meal, you don't know what life someone's coming from when they walk into work that day."

I don't know what to say when he finally finishes, so I end up saying nothing. I had no idea about his past, and I also have no idea how to respond.

"Anyway, I'm going to grab an Uber," he says, jacking his thumb out over his shoulder. "Thanks, Nick, see you next week."

"Bye, Sam," he replies, "wish Harry luck for me on Sunday."

"I will, thanks."

I watch him march away on his long lanky legs before turning off around the corner to catch his ride home.

"Who's Harry?" I eventually ask Nick, who has now come to stand beside me.

"Sam's kid brother, still in high school but a whizz on the football field," he tells me.

I say nothing at first, just remain staring in the distance, not wanting to face him, for I know he doesn't think a lot of me at the moment.

"See you next week, Nate," he says with a sigh.

"Yeah," I huff before walking away.

———

Bea

I didn't tell Leah or Ben about what happened while I was away because I didn't want to hear about it anymore. I pretty much went home on Friday and slept for most of the day. Leah went back to her place to study, and Ben was at work, so I was left pretty much unbothered. Well, not until about four o'clock when I received a text message from Callie:

Hi Bea, hope you can still make it tomorrow night? C x

I'd totally forgotten about agreeing to go to Lily's bachelorette party, but I find myself smiling over the thought of being able to go out with some female friends. I can't remember the last time I went out without Finn by my side. Ben and Leah spend every waking moment together, usually eating one another's faces, so I tend to leave them to it. It always used to be Emma and me, up until she turned into someone I no longer recognized. The only thing that turns my mood sour is the realization that they are also Nathaniel's friends. In fact, he's practically family to Lily. But still, I can kick back on a girls' only night; surely, he wouldn't care if he's not even there.

Absolutely. I could definitely do with a night out after the week I've had. X

As soon as I press the send button, I slap my hand to my face, knowing they are bound to question me on it, and what do I say then? '*Your soon-to-be brother-in-law and longtime friend is a total ass wipe, but please don't tell the big boss that.*' I blame the fatigue for not being able to filter what enters my head before sharing.

Intriguing! We must talk about it tomorrow. Meet us at Bamboo 21 at 9pm. X

Of course, now I have to figure out what the hell to wear. What *do* you wear when you go clubbing? I've never been before, not even with Finn. We usually frequent bars and restaurants, avoiding places that remind me of high school parties where the popular kids would show off their fancy outfits while gyrating against one another. The thought of volunteering to go to a place like that has always brought me out in hives; Finn's going to have a field day when I tell him where I went. Not that I'm yet talking to him after the stunt he pulled.

Unfortunately, this means I'm going to have to consult Leah and Ben, which is so not what I want to do. I'm sure Ben will insist I dress in a boiler suit, perhaps even carry a small weapon in the heel of my boot. I think back to when I used to be able to consult Emma on these sorts of things, but that was such a long time ago now. I'm sure she now has friends who are far better at all that girly stuff. Luckily for her, she no longer has to slum it with her big, dowdy sister who she found so easy to betray.

Bea

That evening, still wearing my PJs, I hear the buzzer to the apartment and practically jump out of my skin. Ben and Leah are both working, and, sad as this is, I cannot think of who else would be coming around to see me. I half-wonder if it might be my mother coming over to make peace with me after our phone call last week. However, when I finally pick up the phone, it's Finn's sheepish voice that is begging me to let him come up. I can't imagine how he managed to get a Friday night off but I'm glad he's here; it's about time we made up. I'm not going to let Nathaniel Carter spoil a perfectly good friendship.

"Come on up," I tell him, then press the entry button to let him in. I open the door for him to walk straight through while I set up a couple of glasses and a bottle of wine that Ben hasn't emptied.

Then, just to tease him, I stand in sight of the doorway with my arms crossed, looking as though I'm about to give him hell like a girlfriend might do with her cheating lover. It works, for when he steps inside, he looks straight to the floor and rocks on his feet for a moment or two, obviously not knowing what to say for the best. I let him sweat it out for but a few seconds before I burst into laughter and bound up to his slumped body so I can kiss him on the cheek.

"I guess you're forgiven," I laugh. He releases a sigh of relief before surprising me with a bunch of flowers and a bottle of 'sorry' wine.

"Ah!" I gush, relieving him of the beautifully long, purple flowers and the bottle of red. "You totally should have!"

"Well, I know irises are your favorite," he says with a shy shrug before taking his usual place on the sofa. "This for me?"

He lifts the glass of wine before I can answer and takes a sip of it anyway.

"It is now," I reply, nudging him as I take my seat next to him. "Jerk!"

"I'm sorry, Bea, I mean it," he says, now looking serious, enough to make me stop smiling. "It was shitty of me to blow you off like that. Especially from what you've told me about the way he treats you. You're my best friend and I should have had your back."

We look at one another for a moment before I crack a smile and we hug it out, effectively accepting his apology.

"So how was the night out anyway? See plenty of stripper action?" I tease.

"Ho-lee shit!" he says with bulging eyes. "There was so much pussy on display, even I blushed. I think it was my first and last time inside of a strip club; it just wasn't what I thought it would be."

"Finn, it's a strip club, what the hell did you expect?" I laugh at him.

"I dunno! Perhaps…I don't know. Besides, you need to be seriously loaded to last long in one of those places."

"I bet Nathaniel is a seasoned pro!" I sneer before taking a huge gulp of wine.

"I couldn't tell you," he says, shrugging again. "He stayed for one drink, then left. He didn't pay attention to one single girl in there. Instead, he asked me about how we knew one another. As soon as I told him the very scaled-back version, he said he had to go; something about a family emergency or some such excuse."

"You didn't tell him about therapy or anything else, did you?" I blurt out, my eyes now the size of saucers and my chest heaving with anxiety.

"Of course not," he quickly replies, screwing up his face at me for even thinking such a thing. "I would never tell anyone about your personal business, babe."

"Ok, good," I sigh with relief, "that would be so humiliating. He'd no doubt use it to make my life even more miserable if he knew my background."

"Hmm, maybe," he murmurs, then turns to look at me. "Bea, is he really that bad to you? Cos I just don't get it. He comes to our place a lot and is always so respectful of all the staff. He always tips, like incredibly well," he explains, his eyes bulging over the thought. "And he is always the first person to put someone in their place if they act all high and mighty with the staff."

"I don't know, Finn," I sigh, "perhaps I just rub him up the wrong way. It feels like I'm at high school all over again; he's the school bully and I'm his victim. I can't even begin to imagine what Ben would do if he managed to get his hands on him."

"Maybe I should ask him what his problem is the next time he's in," he says, looking like a little boy who's just come up with what he believes to be the greatest idea on the planet.

"No, no, no," I rush out, gripping his arm tightly so he winces a little. "You can't do that; he'll know I bitch about him. Promise me, Finn," I demand whilst pointing at him. "Promise me that when it comes to me, you keep schtum!"

"Ow, shit," he says while rubbing at his arm. "Ok, I'll pretend like I don't even know you. Christ, who's the bully now?"

"Sorry, but he makes me insane," I huff as I throw myself back against the couch. "What am I going to do? I can't carry on like this, it's killing me!"

"But Bea, you deserve this promotion," he argues, "don't let some dick like Nathaniel Carter bring you down just because he's got some weird hang-up about you. Drink wine and say, 'fuck you' to him."

"Ok," I laugh, then gulp back another mouthful. "Fuck you!"

At that moment, Ben walks through the door in his work uniform, obviously having just got back from a local flight; he only left this morning. No matter how many times I see him dressed in his pilot's uniform, it always looks strange to see my big, goofy brother wearing something that looks so grown up and responsible.

Even I can admit, Leah is a very lucky gal. Not only is Ben an attractive man, but he is also smart, loyal, and incredibly protective.

Though, having said that, I'm starting to think his feelings for her are waning. He's so adamant about not moving out with her, and it can't just be because of me. They've been together forever, so what else could possibly be stopping him from taking that next step?

"Hey, Finn, she's forgiven you then?" he smirks at the same time as he ruffles my hair, completely snapping me out of my thoughts about how grown up he is. "Not cool, man. Who are we 'fuck you-ing' anyway?"

"Nathaniel Carter," Finn and I both answer in unison.

"I'll drink to that!" Ben grins as he pours himself a glass. "Fuck you, Nathaniel Carter, and pray I never get my hands on you."

Chapter 8

Bea

When I eventually brave it to walk into the living room, Leah makes me feel even more self-conscious by emitting a loud wolf whistle. Ben, on the other hand, looks as though I'm about to go and serve myself up before a group of randy guys in a strip club. In the end, I had to borrow something from Leah which she had handpicked herself. Contrasting completely with what I would normally wear, I am now dressed in a short, fitted black dress, covered in sequins, coupled with a pair of ridiculously high, black stilettos. I can foresee me having to visit the Emergency Room tonight with injuries to my back and neck, obtained from falling spectacularly in front of a club full of beautiful people.

"I can't let my little sister go out looking like that!" Ben gasps.

"Oh, shut up, she looks totally hot," Leah whoops, whistles, then signals for me to turn. "Work it, Baby!"

"Oh, God, do I look like a complete slut?" I ask, blushing in front of my big brother. "This is really short; people are going to see my hoo-hah!"

"Hey, those are my clothes!" Leah cries, feigning insult before laughing at me.

"And while they're as sexy as hell on you, baby, I can't say that about my little sister," Ben says directly to her, trying his best to smooth things over. He then looks at me one more time and runs his hand over his face before groaning. "Jesus, have you at least got your mace?"

I take a little spray bottle out of my bag and waggle it his way. He nods his head with his serious, pilot expression, then signals for me to put it safely back inside of my bag. Ever since I moved in and got a job, he's forced me to take this thing with me everywhere, along with a rape alarm. Thankfully, I've never had to use them, but I will admit having them to hand makes me feel a lot safer. Once inside my bag, I look at my watch and curse under my breath at the time. I throw on my leather jacket and begin walking down the hallway, ready to go and catch the taxi downstairs. Ben insists on escorting me down to the roadside where the cab is already waiting.

"You call me if there is any trouble, Bea," he says sternly. "I don't care what time it is, where you are, or who you're with; you call me."

I give him a teasing salute before going up on my tiptoes to peck him on the cheek. He merely tuts before opening the door to the cab so I can hop inside. As it begins to pull away, I wave out of the window and giggle over his panic-stricken face. He's such an idiot but I do love him.

Bea

As soon as I step outside the cab, I feel like running back to the apartment again. 'Self-conscious' doesn't even begin to describe how I feel at this point. In fact, I feel like if anyone so much as sneezes, my minuscule dress is going to fly up and reveal my vajayjay. No wonder I feel like dozens of eyes are on me, assessing me, judging me, thinking I'm not good enough to be here.

She's not pretty enough to be with Dean, not like her sister. Emma's a much better fit for him.

I shake those ugly thoughts away, trying to be in the here and now so I can move without toppling over. When I finally walk inside and onto the main floor, I take a good look around; I've never been in a place like this before, although I've heard a lot about this particular one from some of the girls at work. Right in the center of a barn of a room, there is a large, circular bar, packed with customers shouting out their orders to the poor bar staff. The dance floor is further toward the back but is fairly empty at the moment. A DJ is playing warm-up music on a raised podium to the side of it. He appears to be lost to the music, looking extremely pensive while he moves disks, presses buttons, and flicks switches. You can see it's a real science, as well as a passion for this guy.

Once my eyes have grown accustomed to the sheer magnitude of this place, I stop studying the interior, and instead, try to spot Callie and Lily. A sudden and unwanted thought crosses my mind; what if they haven't come and I'm here all alone? I might be standing here like a complete idiot, waiting to see people who aren't even here. Perhaps I got the wrong day, the wrong club, or the wrong time, or they simply changed their minds.

"Bea!" I hear someone call out from behind me. "Bea, you sexy bitch, get over here!"

I immediately turn around to see Callie shouting at me from the other side of the bar. She, Lily, Ellie, and a few others are all standing around a tall circular table; I've never felt so relieved to see a group of girls my age before. I begin shuffling over as fast as I can in these ridiculous shoes and begin saying my hellos.

"Holy hell, Miss Summers," Lily exclaims, "where did this body come from? And your hair is stunning!"

I instinctively ignore her flattery; sadly, I can accept insults more easily than compliments. I suppose I can more readily believe all the bad stuff.

"Hi, sorry I'm late, my brother made me spend half an hour trying to find a can of mace!" I lie. It sounds a little better than telling them I was freaking out for an hour before I could bring myself to get ready.

"Ahh," Lily says, placing one of her hands over her heart. "I wish I had a big brother."

"Is he hot?" Callie asks, to which Lily taps her on the shoulder while rolling her eyes in an exaggerated fashion.

"I have to admit, he is attractive to the opposite sex, but very much in love with his long-term girlfriend," I break it to her, even though I am no longer sure about the two of them. Something is off; I just can't put my finger on it. However, now is not the time to ponder on such things, so I pull out my phone to show them a picture.

"Damn," Callie says with disappointment, "I could have done bad things to him."

"Ignore Callie creaming her knickers over your brother," Lily grins, "you know Ellie and Hels from work, but this is James, my super-hot best friend." She gestures to an attractive guy with warm eyes and a dazzling smile. He looks friendly but so handsome, I end up giggling through nerves.

I recognize Helena as the Carter sister who took over reception from me. Unfortunately, ever since I handed the desk over to her, we've barely spoken. When we first met, I couldn't believe she was related to the Carters; she might share their good looks, but she certainly doesn't share their confidence. In fact, I don't think she has any; she's a totally different person from them. And I know she doesn't ever socialize with anyone, not that I have much room to speak on that subject.

"So, what's your poison?" Callie asks me.

"Oh, I'm easy, I'll have whatever the group is having."

"No, no, no, baby," James says with a dangerously sexy voice. "You say what you want and you own that shit. You ain't at work now; you be the confident, beautiful woman you are!"

I giggle, knowing I instantly like this guy. He's the type of person who builds you up and gives you life, not the kind of person who knocks you down and bleeds you dry. I've had the misfortune to have a lot of those come into my life, but James, Lily, and Callie are like Ben and Finn, and I hope I can keep hold of them, even if they are Nathaniel's friends too.

"Come with me and we will get you something you truly want," James says as he links his arm through mine, already beginning to march us toward the bar. *God, he smells divine too.*

"Erm, James… I really don't have a specific drink. I really am that easy," I whisper.

"Oh, we're about to change all that," he declares while signaling to the attractive bartender, who could easily audition for the role of Thor, should Chris Hemsworth suddenly decide he wants to retire. "Hey, man, this beautiful woman has no idea what she wants and says, get this, she's 'easy'!"

I cannot help but blush with a wince in front of the insanely attractive barman. Conversely, he emits a laugh that sounds like pure velvet, then leans in closer to look me up and down. He narrows his eyes, as if in deep thought, before smiling flirtatiously. I think I'm holding my breath but can't really be certain at this moment in time.

"Hmm, I think something with Disaronno, a sexy Italian liquor, with crushed ice and…citrus," he suggests, "sound any good?"

"Sounds awfully tempting," I sigh, feeling something close to flirting with this man who obviously has a lot of confidence with the opposite sex. Someone who will humor me if nothing else. He holds my eye contact a little longer than is considered normal barman etiquette, then begins to make the delicious-sounding cocktail. I watch as his muscular body moves around under his beautiful, flawless skin, all the while he shakes, pours, and throws. I bite my lip, considering what he could do to a girl in the bedroom, or maybe just right here on the bar.

"One Disaronno cocktail for the beautiful lady," he says seductively.

"Th-thanks," I reply awkwardly before taking a small sip. "Holy fuck! That's amazing."

"That's on me, beautiful," the bartender says with a saucy wink, "but maybe a dance later?"

I shyly nod and giggle at the same time, looking extremely uncool in front of the mythical god-like creature. James is grinning from ear to ear by the time I let him lead me back to the table, looking extremely proud of himself.

"Oh, this one works fast, ladies," James tells the group, "she got a freebie and a promise of a dance with the hottie bartender."

"Ah, the force is strong with this one!" Callie makes her bad joke, but we all giggle anyway. I glance back at the bartender who is still looking at me; he eventually winks, smiles, then continues to serve other people at the bar. That was so the confidence boost I needed.

———

Bea

An hour or two passes by and I am having the best time with my new friends. I haven't laughed this much in ages, which admittedly, is partly down to the four glasses of my new favorite cocktail, along with a few shots in between. Lily is having a brilliant time having to do naughty dares, but now we're onto a new game. An old classic - *Never Have I.*

"So, we all know the rules ladies, and James," Callie announces. "We take turns to say something we have never done and if you have done whatever it is, you drink either a shot or two fingers of your drink. We all know I will be the loser, but the question is, who will be the next loser?"

"Ok, me first," Lily says, now slurring her words a little, "never have I had more than one sexual partner."

Apart from Lily, we all slurp our drinks. It's a fact I'd rather not have to acknowledge, but what's the point in lying to them?

"Wow, so Cameron was your first and only?" I ask, to

which she nods shyly but with a silly grin on her face.

"And at the old age of twenty-four," she admits.

"Wow, that's kind of cool. Though, I'm guessing you weren't *his* first and only?"

Of course, I already know the answer to this after having been on reception for a few years before Cameron started seeing Lily. The table erupts into fits of laughter, including Lily, so I'm guessing they're all aware of how much action he used to get before gifting his heart to her.

"No, the Carter men are well known for their sexual appetite," she giggles, "but I'm definitely his only woman now. If not, I will be cutting it off!"

"Never have I had a one-night stand," Ellie announces. Just Callie and I drink this time, which sets all eyes on me.

"Really?" James asks and I nod with feelings of deep-rooted shame. "Go bartender!"

"It was horrible though," I admit, "I was drunk, very drunk, and felt so dirty afterward."

"That's not my experience," Callie grins before taking another swig of her drink.

"Well, I don't like to think about it," I sigh, admitting to things I really shouldn't. "I promised myself I would never do that again."

"Oh, baby," James says soothingly as he rubs my arm in sympathy.

"Erm…" Helena begins, trying to bring us out of our funk, even though she sounds painfully uncomfortable over having to speak out over us. "Well, I can safely say I have never had impure thoughts about my boss."

"Yeah, that would be a little incestuous of you," Lily giggles at the same time as wrapping an arm around her.

Callie drinks yet again but I keep my glass firmly on the table.

"Nothing at all, Bea?" Callie asks with a wiggle of her eyebrows. "Nate is totally gorgeous, just like all you Carter folk," she says, gesturing to a blushing Helena.

"God, no!" I blurt out, screwing up my face in abhorrence over the idea. They all look at me with surprised but amused faces, including his sister and cousin. "Oh, Jeez, sorry," I fluster, "I didn't mean to offend anyone. He is extremely pretty to look at, but, well, your brother isn't afraid to let me know how little he thinks of me."

"Really?" Helena gasps. "But Nate's the easy-going one, the fun-loving one. It's always been Cameron who is more serious. Well, until he met Lily, of course."

Lily merely grins with a drunken look all over her face.

"Oh, Cameron is absolutely lovely to me, and all the staff. To be fair, I think Nathaniel is exactly as you described to everyone else. It's just me he hates."

I shrug my shoulders and give her a smile that doesn't reach my eyes. In fact, I can feel them beginning to well up over the realization that there's yet somebody else hating me. I don't know what I did to deserve this, or what I am doing to warrant such intense feelings of dislike toward me, but I wish it would just stop. I just want it all to stop, to be who I once was, and not have some mean asshole making my life hell.

"I'm really sorry, Bea, you seem like such a lovely person. Do you want me to have a word?" Helena offers, obviously sensing my pain, even though I'm trying really hard not to show it. "Nate and I are sort of close, not like we once were, but…" She looks sadly at the floor before shaking it off.

"Yeah, I'll talk to the idiot too," Callie pipes up, sounding as though she's ready to go to war if she has to.

"Oh, God, no, no, no," I rush out in a panic. "Please don't, it's fine, honestly. It's a working relationship and I can manage it. Please just ignore me; pretend I didn't say anything."

"Ok, fine," Callie huffs, "but you need to start standing up for yourself. I saw the way he was with you; he was bang out of order!"

The table falls silent, and I inwardly curse myself for ruining the atmosphere.

"Never have I used sex toys during sex," I push out, trying to get the mood back. Thankfully, it works because our bride-to-be knocks back a shot, to which the whole table gasps.

"It was Cam who brought them in," she cries out, "along with a few other things."

"You little dark horse," Callie teases, "I knew I'd rubbed off on you somewhere. Here's to sex!"

"To sex!" We all cheer, including the people all around us.

Bea

With sex having been officially toasted and Lily having completed no less than ten ridiculous dares, we are all now officially drunk. Lily and Callie perhaps more so, and Helena less so. I am not so sure where I am on the drunk scale, but I am still managing to remain upright on my stilettos. I am certain I have fresh blisters on the backs of my ankles, but with the alcohol currently floating around my system, I am virtually numb to the pain, for now at least. Tomorrow, I'll be cursing myself.

"Let's go and dance!" I suggest, which is totally out of character for me. I even jump out of the booth and begin wiggling my hips in the direction of the dance floor.

"Oh, yeah," James replies enthusiastically, "now you're talking. Did you know I teach a little dance?"

"No!" I gasp, immediately latching on to his strong arm. "Oh, please, teach me. I'm a totally shit dancer."

"Lead the way," he says, so we turn to go and make fools of ourselves on the dance floor.

"What the fuck is she doing here?!"

No sooner have we turned to march ourselves away, do we run into the tall and broad frame of Nathaniel Carter. He looks me up and down with an expression that appears to be beyond pissed. I'm taken right back to the office, feeling as I do every Monday to Friday when I have to work under his stern glare.

"Nate!" Lily exclaims, looking completely drunk, but excited to see him. "What are you doing here? Is my baby here?"

"Oh, no, no, no, you're not supposed to be seeing him tonight; this is girls' night only!" Callie snaps, wagging her finger from side to side.

"Yeah, he's over on the other side of the bar," Nate replies sulkily, completely ignoring Callie's warning.

"Sorry, ladies, but I'm going to go and dirty dance with my fiancé," Lily announces, then begins wobbling over to the bar.

"Go get her, Ellie," Callie orders, "she's totally breaking the rules!"

"On it," Ellie salutes before running after Lily who has already spotted Cameron. She's crooking her finger toward him while wiggling her hips. From the look on his face, there's no way either of them is going to let Ellie tear them apart; it's a lost cause.

"So, what the fuck is she doing here?" Nathaniel snaps my attention away from the saucy couple with his angry eyes solely on me.

"Fuck, Nate, what blew up your ass and died?" Callie scowls.

"Nate," Helena suddenly speaks up, "why are you being so rude?"

"Because she's my PA, for Christ's sake! I don't want to see her mixing with my family on a personal night out. It's inappropriate."

"For God's sake, Nate, don't be such a fucking buzz kill!" Callie pipes in. If I'm not mistaken, she looks genuinely angry with him, a look I've never seen on her before. Though, from the way she's trying to stare him down, I'm glad she's on my side.

"*Buzz kill*? What about my fucking buzz kill right here?" he says, pointing at me without even having the decency to face me.

"It's fine, Callie," I finally speak up. "I'll leave, he's right, this is a family affair and if my being here is making things uncomfortable, then I'll go."

I begin to turn around, getting ready to run far away from this humiliating scene, but James grabs my hand and pulls me into him, his own anger now coming to the surface for all to see.

"No fucking way!" James says eerily quietly, looking at Nate the whole time. "You were invited, Bea, he wasn't. In fact, I would say you are the one being inappropriate, wouldn't you?"

"Stay out of it, James, this is none of your business," Nate grits through his clenched teeth. *Oh, God, this is getting way out of hand; I almost wish Ben was here.*

"Yeah, well, I'm making it my business," James retorts, stepping toward him.

They have some sort of alpha male stare down, all while we watch on, wondering what the hell is going to happen next. Callie is slurping her drink, looking a little amused by all the testosterone floating around. Helena has sunk down, as if trying to avoid the whole confrontation, whereas I'm just glad the bride-to-be isn't here to see this all going down at her bachelorette party. I take a quick glance toward the bar, only to find Lily and Cameron practically dry-humping on the dancefloor.

Feeling relieved, I turn to see Nate and James still having a glare-off, so tug on James' arm to try and break it up.

"Come on, James, let's go dance," I practically beg him, then look up to see Nate staring down at me. His eyes remain on mine for an uncomfortable amount of time, to the point whereby it looks like his anger is turning into something else, something arrogant, something wanting. Eventually, he steps back and gestures to the dance floor, effectively letting us go.

"That's what I thought," James says to him before taking my hand again. "Come on, beautiful, let's go and dance."

Monday me is definitely going to be bricking it when she goes into work!

Bea

Half an hour later, and the glare off incident is firmly behind me. The music is pumping, James is swinging me about the floor, and every now and then, I catch Lily having a good time, even if it is on her future husband's lap. At first, I felt a pang of jealousy when I saw how besotted they were together, but now I am beginning to realize that if what they have is something I want, then maybe I should take a chance on someone and begin to trust again. I've just got to be more careful about who I trust my heart with this time.

As if the universe is listening into my private thoughts, the music slows and I notice Thor sauntering my way, and with a wicked grin plastered all over his handsome face. A mixture of nervous anticipation and nausea runs through me, and my wiggling slows down into virtually nothing the closer he gets to me.

"I think I'm going to go and get another drink," James whispers inside of my ear, with the sound of a smug smile in his voice. He kisses my cheek, so I turn to try and grab his hand, but he slips away before I can even touch him.

"James!" I whisper shout with urgency, but his back continues walking away toward the bar, purposefully ignoring my desperate pleas to not leave me here alone.

With no other option to hand, I turn away from Thor and begin swaying my hips to the music. I try to lose myself to the beat and ignore the fact that a Nordic god is marching this way, as well as the sad realization that I haven't been close to a man since

Dean. It doesn't stop me from jumping when I suddenly feel warm hands beginning to snake around my hips, and it certainly doesn't stop me from gasping when he begins swaying with me from behind. Intimacy like this, with anyone, feels a little weird after all this time, but I let it happen because it also feels nice, like I'm finally beginning to move on.

"I was hoping you would still be here," he whispers inside my ear, "I've been watching you all night. Do you know how hard it is trying to hide an erection when you're serving drinks?"

I emit a burst of laughter at the same time as he takes hold of my hand and spins me around to face him. I'm then pulled in close so he can prove that what he just said about his 'problem' is true. I think I had forgotten what one of these felt like, but now that I'm here, I may as well throw caution to the wind and enjoy myself. Throwing my hands around his neck and moving in close, I expose my neck and indulge in the sensation of him delivering little kisses over my skin. My eyes fall closed when his kisses become a little less chaste, and a little more hot and passionate.

As he moves up toward my jaw, getting closer to my own lips, I open my eyes, only to discover Nathaniel Carter slow dancing with a woman only a few feet away from us. The two of them are dancing close, looking almost identical to Thor and me. Nathaniel's dark green eyes look straight into mine as we continue dancing with our partners. He maintains his eye contact even when he moves his hand down her back to caress and cup one of her ass cheeks. I try to look away, but for reasons unknown to me, I can't. In fact, I don't even feel Thor's hands on me anymore, just Nathaniel's intense stare. He smiles at me before moving down to kiss his partner's neck with his open mouth, the whole time looking at me, taunting me with his brand of arrogance.

I begin to feel prickly heat spreading out over my neck, my

hands are clammy, and my pulse is speeding up, along with my breathing. My discomfort only intensifies when I watch him tongue-kissing her, but still with his devious eyes on mine. The corner of his lips kicks up as my mouth drops open in shock when he suddenly lifts her leg up to wrap around his thigh. His hand caresses her exposed flesh as he moves up closer toward her ass. Why is he still watching me when he's giving this woman foreplay in the middle of the dancefloor? What is he trying to achieve? Intimidation, lust, humiliation? Whatever it is, it's making me feel all kinds of messed up; I don't know whether to feel turned on or just scared, but I think I feel both.

Without warning, Thor turns us round so I am facing in the other direction, and no longer able to see Nathaniel. The sudden change has me feeling faint, so much so, I break away from his embrace.

"I'm really sorry…I've got to go," I blurt out and begin to move away from him, but he catches hold of my hand before I can escape.

"Where are you going? What's wrong?" Poor Thor seems genuinely concerned and I begin to curse myself for letting Nathaniel Carter get the better of me.

"Nothing, you're amazing, but I…I've just got to go," I fluster, this time managing to pull away from his grip. Trying not to see his disappointment, I walk off the dance floor as quickly as I can without looking like some sort of messed up Cinderella.

"Hey, babe, what's wrong?" James asks when he catches hold of me at the edge of the dance floor. I hardly know how to answer him; I feel so ridiculous over what just happened between my bully of a boss and me, not to mention the insanely attractive guy who I just left hanging on the dance floor.

"I need to go, James, I'm not feeling…but I'll see you at Lily's wedding, thanks for everything…I've just got to…get out of here!"

I can't help but take a glance in Nathaniel's direction, only to find him still standing where he was, hands in his pockets, legs apart, looking very much the alpha in his expensive clothes - dark jeans, dark shirt, dark jacket, dark everything, just like him. His expression is no different from before as he stares at me with a sardonic and menacing grin all over his face.

I just about manage to turn away and look at James, but from the expression on his face, I know he's correctly guessed as to what's happened. Shame takes over me again, and he pulls me in for a hug, no doubt glaring at Nathaniel from over my shoulder.

"Ok, baby, I got you," he whispers. His kindness is the final push for my tears to run over my cheeks, revealing just how much I've let Nathaniel get to me.

"I'll get Lily to send my number. Bea, call me if you need me," he says before kissing my forehead with so much warmth behind it, I want to evaporate into a puddle on the floor. He seems to see this in me, so walks me toward the exit where there is a line of cabs already waiting. "I *will* see you next week because if you let him stop you from going, I will come and drag your ass there myself."

"I will, thank you so much, James," I reassure him with a sniff, knowing I need to leave soon, for the hard and ugly crying is just a moment away from exploding out of me. "Tell the others I threw up or something and I'll see them on Lily's big day."

Chapter 9

Bea

When I arrive home, sometime at around one in the morning, Ben and Leah are still up watching a movie while polishing off my bottle of wine from Finn. At first, Leah looks at me with excitement, hoping my evening has gone well and I have gossip to share. My evening had been going well; I was beginning to feel like the me from before life dealt me the blow that it did, but then Nathaniel Carter happened. She sees my puffy red eyes and jumps up to wrap her arms around me.

"What the hell happened?" she asks, holding me in a sisterly-like embrace. Kindness only undoes me even more, so I end up whimpering and shuddering all over her.

"Did someone do something to you, because if they did, I swear to God, I will draw blood!" I hear Ben starting to growl from beside me.

"I'm fine, I just ran into Nathaniel while I was out," I explain, not having the strength to lie. "He asked why the fuck I was there and accused me of being 'inappropriate'."

"Oh, that's it!" Ben snaps, now beginning to pace about with his entire body looking clenched. "This dude has got to seriously pay! I'm talking shoving a red-hot poker up his ass, tying his balls to a lead weight, and watching him fall down into the Grand Canyon or something."

"You paint a pretty picture, you idiot," I manage to laugh through my tears.

"Bea, I'm going to have to agree with your brother on this one," Leah says softly, all the while stroking my hair. "This is getting out of hand."

Sighing heavily, because I have to admit that she's right, I nod in defeat, even though I really don't want to jeopardize my job.

"Look, I'm going to talk to Cameron; I decided that last night with Finn, but not in the week leading up to his wedding, I don't think that's fair. I'll wait till he's back from honeymoon and then I promise to go and talk to him. It will be a few weeks of keeping my head down, but then, hopefully, I can get something sorted."

Yes, this is what I'll do; it's a plan of sorts. For now, I just want to get washed, go to bed, and sleep for the next month. After which, I can try and talk it through with Cameron.

Nate

I spy Lily and Cam getting hot and heavy; he's already ordered a car; I saw him speak on his cell only about ten minutes ago. They can't get enough of one another. Don't get me wrong, I'm over the moon for their happiness, but I wouldn't be human if I didn't admit that I was jealous...***crazy*** jealous. I thought it was because of Lily, that maybe I regretted letting her go to Cameron when it could have been me getting ready to take her home and make love to her, just like he is now. But it's not Lily, it's what they have with one another. An unaltering faith in their love, knowing it's strong enough to commit to the other one for the rest of their lives. A love like theirs makes me both envious and terrified at the same time.

"Just what in the hell is your problem, Nate?" James starts yelling at me, not giving a shit about the fact we're surrounded by people. If looks could kill, I'd be dead in a dumpster right now.

"Not now, James," I sigh, for in all honesty, I have no idea how to even explain myself. What I just did only confirms something I've been trying to deny for a long while now; Beatrice Summers has crossed over from being the object of my frustration through hatred, into the object of my frustration through desire. I couldn't even tell you when it happened, but what I feel for her is driving me to distraction – in the office, in the bedroom, in the shower, pretty much everywhere. It's a feeling that needs to be squashed, just like I did with Lily. However, there are two major differences between her and Lily - I don't have any more brothers, and Bea is everywhere. Hence why I lost my shit when I saw her here tonight, which admittedly, wasn't my greatest moment, but seeing her in a ridiculously sexy dress and a pair of heels that took my line of sight straight to her beautifully sculpted legs rendered me temporarily insane.

"No, let's!" he snaps. "When the hell did you stop being the Nate Carter who is loved by everyone, who gave everyone a chance, and who would never, ever, treat a woman the way you did tonight? Where is that guy, because the asshole before me is nothing like him. That Nate was someone I was proud to call my friend."

"You wanna know where he is?" I shout at him, to which he nods, almost sizing me up and getting ready to make this physical. "I have no idea, James, I don't know where he's gone!"

He looks at my sorry-looking expression and eventually moves back. I take the opportunity to get the hell out of this place so I can get some air outside, far away from the noise and flashing lights, the eyes, the sweaty bodies, and the expectation to be something I'm not. As soon as the coolness of early morning hits my tired eyes, I let out a breath of relief.

"Shit," James says with a long sigh, "you gonna tell me about it then?"

"Will you let me say no?" I laugh mirthlessly. He laughs with me before shaking his head but also places his hand on my shoulder in a gesture of friendship. "Fancy a coffee back at my place?"

"Well, you're not really my type, but sure, ok."

"Ass, I'm everybody's type," I joke, just as a taxi pulls up so we can jump inside.

Once inside my house for one, I begin making some strong coffee for the both of us. James emits a whistle as he walks around, taking in the interior that was designed by a professional. I've added my own personal touches, but it's never truly felt like mine. It's a show home, a generic version of all the other houses in this gated community for the wealthy. Cam's house was the same, up until Lily moved in at any rate. Since they shacked up together, it's slowly transformed into something that reflects who they are together. I haven't yet had the time or the inclination to do anything to this place. And therein lies the problem; my life is work, nothing more.

"Dude, your house is not at all like your old place," James observes, still looking around in awe. "For starters, it's clean…like, obsessively clean."

"I know," I laugh, thinking back to when I had lived with my friends, a time I sometimes miss. Back then, I couldn't wait to have my own space, but now I have so much of it, it feels empty.

"So, you have a top-notch job, a fancy pants home, you're a Carter, and you look like a magazine model," he laughs at me, "tell me, you poor dear, what's making you act like a tool?"

"Why did I invite you back here again?" I tease as we take a seat on my leather couch. He laughs at me but soon turns serious again, silently telling me to get on with it. "I guess I feel like I'm living two lives at the moment – the fun-time guy who I used to be and the guy who is forever trying to catch up with my big brother."

"So, the fool who's there to entertain everyone else, and the hard-ass boss who's trying to live up to a certain standard?"

"Exactly!" I gasp, relieved to have someone who gets it.

"And you don't feel like you're either one," he says like he can read my mind. In fact, he's saying it better than I ever could. "Shit, Nate, that must be exhausting."

"That's not the worst of it, James," I admit, taking in a mouthful of coffee because what I'm about to say is hard for me to admit out loud. "I'm so lonely, I've begun to question what the point of it all is."

"Nate, you've got really good friends, and this perfect family from what I hear, so why can't you talk to them?"

"Because I sound like a whiney bitch with first-world problems. You said so, yourself, what have I got to feel sad about?

Besides, no one ever takes me seriously."

"Well, first off, everyone's problems are important to them, no matter who you are. Yes, there are many people who are worse off than you, but that doesn't make your problems go away. If something's broken, you don't just ignore it because your neighbor's got something even bigger that's broken."

"True," I reply, nodding along because what he's saying does make sense.

"And as for taking you seriously, the first person who saw you as someone serious, you treated like crap. You can't have it both ways, Nate, you can't want someone to treat you like fun Nate but also fear you at the same time."

"I don't want Beatrice to fear me, I just wanted her to treat me like she respected me; someone who was worth talking to."

"What made you think she didn't?" he asks with a curious look on his face.

"When we first met, she could barely look at me, talked about me having a reputation for being a party boy, and how it was so great that I was now working for my brother. Then she ran off before I could even tell her how I liked my coffee," I explain. "I tried to be friendly, but she was having none of it."

"You're her boss, Nate, she was bound to be nervous of you," he laughs. "Dude, you read far too much into it. She was apprehensive when she met me tonight, as well as the barman, and she really liked him!"

My jaw involuntarily tenses up over the thought of her liking him, of them dancing together the way they were, of him placing his hands and lips all over her. My fists are now clenched, and I feel inexplicably hot and bothered.

"What's this?" James says, gesturing to my constipated-looking expression. "Why are you clenching your ass together?"

"I am not clenching my ass together!" I snap, causing him to laugh at me.

"Yes, you are," he says with incredulity, "you're all clenched up like one of those musclemen trying to lift a car or something. Nathaniel Carter, you like your PA, and rather than face it, you've been a complete asshole to her. Jesus, Carter, that's funny!"

"I haven't always liked her, I really did dislike her in the beginning," I pout like a miserable teenager, "but I guess I've been getting to know her a little, seeing her as a person. She's sparked my interest, that's all. I mean, she's always been hot, but I couldn't see beyond the way she treated me."

"Nate, I think you win first prize for treating someone badly, I can't feel sorry for you over that one. However, what I will say is this, Beatrice Summers is not the snooty mean girl you think she is. In fact, she reminds me of Lily when I first met her; she even reminds me of your sister. That girl has a past, and her acting shy and unwilling to show you her true self is more about that than what she thinks of you. Not that you could blame the poor girl for thinking you're an ass, you kind of have been."

"Shit, I know," I sigh with frustration.

"Perhaps you should talk to her about all of this," he suggests with a shrug, "tell her how you really feel."

"God, no! Are you insane?" I look at him in horror over his seriously bad idea. "I'm her boss and I need to maintain distance. Perhaps you're right about me taking it too personally though. I guess I could arrange a meeting so we can clear the air;

I'll admit that before her, I'd never really been anyone's boss before. Jack was more of a guide to the company than my employee. But I'll promise to try and be a better one. How about that?"

"Well, yeah, that is the least you can do," he says with a shake of his head. "I'd do it soon though. If you had been my boss, I would have gone to HR before now. That or punched you in the face."

"Gee, thanks," I laugh sadly. "Let me get through the wedding of the year first, then I'll fix it. Until then, I'll keep my distance and try not to be such a dick."

"That might be a challenge for you, Nate," he teases.

Insulting though he is, I'm glad I've had this talk to clear things up inside of my head.

Bea

The week passes by slowly, but thankfully, uneventfully too. To my utter shock, Nathaniel pretends like Saturday never happened. He's even said *please* and *thank you* on several occasions, though he completely avoids eye contact altogether. Perhaps he feels bad about it, or maybe he was more intoxicated than I previously thought, or maybe they all laid into him after I left. Whatever the reason for his sudden distance, I'm beyond grateful for it. In fact, if this continues, I might not need to have that conversation with Cameron after all.

When the day of the wedding finally arrives, I begin to feel nauseated. There're going to be so many people there with their eyes on me, not to mention the entire management team. The last party I attended didn't go so well, in fact, if things had gone according to plan, that night would have been my last. My hands begin to tremble over the thought of it all and I end up getting shampoo in my eyes and shouting out a torrent of curses, which only leads to me slipping over and landing on my butt.

"Bea? Bea, you ok?" Ben shouts as he comes rushing in, looking concerned and ready to draw blood. Unfortunately, he catches me butt naked on the floor, my wet hair everywhere, and tears streaming down my cheeks.

"Oh, God, oh, shit," he gasps, flustering in an attempt to help me up, even though I'm flapping him away from me.

"Ben, for goodness' sake, can you get me a towel or something?" I yell, knowing a lovely purple bruise is now forming over my right thigh.

"Yeah, right, sure," he blurts out before grabbing for my robe that is hanging on the back of the door. He quickly wraps it around me before helping me back into my room where we both end up lying against my headboard, staring at an old family portrait, the only one I have. Ben is about seventeen, so I must be twelve, and Emma would have been ten, nearly eleven, just one year behind me. I keep it out because the girl in that photograph is happy. She's happy because right next to her is her best friend. That little girl will always be my best friend, even if I no longer talk to the woman she grew into.

"So, why did I just have to rescue my little sister off the floor?" Ben sighs. "The fact that you were naked is even more disturbing for a big brother to see, but I can bypass that for now."

"Ben, do you know how many times I've had to see your naked wing wang flapping about the place because you can't be bothered to put anything on after you and Leah have been…you know?"

"Stop avoiding the question, Bea," he huffs, "is this about your boss again?"

"Not really, well, only partially," I tell him with an insolent shrug.

"Ok, so tell me, what has you lying butt naked on the floor?" he says with a smug smile, so I nudge him…hard.

"The last party I went to was the one that ended with me ingesting a potentially lethal cocktail," I explain. "I made so many mistakes back then."

"You had good reason to feel like you did, Bea, you were surrounded by assholes," he says, gesturing to the photograph again. "Bea, you were being bullied and betrayed; you needed help; that cocktail was you asking for it. I just wish I could have seen it before it had to get that far."

"I'm not afraid of getting to that point again, Ben, and I know I can come to you now, but it still stirs up a lot of bad memories. Occasionally, I begin to think it might be me. What if I'm the problem? Bullied at school, bullied in the workplace; I'm the only thing in common here."

"No one deserves to be bullied, Bea, or betrayed. Perhaps serial killers or rapists, or whatnot, but not people like you. What can I say? Some people are just plain assholes."

"Yeah, but why do I keep running into them? Why me?" I ask with an exasperated sigh.

"Everyone runs into them, Bea, all the time," he says matter of factly, "you just gotta learn from me, sis, and tell them to fuck the hell off!"

"I can't do that to my boss, Ben," I nudge him for the bad

advice, "I'd be fired."

"A job isn't worth your health, Bea," he says seriously. "And anyway, there are ways to say that to someone without using those words. It's called HR, or maybe the papers?"

"I would never do that to Cameron and Lily," I tell him. "Besides, Nathaniel has actually been ok this week. I have a feeling James might have talked some sense into him. I'll be fine, honestly."

"Well, if it isn't, I'm going to hold you to that meeting with Cameron when he's back from honeymoon, got it?"

"Yes, Mom," I salute him with a silly grin on my face. "You seeing Leah tonight?"

"Er…no," he says, now beginning to fidget with his fingers and avoiding all eye contact. "We had a huge argument yesterday, so we're just taking some time to reset things."

"Ben, is everything ok with you guys? Things seem different between you."

"We will be," he says, shrugging it off, "she's just pissed at me for not wanting to move out with her."

"Why don't you want to move out with her, Ben? You've been together for years; don't you think it's time?"

"You know why, Bea!" he sighs sadly, but it only causes me to groan with frustration.

"I'm fine, Ben, I don't need you to babysit me anymore!"

"But *I'm* not!" he cries out, silencing me with just those three words and with what looks like tears in his eyes. "I can't forget about seeing you that night, or even the shaky, slurred voice on the end of that telephone call. You literally died, Bea, they had to revive you. I was in the room next door having to listen to the beeping of your heart monitor running solid. I can't forget it, Bea, I still have nightmares about it. I love you so much and none of us were there for you, none of us even knew there was a problem, you kept it so well hidden. And I just worry that if I'm not here, keeping an eye on you, being here for you, then it could happen again."

"Ben," I whimper while reaching out for him, "I am so sorry. You were the only one I could think to call, the only one I could rely on. But I shouldn't –"

"Don't you get it, Bea? Yes, you should have! I just wish you had come to me sooner." He takes my outstretched hand and pulls me against his warm body and hugs me so tightly, I know just how painful this is for him. "I'm not ready to leave you alone yet, not when there is still some doubt in my mind. I will not lose you, sis, never!"

"Ok, ok," I try to soothe him, "ok. I love you, Ben."

"I love you too," he mumbles against my hair. "Though, I'll deny it if you tell anyone."

"Idiot," I laugh.

"Now," he says, pulling back to look at me, "are you gonna go?"

I notice my phone flashing a message at me from an unknown number so tap the button to open it.

I better see you there today! No excuses, beautiful. James x

His message makes me smile and I give myself a silent talking-to before I give Ben a nod. It's time to prove to my brother that I can survive without him, that I'm not ever going to make him worry like that again. He deserves it after everything he's done for me.

Chapter 10

Bea

It took me thirteen minutes of staring at the church from where the taxi had dropped me off to have enough courage to walk in. As expected, the place was full to the brim with family, friends, and colleagues, the sight of which almost had me running back out again. However, I remembered the memory of Ben's terrified face and forced myself to continue walking inside.

Once through the door, I immediately sidestep so I'm out of the way of the aisle, then have a look around for somewhere discreet to stand. My 'date' is the head bridesmaid so I can't exactly sit with her, but, to my relief, I soon feel an arm slip through mine and with a familiar voice to go with it.

"You are lucky you are here, Miss Summers, because I was about to get in my car to come and get you," James tells me with his handsome smile in place.

We walk up the aisle, getting closer and closer to the front where the close family usually sit. I keep looking back at those sitting behind us, unable to comprehend how or why I am being led in front of them.

"James, where are we going?" I whisper, just before he directs us into a pew that is right behind the one at the very front.

"I can't sit here, I'm not family!"

"Neither am I, but that doesn't mean I'm not important," he says with a smug smile on his face. "My boyfriend couldn't make it so that means you're sitting with me."

"Ok," I reply slowly, not being at all convinced by this. He laughs softly before gesturing for me to sit down next to an older man who has so much facial hair, you can't tell if he's smiling or grimacing.

"Beatrice, may I introduce you to Mick; Mick, this is Bea," James says, and we shake hands.

James goes on to explain that Mick used to own the bar that he now runs, then we talk about Mick's retirement, and how he plans to travel around the country. He seems friendly enough, and strangely comforting, even with all the facial hair and expletives that escape from his mouth after every other word. I soon recognize the different shapes of his moustache and whether they mean he's smiling, grimacing, or simply looking straight-faced. It's as though it has its own morse code.

The two of them distract me for a while and I hardly notice the church filling up even more so than before. In fact, it isn't until a lady, who the boys call Jane, appears before me, that I realize the church is virtually full. She smiles kindly at me while James introduces us, her as the mother-of-the-bride, and me as his friend. I can't help blushing when he calls me that. I learned a long time ago to appreciate real friends; friends that would never turn their back on you, no matter what lies were being spread about you.

About ten minutes later, I watch Cameron and Nathaniel walking down the aisle to take their places at the altar. God, they must be the sexiest brothers I've ever seen; Lily is a very lucky lady. She bagged the brother who has both the looks and the personality. Thinking that has me feeling a little guilty, for I'm sure Nathaniel will make some lady very lucky too, one day. After all, he has the potential to be just as lovely as Cameron, just not with me.

I watch the family coming together, with Cameron's mother fussing over his tie and suit, dabbing at her eyes every now and then, before returning to flustering over her baby boy. Nathaniel is silently giggling from the side, looking entirely smug and just as a little brother should when his older sibling is being embarrassed by their parents. Their father then comes up to shake hands with them both, and they turn serious all of a sudden. Even Cameron makes himself a little smaller in this man's presence. It's extremely fascinating to watch, though not as interesting as when their sister, Helena, comes up behind her parents, but very much keeps to her mother's side, and with her eyes always diverted away from her father. He smiles at her, but she doesn't return it. He even reaches out to help her into her seat, but she flinches before he can make contact. Once she turns her back on them, he looks at their mother, appearing confused over his daughter's reaction to him. She says nothing, just shakes her head before going to sit beside their daughter.

But that's not all, for as soon as Helena is sitting, she looks up at her brothers. Nathaniel offers her a warm, brotherly smile, one that reminds me of Ben when he's looking at me. It's the first time she displays something that at least resembles a smile, but then it vanishes the moment Cameron and her lay eyes on one another. Something passes between them – hurt, guilt, the loss of a relationship that was once there. It's sad. Heartbreaking in fact.

When the wedding march finally begins, I drop my gaze from them, and we all stand to face the doors. Callie is the first to walk in, wearing a purple knee-length dress that is simple and elegant. Behind her, walks a girl in her early teens, and with the same beautiful dark hair as Helena; this must be her daughter, Jess. Then, a woman with the same hair color as Lily walks in, and I'm guessing she's Lily's sister, Rachel.

After that, we begin to hear gasps of awe, signaling the arrival of the bride. Like nearly everyone else in here, I instinctively begin to crane my neck, trying to get a glimpse of Lily in her dress. But then I remember to look at the groom, just like people tell you to do, for this is when you'll see his true reaction. The man is positively beaming with a smile that is so beautiful, it has me feeling a little emotional. To his side, his best man, Nathaniel, rolls his eyes but is smiling proudly as he does so. He looks genuinely pleased for both his brother and sister-in-law to be.

Lily begins to ascend the aisle with her father, a man who looks a little awkward from all the pairs of eyes on them. Their physical contact appears unnatural. They're obviously a family who doesn't hug and kiss at any given opportunity. Come to think of it, Lily rarely offers physical contact unless it's with Cameron. I can appreciate that.

The bride looks absolutely stunning in a floor-length, lace gown. It's a halter-neck white dress with a train and a simple veil. Her hair is long and curled, with a small section pinned to the side with a few flowers. She looks stupidly happy while her eyes remain firmly fixed on Cameron's equally stupid happy face. As soon as she reaches him, he wastes no time pulling her into his arms so he can kiss her. The crowd begins to laugh over their rather passionate embrace that breaks with tradition, prompting her to pull back with an obvious blush on her cheeks. While the minister grins at the happy couple, I cannot help but feel a pang of jealousy; will I ever have someone feel that way about me?

I try and shake it away, to be here for the couple rather than focusing on myself, so look at the best man, who is sure to snap me out of my romantic slump. However, when I do, I see that he is looking right at me, just like he did last Saturday evening. And just like then, I cannot make out what the hell his goal is. With little else I can do in the middle of a silent church, I decide to look right back at him, remaining expressionless and defiant, daring him to make the next move. After a few moments, he quirks up the side of his lips, then looks back at the happy couple. I decide to take this as a win, even if I'm the only one who sees it that way.

After the ceremony, we head over to Cameron and Lily's house which stands tall and grand in the middle of a well-to-do gated community. Bunting and wildflowers decorate the grounds, and I hear the little girl, Jess, proudly explaining that she and her mother made all the decorations themselves. She's a carbon copy of her mother, apart from the color of her eyes, an icy blue, that makes her look all the more stunning with her dark features and long, mahogany-colored hair. Right now, she's sticking close to the bride, completely in awe of her, which Lily indulges by taking hold of her hand and making her the chief bridesmaid. Cameron continues to look like the proud groom and can't stop plastering Lily with little kisses, some being more passionate than others.

After a while, taking in all this romantic display of affection becomes too much, so I decide enough is enough and go to find my 'date' at the bar. To my utter delight, I discover Callie was right, this is a free bar. Someone is finally on my side for a change, so I walk over with gusto and a huge smile on my face. Alas, the closer I get, the more I can make out the figure of my ray of sunshine boss, Nathaniel. Of course, he is the best man, as well as the groom's brother, so I was bound to run into him. I just wish it had been after a few glasses of Dutch courage.

"Hey, date," Callie laughs with a glass of champagne already in hand. "You are looking shit hot!"

"Oh, my, Callie, how much have you had to drink?" I cannot help but laugh at her.

"Been drinking since ten this morning," she replies with a cheeky grin.

"Well, you look beautiful, as do the happy couple. I love Lily's dress," I comment as I look her way again. "Everything looks so romantic."

"Getting caught up in the moment are we, Miss Summers?" Nathaniel asks before taking a swig of his beer. "You never know, you might meet your future husband here; what a romantic story that would be."

"Oh, hush up, Nate! Bea, you need to catch me up. Drink, drink, drink!" Callie chants at the same time as handing me two glasses of champagne.

"Where are they going on their honeymoon?" I ask to make small talk.

"Hawaii," Helena chimes in as she walks over to the bar with her daughter, Jess. "Jess this is Bea; Bea, this is my little girl, Jess. She works with your Uncle Nate."

"Mom, I'm not a little girl," Jess laughs softly, and I can tell straight away that she shares a really close bond with her mother. "Hi, Bea, I love your dress."

"Thank you," I reply, "but I must say, you look stunning. The color of your dress really compliments your eyes."

"Dear Lord, I need to get out of here," Nathaniel mutters, then quickly ambles away.

I take a glance at Callie, wondering if I said something

wrong, though I can't imagine what. She simply shakes her head, then grabs my hand to begin walking us over toward the marquee, presumably where the wedding breakfast is about to be served. At least, I hope there's some kind of food, otherwise, I'm going to lose my head with the number of drinks Callie is serving me.

Once inside, I lose my date again, being that she's sitting at the top table with the wedding party. However, I'm still in good company with James, Mick, and Lily's sister and partner. The atmosphere is laid back and the conversation extremely amusing, especially with Rachel's dry sense of humor and Mick's muttering obscenities every few minutes.

Sitting along the top table is the bride and groom, Callie, Nate, and both sets of parents. Callie soon offers me a wink and the eating begins. Against my better judgment, I eat very little. I can't help it, I'm still feeling beyond nervous, so I drink instead. Callie keeps tabs by asking me which number glass I'm on, so I use my fingers by way of sign language. It's no surprise that she is constantly in front of me by one or two glasses, demonstrating how much better she can hold her drink than I can. I would be a collapsed heap in bed if I had been drinking since ten in the morning.

At the end of the meal, the speeches commence. Lily's father begins with a speech that is sweet in its own way, but you can tell showing public affection is uncomfortable for him, whereas Cameron's father is openly proud and emotional about his son. He welcomes Lily to the family and ends up in tears. Callie's speech is as you would expect but generally kept clean and appropriate for most of the audience. Jess occasionally asks her mother what Callie is talking about, to which Helena smiles shyly and tells her she will explain when she's older. Her reaction makes me smile; I can remember being her age, wondering why the adults were laughing at things that didn't seem even remotely funny.

When it's Nathaniel's turn, he stands and charms the room within an instant. He plays everyone like puppets; he will have no doubt planned when he wants the audience to laugh, gush, and applaud. To begin with, he tells funny anecdotes about Cameron's misspent youth, such as getting into trouble with Mick and having to avoid girls who he had inadvertently wronged. To be honest, I try to avoid his face, which is unfairly gorgeous. Even his voice is smugly perfect, so I switch off to most of it. But then he says something that grabs my full attention:

Seeing as the happy couple is now married, I can admit that I once had a crush of my own on Lily, my now sister-in-law. One might have even said I was falling in love with her.

Lily looks painfully awkward at this point, while Cameron's jaw ever so subtly clenches. It's like watching a car crash, oddly fascinating, but oh, so terrifying.

However, I knew I wasn't good enough for this wonderful woman. I am far too reckless with hearts, even my own. Besides, her best friend, aka American mommy, Callie, said it was a terrible idea for me to try and settle down; she was dead set against me trying it out with our dear Lily. Though we did decide that she needed some intervention; it is of no surprise that she was inexperienced with romance and…

The crowd sniggers when he theatrically coughs into his fist, meanwhile Jess is looking even more confused than ever.

So, I came up with the perfect solution; I decided this man here, my big brother, was the only man I knew that truly deserved her heart.

Cue a collective 'ahh' from the audience.

After all, unbeknownst to her, the both of them had history. And I think you'll all agree with me when I say, Cam, you proved me right, for you make the most perfect couple. If I couldn't have her, then I'm glad it was you who could.

Cameron's clenched jaw has now eased and he's standing to embrace his brother; their mother is in tears, and Lily is blushing brighter than a ripened tomato.

To the happy couple, he toasts, **and to me, the forever bachelor!**

The crowd either offers their laughter or throws a napkin his way.

Hmmm, interesting.

I never knew Nathaniel had feelings for Lily and I certainly didn't know he'd been abstaining from relationships because he thought he would suck at it. I might have to discuss this little nugget of information with Callie, for I know they were in some sort of something before Lily paired up with his brother. Of course, it's none of my business, but the champagne has made me incredibly nosey about it all.

Snapping me out of my Nathaniel Carter musings, the groom stands to the sound of cheering and clapping. His first few words reveal how beautiful he thinks his new wife is, causing her to look even more embarrassed. However, he doesn't seem to care. Given his goofy expression, it's as if they are the only two people in the room. I can only imagine what the wedding night is going to be like; there won't be a lot of sleep is all I'm going to say on that matter. After he's calmed his gushing to a reasonable level, he does the dutiful thanking of the bridesmaids, the family, Nathaniel, and finally, everyone for coming. He hands out a few special gifts to the bridesmaids, Helena for her decorations, Nathaniel for being his best man, and the mother of the bride, before finally embracing his own mother with an elaborate bunch of flowers.

Now, before I finish, he begins, looking mischievous with blushed cheeks and a guilty smile, **I know a few of you have been a little shocked by how long Lily and I have waited to finally tie the knot, seeing as I've been very vocal on the matter. You know me, I don't hang around when I want something. After all, we got engaged fairly quickly after meeting.**

He pauses when some of the guests begin their mumbles of agreement.

Some of you feel that I've let my bride keep me waiting for longer than I am used to, that I am already 'brow beaten'.

Cue more giggles.

Though, I think I have permission to now let you all in on a little secret.

He looks at his new wife, who gives him a subtle nod. He picks up his tumbler of hard liquor as if bracing himself with liquid courage. Once he's placed the crystal glass back onto the table, he gifts everyone with a cheeky smirk, drawing out his announcement, and making the impatient crowd wait that little bit longer for his surprise.

Lily and I are already married. Have been for years.

Lily immediately covers her face with both hands, while the crowd gasps with shock.

I'm afraid we were married just after Christmas, the year we got engaged.

He laughs at Callie and Nathaniel, who are now exchanging

horrified expressions.

To my beautiful wife, who, by the way, is wearing a dress that I personally chose for her, I love you, and always will.

The crowd cheers and Lily stands to kiss her already husband.

"So, no need for a wedding night then?" Nate calls out over the roar of cheers, which then turn into rounds of chuckles.

"Oh, there will be a wedding night alright, right, babe?" Cameron grins at Lily, who is gulping back her own glass of champagne.

Fuck, that's romantic! I'm feeling so jealous right now, I have to pour myself another glass of wine and slurp it down continuously until it's all gone.

Chapter 11

Bea

After the room has been cleared, Cameron and Lily take to the dance floor for the first song while we all look on and sigh. Callie and I watch for a while, taking in the happy couple with their silly grins, then high tail it to the free bar outside. There's only so much love and happiness I can take before I slip into a deep depression. I follow Callie's lead and take up a position near the bar with quick access to booze and a good viewpoint. Callie wastes no time in ordering a couple of shots, as well as two margaritas. Just as we knock back the first shot and giggle a little, James comes up behind us with Nathaniel trailing behind. From the looks of things, it would appear the two of them have made up since last Saturday.

"I see you two are taking full advantage of the free bar," James comments with his soft smile and his arm planted firmly over my shoulders.

"It's only polite, my dear James," Callie says with such a serious expression, I end up laughing at her. "Besides, we plan to dance soon and that means we need some good old fashioned dancing juice," she declares, then turns to give me my second shot. "Cheers!"

"Anyone caught your eye, Callie?" James asks, looking around and gesturing toward a group of suits out front.

"Hmmm, there're a few older guys who have peaked the material girl in me, but I'm keeping my options open at the moment. Sheesh, there sure is a lot of money floating around here, including Mr Best Man behind you." She points over my shoulder, so I turn to see Nathaniel, who has now lost his jacket and tie.

"Darling, never go back, only move forward," Nathaniel replies, to which she winks with a wicked smirk.

"What about you, beautiful?" James asks, snapping me back to look at him. "I can't believe you ditched the barman last week; he was seriously hot."

"I'm sure Miss Summers saw that he had 'one night only' written all over him," Nathaniel pipes up, smiling wickedly as he does so. "And I'm guessing Miss Summers only participates in romcom fairytale endings, don't you, Miss Summers?"

I try to ignore his jibe and pretend it doesn't bother me by putting on a tight smile and holding my tongue. Though, Callie's dousing me with alcohol might encourage me to loosen my tongue and say something that will lead me into unemployment.

"Tell me, when was the last time you dropped your panties for some poor bastard?" he asks as he chuckles inside of his glass, before taking a large gulp of something that I hope chokes him.

Meanwhile, Callie hits him in the chest with her purse which is the same color as my flushed cheeks.

"I'm joking, I'm joking!" he laughs, shooting his hands up

in a defensive stance.

"Still being an asshole," James says, making me smile to myself.

"Hey, all I'm saying is that I bet Miss Summers has to wait for a man to say he loves her before she lets him see the goods, am I right?"

"Actually, the last time a man told me he loved me was just before I walked in on him having sex with my sister," I reply bluntly, prompting all eyes to zero in on me, though mine remain right on his smug face, just daring him to say something that will finally make me lose it. "So, to quote my namesake and all out hero in my eyes, 'I had rather hear my dog bark at a crow, than a man swear he loves me'."

I savor this moment, staring at him as he drops his mouth open in shock over my tragic little anecdote, then walk away without another word.

Fuming mad, I keep walking until I find a small garden table that faces the gentle river which runs along the back of the house. I perch my butt against the ledge, cross my arms and try to take in the ambience of the splashing sound of water. I probably look like a spoiled child who's throwing a tantrum over something completely insignificant, but I had to get out of there, away from all the people, if only so I could calm my nerves and try to forget what has plagued me for the last nine years.

How dare he ruin every bloody event I go to? It might be his brother's wedding, but why can't he just leave me the hell alone? I'm so sick of this jerk taking over my life and constantly making me feel inadequate. He's such an arrogant prick, thinking he knows me, when in fact, he knows so little about me that what he does know wouldn't even fill a thimble.

After about five minutes of silent venting, I hear the crushing sound of heels on gravel gradually approaching my little lonesome, pity party.

"Damn, girl!" Callie declares, handing me another drink. "That was fucking awesome, I shit you not!"

Her words have us both erupting into laughter over my little outburst. In fact, as my anger begins to dissipate through laughter and Callie's wicked smile, I realize that it had actually felt pretty good to speak up for myself. I've been waiting over eighteen months to say something back to him and I finally got the opportunity. The best bit is I didn't even swear or lose my shit; I kept it cool and classy. I quoted Shakespeare for Christ's sake!

"I'm sorry, I didn't mean to bite here of all places, but you've got to understand he's been awful to me ever since I started working for him…eighteen months ago! I blame you and the alcohol."

"No, don't apologize, that was a great show," she practically beams, "and very nicely done."

"I don't understand; why does he hate me so much?"

"Maybe he likes you?" she replies contemplatively, then takes a long sip from her cocktail straw.

"Nope," I reply, shaking my head. "I don't buy into that shit, you can't be a total bully to someone, and then say, 'oh, it's because I like you.' That crap just excuses bad behavior. If I'm ever a mom, there is no way I will ever excuse some ass who is being a little turd by saying, 'oh, it's because he likes you.' I mean what am I supposed to say? Oh, well, that's ok then, you continue making my life a misery."

"I love your bluntness, Bea, and you're totally right. I have no idea what his fucking problem is but forget him! We're here to party and I've run out of fingers to count my drinks on."

"Where are the bride and groom anyway?" I ask, noticing I haven't seen them in a long while.

"Who knows with those little fuck bunnies, probably consummating the fake wedding. I know I would be; the Carter brothers are hot," she says with a far off look in her eye. "Sometimes the hot ones ruin it by speaking though."

"Did you really tell Nathaniel he was no good for Lily?" I ask, to which she nods with a sincere expression on her face.

"Would you still say that now?"

"Yes, but only because I personally think he only liked her because he fell for the story of how Cameron and Lily first met, as well as their first kiss. He got swept up in the romance of it all. He is different now, grown up a little bit...well a lot actually. Apart from when it comes to you of course."

"Yeah, I am one lucky bitch aren't I!"

"Oh, shit," she giggles, "he's back for more. Quick, think of some more witty comebacks, it's so amusing to watch."

Panic begins to infiltrate my lungs and I start breathing quick and shallow, preparing myself to down the rest of my drink and make a run for it. I manage the drink part but before I can run, he's there, in front of me, with his hands in his pockets, his top two buttons undone and a stern and purposeful look on his face.

Shit, Bea, don't let tequila and a hot bod make you fall for his pretty boy looks. He's an ass, remember that!

Placing my glass on top of the table, I stand up straight in preparation for his cruel words, whatever they may be. However, to my surprise, Nathaniel says nothing when he stops in front of me. Instead, he takes my hand and pulls me away from the table, all the while Callie looks on with amused interest. Then, still without saying anything, he leads me over toward the dance floor. My brain ignores my earlier warning and fails to stop my feet from following his.

As we approach, the music changes to something a little slower and extremely inappropriate to be dancing to with your boss. Nathaniel, however, continues to lead us right into the middle of the dance floor where he swings me around in front of him. As his arms wrap around my waist and bring me in close to his hard body, he smirks at my questioning frown. He waits, not moving an inch until I nervously reach my hands up to rest upon his upper biceps, which flex and stretch as he begins moving me around to the music.

The beat kicks in and he pulls me even closer, so close, I can feel his entire hard body pressed up against mine. And I do mean *entire* hard body. His hand gradually moves down to my ass cheeks, and my sex betrays me as it starts to throb with need for the beautiful bastard now dancing with me. My eyes close to everyone and everything else as I indulge in a lust, I have no business in feeling toward him.

As the instrumental takes over the song, he spins me around, so my back is to his muscly chest. He begins grinding his hips against my ass in such a way, I can feel everything. His body moves us side to side, all the while his hands are exploring my body. I let him, not even thinking about what we must look like to all the other guests. I'm guessing he's not either; this is his entire family after all. His face nuzzles into the side of my hair, and he takes a deep inhale of my hair. I expose my neck to him, inviting him to kiss my skin with those soft lips of his. He accepts, with nips, open mouthed massages and groans of need.

Eventually, the music comes to an end, and my eyes open to see dozens of faces looking right at us, including Callie, James, Lily, Cameron, and Nathaniel's father. I instantly want to run, to hide away and never come up for air. My cheeks heat with a blush so strong, you could use me as a flashing beacon out at sea. All those faces gasp in shock, all except Callie who is grinning from ear to ear. No one moves and it feels like we're frozen in time, forever facing our shame in front of all these people.

It is Nathaniel who moves first, disentangling himself from me and stepping away. I can't see what he does next, I only hear him offer a cough before his shoes tap away across the floor behind me.

The realization hits me like a freight train; I have been literally left alone in the middle of the dancefloor looking like the world's biggest slut. Without anything else to cling onto, I slowly wrap my arms uncomfortably around my midriff, take a breath, then run like the wind. I grab my bag and find the quickest route to the front of the house so I can retrieve my phone and dial an Uber. With tears streaming down my face, I soon lose my patience with my fingers that are shaking too much to dial properly.

"Hi, please can I get an Uber?" I eventually sob down the phone to the poor man on the other end. I can't even remember giving him the exact details, but when I hear the magical confirmation and a promise of being here within the next ten minutes, I let out a sigh of relief and wipe my face. I then begin marching down the road, not wanting to face anyone, not even Callie.

What the hell was that? Was that to make me look bad again? Was it to get back at me for standing up to him? Whatever it was, I can't take it anymore. I'll be calling in sick on Monday and getting some legal advice about how to leave without notice. I don't want to do it to Cameron and Lily, and I know I should have gone to see them sooner instead of waiting for it to end in tears, but I haven't felt so humiliated since the night I caught Dean in my bed with my sister. Though, this is marginally worse, for at least there wasn't an audience back then; this had the entire wedding party watching on.

That's it, I'm done!

Nate

"Get the fuck inside now!" Cameron practically screams at me.

I don't even try arguing with him for I literally have nothing. Not a single thought to try and excuse what I just did. I should have left well alone, especially at my own brother's wedding. Beatrice Summers is a temptation I need to fight, for everybody's sake, especially hers. I've treated her abysmally so why did she let me dance with her like that? Why did she turn to putty in my hands? Why did I feel like everyone else had vanished the moment I touched her?

This is exactly why I never go past two nights; I mess everything up. It's also why I listened to Callie when she said not to pursue things with Lily; I would have ruined everything. She was meant for Cameron, I more than know that. However, what I knew they could have, what they will have, is precisely what I've always wanted from someone. But I'm not capable, not built for it. I'm precisely like Dad, weak-willed when it comes to a pretty face and an offer of no-strings sex. Helena and Cam might think they kept his affair a secret from me, but little brothers are nothing if not sly. Being able to eavesdrop without detection is perhaps one of the only weapons the baby of the family has at their disposal. How else are we meant to survive? I kept their secret safe, and pretended not to know, but I still mourned the loss of my parents' seemingly perfect relationship. If my father, the so-called perfect husband, couldn't be the perfect guy, what chance do I have?

"Cam, calm down," Lily says when she joins us in the living room, "the guests can see."

"She's right, we'll go upstairs, to one of the front rooms," he says, running his hand through his hair, all the while his jaw clenches in frustration. I feel like I'm thirteen years old again, with him having caught me in his room trying to look for any spare change he might have left lying around. "Jesus, Nate!"

Now, Cameron is different; he really is a nice guy. Yes, he had his years of partying and sleeping around, but he never made promises. Besides, ever since he got together with Lily, he hasn't so much as looked at another woman. He admitted to me that the idea of touching another girl makes him feel uncomfortably itchy. Lily is the only woman on his mind.

I follow Cam upstairs and into the spare room, right at the front of the house, probably so he can let rip. He should, I have been a complete prick. Still, the fact Cam and Lily have just led me into a room where Dad is waiting to give me one of his lectures doesn't seem altogether fair right now.

"What the flaming hell was that, Nate?" Dad shouts at me with the same tone of voice he used to use when we were little. Usually, Cam would be making me laugh by mocking the old man behind his back, however, this time, he's not exactly in the right mood. In fact, I'm sure he's going to be joining in with the verbal spanking, and the 'I'm so disappointed in you' speech.

Avoiding his angry pacing back and forth across the room, I turn to find Lily sitting on the end of the bed with her arms firmly crossed. She's the only one who is looking vaguely sympathetic; still pissed with me, but not totally ready to kill me yet.

"I'm sorry, I lost my head," I answer quietly, all the while looking sheepishly at the floor.

"No, you thought with your dick, that's what you fucking did!" Cam says through his clenched teeth. "We've come to expect this from you, Nate, but you don't do it with your PA, and you certainly don't do it at my fucking wedding reception!"

"Do you wanna hit me? Is that it? Go right ahead, I deserve it," I tell him, being genuine with my offer. I even turn my cheek to his awaiting fist.

He comes pacing toward me, only to come to a standstill when Lily jumps up between us, essentially stopping us from meeting in the middle.

"Please," she says, sounding completely exasperated, "there'll be no violence at our wedding. I think there's already been enough drama."

"That poor girl," Dad says softly, shaking his head in despair. I want to throw his mistakes in his face, but then his words remind me of what I just did to Bea in the middle of a crowded dance floor. So instead, I hang my head in shame.

"Nate," Lily says softly, "you practically dry-humped her in public, then left like a one-night stand in front of everyone."

"I know!" I admit through clenched teeth, feeling beyond angry with myself.

"Not to mention you've been a hideous boss to her

for…well, since you got her," she continues, making me feel even worse than before.

"You're a piece of work, do you know that?" Cam points at me with his judgmental finger, but I let him. He's right.

"What the hell is wrong with you, Nate? I didn't raise you to treat women this way," Dad says with disappointment. "I mean, I know you have a lot of 'girlfriends' but you have always been polite and charming with them. As far as I know, you've never treated them like that, and certainly not in front of an audience. If that had been Helena, I would have laid you out flat, no questions asked."

Dad's words only make me feel like a bigger pile of shit than I already do.

"Look, I'm a complete dipshit," I snap, "we all know this, the baby of the family who has to rely on his big, perfect brother."

"Fuck, grow up, Nate!" Cameron practically spits.

"Look," Lily, the voice of calm, says to me, once again providing a barrier between the two of us. "Let's just calm down. Nate, what are your feelings toward Bea?"

"None! I feel nothing towards her. I just got caught up in the moment, you know, weddings and shit."

Lily sees right through my lie and with her expression saying as much.

"As much as I know how you love to feel up a woman, feeling up a woman who you have acted like you hate for the past eighteen months, and at your brother's wedding no less, does not really seem altogether rational."

Knowing I can't win against Lily, a self-confessed surveyor of people and how they behave under stress, I sigh heavily and slump onto the bed next to her, ready to bear all.

"The last time I felt like this was with you, Lily, and I knew then I would screw it up. Everyone knew and told me so in the bluntest way possible. So, I set you up with the next best thing, my brother." I pause to point at Cam's angry face; my confession has done nothing to ease his temper from the looks of things. "Trouble is, I've run out of brothers."

"Oh, my God, Nate, that was a few years ago! Do you not realize how much you've grown up since then?" she says, laughing at me as she does so.

"Maybe, but not when it comes to women," I argue. "I don't want to hurt anybody, especially if I feel strongly about them. I didn't mean for it to happen, I literally forced myself to hate her. It's your husband's damn fault, putting her with me so I'd be working with her day in, day out. Hatred was bound to turn into something else. You should have left me with Jack."

"God, you're an idiot!" Cam snaps, throwing up his hands over my stupidity.

"Please don't tell me you've done the whole 'he's being horrible because he likes you' routine, because that's a pretty shitty reason to be vile to someone."

Lily is now looking at me in much the same way as Cameron. Good, I deserve it.

"It seemed like the only option I had at the time," I reply sulkily, shrugging my shoulders with embarrassment.

"Bullshit!" Dad pipes up. "Man the fuck up and tell her how you feel and that you are sorry for being a complete idiot."

"Gee, thanks, Dad," I gasp, with Cameron and I both looking at him in shock over his use of expletives.

"He's right, Nate," Lily says more softly, not thinking anything of my father swearing in front of us. "And for the record, you never even gave you and me a shot. You were too busy convincing yourself and everyone around you that you were incapable. Trouble is, Nate, if you don't try, you'll never know."

"Hey!" Cam says, turning to glare at Lily. "What do you mean, give *you* a shot?"

"Calm down, honey," she says as she glides over to give him a calming kiss. "I'm glad he didn't because now I have you. I will always love your brother for that," she says, before turning to offer me a wink. "Now, get lost, Nate, and go and think about how to fix all this."

I get up to walk out, Dad follows but pauses at the door to hold it open for the bride and groom.

"You guys go ahead, my wife is going to show me how glad she is," Cam says as he grabs her ass and starts tongue kissing her. I can't help but roll my eyes, but I do know I made the right choice about Lily and him. They're sickeningly great together.

Chapter 12

Bea

When I got home last night, I was so wound up with anger and hurt, I immediately took to my laptop and wrote my letter of resignation. I then crawled into the shower and tried to wash away my shame, and my humiliation, but to no avail. In the end, I made up a bed on the couch and watched old re-runs of 'Friends'. Not for comedy, but for the nostalgia. I remember watching those on repeat as a child while sitting next to my mom on the couch. Emma would be coloring on the living room floor. Things were so much simpler before the onslaught of hormones, things I never appreciated at the time. Ben used to come home and roll his eyes at us, complaining about how frequently we watched the same episodes. We ignored him completely, much to his annoyance.

Speaking of which, Ben must have been on a late shift, for I never saw him. I gave up waiting for him to come home and fell asleep. It was a broken sleep, one consisting of my usual anxious dreams.

Beatrice Summers, do the world a favor and go and die!

This morning, I woke up with a start, my breath quick and shallow and my heart beating much too wildly inside of my chest. Waiting for my breath to even out again, I grab my phone and check the time. It's only eight, but I need to get up and drink some water to try and halt the threatening headache that's already trying to spread over me. By nine, I still don't want to eat, but at least my headache hasn't progressed.

I listen to Ben getting up to go to his bathroom, only for him to slump off to bed again. I can't blame him; it's precisely where I would be if it wasn't for fear I'll have more bad dreams. Though, the feeling of my heavy eyelids has me resting my eyes for a moment or two, causing my willpower to not succumb to sleep to wither away. I can feel myself slipping, right up until the sound of someone thumping on our apartment door has me jumping in surprise. It must be Finn, having sweet-talked one of our neighbors into letting him in through the outside door. I find myself smiling over the thought of seeing him, of being able to vent to someone who wasn't there to witness me making a fool of myself last night.

However, when I open the door, I'm taken aback by the sight of Nathaniel Carter filling up the door frame, all the while grinning sheepishly at me. Not quite believing he is here, looking casual in a pair of black cargo shorts and a fitted white t-shirt, I look over my shoulder to see if I'm still lying on that couch, stuck in the land of dreams.

"Good morning," he says in a deep, husky voice, giving away how much he must have had to drink yesterday. The genuinely friendly tone in his voice has me turning back to face him with a thoroughly confused look on my face. His presence is so disarming, I don't even think to care about the fact that I'm standing in an old pair of checked PJ shorts and a faded pink tank top, or that my hair is pulled up in a messy bun.

"Bea?"

"Morning," I answer curtly, still with my eyes trying to search for some sort of explanation as to why he's suddenly here, looking so out of place in my building's narrow corridor. But then the memory of writing my letter of resignation comes to mind and I realize I no longer have to answer to his bullshit. The decision to end this has been long overdue, but now that I've come to it, I'm more than ready to show him that he can no longer get to me.

"Have you now decided to come and humiliate me in my own home? Does work not cut it anymore?"

Surprisingly, he laughs with an awkward rub of his neck, looking just as embarrassed as I have been feeling since last night. Specifically, when he had left me to face everyone all alone.

"Er, yeah, I deserve that. But no, I came here to apologize. I was kind of an ass to you."

His squirming is immensely satisfying, even if I don't have any idea as to why he's suddenly making an effort to put things right.

"Oh, you were, were you? How very…*gracious* of you!"

"You're not going to make this easy for me, are you?" he asks with a schoolboy smile, still scratching nervously at the back of his neck. I merely gift him with a momentary fake smile before returning to my neutral expression again.

"May I come in to explain?" he asks and begins to take a step forward.

"No!" I snap, moving so he is forced to step back again.

Alas, this is the exact same moment that Leah and Ben

decide to serenade us with their animalistic chorus from upstairs. We both look inside the apartment, him smirking awkwardly, me closing my eyes through yet more humiliation.

"For fuck's sake, Ben!" I mutter through my teeth.

"Ok," he says slowly when I turn back to face him. "Why don't I take you out for breakfast to say sorry and to explain," he suggests with huge, pathetic, puppy dog eyes. "Please?"

"I don't think…"

My voice trails off when their screams and thumping of the headrest become so loud, I can't even pretend to act even vaguely nonchalant over it all. The worst part is, I know Ben has amazing stamina. This is something a sister should never know about her brother.

"Actually, you can," I reply with an exasperated sigh, to which he looks genuinely relieved. "I'll just change. I'll meet you at the café on the corner."

"Yeah, sure," he says, smiling like a teenager who has just scored his first date. "See you in a bit."

I smile tightly, then walk back into the apartment, closing the door behind me, and not even caring if he had gone or not. The door could have slammed on his nose for all I care.

Bea

Half an hour later, I'm walking up to a table to sit with my asshole boss, soon-to-be ex-boss. He looks nervous, fiddling with a packet of sugar while bouncing his leg up and down. I smile for a moment, enjoying the sight of him not looking like his usual confident self. He probably thinks I'm going to lose my shit and cause a scene by screaming the place down. Fortunately for him, that's not my style, it never has been, not even when I caught Dean screwing Emma in my very own bed. Not that I'll let him know that any time soon.

When I finally slide inside the seat opposite him, he immediately stops his leg from bouncing up and down and offers a smile with the same awkward, little boy grin from before. It's a little unsettling after everything he's put me through, so I find myself instinctively avoiding his gaze. In fact, I have to give myself a pep talk to make myself face him eye-to-eye if only to prove to him that I've had enough.

"Morning, Bea," Marge, the waitress, says to me with her usual friendly voice. "Tea or coffee, dear?"

"Morning, Marge, I'll have tea this morning," I reply with a smile. "How are you this morning? Leg all better?"

"Yes, thank you, dear, still going," she chuckles. "Anything to eat?"

"No thank you," I answer, looking back at Nathaniel before telling her, "I'm not feeling myself this morning."

"Oh, dear, well, I'll get you that tea," she says kindly, then marches off. I assume Nathaniel must have ordered when he first got here.

"Are you ok?" Nathaniel asks, looking concerned for me, which is not something I am at all used to.

"I'm just feeling a little nauseated after being so publicly displayed in front of my work colleagues and friends last night," I reply bluntly. I then smile at Marge who is already bringing me a much-needed cup of tea.

When I finally turn back to face him, I find him looking down at the tabletop, still playing with the same packet of sugar. I can tell the paper isn't going to last much longer; there'll be sugar everywhere. But I'll let him find that out on his own.

"I'm very sorry, Beatrice, it was not my intention to embarrass you like that."

"So I'm Beatrice now? What happened to Miss Summers?"

The way he looks at me reminds me of a puppy in an animal shelter, or a small boy being told off by his parents for whatever misdemeanor he's just committed. With a long sigh over this man's ability to melt my anger, and with only his eyes, I force myself to take a sip of my soothing tea.

"What was your intention, Mr Carter?" I ask, relenting in my initial plan to offer him nothing but contempt.

"Please, call me Nate," he says, looking genuinely relieved and happy over my tiny olive branch. However, when he tries to reach for my hand, I withdraw it far out of reach. He retracts his own hand and looks somewhat embarrassed by my rebuttal. "Would you believe me if I said I danced with you because I wanted to? That there was no malice in it?"

"No," I reply with a shrug of my shoulders. "Why would you want to do such a thing with me? The woman who you take great pleasure in humiliating on a daily basis, even at the weekends it would seem."

"I don't enjoy doing that," he sighs. I can't help but stare back at him with incredulity, not believing him for one moment. "Look, Beatrice…Bea, at first, you did rub me up the wrong way. I thought you were snooty, that you were making judgments based on my 'party boy' reputation, so I decided to punish you for it; to make you see that I am where I am for my own merits, not just because I'm the CEO's little brother."

"What?" I ask with a thoroughly confused look on my face.

"Somewhere along the way, I stopped hating you. In fact, I began to respect you for not being like all the other women who have always tried to pander to Cameron and me, purely because of the Carter name and Medina Technologies. You got where you are all on your own, Bea, and you never ask for anything other than what you earn."

"Get to the point, Mr Carter," I tell himhau impatiently, letting him know I won't be charmed like all the others.

"Something changed the night I saw you in your friend's restaurant," he says with a sigh, still fiddling and not acting at all like himself. "I saw you in a different light; something just sparked."

"So, you're saying…?" I push further.

"I'm saying that ever since London, the thought of you has been making me feel completely insane! Bea, I don't fall like this, not since Lily, and it scares the shit out of me. In fact, it's worse than Lily, because it makes me want to draw blood when I see you dancing with some barman. I wanted to rip out my own hair when I saw Sam trying to kiss you, and when Nick flirted with you, and when I thought the guy on your phone was a boyfriend. I even hated it when you were dancing with James, who bats for the other team for Christ's sake!"

"So, you're saying you have made my life a living hell, humiliated me, bullied me, stripped me of any confidence, all because you're scared of your *feelings*?"

I immediately narrow my eyes at him as extreme rage begins to rise to boiling point. His face loses its Californian suntan glow at the same time as I grab a note from my purse and slam it onto the table.

"Expect my letter of resignation tomorrow; I'm done!"

Before he can respond in any way, I get up and begin marching toward the door, completely going against the grain and causing the scene I usually avoid at all costs.

"Beatrice, please wait!" he shouts from behind me, scrambling to get some notes out to pay his bill and come after me.

When I'm halfway back home, I begin to feel relieved, thinking I've safely escaped him. However, just as I pass by a less-than-savory-looking alleyway, I feel someone grab my wrist.

"Get off me, Nathaniel!" I snap, trying to shake him off but he only continues walking toward me so I end up being flat up against a wall. He then pins me in by placing each of his hands on the wall next to my head.

"No!" he shouts back, then holds me there all the while I try to struggle free of him. "I'm not going to let you throw your job away because of me. I promise I will treat you differently from now on. I know I've been awful, but… Look, don't go, just give me a chance to prove to you I can be a decent boss, please?"

I breathe short and shallow breaths all the while I consider what he is saying. It would make things a hell of a lot easier to not have to leave and find a new job, and I do like working for the company. I wasn't exaggerating when I said I wouldn't find a package as generous as the one I have.

"If, and I mean ***if***, I stay, I get to tell you when you're being an ass," I finally reply, keeping continuous eye contact with him.

"Agreed," he answers.

"And you stop making me look like an idiot in front of my colleagues?"

"Goes without saying."

"And you use manners," I tell him with a set of eyes that probably look like my mother's did when she was training me to use 'please' and 'thank you'.

"As long as you never tell my mother I did otherwise. Yes, to everything, Beatrice."

"And it's Bea," I tell him, which earns me a soft smile. "Beatrice was only ever used when my parents were mad at me."

"Only if you call me Nate. Nathaniel is when my parents are mad with me," he replies with a wider grin on his face.

"Well, maybe when I stop being mad at you, I'll call you Nate."

"Fair enough," he laughs.

We stand still for a moment, his eyes turning darker as they slip down to look at my parted lips. The way he's looking at me is so intense, I feel a sudden need to break his hold on me, so I look away and sigh.

"Are you going to let me go, Nathaniel?"

"No," he whispers, to which I answer him with a furrowed brow, effectively snapping him out of his staring at me. "I mean…yes, of course."

"May I walk you back to your apartment?" he asks politely, releasing me from his arm cage and finally stepping back.

"Probably best you don't," I tell him honestly before wincing over what I'm about to say. "My brother will either be engaged in bumping uglies with Leah, which is highly embarrassing, or he'll want to kick your ass. I'm pretty sure you could take each other but there's no way you can take on Leah - she's feisty."

We both laugh, then stand still in silence, right up until it becomes awkward.

"Why did you let me dance with you like that?" he asks out of the blue. "I didn't make you feel forced into it, did I?"

"No," I whisper, scratching at my arm through embarrassment for admitting such a thing.

"Good, I'm glad," he says. "Then why?"

"I suppose…" I can feel myself blushing while struggling to articulate myself.

"You wanted to?" he asks, and when I look at him, he grins at the answer my expression is obviously giving away. He steps closer again, which has me feeling incredibly nervous, but maybe in a good way. His hand slowly reaches up and pushes a stray strand of hair behind my ear before he leans in further, to the point where our lips are so close, we're going to end up kissing.

"What are you doing, Nathaniel?" I murmur, trying to catch my breath. *Bea, don't fall for an asshole just because he has a hot bod and is giving you seductive eyes.* "I, er, think I should get going."

He remains fixed, letting his thumb drop down to my bottom lip, tracing it along my skin ever so gently. He looks conflicted, as if locked in his own silent battle.

"I really want to…" He sighs, still tracing my lip. "Let me kiss you, Bea," he whispers. I silently curse myself for wanting him to; I even close my eyes, readying myself to do something I haven't done in years. But then sense prevails and I force myself to step away.

"I can't," I reply, and he frowns before dropping his arms to the side and stepping back. "I think I need to get back before we complicate this even further. I…I have to go."

"Wait, Bea?" he calls out as I begin stepping away from him. "I *will* see you tomorrow, won't I? At work?" I smile sheepishly but then nod my confirmation. "Goodbye, Bea, enjoy your Sunday," he says, sounding professional again.

"You too," I reply before getting my ass out of there.

Nate

"So, she knocked you back?" Cam laughs with far too much enthusiasm. "I knew I liked her!"

After meeting with Bea, I came over to catch Lily and Cam before they go on their honeymoon. Actually, I suppose they already had their honeymoon, so it is essentially just a run-of-the-mill vacation. I still haven't given him shit for that, but it will have to wait; I'm not in the mood to put in my best work. Besides, I might wait until we're all around my parents' place so I can wind Mom and Dad up about it too. It's not often Cam's the guilty party so I need to make the most of this one.

Anyway, I'm now sitting on their couch with him while Lily runs around packing everything for their honeymoon. I give it about ten minutes before she snaps at him to get up and help. Either that or I'll be given my marching orders while he picks her up and has his wicked way with her on the living room floor. I know they've done it on virtually every surface in this house, lucky bastard.

"I have to ask, Nate," Lily chimes in, "what did you expect? You've been horrible to her."

"Gee, thanks, Lils," I huff, "I'm so glad I can come to family for sympathy and support."

"You have my full support," she says before kissing me on the head. "But as for my sympathy? Well, I'm afraid you kind of brought this on yourself."

"Plus, is it really a good idea to enter into a relationship with your PA?" Cam asks, being the top boss and all.

"Remember Jill?" I remind him.

"Who's Jill?" Lily instantly freezes in her packing and looks up with her hands on her hips.

"Oh, that was just fucking," he says nonchalantly, "and way before I met you, baby."

"Technically it wasn't," I point out, "seeing as you guys met when Lily was still at school."

"You know what I mean," he replies casually.

Seemingly placated, Lily merely shrugs and continues packing.

"You know what, why don't we just say you and Bea are right about everything, and I'm wrong," I sigh, feeling defeated and frustrated.

"Glad you can admit it, bro," Cam says before slapping me

on the shoulder. "Honestly, Nate, if you were truly serious about her, I would be all for it, we can always work around these things. But if you just want to bang her out of your system, it's a firm no from me."

"I second that," Lils shouts from the kitchen.

"Well, thanks, I guess," I mutter moodily. "In any case, she's not interested. Well, I think she is interested but doesn't want to go there so what else can I do but respect her wishes?"

"Maybe you should just be patient," Lily suggests, to which Cam and I both frown at one other like she's talking crazy.

"Not really our strong suit, babe," Cam states.

"Hmm, well, it sounds like the only choice you have right now," she points out while wrapping her arms around his shoulders. "So, you think you can keep it in your pants while you give her time to think about it, Nate?"

"Haven't touched anyone since before London," I admit with a frustrated sigh. "I hate this."

"Wow, are you saying you're prepared to give up all pussy for her?" Cam asks with genuine shock in his voice.

"I don't get it," Lily says, "isn't one vagina much the same as another?"

"No!" we both reply in unison.

"Would you say that about a dude's penis?" I counter.

"Well, I can't really comment, I've only ever been up close and personal with your brother's penis," she says matter of factly.

"And that's the only penis you'll ever be up close and

personal with!" he declares, trying to act as some sort of authority. "Starting in about half an hour when I throw Nate out."

"Oh, really?" she says with a mischievous grin on her face, then slides herself around onto his lap where they begin kissing and pawing at one other.

"That's it, I'm out," I declare as I stand to leave. "I don't know whether I'm going to get a hard-on or vomit."

Of course, they ignore me and continue dry-humping one another, which only has me rushing to get the hell away from the sight of my brother going to town on his wife.

"Laters, enjoy Hawaii," I call out as I quickly pace toward the door.

"Nate," Cam shouts, all the while Lily kisses his neck, "don't let me come back to a complete legal mess if you know what I mean."

I sigh with a nod before walking out the door. *What the fuck am I going to do?* Nothing, I'm going to do nothing except try and be nice to her without throwing myself at her feet.

Chapter 13

Bea

After hours of deliberation, hovering my finger over the send button with my letter of resignation attached to an email addressed to Cameron, I finally decided to give Nathaniel Carter one shot – just one. After all, things between Leah and Ben have hit an all-time low; perhaps if I can convince him to move out, that I'm ready to stand on my own two feet, he and Leah can get back on the road to their usual animalistic kind of love. If I have no job and no means of income, then he'll definitely refuse to move out with her.

So, I get up, get dressed, and go to work as usual. Nathaniel is already here, tapping away on his computer, so I knock on his door to ask if he would like his usual coffee. I figure I can gauge what kind of mood he is in while appearing professional at the same time.

"Good morning, Mr Carter, would you like a coffee?" I ask him in a timid tone of voice.

"Ah, Bea," he says with a beaming smile, which is a little

unnerving. Truthfully, I was expecting him to be back to his usual mood. "A coffee would be lovely, thank you, though only if it's not too much trouble."

"Er…no, no trouble at all," I stutter, trying my best to smile back at him.

"Next one is on me," he says before turning back to tap away on his computer again.

After that interaction, he went out to get his own lunch but shocked me by offering to pick me up something too. He used 'please' and 'thank you' and spoke politely to me in front of other people in the office. It was unsettling at first, but by close of day, it felt kind of nice. Refreshing, one might say.

The following day, I'm called into his office and asked if I can do a working lunch with him this Thursday. Apparently, we are to attend a meeting together that same afternoon and he wants to run through the specific points I need to pick up on so I can record them word for word. I agreed that this would be ok. Not only was he polite the entire time, but he also said I could have Friday afternoon off for time in lieu. When I returned to my desk, I have to admit I felt a little lightheaded. Everything seemed to be going along so easily and so normally, that I immediately felt suspicious. But perhaps this is simply because I'm not used to it and I'm now trying to find faults in places where there are none.

That evening, after hours of overthinking, I decide to call Callie to get an outsider's opinion on things.

"So, what do you think? Am I being paranoid?" I ask in between chewing on my fingernail.

"Probably," she replies bluntly, "but it's completely understandable. Nate is one of my closest friends, but even I'll say he's been an asshole to you."

"He kind of explained why, then went off on this weird tangent, suggesting that he has feelings for me," I tell her, my cheeks blushing over the memory of him caging me in. "I was too angry to take any real note of it, but even if I did, how could I possibly trust him? The idea of me and him is ludicrous after all that has happened."

"Guys are funny creatures, but what I will say is this, the Nate you've been having to deal with over the last eighteen months, is not the real Nate. Unfortunately, he took your shyness, your standoffish demeanor, as some sort of insult, which, to be fair, was only reinforced by his own insecurities. Now, you can either remain cautious and keep your distance, or you can decide to start again with him. And I'm not talking about a romantic relationship, I'm talking about two people who have got off on the wrong foot."

"Look, I can admit, I find it hard when meeting new people, Nathaniel in particular. I knew about the Carters before I even started working for Cameron; I felt deeply intimidated by them."

"Not so much with Cameron, though, why is that?" she asks me with curiosity in her voice.

"I don't know, maybe because we're the same age," I quickly reply, trying to get around mentioning my sordid past.

"Hmm, maybe," she says, not sounding quite so convinced. "Baby steps, Bea. Though, I am almost certain that his behavior now isn't some sort of attempt to get at you. Of that, I think you can trust him."

A silent pause ensues while I try to process it all.

"So, seeing as I have Friday afternoon off, and I know you leave work early on a Friday, do you fancy meeting in town to do some light shopping?" I ask with hope in my voice.

"Of course," she replies, "I'm always up for retail therapy. Anyway, I've got to go, babe, but we'll continue this conversation on Friday," she says in a rush. "You can also tell me what happened at this working lunch."

Oh, crumbs, yeah, the working lunch!

Bea

Thursday arrives much sooner than I expected. I barely slept, and I've been a bag of nerves all morning. Believe it or not, I've never had to spend that much time with Nathaniel just by myself, which was something I was always immensely relieved by. But now that we're about to spend at least an hour together, I feel strangely excited about it. Something is telling me that this hour will be a turning point in our relationship. Perhaps Callie is right, and we can begin again. Forgive and forget. Let bygones be bygones.

"Nathaniel, would you like me to go and get some sandwiches in for our meeting?" I buzz through the intercom.

"Er, thank you, Bea, but I thought we'd go out for lunch," he suggests, "just give me five."

"Oh, ok," I reply, though these are not the words currently running through my head. However, those words would not be deemed acceptable in a workplace environment. "I-I'll just wait here until you are ready."

"Great, just signing off now," he says and within moments,

I hear his door creak open. He's never looked so intimidating, but with a beaming smile aimed directly at me. Nathaniel Carter has always been extremely attractive, even when he was at school and chasing after cheerleaders.

"Oh, my God, Bea," Emma gushes as she comes running in wearing her yellow and bright blue cheerleading outfit. I merely quirk a brow at her for further explanation, for this sort of dramatic greeting is not at all unusual since she discovered boys last year. We could not be more different, though perhaps this is why we get along so well.

"Who now?" I ask in a bored tone of voice, only to end up laughing when she throws her hands over her chest and begins batting her eyelashes in my direction.

"No, this one is the one, Bea. I am totally, undeniably, unequivocally in love!"

"Oh, Lord," I groan at the same time as she comes flying over to the couch where I'm reading 'Much Ado About Nothing' for perhaps the fifth time. Dean and I are going on a date tonight; he has big expectations, and I no longer feel like I can deny him. Hence reading my comfort book and trying to channel my inner favorite heroine, Beatrice.

"The girls and I went to that diner over on the posh part of town. You know, the one where they serve shakes that are ridiculously good," she begins explaining.

"Sure, I know the one, you better not eat any more sugar for at least the rest of the week," I warn her. Though, those shakes are totally worth the health hazard of consuming your weekly recommended calorie intake in one sitting.

"Well, some of the kids from Westlake were there, and oh,

my God, were they gorgeous!" she beams, looking up to a higher power as though thanking them for creating such works of art. "So, of course, we had to pick which one was ours."

"Of course," I tease.

"And being the youngest, I had to wait until last," she says with an eye roll. "But the joke was on them because just as I was about to choose none other than Nathaniel Carter walked in!"

"Nathaniel who?" I ask, screwing up my face with a genuine lack of knowledge as to who he is.

"You have to know Nathaniel Carter," she says, looking at me like I'm some sort of grotesque alien species. "As in Cameron Carter, Helena Carter? They always attend the Christmas pageants. Cameron was chosen to turn the lights on a few years back; he had won some big competition and earned a butt load of money for some charity or other."

"Oh, ***those*** *Carters!" I reply, their names and faces finally clicking into place. "Me and Helena had a brief conversation about her book; she was reading about –"*

"Yeah, yeah, blah, blah," she says, cutting me off to talk of more important things, like boys. "So, after a while, I walk up to the counter to order some water, after the sugar high had officially worn off, and he appears next to me."

She looks at me, grabs my arm with both hands, and emits a high-pitched squeal.

"I sure hope this is going somewhere because him standing next to you does not warrant this kind of excitement," I deadpan.

"He said hi to me," she cries and begins tapping her legs up and down in excitement.

"Is that all?"

"No, he smiled and asked if I had the time," she says with her mouth left hanging open.

"Oh, my gosh, you're like practically married now!" I mock her. "And when you gave him the time, did you orgasm on the spot?"

"No, but he did say he'd maybe see me around sometime," she says, looking a little less excited.

"Emma, do you have any idea how many girlfriends a boy like him would have hanging around him?" I tell her truthfully. "All of them without a feminist bone in their body. Don't pin your hopes on some boy who hasn't yet learned to respect a girl as a human being; I bet he only sees them as toys he can pick and choose from whenever he so pleases."

"I think you're wrong about him," she pouts, getting out her phone to let all her friends know about her new budding relationship with Westlake Prep's golden boy.

"No, you ***hope*** *I'm wrong about him; there's a difference, Emma."*

"We ***will*** *run into each other, and he'll see me, Emma Summers, and only want me."*

"For your sake, I hope he does," I utter, feeling a little sad for her all of a sudden. She doesn't ever feel seen, not even with all the pictures she puts on social media, she still doesn't feel enough.

Emma never did run into Nathaniel Carter, and I didn't let Dean take my virginity that night either. Unlike my sister, I didn't want to be seen. I was happy with myself and knew I'd regret letting a boy talk me into doing something I wasn't yet ready to do. Though, perhaps if she had met him and he had fallen for her like she had hoped he would, I would never have lost her.

"Ready?" Nathaniel asks, snapping me out of my daydream with his hand gesturing toward the office door.

"Yes, sorry, yes," I fluster before picking up my iPad to take the necessary notes.

"Let's go then," he says, letting me lead the way to the elevator. He slots in behind me as the doors close with just the two of us inside. The silence is deafening, his aftershave intoxicating, and his close proximity is making my hands clammy.

"Are you ok, Bea?" he asks in almost a whisper against my ear, making me gasp over the closeness of his lips to my skin. "You look a little…flushed?"

"I'm fine, thank you," I snap, only to end up laughing awkwardly. Keeping my eyes trained forward, I can see his reflection smirking with self-satisfaction.

Moments later, the doors open, and I end up taking in a gulp of fresh air to try and steady my nerves. He puts his hand on the small of my back and directs me through the underground parking lot. Nate's black Mercedes convertible is sitting almost directly in front of the doors when we step out of the main building. Being a gentleman, he opens the door for me, then walks around to get inside himself. I have to smile when I take a few moments to look around the luxurious interior. How many women has Nathaniel escorted to dinner in this very car?

"Something funny, Miss Summers?" he asks.

"No, not at all," I quickly respond, shaking my head and re-establishing my neutral composure.

"Spill," he says with a cheeky smile on his face, the same one I've seen him give to countless other people, but never to me. "Or I won't let you out of the car."

"I believe that is considered a punishable offense in the eyes of the law," I tell him with a casual shrug of my shoulders. "But just in case you are willing to do jail time, I was wondering how different things are from a week ago."

"I promised you that I would be different from now on. I want to show you I can be someone better to you, hopefully, someone more than a rude asshole."

We share a moment and just look at each other, me seeking truth, him seeking acceptance and trust. It feels too intense, so I pull away first.

"So where are we going?"

"My place," he answers and grins widely at the same time as he revs the engine to go. "I hope you don't mind."

"Er…no, fine with me," I reply nervously.

We drive through the city until we reach a more suburban area. The houses are gated and beyond luxurious to even look at, let alone live in. It's the type of place you would want to bring up a family with the picket fence and customary pet dog. It's not where I was expecting someone of Nathaniel's reputation to be residing, something that my expression must convey without any sort of subtlety. He laughs over my wide eyes and confused expression but continues driving past rows of ridiculously expensive homes without comment.

"You realize Lily and Cam live just through there," he says, pointing in another direction, the houses now looking more familiar. "If I was going to be moving away from my youthful days near the coast, I was at least going to live near the people I care about."

"Oh, well, that makes sense, I suppose," I reply with a simple nod. "You really love your brother, don't you."

"Most of the time," he says with a smile. "Me and Helena used to get on pretty well too, but then she got married and things changed. Cam and I have always been close, but after Evan, we sort of lost that relationship with her."

"Hmm, well my brother and I are very close too," I begin to explain, "and I was close to my sister until…well, you know."

"Wanna talk about it?" he asks, but from the look on his face, I think he already knows the answer.

"No offense," I reply, "but discussing my family problems with my boss isn't really on top of my list of things I want to do."

"Fair enough."

When we finally arrive at his house, I am overwhelmed by how big it actually is. It's modern and imposing but it does have a beautiful garden with wildflowers growing out front. Someone has planted a climbing flower at the base of the house, wisteria and clematis, if I were to guess. I wonder if Nathaniel has the green fingers or if someone else has done it for him. I would hazard a guess at it being the latter of those two options.

Nathaniel opens the door for me while I sit here gawking at his abode. As soon as I tear my eyes away from the magnificence of this place, I shuffle out behind him and wait while he walks up to the front door to enter a security code. I wait until he invites me in, remembering that the last time I went inside the home of Nathaniel Carter, I was drunk and distraught.

When we enter the marble hallway that leads straight to the living/kitchen area, my eyes are overwhelmed by the sight of the over-the-top show home of a room. It's typically masculine with its dark wooden edges, stainless steel appliances, and marble countertops. It's magnificent, enviable, and expensive, but it's still a show home. I half wonder if he simply moved in and forgot to make it his own. The only thing I can see that he might have purchased separately is a huge television that's hanging on the wall in the living area. Beneath it is a grey sofa and one navy armchair. Everything is straight lines and hard.

I almost return to looking at the one human touch in here, Nathaniel himself, when something catches my eye. Just like me, he has one solitary family portrait sitting on a dark wooden sideboard. I cannot help but walk straight over to study it in more detail, not least of all because it shows a child version of both him and Cameron.

"I'm about eight years old in that one," he says, pointing to the photograph in question. "Cam would be thirteen, which would make Helena eleven or twelve; there's only a year between the two. Poor Hels wasn't planned, though it didn't make her any less loved. Dad's always been highly protective of his little girl, much like Cam or I would be with a daughter, I suppose."

"My dad's the same," I tell him with a smile, remembering the games we used to play where he would be the monster and Emma and I would be his victims. Mom would constantly shout at him for being too rough, though we'd always end up laughing. My parents love one another, as well as us kids, more than any family I know. It's why I didn't tell them the full story of what happened; I didn't want to be the one to spoil the illusion of their perfect family.

"Which one of you was the biggest headache for your

parents?" I eventually ask, guessing it was one of the boys.

"Definitely Cam," he says with a smirk. "Trouble is, I always got roped into his dastardly plans, so more often than not, I'd get it in the neck too. I remember when we were on holiday once, at the beach, and Cam had got hold of some stink bombs. Don't ask me how; he kept his secrets highly guarded. Cam and I set three of them off in the corner of the beach, then waited for the sand to clear."

"What did your parents do?" I gasp, not being able to picture the top boss being such a terror.

"Mom let rip on us, but Dad gave us a secret thumbs up for allowing us to claim the prime place to set up our stuff," he says, laughing over the memory of it. "Even Helena found it funny."

"I have to ask, what's with your sister?"

"Helena has always been quiet, she never liked being in the limelight, not like Cam and me. To be fair, Cam and I were always encouraged to try everything, to be brave and chase whatever adrenaline rush that struck our fancy. He wanted us to be the head boy, the captain of the football team, and he usually turned a blind eye when it came to us and girls. But when it came to Helena, he worried about her becoming *one* of those girls. He made it clear that boys and girls would always be treated differently; the world doesn't care if that's fair or not, it's still the way it is. Trust me, if you met his parents, you'd understand why he drilled this message home. They didn't even approve of Mom, and she was valedictorian, volunteering extraordinaire, and more polite than the queen. But she didn't dress like a fifty's housewife, so she was considered too 'edgy'."

"Wow," I gasp with wide eyes, having a better understanding of why Helena is the way she is.

"She settled into the role of the swot up until she was seventeen. My parents went away for the summer, so she went to stay with our cousin. When she came back, she was different, sad but also discontented with the way she had lived before. Even though Dad wasn't keen, she went away to college. She went a bit rebellious, dyed her hair pink, partied, and went to work a summer abroad. For a short time, we got to see the real her; she was actually really cool to hang around with, but then…"

He trails off as though he's thinking about whether he should be telling me any of this. I guess it's not his story to tell, not to mention I'm a work colleague.

"It's ok," I reassure him, "you can tell me if I'm being too nosey."

"No, it's just kind of sad," he says contemplatively. "She fell pregnant by her now ex-husband, Evan, who turned out to be a complete douchebag. She was only twenty. He proposed to her, and of course, my father thought it was the best outcome given the situation, so he convinced her to accept. Marrying him so young sucked the life out of her and destroyed her newfound self-confidence. As soon as he put his ring on her finger, she reverted to the quiet, little, shy woman you see today."

"That must be hard to watch," I utter, thinking of Helena hiding behind her reception desk at work. She's always very polite and friendly but also reserved, choosing very much to keep to herself. I've never seen her with any real friends, besides Lily, and, other than Nathaniel, she rarely talks to anyone past a friendly greeting.

"Well, at least she eventually divorced him a few years ago," he says. "He attacked Lily shortly after that."

"What?!" I gasp in shock. "What do you mean 'attacked'?"

"Oh, I thought the girls would have told you," he says, looking a tad anxious over revealing such a thing. "He basically tried to rape her; he blamed her for the breakdown of their marriage."

"Oh, my God!"

"I know I can trust you not to mention any of this. Lily doesn't talk about it; I think it's still quite raw."

"Of course," I reassure him, "it's none of my business. I'm just…shocked!"

"Well, that's what everyone's reaction tends to be," he says with a soft smile. "Anyway, let's get some lunch and we can talk shop for a bit."

"Good plan," I confirm with a nod. "Can I do anything?"

"No, make yourself comfortable," he says, gesturing to the breakfast bar, "and I'll get some bits and pieces together."

Bea

For the next half an hour or so, Nathaniel tells me about the lawyer with whom we are going to be meeting this afternoon. He is representing a company that Cameron is trying to purchase. He tells me what to note down and what to pay special attention to. Apparently, this lawyer has a bit of a reputation for being difficult, as well as being extremely good at what he does. In fact, he is so well known, people try to avoid him if they can. Nathaniel says he's nicknamed 'The Devil', being that he leaves you feeling soulless. I must have looked horrified because he laughed and told me not to worry, that Cameron has already negotiated the main details, so this is merely a follow-up meeting before they finally sign on the dotted line. He just wants me to be prepared.

"Have you ever worked with him before?" I ask.

"Not personally, no," he replies, which comforts me a little, it means we're both in the same boat. "Though, we were technically cousins for about three years."

"Ok. I'm guessing there's a story there?"

"His father was married to my aunt for about three years," he explains. "He's always been an ass, a very entitled ass too, if you know what I mean."

"Oh, you mean very rich?" I smile in response, complete with an accusatory expression on my face. I know how much Cameron is worth, and Nathaniel doesn't appear to be short of a dollar or two either.

"Still is, as far as I know. Honestly, I haven't seen him since my aunt parted from his father," he says matter of factly. "Would you like a tour of the house?"

"Oh, erm, shouldn't we be getting back?" I ask, feeling a little nervous about his offer.

"Nah, we've got at least half an hour," he replies with a wicked grin on his face. "Imagine what we could get up to in that time?"

My mouth drops open over his suggestion, but he simply laughs and grabs my hand to begin showing me around his home. First, we go outside to where there is a river running along the back, the very same one that runs along Cam and Lily's house too. The garden is decorated with flowers and plants and looks very well looked after. When we go back inside, he shows me upstairs to where there are four good-sized bedrooms, two of which are ensuite. When we enter his bedroom, I feel a little intrusive, however, he doesn't seem the least bit perturbed by me being in his personal space.

"It's very neat," I comment, thinking how my room looks like a hovel by comparison. Don't get me wrong, it's not dirty or smelly, and I never have food or drink in there, but every now and then, my entire wardrobe will be lying all over the floor.

"My mother was very particular about how we kept our rooms," he explains, "it's kind of stuck with me I suppose. Plus, I'm a little bit of an entitled prick too," he says sheepishly, "I have a housekeeper who comes in twice a week."

"Ah-ha," I laugh, "it's all coming out now."

Downstairs, he shows me an extensive home gym that would be the stuff of nightmares for me. I own one pair of sneakers and a weighted hula-hoop that is currently collecting dust behind the TV.

"Wow, you must work out a lot," I comment.

"Well, you don't look like me without putting in the work," he teases while throwing up his muscular bicep.

"Hmm, you don't get to be as vain as you either," I reply, feeling comfortable enough to poke fun at him with a roll of my eyes.

"Hey, I'm a single guy with free time," he says with a shrug, "I like to work out; it zones me out for a bit."

"Well, it appears to have the right effect on members of the opposite sex," I laugh, "considering all the bunches of flowers I've had to send over the last year."

"And what effect does it have on you, Beatrice?" He looks at me with a now serious expression, with him being so close, I can feel the heat radiating from his body. My breath catches and I have to think really carefully about what to say.

"Erm…well, you are extremely attractive if you like that kind of thing," I eventually reply, together with a shrug of my shoulders and a nonchalant tone of voice. "I especially love your modesty."

He laughs, glances at his watch, then widens his eyes in what looks like horror.

"Oh, crap, Bea, this will have to be continued because it's time for us to go. Do you want to go out to the car, and I'll lock up."

"Sure," I answer as I begin to shuffle past his huge, muscular frame. "It really is a beautiful home, Nathaniel."

"Thank you, Bea," he says with what looks like a genuine smile. "I hope you get to see it again…soon."

Another awkward staring session ensues before I sheepishly walk out the door.

Keep your cool, Bea, this can't happen. You're his PA for Christ's sake; it's got stupid written all over it.

Chapter 14

Bea

We arrive back at the office earlier than expected, and as I walk in, I glance over at Helena and think about what Nathaniel had said about her. Looking at her hair pulled up in a neat bun, dressed conservatively with little to no makeup, I wonder how on earth she was ever the type of girl to dye her hair pink and work abroad by herself. She seems like she'd rather be completely invisible, and yet her brothers are so confident. Even with her father's sexist upbringing, what happened to her?

"Hi, Nate, Bea," she says, smiling at us before picking up her glass of water to sip, which looks more like a nervous reaction than a need for hydration.

"Hey, Hels," Nate beams at her, "has Lucius Hastings arrived yet?"

At the sound of that name, Helena freezes mid-sip, then takes a few moments to gulp down her rather large intake of water. She then stares in shock at her brother, with color quickly draining from her face.

"What? I mean wh-who?" she flusters, shaking her head like she must have heard him wrong.

"Lucius Hastings, you remember him, don't you? His father was married to Aunt Jen. You even stayed with them when you were seventeen. You must have run into him now and then?"

"Er…yeah, no," she gasps, now flapping over some papers. "No, he's not arrived yet; is he due in now?"

Nathaniel silently nods his head, looking at her with a deep-etched frown of concern. He then looks at me as though I have the answer to his sister's sudden anxious behavior. All I can do is shrug my shoulders; I know even less than he does. Just as we're having this strange telepathic conversation, she snaps our attention back by suddenly dropping her glass, which hits the floor with a smash that echoes all around the reception area. I emit a gasp of shock before I spin around to see who she's staring at.

Standing in the doorway is perhaps one of the most intense-looking men I've ever seen in my life. If this is Lucius Hastings, then Nathaniel's description of a soul-sucking devil is spot on. With dangerously good looks, he exudes masculinity and power in a way that's different from Nathaniel and Cameron. I would not want to go up against him in a courtroom. Actually, I wouldn't dare go against him in *any* room.

Initially, he looks at Nathaniel, offering a nod of acknowledgment, but then he bypasses me altogether and stares right into Helena's wide eyes. The wad of envelopes she was holding out for Nathaniel is now trembling within her white-knuckled hand and she looks sickly pale. When no words are exchanged, just Helena staring at him with an unreadable expression, I turn back to see what this strange man is doing, only to find he is beginning to smirk in such a way, I almost think I'm intruding on an intimate moment between the two of them. It's so intense, that even I feel a shiver run down my spine.

"Nathaniel," he eventually says in a deep voice, a voice that could command anyone in any room. "I hope you are well; how is the family?"

He glides over with purpose, and they grasp hands in a manly handshake. It feels like the testosterone levels are suddenly rising to dangerous heights in this already male-dominated building.

"Great, thank you, Lucius," Nathaniel replies with a deeper-than-normal voice. I sense the competitiveness in masculine authority and find it fascinating to watch. It's like observing two male lions pacing around one another, ready to fight it out. Helena, on the other hand, looks so uncomfortable, I can tell she would like to vanish into the wall behind her.

"Helena," Lucius addresses her in a strange, but commanding tone of voice, "it's been a while."

"Yes," is all she manages to say in barely more than a whisper.

"How is the family? Your husband and daughter are well, I take it?" he asks, taking her hand to kiss the back of it. It's still shaking but Lucius holds it firmly, then watches it until it eventually stills within his grip.

She clears her throat in an attempt to answer, but her brother jumps in for her. Something I'm beginning to think she's had to endure her whole life, especially with two brothers and an overbearing father.

"Thankfully, she got rid of her ass of a husband, didn't you, Hels?" He grins at her playfully, but she merely gifts him with a cold, hard stare, all while blushing with embarrassment.

"Really?" Lucius says, raising his brow in surprise. "That is...*interesting*."

"Nate," Helena manages to push out, "is it ok if I take my lunch now?"

Nathaniel frowns with concern over her sudden change in demeanor but eventually nods his head in reply.

"Course, you don't need to ask if you have it covered. She is my big sister, after all," he says, now looking at Lucius, and they both laugh politely at one another. Helena nods her thanks before scurrying out back to grab her bag.

"Shall we make our way up to my office?" Nathaniel asks Lucius. "It's just going to be you, me, and Beatrice today. Cameron is on honeymoon."

Lucius finally acknowledges me and shakes my hand politely, though his main attention seems to be elsewhere. It is most likely with the Carter sister who has just rushed out the door to get away from here as quickly as possible.

"Sure, but can I meet you in a moment?" he asks. "I just want to ask your sister something about Meriel. I haven't heard from her in a while and thought Helena might know what's going on with that cousin of yours."

"Ok, sure, I'm at the top, straight ahead once you leave the elevator. I'm pretty much next door to Cameron's office," he explains, to which they both smile before Nathaniel leads me over toward the elevator.

"Was that normal?" I ask. "Between him and your sister?"

We enter the confined space of the elevator but this time he is standing in front of me; I am literally pinned to the wall, enclosed by his muscular arms. I'm not sure if this is an intentional move on his part, but now I feel a sudden throb of lust between my thighs. I don't even feel guilty for it, not when I am close enough to be inhaling his delicious aftershave. The mix of woody and citrussy scents is enough to make anyone feel a little woozy and reckless.

"Who knows, who cares?" he says with his eyes suddenly appearing much darker than usual. "Kiss me, Bea."

I look up, trying to keep my senses about me so as not to fall for his ridiculous muscular arm cage. When I manage to escape the first overpowering urge to give into his demand, I nervously shake my head. I have a feeling if any words escaped from between my lips, they might betray my more sensible thoughts. At my silent rebuttal, he places a hand on my waist and pulls me in a little closer.

"Kiss me, please, Bea," he says again, sounding a little urgent, and I cannot help but look straight at his lips. He darts out his tongue to wet them, which doesn't help my throbbing situation at all. As my mouth gets closer to his, with my lips begging me to just give in, I force myself to close my eyes and snap myself out of his seductive fog.

"Please, Nathaniel," I whisper a plea, "you know this isn't a good idea."

"I know but every minute I'm with you, I no longer care," he says, leaning even closer to me; so close, I think he's going to actually make contact. Then…then I will be lost to him. There's only so much willpower a girl has.

Thankfully, the elevator doors ping and open at our

destination. He smiles at me before straightening up to redeem his normal composure, looking as though he hadn't just propositioned me inside of the elevator. He marches out, so I shake it off and sheepishly follow behind, probably not looking quite as innocent as he is.

The rest of the afternoon is filled with meeting Lucius Hastings. I try to avoid eye contact with the man; I'd like to keep hold of my soul, such that it is. The man is very professional when it comes to talking business, but his eyes appear to have the power to lower your life expectancy. Other than his demon-like powers which I've made up inside of my head, the meeting runs as smoothly as any other. Still, I feel a huge weight lifted from my shoulders the moment we bid Mr Hastings adieu.

When the end of the day comes not long after, Nathaniel tells me I can go a little earlier, then simply says goodbye to me, just as he would with any other employee. I feel a strange mixture of relief and extreme disappointment. Maybe my refusals have cured him of his attraction to me. It's probably for the best though. I can't seriously date my boss, can I?

With these conflicting thoughts, I walk toward the door onto the street and see Helena sitting on a nearby bench with her head between her knees. She appears to be taking deep breaths, as though trying to ward off sickness.

"Are you ok?" I call as I rush over to where she is. She slowly looks up in my direction with a sickly-looking complexion and red, puffy eyes. "Helena, have you been crying?"

"Oh, no," she whispers, even though she's blinking away tears. "I think I'm getting a migraine. I used to get them a lot, but this is the first I've had since Evan. I'm just trying to breathe through the nausea."

"Shit, er, ok," I reply rather awkwardly, "let me get Nathaniel."

"Oh, no, don't…" she begins but then seems to slump in defeat. "Actually, yeah, could you? I don't think I can drive in this state. Jess will be home soon too."

I nod, then run inside to find him. He's still in his office, talking away on the phone to someone. At first, I hold back, not wanting to interrupt. Such a thing would have earned me a verbal lashing not long ago, but then I remember Helena's face just now, so I continue marching up to his door with determination.

"Yeah, still a no-go," I hear him say with a sigh, "but I'm not giving up…Yes, I fucking know what I'm doing, it's totally worth it!" He pauses to laugh. "Well, you don't have to fuck each other every day and night of the honeymoon, Christ!"

Assuming the conversation isn't urgent business stuff, I knock on the door and wait for him to respond.

"Yep, come in," he calls. "I'll see you when you get back," he says into the phone as I walk in.

"Bea?" He frowns, looking deeply concerned.

"Sorry, but your sister is in real bad shape outside," I gesture with my thumb over my back. "She says she thinks it's a migraine and doesn't think she can drive."

"Oh, ok," he says, now flustering as he grabs hold of his phone. "Let me call my mom, and then I'll come down with you. Thanks, Bea."

I wait in my office while he talks to his mom, arranging for her to be at Helena's house for when he drops her home. He then turns off his computer and walks past me, gesturing for me to follow. He doesn't say anything in the lift but keeps checking his watch. I find myself beginning to wonder, irrationally, if he's supposed to be seeing someone. A female? Pools of jealousy begin to gather in my stomach and it's not a pleasant feeling.

We find Helena in the same position as where I'd left her about ten minutes ago, still clutching hold of her head and trying to gasp for air to soothe her nausea.

"Hels," Nathaniel says gently at the same time as he puts his arm around his sister's shoulders. "What's up?"

"Migraine," she murmurs, the one word sounding like it's painful to utter. She looks even worse than she did before. "There're sparks in my eyes, and I've already thrown up in the bin. Sorry to be a pain."

"Shut up," he says, sounding just like Ben would with me in the same situation. "You're not a pain. Mom's going to wait for Jess while I drive you home. Got any medication?"

She nods, seemingly no longer able to bear talking. Nathaniel looks back at me and smiles.

"Thank you, Bea, I can take it from here," he says, and I nod quietly before taking my cue to go.

God, what is wrong with me? Am I being an idiot for even contemplating doing anything with my boss? Or am I a fool for not leaping on top of this genuinely caring Adonis? I sigh heavily as I walk home. An apartment where I live with my brother and his girlfriend humping at all hours, in a room for one. Perhaps it's time to re-evaluate my life; to finally move forward.

Chapter 15

Bea

"Morning Nathaniel," I smile as he walks into the office. "How's Helena?"

"Morning, Bea, she's fine, thank you," he replies, then walks straight past me and into his office. I think I'm just another employee again, which is good, isn't it?

The morning drags on and I don't hear a peep from my boss, otherwise known as my missed opportunity, so I'm literally counting down the minutes until I can leave for my retail therapy session with Callie. I flip from cursing myself for turning him down to praising myself for doing the right thing for the sake of my career. By lunchtime, my head is beginning to ache from all the over-thinking. Luckily, my new gal pal arrives and it's enough to take away some of the strain.

"Aren't you early?" I grin at Callie as she perches on my desk. "I thought you didn't finish until one."

"I know but I had some flexi and work was dull, so here I

am!" she sing songs.

"Well, I *am* here till one, so you might have to entertain yourself for a bit," I tell her with a long sigh.

I get back to writing up some emails, only to still when Callie gets up and grabs the intercom into Nathaniel's office from my desk.

"Mr Carter, your twelve o'clock call girl is here to do unspeakable things to you," she purrs in a seductive tone of voice. I can't help but giggle over her antics.

"Mr Carter is busy right now but if you'd like to call back later, I still won't be in," he replies jovially.

"Nate, get out here now!" she shouts through the door playfully. "There he is!" she sings out to him when he opens the door to reveal a smirk on his face. "Can I steal your girlfriend away early, pretty please?"

"Beatrice is not my girlfriend," he says dryly, "but you may take my PA early, on one condition."

"And what is that, Mr Fancy Pants?" she continues, all the while she grins innocently at him.

"You both have to accompany me to Helena's house tonight while I watch Jess," he says in his usual commanding tone. "Hels is still out of it and my parents are at one of their soirees tonight, so it's been decided that I need to step up. I know fuck all about entertaining a pre-teen, so I'd be grateful for the reinforcements."

"Sure, we can do that can't we, Bea?" Callie says, turning to offer me a cheeky wink. He looks at me expectantly, so I take a risk and nod.

"Good, I'll pick you up at half four?"

"Sure, just text or call when you want us," Callie grins as she grabs my bag for me. "Switch off that computer, Miss, we're out of here."

Bea

The afternoon was more fun than I could ever have expected. I've not stopped laughing the whole time and I feel blessed to have actually reached out and made a new friend. I know she's missing Lily, but I think I'm making a good substitute. Callie is the funniest, most ridiculous person I have ever met, but I also think she is loyal and genuine. If the chips were down, she'd be there for you, no questions asked. I've come to value that more than anything when forming relationships with people, it's what first drew me to Finn.

At about four o'clock, we head over to a little boutique where Callie tries to make me break out of my comfort zone. She picks out a whole bunch of skimpy dresses, the sort that I would never wear, not even when I was in my teens, and begs me to try them on. No one but us two and the changing room is going to see me, so in the end, I concede. The first three don't even make it out of my cubicle, they look that awful; the next two earn me a burst of laughter from Callie, and the last one won't even do up.

After trying no less than three times to make the zipper work, I decide to take it off. Alas, as soon as I try to pull it up and over my head, I become stuck. In fact, I'm becoming acutely aware of the fact that I am now completely immobilized from the neck up. My arms are up in the air, I can't see anyone, and I have the heart-stopping thought that someone is going to have to come in and cut me out.

Shit, what the hell do I do?

"Callie?!" I shout frantically. "I'm stuck!"

Nate

"Please, let me go in," I whisper to Callie when we hear Bea's desperate pleas coming from the changing cubicle. I had finished a little earlier than expected so arranged with Callie to meet the them here. I couldn't have organized a more perfect situation if I'd tried; to rescue the damsel in distress who is currently wrestling to get out of her clothing in the changing room? *Perfection.*

"What? No, perv!" she whisper shouts. "Every time I meet this poor girl, she ends up being accosted by you!"

"Please, Callie, I'll pay for a spa day for you," I bargain, "for you, Lily, and Bea."

She pretends to think for a moment, but I already know I have her; it's not that she couldn't afford it herself, nor Lily for that matter, but who doesn't like a treat on somebody else's credit card?

"Fine, but if you end up being sued for sexual harassment, don't come crying to me. I'll see you guys outside, hopefully together and without any black eyes. Behave, Nathaniel!"

Bea

"Callie?" I shout again. "Where the heck are you? I'm well

and truly stuck in this hideous dress that you chose."

I no longer care if the sales assistants can hear me, I need to get out of this ridiculous dress. I don't want to die in a skintight leopard print dress wrapped around my neck, my life has been sad enough as it is.

"Now there's a sight for sore eyes," a familiar, deep, and masculine voice says, making me freeze in my jiggling on the spot.

"Nathaniel?" I ask, hoping I'm wrong and the once-upon-a-time object of every teenage girl's fantasy from Western High, isn't standing before me whilst I'm in this thoroughly compromising and humiliating position.

"This is Nate," he confirms, "do you need some help, Miss Summers?"

"Where's Callie?" I gasp with horror.

"I told her I could handle whatever situation you were in," he says. "Would you like me to free you from your restraints or…not?"

"Nathaniel, please help me get this off," I practically beg, "I don't want to have to ask for scissors and spend what little cash I have left on the remains of this hideous dress."

"Are you sure? The view is very tempting," he whispers with dark intent. Jesus, I can feel his breath on my right arm, which is currently being restrained by leopard print Lycra. I take a deep, albeit shaky breath as he runs the tip of his finger along my naked spine.

"Nathaniel…" I gasp, trying to sound like a warning, though not being entirely successful in that feat.

"Imagine giving in, Beatrice," he whispers with temptation dripping from his lips.

I breathe in deeply if only to try and get some much-needed oxygen to my brain so I can stop myself from giving into him completely, right here in this changing room. It doesn't work that well, and I even open my mouth to give him the green light, but then I feel him pull the fabric away as he releases me from my ugly dress prison. With my hair flying back into place, static from the horrendous fabric of the dress, I take in my boss, who is wearing a three-piece charcoal suit, white shirt, and silk tie. His intimidating muscular frame is doing unspeakable things to my insides, especially with him staring at me with a ghost of a smile. After taking much too long to come to my senses, I grab my dress and hold it in front of me, even though he's already seen my underwear.

"Thank you, Nathaniel," I breathe out awkwardly.

"Believe me, Bea," he begins with a beaming smile, "the pleasure was all mine. And I have to say, I do love a woman who wears matching underwear, even if it's just for herself."

"All my underwear is black," I say for some unknown, stupid reason. It wasn't to be sexy; I don't even know how to be sexy.

"Duly noted. I'll meet you out front."

He then looks at me one more time before turning to leave.

When I finally get outside, Nathaniel is on the phone, so I take the opportunity to glare at Callie, who simply giggles over my flushed cheeks.

"How could you do that? That was so embarrassing!" I

whisper angrily to her.

"Oh, come on, you so like him," she teases, "you just need to live a little dangerously and that's where I come in. You do know I set Cam and Lils up, don't you? Just call me Cupid!"

All the while Nathaniel has his back to us, she performs a little rendition of Cupid flitting his wings while dancing on tiptoes. She looks ridiculous but couldn't care less what anyone thinks of her, not even the group of teenage girls who laugh and whisper as they walk past. I shake my head at her but with a huge smile on my face.

"You girls ready?" Nathaniel asks, now turning to face us with a star-studded smile and a pair of sunglasses that only add to how sexy he looks in that exquisite suit he's wearing.

"Lead the way, Sir," Callie says in an appalling British accent, "let us tame the teenage girl who goeth by the name of Jessica!"

Oh, my Lord! But thank God she is with us tonight. Nothing too bad can happen if someone is there to be a third wheel, can it?

Bea

Helena's house is beautiful - plain and simple! There are handmade decorations everywhere, all created by Helena and Jess. In addition to these gorgeous personal touches, there are family photographs adorning virtually every wall. Someone definitely has a passion for photography in this house, if not, both of them. There are multiple artistic shots of people and landscapes that wouldn't look out of place in a professional art gallery. It couldn't contrast more with Nathaniel's impersonal show home. He should definitely ask his sister to help him decorate. Though, from the look of the garden, she's already lent some of her artistic skills to him.

Of course, Helena doesn't let us in herself, she's still really sick with her migraine. Nathaniel told us they can be known to last for days, so she takes medication that will literally knock her out. However, her daughter, Jess, is more than eager to welcome us in with a huge grin on her face. From the moment we step inside, she begins explaining that her grandmother had left about half an hour ago, but not to worry for she's already set out some nibbles, as well as some glasses to serve us drinks. Bless her, I don't think she draws breath until we're all safely inside their quaint cottage-style kitchen.

"So, what do you wanna do tonight?" Nathaniel just about manages to ask when she finally puts a glass of lemonade to her lips.

"Well, there're some movies over here and Nanny got us some pizzas," she says, gesturing to all her listed forms of entertainment. "But I really want to show Callie and Bea my newly- decorated bedroom."

"Hey, why can't I see it?" Nathaniel gasps while feigning offense.

"Because you're a boy and Mom always says, 'Jess, you cannot positively, absolutely not have boys in your room yet!'" she parrot fashions her mother's words, making me giggle. She's cute and gorgeous, so Helena is totally right to say this to her. We're all forced to grow up much too soon. Some of us survive it, some of us come out bruised and battered, whereas some of us barely make it out alive.

"That's very good advice," Callie chimes in, sounding matter of fact, "boys *are* trouble! Fun, but definitely trouble."

Nathaniel glares at her for a moment or two before turning back to offer Jess a smile of understanding.

"That's fair enough. Why don't you take Callie upstairs now? I just want to talk to Bea for a minute."

As soon as Jess leads Callie into the living room, walking in the direction of the staircase, I turn around to question him with a furrowing of my brow.

"Nathaniel?" I ask, finally finding the words when he says nothing. "Is everything ok?"

"No, actually, it's not," he says, walking toward me with such a serious expression, my hands begin to feel clammy. Eventually, when he reaches me, he places a hand on either side of the sink where I'm standing, caging me in once again. He moves in close, so close I can feel the breath from his parted lips, and a buzz of something inexplicable running between us.

"What's it going to take, Bea? What's it going to take to let me kiss you? I'm going out of my fucking mind here. Do you know how crazy I am about you? How long I've literally been going insane for you?"

I grin, biting my lip, trying to lighten the atmosphere, though the intensity is much too much for me to break through.

"Er, well, not really, you've been kind of an ass for so long," I tease, "how was I supposed to know when you started thinking naughty things about me?"

"Are you flirting with me, Bea?" he says, quirking up his

lips into a breath-taking smile. I breathe in and out for a few moments, trying to consider what answer to give. Should I give this a go, or should I keep my distance? Why am I so damn indecisive?

"Maybe," I reply with a long breath.

His eyes immediately turn darker, and I suddenly see his desperation for this to go further, which I have apparently given him the green light to do. He leans in closer and our lips just about touch when Jess suddenly bursts into the room, prompting us both to jump apart. Nathaniel steps back and scratches the back of his neck, all the while I try to cover my smile from behind my hand.

"Come on, Bea," Jess says impatiently, "Nate can smooch with you later."

Nathaniel gasps, but we both smile at each other before following the little passion killer up to her bedroom. We find Callie looking through some of Jess' schoolbooks at the end of her bed.

"Were they?" Callie asks, not even bothering to look up from Jess' exercise book.

"About to," Jess replies nonchalantly, and with a shrug of her shoulders. "I got bored of waiting so interrupted before the real show began."

"Oh, my God! You two, nosey much?" I laugh.

"It really is like a soap opera," Callie comments, completely ignoring me.

"Well, I made them end on a thoroughly frustrating cliffhanger," Jess giggles, then gestures all around her room.

"Anyway, what do you think? I want to get some lights to go around the mirror and some wall stickers to break up the color, but this is basically it."

"Wow, you are one lucky lady," I tell her. "I never would have been allowed to decorate like this, it's so…so grown up. You have a walk-in wardrobe for goodness sake!"

"You know, you could do with some throws for over here, maybe?" Callie suggests, gesturing to her mini sofa that sits along the end of her bed.

"I love all of your photographs," I add, looking carefully along each one.

"Yeah, Mom likes her photography," she replies casually. "She's teaching me as well, but I like finding strange objects in nature, whereas she likes photographing people, especially candid shots."

"They're amazing," I tell her. "Perhaps your mom should consider a career in it."

"Yeah, I keep telling her that, but she doesn't think she's good enough," Jess sighs, shrugging her shoulders. This is obviously a conversation that she's had many times but has perhaps given up on.

When I reach a photograph of Jess as a baby, I smile over how cute she is, with lots of dark hair all over her tiny head, looking like it's just been attacked by static electricity. I then take a careful look at the man who is cradling her, holding her little fist with just his forefinger while grinning like an idiot, as most fathers do with their newborns. I'm sure there's a similar picture of my own father holding me like this somewhere. However, when I look at his eyes, his hair, and the way he smiles a little lopsidedly, there's something eerily familiar about him. I squint my eyes to really try and focus in on his face, which only gives me a stronger sense of déjà vu. Where the hell do I know him from?

"Who is this, Callie?" I whisper, even though Jess has left the room to skip off to the bathroom down the hall. She leans in to look more closely at the picture, then immediately groans.

"That is Jess' father, Evan, a complete asshole in other words."

Oh no! I know who he is.

"What's wrong, Bea, you look like you've seen a ghost."

"Oh, God, Callie, this is bad, really bad," I gasp before slapping my hand over my face. "This is him, the horrendous one-night stand I had once upon a few years ago. God, things went so bad after that."

"Oh, shit," she murmurs, then appears to think about it for a few moments. "I think best keep that information to yourself; no one needs to know about that from this household."

"Yes, yes of course," I tell her while nodding my head with too much force. I'm about two minutes away from hyperventilating.

"That was good, cutie, but I have to get home to my wife and kid. Stay in school, or college, or whatever."

"What the fuck did you just say?!"

We both turn to see Nathaniel's fuming red face and clenched-up body, which is now filling up the entirety of Jess' door frame.

"Look, hold on Nate-" Callie begins, trying to calm the beast that looks like he cannot be tamed right now.

"Callie, don't even try it!" he snaps in such a way, not even she tries to argue.

The whole time he takes to walk up to me, I feel like throwing up, only I have no breath with which to do it. Approaching me, he breathes heavily and angrily, his eyes turning darker by the second, and not at all in a good way. I begin to tremble, just needing to find the nearest exit. Just like back then, when I was barely eighteen, I need to get away from this place and everyone in it.

"You have turned me down flat at every advance I've made, even though I know you want me and yet you slept with that…that piece of shit rapist, just like that?! What the fuck is wrong with you?" he snarls, looking at me with utter disgust.

"Nathaniel, I…it was-"

"Save it!" he yells. "I'm done! If you can sleep with someone like that, then you're right to turn me down. In fact, I think it's best you leave, especially while his then-wife and daughter are under the same roof."

Tears well in my eyes as I shove him to one side before flying out of the room. Ignoring Callie yelling after me, I jump down the stairs two at a time, grab my bag and run out the door, not even stopping to shut it behind me. I run as fast as I can, with tears streaming down my face over his words, his revulsion, and his anger. I feel it all over again - the pain, the shame, the sick feeling that hung around me for months afterward. The reasons for never dating anyone all slam into me at once, reminding me of why I try to keep myself safe by not engaging in anything that will threaten my heart ever again. How could we have gone from virtually kissing and giving into passion, to him shouting at me to get away from him?

When I've run so far that I'm now out of breath, I finally stop to rummage around in my bag so I can grab my phone. At first, I find Ben's number, for he's always been my go-to hero, the one guy who I can rely on. However, if I phone him, he'll go insane and probably end up in prison for brutally murdering Nate. No, I'll have to call Leah and beg her not to tell him. I just want to get home.

"Hi, babe," she says, sounding somewhat tired. "You ok?"

"No," I just about manage to say through my tears. "Please, Leah, can you come and get me?"

"Honey, what's happened?" she asks with deep-rooted concern in her voice. "Where are you?"

"He…he screamed at me, told me to get away from him, and he made me feel so dirty, like I was some kind of cheap whore," I sob loudly.

"Who are you talking about? Not that asshole boss of yours?" she says with the sound of concern morphing into angry frustration. "I thought you were off work? Why are you with him?"

"He told me he liked me, that he wanted me, has done so for a while." I smile sadly, realizing just how ridiculous this sounds. "I began to like him back…I'm such a fucking idiot!"

"No, you're not, Bea," she says softly. "But what

happened? Why did he go mental at you if he likes you?"

"I've been saying no to him, you know, because of everything, but then he heard me tell Callie that the one night stand I had - you know the *one* I'm talking about - was his sister's ex-husband. God, what did I do to deserve all of this?"

"Nothing!" she cries. "Look, sweetie, text me where you are, and I will come and get you as fast as I can. Just hold on!"

"Leah, please don't tell Ben, he'll go ballistic," I plead with her.

"Er…ok, I won't," she replies. "Text me where you are, and don't worry."

Chapter 16

Bea

Fortunately, I don't have to wait too long before Leah's motorbike comes revving down the road. Though, when I listen more closely, it's not just the sound of one bike, it's the sound of two engines coming this way. I sigh, closing my eyes tightly, realizing that Ben has obviously come with her, which means he knows what's happened.

The two great big bikes skid to a halt on the gravel track just in front of where I'm standing. Leah switches off her engine and dismounts her bike before pulling off her black helmet. She says nothing but grabs hold of me in an all-encompassing hug while I break down and sob onto her shoulder. The second bike, however, snaps me out of my crying when I hear it revving away in the direction of Helena's house. Holy shit, this won't be pretty. Helena's house is the only one down here and with Nathaniel's car having a personalized number plate, it's pretty clear as to where he can find him.

"Leah!" I pull back to look at her with bleary eyes and a puffy face. "What the hell?"

"I didn't tell him!" she cries back, looking a little sheepish. "You were on speakerphone; unfortunately, he heard everything."

"Then why didn't you warn me?" I ask, slapping my hand to my forehead.

"Cos…cos I kind of think the asshole has it coming to him," she says without any hint of an apology for her statement. "Bea, we are all tired of this douchebag being a total mindfuck to you."

She watches me pacing with nervous anticipation, then eventually holds out the spare helmet for me.

"Come on, I'll drive you back. There's nothing you can do about it now, Bea."

Sighing in defeat, I take the helmet and put it on, letting it hide my face from the world and the world from me. To be honest, I don't have any energy left in me to fight it. So, as I climb onto the back of her bike, I watch my brother in full leathers, getting smaller and smaller as he closes in on Helena's house, then shut my eyes to it all.

Nate

I'm literally shaking with rage as I pace up and down the length of Hels' living room, all the while I run my hand through my hair. I can't believe that fucking sleaze bag not only destroyed my sister, and attacked Lily, but he also slept with Bea…***my*** Bea. I don't care that she's not actually mine, it still makes me feel sick to know that his hands have been on her. And now I've gone and lost it with her. Knowing that I shouldn't have, I'm damn well angry with myself too. Callie tried to call after her, but she just ran away as fast as she could, and all because of my big, stupid, and impulsive mouth. And to top it all off, Jess is sulking up in her room because her uncle 'ruins everything'. To be fair, I can admit that this time, I have.

"Good job there, Nate," Callie says, returning to the room with a sigh. She's now looking at me like I'm the biggest idiot in the world.

"I know, alright!" I yell back at her. "I'm just...frustrated. She won't even give me the time of day, but she slept with that piece of shit?"

"You heard one little piece of information and instead of talking to her about it, to hear all the facts, you had a toddler tantrum," she says, shaking her head over my stupidity. "And now you've pretty much blown it. I wouldn't put up with that kind of shit from anyone, let alone my asshole boss who has systematically destroyed my confidence over the past year and a half."

"Fuck, I am an asshole, aren't I?" I sigh. "I've screwed it up again with my stupid short fuse, fuck!"

"Well...yeah, I have no other words I'm afraid," she replies bluntly.

As I breathe out another heavy sigh, we begin to hear thudding coming from the front door. Callie and I both look at each other with matching confused expressions.

"It might be Bea," Callie says, jumping to her feet to answer the door. "She sounds pissed too; prepare yourself and take it like a man. You owe her that much."

I listen as she walks to the front of the house to open the door, expecting to hear her greet the poor girl who I just lost it with...again! I stand, getting ready to accept her wrath, for Callie is right, I owe her this. However, when I don't hear that greeting, and instead listen to the sound of boots stomping across the floorboards, I brace myself for something I wasn't expecting – a man dressed all in leathers and with a rage-filled expression on his face. This is Ben, Bea's older brother, probably come to murder me all over my sister's beautiful house.

He paces right up to my face and grabs hold of the lapels of my suit jacket. I don't try to fight him, instead, I remain rigid, just waiting to accept whatever he's about to deliver; I deserve it.

"Listen, asshole," he begins with a sneer on his face, "you don't come near my sister, you don't look at her, you don't even think about her, do you understand me?"

"I can't promise that I'm afraid," I reply, the audacity of my words shocking even me as they flow out into the space between us.

"You arrogant son of a bitch, you are not nearly good enough for her, and Lord knows, she's been through enough shit already. Stay the fuck away!"

"No!" I snap back.

At first, he smiles, but then he lands a large fist in my gut, enough to make me hunch forward and cough out.

"Shit! Nate, you ok?" Callie whimpers. "Stop it, please!"

"It's ok, I deserved that," I reply with another cough, putting my hand up in surrender, "but I can't promise to stay away from Bea."

The hulk of a man laughs before forcing himself back with what looks like anger running all the way through his body. For a moment, I think he's going to jump on me, but he ends up walking about in a small angry circle, flexing his hands as if trying to calm himself down.

"Look," I begin, taking the opportunity to try and reason with him, "I'll admit, I've handled everything horribly. Today, I found out she had an...*intimate* encounter, with my asshole ex-brother-in-law and I saw red. I couldn't help it. You don't know what this fucker is like. I'm sorry I took it out on her, I just couldn't believe she would sleep with someone like that."

"Oh, really?" he snaps, looking at me like I'm the lowest form of being. "Well, maybe get off your high and mighty pedestal up there because I know exactly what that asshole is like. I had to pick up my baby sister when he did a number on her. She was in a fucked-up place back then, ran off to some stupid kid's party, drank herself into an even darker place, and blacked out before waking up with him on top of her. Maybe it wasn't her best move to get into that kind of vulnerable position but look me in the eye and tell me you have never made bad decisions."

I stay silent, letting his words sink in. Of course, I can't tell him that, I'm a guy with a party-boy reputation. You don't get there without making a few wrong turns along the way.

"As soon as he had finished, he put on his wedding ring and told her he was married, that she had been a great fuck, but he was going home to his wife. He left her there in a crumpled heap, feeling cheap and dirty, all at the age of eighteen. *Eighteen*, asshole!"

I close my eyes, imagining how on earth she must have felt after having had that happen to her.

"The day after, in the early hours of the morning, I get a phone call from her, sounding drunk, lost, and alone. It took some time, but I finally managed to get out of her where she was, some diseased-looking place out in the middle of nowhere, hidden away in a room that she had paid for on my emergency credit card. She'd been ingesting a deadly concoction of painkillers and neat vodka. She was completely out of it, with puke lying all around her body, an erratic pulse, and a desire to never wake up again. Can you imagine that? Can you imagine finding your baby sister in that state, not knowing if she's going to make it or not?"

"No," I reply quietly.

"And the worst part is," he says, sounding like he's close to tears himself, "none of us knew what the hell she had been going through. She masked her pain, her sadness, her desperation, with her usual smile and laid-back façade, and we all fell for it. Not again, asshole, I've been with her ever since, so I won't let some shitty boss with a power trip destroy her again. Stay.The. Fuck.Away from her!"

"I can't do that," I murmur with a sigh, not able to lie to this guy while he relives it all.

"Why the hell not?" he yells.

"Because I've fallen for her," I tell him flat out.

Ben shocks us both when he throws his head back and laughs, sounding almost hysterical, while placing his hands on his hips to steady himself.

"This is your idea of falling for someone?" he says incredulously. "Cos if it is, she doesn't need any of it!"

He then shoves his hand into my chest, causing me to step back from the force of it. Unfortunately, he has a point. I've been the worst boss and an all-around crappy person to her.

"You're right and if I were her brother, I would be trying to protect her from someone like me as well," I begin, "but I'll be completely honest with you, I've never been here before. The last time I was even close to feeling like this about somebody, I gave her to my brother."

"Hey, man, I don't need to hear about you sharing fucking women," he snaps at my inability to get my point across, "all I care about is my sister!"

"I'm not going to let anyone else go near Beatrice, she's mine and I will do everything in my power to protect her, so you won't have to anymore."

"Yeah? And who's going to protect her from you?" he spits back at me. "Look, this is all bullshit anyway, you've blown it Mr Big Balls, she's never going to want to come near you again. Did you know she's not even been near a man since that fucker pushed her over the edge?"

Her reactions to me begin to make more sense now. Of course, she doesn't want to come near me after the way I behaved, she must think I'm as every bit of an ass as fucking Evan!

"You're done," he says matter of factly. "Don't expect her in on Monday…or ever! And if you don't want a lawsuit for sexual harassment and bullying in the workplace, you'll let her leave from immediate effect and with a fucking glowing reference. I know how good she is at her job, especially having worked under you. It's the very least you can do."

Reluctantly, I nod, knowing I've lost the argument with Ben. Not that I can blame him; I would be the same if Bea was my sister. He turns and glances at Callie and they politely nod at each other before he leaves the room. Once I hear the door bang, I sink into one of Helena's armchairs and sigh heavily, covering my face with my hands over my shameful behavior toward someone who has already had to endure so much.

THE FOOL

Chapter 17

Bea, eighteen years old, therapy

I don't want to be here; I do ***not*** want to be here!

My leg has been jiggling up and down since the moment I sat down in the generic-looking doctor's reception room. The only piece of art to break up the sheer whiteness of the walls closing in on me is a Jackson Pollack print. I can't look at it; it reminds me too much of what my head had looked like on that night.

"Do you want me to stay with you, Bea?" Ben asks with a softness he's never used with me before. He even places his hand on my shoulder with a comforting touch, from which I shy away. My reaction causes him to tense up, which I cannot blame him for.

"Sorry," I whisper, trying not to cry all over again.

"Don't," he says with his jaw tightening and his fists curling up with white-knuckle anger. "Don't you apologize, Beatrice Summers, just let me in."

"I'm trying to, Ben," I whimper, and he grabs hold of my hand to squeeze.

"I think we need to tell Mom," he says in an agitated whisper. "I'm not…I just…I really think we need to, Bea."

"No!" I snap, shaking my head with such ferocity, he squeezes my hand harder and starts stroking back my greasy hair. I guess good hair hygiene hasn't been a priority recently.

"Ok, Bea, ok, I won't tell anyone," he says as he leans down to kiss my head, the action causing my emotions to spill over again. But at least his reassurances calm me down enough to stop my erratic shaking.

"Beatrice Summers?" a friendly lady announces as she walks into the reception room. She smiles at me in such a way, I feel a little more at ease with the situation. Being here wasn't my idea, but if I was going to be forced to divulge all the ugly details of that night, I at least wanted it to be with someone who felt like a friend, not a judge.

"Do you want me to come with you?" Ben asks again, his eyes boring into mine. He wants to give me time and space, but he's also terrified to.

"I'm sure Bea will be ok," the kindly lady says, "I won't let her out of my sight. And you are welcome to stay out here," she says to him, her expression still kind but also serious, as though she is trying to tell him that she understands, that she will keep me from trying to kill myself for at least the next hour.

He looks at me one more time, seeking my permission above all others. I nod just once, not feeling entirely sure of being able to function without him.

"B-Ben? Ben, I think….ohhhh…I think I've done something…"

"Bea? Bea, what's wrong? You sound weird. Are you

drunk?"

"I think so, but I think I might be dying too."

"Jesus, what are you talking about? What's happened?"

"It's ok, Ben, it doesn't hurt; it won't hurt anymore."

"Beatrice, what did you take? What did you take?!"

The chair is comfortable, and I suddenly wish I had one back at Ben's apartment, my new home. My old home is gone, no longer mine, just hers, all hers. I can no longer think about it without feeling the swell of tears in my eyes. The doctor chooses not to say anything about them while she follows me in. She takes her own seat, one that is similar to mine but with a straighter back.

"Before we begin, Beatrice, I want you to know this is a safe space with impenetrable walls; no one can hear our secrets, and no one can hurt us in here. Anything you share with me and these four walls is for our ears only. We can share everything here, from what makes us sad and angry, to why toast will always land butter side up."

She smiles, and I try to, but I know I haven't succeeded. Happiness seems like an emotion that will be forever out of reach.

"Now, my professional name is Doctor Carrow, however, I ask my patients to call me by my Christian name, which is Sonia. But if you would prefer to call me Princess Moonbeam, I won't question it. I am here for you, nobody else, ok?"

I nod, again just once, before she begins her interrogation, right from the beginning.

Bea

Sonia and I don't get onto that night until our second session, the first being taken up by small talk, as well as my childhood. It was like the boring build-up to the heart of the story, when everything is infuriatingly nice, easy, and absent of any twists or turns. Fictionally, this part is the decider; do you go on with the syrupy goodness in the hopes that something eventful is going to happen? Or do you give in before the possibility of one of the characters doing something epically stupid to make it worth reading? In reality, it was my world, my happiness, a time I would give anything to return to.

"You told me last time that you had a lot of friends, but that most of them were boys," Sonia says, looking over the top of her glasses at me. "And that your sister is perhaps your only friend who is a girl."

"Was," I mutter, to which she looks at me as if waiting for me to elaborate. "Emma ***was*** my friend; she isn't anymore."

"I see, she hurt you," she says, forcing me to say what her betrayal was out loud, even though I would hazard a guess that she already knows. When I offer her nothing, she removes her glasses to look at me more intensely. "But things started to go wrong before that, didn't they?"

Conspiracy theory: Beatrice Summers is a dude and Dean is forcing her to dress up because he's too afraid to come out!

"Yes," I reply at the same time as coughing into my jumper sleeve. "Though, it didn't bother me that much before they did what they did. You tend to think the injured party would garner people's sympathy, but not even their betrayal softened their blows. If anything, it only made it worse."

"Tell me about it," she says, gesturing with her hand for me to continue. "The bullies, what sort of things would they say about you?"

"Anything they could think of," I reply with an insolent shrug. "I used to get it face-to-face, but it was especially nasty online. I guess it was so much easier to say such things from behind a screen. Even the good kids could turn bad there, and the best part was no one would think anything differently of you in real life. You could be a villain in secret."

"And how did it make you feel before what happened?" she asks.

"I don't know," I reply truthfully and with a sigh. "I guess I had Emma, Dean, and people who I thought were my real friends on my side, so I tried not to let it get to me."

"But it did, at least to some extent, didn't it?" she asks, prompting me to think back to before. I suppose it did hurt to see those words. Those nasty words all grouped together, talking about me and calling me the most horrific names imaginable.

"It made me feel segregated, cut off, alone," I admit. "Dean and Emma might have been there to tell me not to take any notice, that those people were assholes, but they weren't the object of someone's venom. Nobody thought that about them, just me."

"Did you tell anyone about it?" I cannot answer her with words for I know I will cry if I try to, so instead, I shake my head. "Do you know why not?"

"I was afraid," I whimper, closing my eyes and allowing the tears to fall. "I didn't want it to get any worse. I thought if I ignored it, if I played it down, it would all go away. I begged Emma and Dean not to say anything, even threatened to break up with Dean if he did."

"Do you think you would do things differently now?" she

asks.

I already know the answer, of which I'm ashamed to say, but in the end, I have to concede and admit what still feels so shameful.

"No."

Bea

On our third session, Sonia jumped right into what happened between Dean, Emma, and me; the incident that caused me to not only lose my boyfriend and sister but also myself.

"I didn't initially realize at the time, but I had heard them before I saw them," I begin, taking in a deep breath to steady my emotions. "Muffled breathing, groaning, the squeaking of a bed…*my* bed."

"Why do you think they chose your bed?" she asks, her brow furrowed.

"I don't know," I reply with a shrug and far-off gaze, not being able to escape the image of my boyfriend, a guy who had told me he loved me on multiple occasions, grinding on top of my sister, my best friend. The girl who I used to cover for when she was in past curfew; the girl who told me about her horrible first time and who I had held when she finally admitted that it was a mistake; the girl who had snuck into my bed whenever there was a thunderstorm. The girl who gave me up in an instant.

"It seems like an added twist of the knife to do it in your bed, Beatrice, whose decision do you think that was?" she asks, poking at the wound until I bleed.

"I guess he had been waiting for me and she turned up first," I suggest, though I think the added cruelty runs deeper than that.

"You're not sure though, are you? Why not?"

"When they realized I was there, after a good few minutes of me staring at something I wasn't entirely sure was happening, Emma ran to the bathroom and hid, burst into tears, or whatever. But Dean…Dean just laid back and smiled," I recall. His smug face was one of the last things I remembered when I took the final tablet and passed out not long after. "It was like he was reveling in my pain; I gave him everything and he wanted to hurt me."

"And what happened in the week leading up to the party?" she asks as if she doesn't already know.

"Word got out about Dean and Emma. People either congratulated Dean for trading up, or they questioned why he had chosen my sister to cheat with."

I smile momentarily, for the latter might have shown some empathy for me, had it not been for the rumor Dean started.

"He accused you of sleeping with someone, that he had caught you with his best friend," she says sadly.

"Martin went along with it; said I came onto him when he was drunk. He was forgiven, and I was declared a slut who didn't know how lucky she was to have Dean in the first place."

"Oh, my God, what a disgusting whore! No wonder Dean finally opened his eyes and saw the true catch in that family."

"That's when the online attacks really started to get to me," I admit, tears welling in my eyes once again. "Emma avoided me at all costs, or she stuck to my mom's side, knowing full well I wouldn't say anything in front of her. My phone was pinging with notifications all the time, all through the night and day. People would shout at me at school and accuse me of the most horrible things. Dean would just stare at me, smiling through most of it. As for my friends, who I guess were more his than mine, they all turned on me too."

"Beatrice, your medical notes showed something else too. Were you aware of your condition? Were you aware that you were pregnant?"

I look up at her, the shame hitting me full pelt in my chest, and words escape me. Instead, I nod my head, just once.

Bea

"Are you ready for this, Bea?" Sonia asks after our initial greetings, and although I would dearly like to say no and run away, I know I need to do this; to face all that I haven't been able to over the last few weeks.

"I'm not sure I ever will be, but yes, I'm ready…sort of," I finally reply with a nod.

"What made you go to that party, Bea?" she asks softly.

"Friday had been a bad day, a really bad day," I admit. "Someone had graffitied all over my locker, which once upon a time would have made me roll my eyes over how unoriginal it was, but after being called a slut all day, it got to me. It made me hurt; it made me cry; it made me run. And that's what hurt the most, the fact that they had finally broken me. I was so close to the end of school, to leaving them all behind, and just when I thought I had survived it all, they got me. I was angry, so angry."

"Who were you most angry with do you think?" she asks at

the same time as I brush away my tears.

"At first, Dean," I admit, "I was never well-liked because I chose to stick with the boys, to not be what they wanted me to be, but I made it all the worse when I agreed to go out with him. I thought we could make it through anything…which was stupid."

"He left you when you needed him most," she answers for me.

"Not only that, but he made it worse; he wasn't the person I thought he was. That person was gone…forever."

"So, what happened when you got home, Beatrice?"

"I walked in to find them kissing on the couch, in broad daylight, as if being caught didn't matter. My anger changed direction at that point, from then on it was all on Emma. I confronted her, ignoring the smug smile on Dean's face, but she'd convinced herself that I had done what Dean had accused me of, that I had cheated on him with Martin."

"You brought this on yourself, Bea!"

"Do you think she really believed him?" Sonia asks, the answer to which only makes the tears fall down my cheeks.

"No, it was just convenient for her to believe him, she knows I didn't do anything," I reply with a shrug, "it's not who I am."

"What was the thing that sent you running to that party?"

"Emma ran off crying to her room; her classic avoidance tactic and all-around sympathy winner, leaving me with Dean. At first, I said nothing, just looked at his wicked smile and wondered how on earth he had changed so drastically in the space of one day."

"Why?"

"You started this, babe. Besides, your sister is a little more in my league and a much better fuck than you. I can get her to her knees with a click of my fingers."

"I hate you; you could have chosen anyone else, but you chose the one person who meant the world to me. And don't give me your bullshit about me cheating on you with Martin; I deserve to know the truth, Dean!"

"Because I knew it would sting just that little bit more, Bea. The feeling's mutual, I hate you too!"

"It was like a bad dream, a nightmare I couldn't wake from, so I ran. I grabbed Ben's car keys, jumped inside, and drove to where I knew Nathaniel Carter was throwing one of his end-of-term parties. No one ever checked who went in, as long as you bought a bottle of something, you could walk straight in."

"Where did you get the Vodka from, Beatrice?"

"Some little store on the way there, no one asked for ID, no one cared," I laughed mirthlessly, "***no*** one cared."

"How much did you drink?"

"I can't remember…a lot. I couldn't even tell you if I recognized anyone there, all the faces were a blur. The sound of music, laughing, shouting, and chatting muffled into a percussion of ear-splitting noise."

"Are you ok, sweetheart? Woah, baby, let me take you somewhere quiet; I'll look after you."

"He didn't look after you, did he?"

"Shhh, it's ok, you have a beautiful body…let me take care of you…"

"Mmm…No…No…Stop…"

"But you feel so good, doesn't this feel good?"

"By the time I came too, he was zipping himself up, telling me he was married and needed to get home. I felt sick to my stomach, but I couldn't move, I was too stunned. But then the notifications started beeping through on my phone, one after the other, over and over."

"Someone had been at that party from your school," Sonia said, and I nodded.

"I ran out as fast as I could, but when I finally got inside of Ben's car, I had no idea where to go. I couldn't go home, so I just drove. I drove and drove until I came across the roadside motel, looking sleazy, dirty, and cheap, just like they said I was. And I did feel dirty and full of shame. My head was hurting from all the shame I felt so I grabbed a few boxes of painkillers and a credit card from Ben's glove compartment, as well as the bottle of Vodka from earlier, and booked a room."

"And the notifications?"

"I couldn't not look at them, not with the persistent pinging; I had to look."

"Did you see that slut at the Carter party?"

"What a bitch, Dean is so much better off."

"She's nothing but a cum bucket."

"Hope she doesn't reproduce – what baby would want her as a mother?"

"Skank."

"Hoe."

"Bitch."

"Whore."

"All of their words were fogging up my thoughts, just going round and round along with Dean's smug smile, Emma kissing him, the blurry man on top of me, their judgmental faces all on me. I remember feeling dizzy from it, screaming at it to just stop."

"When did it stop, Bea?"

"Beatrice Summers, just kill yourself!"

"It was such a simple instruction, such clarity in a storm of sadness and anger, it seemed like the most logical thing to do; a way out of it all. After all, no.One.Cared. Why should I?"

"What made you call Ben?"

"After the first packet, I began to feel good, light-headed, and ready to fall asleep. I couldn't even hear the pinging anymore; I can even remember smiling over the relief. I took another pill, then another, and another, each one promising to make all the pain go away. But then I fell, slumped over on the bed where I could see sick coating my hair and my phone flashing up with a picture of us – him, me, and Emma. I thought I should call him, to let him know that I was going, and to wish him well and say goodbye one last time. I owed him that."

"And then? After you had talked to him?"

"Nothing; there was nothing."

Bea

"How are you feeling, Bea?"

"Not good, but not bad either," I admit, knowing that this is my last session with Sonia. I think she wanted more with me, but I don't. I just want to move on, or at least try to.

"Well, seeing as this is your last session, I wanted to try something a little different. I've asked Ben to join us today," she says, welcoming my brother into the room. I smile, for life would have been unbearable if it hadn't been for his support over the last month or so. "Now, Bea, things might be a little hard to hear today, but I don't want you to think I'm doing this to make you feel bad, or to guilt you, quite the opposite actually."

"Ben, I need you to be honest, to let Bea know how much she means to you. This is really important; can you do that?"

He nods, then looks at me with a sad smile. I know the next half an hour or so is going to be brutal, but he deserves to have his say. I messed him up that night too.

"What do you remember from that night, Ben?"

"To be honest, I'd only just got back from a flight from Boston; I'm training to be a pilot," he says and I beam at him with a proud smile. "I saw Bea's name flashing up at me so answered as soon as possible; we don't call each other too often so I knew it was important. That's going to change from now on, I'm going to be calling her at least once a day."

"And I will answer," I tell him honestly.

"When she answered, she didn't sound like herself, she

sounded like a ghost of her," he says, looking down at his hands with emotion swimming in his eyes. "I knew almost straight away I was losing her, but I thought she'd been in an accident, I didn't think for one moment that she'd tried to take her own life. I didn't even know anything was wrong, and for that, I will never forgive myself."

"It wasn't your fault, Ben," I tell him with tears in my eyes.

"It's amazing how much people can hide, even from the ones closest to them," Sonia says, trying to reassure him. "What happened when you got to her motel room?"

"It was a…blur. A nightmarish blur of flashing blue lights, paramedics, motel staff, and nosey onlookers, but the thing I will never forget is the smell – puke, alcohol, and the onset of death. When I finally saw her, I thought she had already gone, that I was too late. But then they made her sick, turned her on her side, and she gasped and coughed. I have never been so thankful to see my baby sister throwing her guts up.

"Bea, Bea, what the hell have you done to yourself, baby?"

"I just wanted it to stop, Ben!"

"I followed behind the ambulance on my bike and just prayed you'd still be alive when I got to the hospital. They put me in the room next door and told me to prepare myself, that they weren't sure if they could save you. You took pills over a long time period so there was only so much they could make you throw up. Bea, your heart monitor flat-lined three times."

I watch the pain in his face bring him to tears, right alongside my own. In fact, I crawl out of my chair and onto the floor where I grab hold of his hands and rest my head on top of his lap, all the while I whisper my apologies over and over again.

"Please don't say you're sorry, Bea, I would do it all over again to save you, I love you."

"I love you too," I murmur as he wraps his arms around me.

"I should have seen it sooner; I should have protected you. Bea, I would rip the world apart for you," he whimpers. "I will never let you down again."

"Do you see, Bea? Do you see now that you leaving the world would not only destroy you but also those who truly love you? Your death is not the answer."

"Promise me you'll never do anything like that again, Bea, that you will always talk to me if you are hurting or thinking of doing something stupid. I beg you, please!"

"I promise, Ben," I whisper, still cocooned inside of his arms.

"Remember this moment, Bea, when all the bad thoughts come swimming inside, remember this."

Chapter 18

Bea

"What did you do, Ben?" I stand angrily in front of him as he walks through the door and chucks his gloves and jacket on the side table.

"I told him what needed to be said," he says arrogantly. "What should have been said months ago!"

"Did you hurt each other?" I ask, feeling concerned, even though Nathaniel had reduced me to tears yet again. Even though he managed to make me feel like I did all those years ago.

"I may have winded him a little," he replies with a smirk. "Got to give him that at least, he didn't fight me on it."

As I run my hands through my hair, I feel like every breath leaves my body. I've worked hard over the years to keep it all inside, to not let anyone know my shameful secrets. I especially didn't want the brother of that guy's wife to find out what happened. Though, perhaps this is my penance; perhaps what I've already been through isn't enough after what I did to Helena, Ben, or…whoever was growing inside of me at the time.

"How did you feel when they told you the baby was gone, Beatrice?"

"Numb…I felt numb."

"And now?"

"I don't know; I have no idea how to feel. Perhaps he or she is better off without me. After all, that's what they said - who would want me as their mother?"

"How much did you tell him, Ben?" I ask with a tremble in my voice. "Does he know about that night? Does he know about the baby?" I place my hands on my stomach, to where he or she once clung onto me, their lifeline until I took a bottle of Vodka and countless painkillers. I didn't think about them at the time; I only thought of myself.

"No, Bea, I would never tell anyone about your baby," he says softly, clutching hold of my shoulders to try and ground me. "Beatrice, please don't worry about it," he whispers with concern in his big brown eyes. "I told him to accept your resignation with full pay and to make sure he gave you a glowing reference."

"Ben, you shouldn't have done that," I whimper, shaking my head over everything. One fortnight changed my life forever; Ben is never going to trust me. I've been keeping us in limbo, stopping us both from moving forward. "I never meant for you to hear what happened today, I just needed a ride. It's the only reason I called Leah –"

"It's done Bea, end of!" he snaps, releasing my shoulders and stomping off into the kitchen. "Leah is not your brother, I am. You should be coming to me anyway."

"Ben, you have to let me go sometime; I am not that girl who you found in that motel room anymore. Please, you have to trust me at some point. Yes, I called Leah, but most girls would have called a friend in that situation. It doesn't mean I'm slipping, Ben."

"You never said anything back then, Bea, and it keeps me up at night wondering if you're doing the same thing."

"I do tell you everything, Ben, I promise you, but if you keep making choices for me, I'll be too afraid to."

"You sound like Leah," he grumbles.

"Well, perhaps, instead of arguing with her, you should listen," I murmur, rubbing at my arm to try and soothe myself. He looks at me in such a way I'm not sure if he's thinking about my words or just angry with me for siding with his girlfriend.

"I'm beat, I'm going to lie down," I tell him, and he nods, looking sad and defeated.

"Hey, Bea," he says when I turn away, freezing in my steps before facing him again. "No matter what, I love you. And remember what Sonia said, remember that my life would only be half as full without my baby sister in it."

His words undo me, release the lump in my throat, and force me to run over and wrap my arms around him, all the while having to stand on my tiptoes to reach his shoulders. He wastes no time in hugging me back so tightly, I cry even harder against his shuddering chest.

"I love you too."

Bea

By the time I finish crying, I feel hollow, and my head hurts so much, I can't stop thinking about everything and everyone. It's a feat I cannot even hope to achieve. I know Ben is trying to protect me, but I need him to see that what happened is in the past. I was in a bad place, but I don't think like that anymore. I've moved on, but I guess Ben hasn't. I feel bad for what I put him through, but I can't keep paying for it forever. As for Nathaniel, I don't know what to think so choose not to. Besides, after Ben's confrontation, I suppose it matters very little.

"Bea, I'm heading out to try and work things through with Leah," he says with a heavy sigh, so I pull a face to show some sort of sympathy for him. "I'll be back by nine."

"Ben, you don't need to tell me when you'll be back like you're my parent; I'm a grown woman," I tell him softly. "I'm not going to do anything, ok?"

"I'm trying to be, Bea," he says sadly.

He takes in a deep breath, as if trying to psyche himself up over his impending argument with Leah, then eventually leaves. To be honest, it's a relief. Sometimes I need the silence and alone time, probably because I had so much of it during those hard years. Back then, having few friends made me feel lonely and worried, but now I can embrace the loneliness. Some might call that social anxiety; I call it comfort.

My phone pings through a text message, the sound of which still causes a twinge inside my gut. I don't think I'll ever shift that feeling. The sound of a notification will always be a trigger for me. This time especially; is it Nathaniel or Callie texting to curse me for letting Ben loose?

Hey, Hun, I was going to text earlier but thought you might need some time. How are you, babe? C x

I'm so relieved by her words, her genuine concern, and hints of affection, a lump forms inside of my throat.

I've been better. I am so sorry about Ben, I didn't phone him, I phoned Leah. It was never my intention for him to come in and lose his shit. Was he awful?

He was pretty brutal, but I'm not gonna lie, he totally turned me on! C x

Callie, eww, he's my brother!

I say how I see it. As for Nate, he totally deserved it. I knew it, Ben knew it, but more importantly, Nate knew it. I didn't even need to put him in time out, he put himself there. C x

I can understand where he was coming from, it must have been a shock. It's not something I'm proud of, Callie, you have to believe that.

Bea, we all know that. Now about your resignation...please don't be angry.

Sensing my anxiety beginning to rear its ugly head over her last message, I gulp back a lump of fear and call her. Fortunately, she answers after the first ring.

"Callie, what have you done?" I ask with dread in my voice, to which she laughs nervously.

"I called Cam," she replies bluntly.

"Callie, no! He's on honeymoon, for goodness' sake. How much did you tell him?"

"Kind of everything. I decided this counted as an emergency," she says as I slap my hand over my face. "Lily heard too, and she agreed that they need to come home."

"Callie, why did you do that? It's their honeymoon, they shouldn't be worrying about me!"

"Nonsense, Cameron is beyond loaded; they can fly private jets here and there whenever they want to. Plus, it's not their real honeymoon, is it? They've been married for years."

"But –"

"But nothing, he'll be at yours by ten tomorrow morning. I'll come with because I'm more fun. Your brother will be there, right?"

"I can't believe this," I mutter, completely ignoring her question about Ben.

"Look, I gotta go, but I'll see you in a few hours anyway," she says with her usual smile in her voice. "Don't worry, all will be good."

"If you say so. See you tomorrow."

Bea

An hour or so passes by, and after texting Finn a few times, I manage to occupy my mind with easy TV and a tub of chocolate ice cream. This is how I used to survive in the early days of being bullied, but instead of Finn, I would be messaging Dean. Friends at first, lovers later. Love on my side at least. I thought he was everything I never knew I wanted when he declared his deeper feelings. The high school popular boy who could have any girl he wanted, chose me.

I thought he was playing games with me at first, joshing with me for laughs. After all, I had always enjoyed winding the others up and could take a joke as much as the next person. Though this seemed a step too far, even for me. I pushed him and began to stomp away, letting him know that I didn't find this particular game funny.

"Beatrice Summers, get back here so I can kiss you again!"

"Stop it, Dean, this isn't funny."

"No, it's not," he said before placing his hand to my cheek and kissing me again.

"I'm not pretty, Dean," I murmured, still in a daze from his kiss.

"No, you're not," he said with a smile, "you're beautiful, and you're mine."

God, I could have swooned, it was the stuff of fairy tales. I fell far too quickly and far too deeply. I did everything to try and keep him happy. Date nights where I'd have to play the part of the girlfriend with all the other boys' insipid girls who I knew were responsible for some of the viler messages online. They acted sweet for Dean's sake, but they would have been dissecting me piece by piece the minute we left. I gave him my body before I was ready, and did everything he asked of me in that department, even when I didn't want to. I didn't even dare to say I wasn't comfortable with sex for I was so afraid of losing him. This, at least, wasn't his doing, it was mine; mine and the dozens of messages from people who all liked to remind me of how far beneath him I was.

Before I can sink any lower, there's a knock on the door, and I smile to myself, hoping it's Finn coming to bring me out of my funk. He should be working but I think my earlier messages were enough to convince him to come and save me. I jump to my feet with a reminder to tell Mrs Green to stop letting people in, no matter how handsome or charming they are. Pretty doesn't always equal safe. Another knock has me laughing to myself over his impatience.

"Beatrice?" a voice that doesn't belong to Finn says through the door. It stops me dead in my tracks, for although it's not my friend, I more than know that voice. My breathing speeds up and I can feel my hands turning clammy. "Bea, it's Nate, can we talk?"

"H-how did you get in the building?" I call from where I'm still rooted to the spot.

"Some old lady took pity on me," he says with a soft laugh that holds little mirth in it. "Kept saying I'd be under her spell if she was twenty years younger."

Damn Mrs Green, the randy old cougar.

"She just happened to have been passing by the moment

you came here? Luck obviously follows you wherever you Carter folk go. Us mortals can only live in your shadow."

"No, she wasn't," he says sadly, "been waiting outside for over two hours, just hoping."

"Why?!" I snap.

"Bea, please, I know I messed up," he says, "but you have no idea what that guy did to our family, and the thought of his hands on you…I'm sorry, Beatrice, I shouldn't have got angry with you. I just care about you so much."

"You don't even know me," I sigh, slumping down onto the floor with my back against the couch. "There are things I've done, things you would never understand or forgive."

"Your brother, he explained what happened to you, how you tried to –"

"He shouldn't have!" I snap, feeling angry with the entire situation. "I don't need your sympathy and I don't need your apologies, Nathaniel. You can go away with a good conscience, I'm fine."

"You sure about that?"

"You want the real Beatrice Summers? Well, now you're going to get her, completely unfiltered. You're a spoiled little rich boy, even before Cameron made it big, you got everything you ever wanted – the family, the siblings, the labels, the private school education, the girls, the sports, and the prestige of being a Carter. Everyone from back home knew who you were, and they all worshipped at your feet. All I ever heard was what an amazing guy you were, how handsome you were, and how you could have any girl you wanted; they'd be lucky to have you. Your parents even let you hold ridiculous parties whenever the hell you wanted, but you know what? Nathaniel Carter was a popular boy with a heart, so I tried not to judge. I genuinely believed them when they said you were as beautiful on the inside as you were on the outside. When I heard you were going to be my new boss, I was so intimidated, but I was relieved to know I was going to be getting a boss who didn't discriminate and treated everyone with kindness and respect. But how wrong I was! You were just as bad as they were, Nathaniel Carter."

"Bea, I had no idea –"

"What? That not everyone had such the great experience as you growing up? That I was hounded day in, day out by kids like you, kids who wanted to remind me of how 'tragic' I was. That my sister, my best friend, threw me away to sleep with my boyfriend. That a guy, who had no business being at a high school party, took advantage of me when I was drunk and vulnerable. That I sunk so low, I could only see death as a way out. Apologies for the wake-up call, Nathaniel, but that kid was me. And I've tried to keep it hidden, to leave it behind me in the past, but then you came along with your judgment, your power trip, and forced it to the surface all over again."

"Wait," he says, then pauses for a moment or two, as if taking the time to think, "Beatrice, where did you and Evan…er, happen?"

My teeth are clenched, my breathing more akin to an angry bull, and I'm about ready to let all the frustration out on my apartment.

"Where do you think, Nathaniel Carter?"

"Please don't tell me it was at…shit!"

"You had a beautiful home, Nathaniel, it's a pity you had

no idea who was in it or what the hell was happening to them at the time," I tell him with tears now in my eyes. "I'm sure I'm not the only one who never wants to see the inside of those walls again."

"Bea…" he whispers with horror in his voice.

"Don't feel bad, Nathaniel, it was my choice to make; just another bad one in a long list of them."

"Bea, please let me in," he begs, "I need to see you, to tell you how incredibly brave I think you are, how amazing you are for reinventing yourself, and for surviving everything. You are so beautiful, Beatrice, inside and out, and if I could go back in time, I would go and kick all their asses for you."

"Just go, Nathaniel, please," I practically beg as the tears come thick and fast. Eighteen-year-old Bea would have given anything to have Nathaniel Carter come and rescue her. But this Beatrice doesn't believe in fairy tales anymore.

"Beatrice, promise me you won't leave, you'll come back and give me just one last chance. I will do everything in my power to make things right. Just one more chance, Bea, one more."

"For a moment, I did," I reply, "I gave you a chance, and began to believe in something more than what we are – colleagues. Now, we're not even that. The last guy I trusted broke my heart with my sister; I can't go through that again, Nathaniel."

"I would never do what he did, Beatrice, I swear!" he says, with the sound of his hands bracing against the door. "You are a queen, Beatrice Summers, and I want to help you see that."

"Nathaniel, please, go," I tell him with a long sigh. "I don't want Ben to catch you here; I don't want him to hurt you again."

"Why not?" he asks quietly, sniffing back what sounds like

a whimper, which only causes me to hurt even more. "I deserve it."

"No, you don't, Nathaniel," I whisper, only just realizing that I've managed to shuffle over to the other side of the door. "I need you to go…please."

At first, he says nothing. In fact, he doesn't even move, and I find myself holding my breath in anticipation. My head needs him to go, to be gone before Ben gets home and sees him here. My heart never wants him to leave, no matter how stupid that sounds.

"Ok," he huffs through his nose, "I'll go, Bea, but I promise you I'm going to fix this; you won't have to leave Medina because of me."

"Nathaniel, please…just…"

"And Bea, I'm not giving up on that kiss you almost gave me," he says, and I swear my heart feels like it's stopped beating. "I want you, Bea, and I can't just stop wanting you, even if you ask me to."

"Sometimes we don't get what we want."

"And sometimes, Bea, sometimes you do."

Chapter 19

Bea

I wake with a start; Ben must have put me in bed because I don't remember getting much past the couch after Nathaniel left. I feel huge relief at first, knowing that Nathaniel left way before Ben got back, but then I remember big brother Carter is coming to see me in a matter of hours. Ben has already made it quite clear that he'll be staying, which is going to make things a whole lot more uncomfortable. I'm already feeling the strain of everyone knowing about my past, but having your big boss leave his honeymoon to come and deal with your shit is beyond humiliating. I'm not even sure if I need to dress in workwear or not.

"Ben, let me handle this," I warn him when the buzzer rings at ten o'clock sharp. "I don't need you to interfere when it comes to Cameron."

As if completely ignoring me, he goes to open the door for Cameron and Callie to walk through as soon as they've scaled the stairs. I answer his arrogance with a dramatic roll of my eyes and a long sigh that he chooses to ignore. Before I can call him something unsavory, Callie walks in with a beaming smile and a giant hug for me. She smells of coffee and the fresh outdoors. She pulls back and studies me as if looking for any signs of me losing my mind. Once satisfied, she nods, then steps aside to reveal Cameron, thankfully dressed in casual clothing and a warm smile.

"Morning, Bea," he says, leaning in to shake my hand. "Morning, Ben?" he asks, holding out his hand to shake with my brother, which Ben thankfully accepts.

"Please, take a seat," I say to them both, gesturing to the couch behind me. "I'm so sorry, Cameron, Callie shouldn't have called you, especially on your honeymoon. Really, there was no need to come back."

"I disagree, Bea," Cameron says with a serious expression.

"As do I, actually," Ben chimes in, so I turn to glare at him. Cameron also glances his way, when I notice his smile slips a little, but he remains confident; he must have had to handle many difficult people like my brother over his career. "This has been going on for months and I've had to see my sister upset on numerous occasions. What the hell is going on at your place?"

"Ben, please…" I plead with him.

"No, you're right, Ben, this should have been handled better and for that, I apologize," Cameron expertly replies. "Bea, you are a valued employee and, after speaking to Nathaniel, we both agreed that it would be better all-round if you came and worked as my PA. I've already spoken to Jack and he's happy to work with Nate again."

"Oh, God, Cameron, you don't have to do that. The last thing I want to do is mess people about," I reply in a fluster.

"Beatrice, I don't want to lose you and I have every faith that you will be as effective as Jack; this is not a bother to anyone but you. If you still want to leave, rest assured you will be given a glowing reference. However, if you want to stay, and I hope that you do, I believe this will be a good solution for everyone involved, especially for you, Bea."

I look at all the awaiting, serious expressions on everyone's faces, all the while I scream inside of my head. It does sound like a good solution, and I do want to stay, but the downtrodden girl inside of me is still whispering messages of self-doubt, self-loathing, and all the other ones that were ingrained into me. When Ben places his warm hand over my shoulder, it gives me the courage, if only for a moment, to accept what I want.

"Well," I finally say, "I guess if it's ok with everyone, maybe it's for the best. I hope I can be as good as Jack for you."

"Great," Cameron says softly, looking me in the eye to show that he really means it. "I'm going to spend some time at home with Lily, so I'm also going to give you two weeks paid leave. I'll see you when I return. Are you sure you are happy with this, Beatrice?"

"Positive," I reply with a nod and a smile. "Thank you, Cameron."

When Cameron finally leaves, Callie remains sitting on the couch, so I make her a coffee and settle myself in beside her. Ben takes up the chair opposite, watching the both of us chatting away over nothing. She pretends not to notice, but I can't help staring at him when he fails to say even a single word.

"Spit it out," I huff, folding my arms in question.

"I need to ask Callie a favor," he says, surprising me completely.

"Sure!" Callie says excitedly, all the while I continue

looking at him with suspicion.

"I'm on long haul from tomorrow and Leah is working nights," he explains, "would you mind keeping an eye on Bea for me? It's only until I fly back on Friday."

"Happy to," she replies with a shrug of her shoulders.

"So, now I need a babysitter? Ben, you need to give me a break," I snap.

"For now, I need to know you're safe. I have to get going," he says, effectively dismissing me before leaving the living room.

"Have you spoken to Nathaniel?" I ask Callie as soon as he's gone.

"Bea, don't worry about Nate," she says with a serious expression. "Cameron gave him a good talking to; that was after his father had a go."

"Oh, God, this is all my fault," I gasp, clutching hold of the bridge of my nose between my fingers.

"Not true, this is Nate all over," she says with a reassuring smile. "But on a side note, he only gets like this over things he truly cares about. There's something about you which is driving him crazy. Cameron did the exact same thing with Lily, just ask her. The Carter men can be a little dickish like that. He'll get over it though. Course, it's your choice if you want to forgive him or not."

I choose not to say anything, for in truth, I don't know what to think or feel. Most of all, I don't want the emotions to consume me, I can't let that ever happen again. Nathaniel could be something great, or he could be something I've been avoiding since I was eighteen. With all this whirring around my head, I realize Callie hasn't said a word in response to my silence. When I turn to look at her, I find her smiling at me, her brow furrowed and with a knowing look in her eyes.

"So, you aren't working under Nate anymore," she says in a leading way. "That could be...convenient."

"What are you talking about now, Callie?"

"Well, let's say you and Nate decided to give it a shot..." she suggests.

"No, not happening," I reply sternly. "Ben is right; I can't fall for someone who makes me feel crap about myself. Nate made me feel bad all over again; he's just not right for me."

"Bea," she says softly, "that's not the real Nate, I promise you."

"Oh, so the asshole Nathaniel is just for my benefit, is it? Great, sign me up!"

I grin at her, knowing I've won the battle she was trying to fight on his behalf. For now, at least. She simply nudges me with her foot before laughing with me. After which, we fall silent, comfortably so, as we both seem to get lost in our own thoughts. My thoughts are plagued by images of Nathaniel, evoking a whole arc of emotions. I rarely saw him when we were both teenagers, we were at different high schools and ran in different social circles. He was the popular golden boy, whereas my social circle consisted of Emma and Dean...until it didn't.

"You know, Ben told us what happened with your sister, as well as Evan. He also told us what happened afterward," she says with caution. I try to block it all out by closing my eyes.

"Well, he had no right to do that," I whisper sadly.

"Did you ever have counseling or anything?"

"I had a few sessions, but they weren't necessary," I lie. "I got over it quickly and I'm fine now. Ben should move out with Leah; I don't need his or anyone else's protection anymore."

"Because you've had healthy relationships with other people since then?" she asks, looking curious.

"Have you?" I snap, hating how defensive I sound.

"In my own way, yes. I've loved virtually every guy I've been with, maybe not *in* love with them, but I cared about them at the time. Dating without the desire to settle down is my choice; I don't have any regrets about the men I've been with. But being alone and sad isn't really your choice, is it?"

"Maybe not, but it's certainly a lot easier," I admit. "Safer too."

"Perhaps you need to have a bit more counseling? Now that time has settled," she suggests.

"Why? Because I don't want to go out with Nathaniel?" I huff, still acting like a pouty child over her words, even if they do make sense.

"No, forget Nate if you want; I mean get help for you," she says, reaching over to hug me, "you deserve it."

I hug her back and let the tears escape from my eyes a little because I know she's right, but I'm too scared to face it all. And yet, I desperately want to move on; to experience life and love without fear.

"God! Why do I attract the assholes?" I grumble. "And why did I let this particular asshole get close to me? I mean we virtually…we nearly…oh, forget it!"

"I know," she says sympathetically, "I was really rooting for you guys. I thought once you got past all the bullshit, you two would have been every bit as great as Cam and Lils. Unfortunately, as I said before, they tend to fight off relationships by behaving a bit dickish for a bit. If you can move past that, then it can be wonderful. If you can't, then I think people understand, even Nate himself."

"Well, after his visit the other night, I've not heard anything, not a peep. I think it's safe to say any possibility of Nathaniel and I getting together has well and truly disappeared. Kind of thought he might have texted me though."

"He did," Ben calls out from the corridor leading up to his room, now fully dressed in his pilot's uniform. "Last night, after I put you back in bed."

"Oh, my!" Callie murmurs, then starts to fan herself with her hand. Looking at her flushed cheeks and wide eyes, I think Callie has just orgasmed right here in our living room. I can't help laughing as I slap my hand against her leg, prompting her to at least try and be subtle.

"I blocked his number from your phone and warned Mrs Green not to let anyone up," Ben says arrogantly as he fusses with his tie in front of the mirror. "I hear she got a beautiful bunch of roses from him this morning and she didn't seem to care they had your name on the card."

"Ben, will you butt the fuck out of it?" I snap with my inner angry bull beginning to rear its ugly head.

"No, I'm finally taking control of all this shit!" he says, turning to face me with a stern expression; he looks so much like

Dad it's a little unsettling.

"Hey, Ben, is it?" Callie pipes in after having watched our altercation. "Tell me something, if Leah had a brother who was stopping you from having any contact with her, would you accept it, or fight for her?"

"I would fight for her, but then I'm not a fucking douchebag," he argues.

"Hmmm, I don't know, you're kind of acting like one," she says with a shrug of her shoulders. I don't think I make things any better when I drop my mouth open in amused shock. I think Ben might have met more of a match for him than even Leah.

"Excuse me, but it's kind of none of your business!" he snaps. "She's my sister and I will protect her with everything in me."

"And I respect that, but you're her brother, not her father, not her boyfriend, and not her keeper, yet here we are," she argues, still maintaining a calm exterior.

This is where she and Leah differ; Leah would have bitten his head off by now, whereas Callie is clearly getting under his skin by acting indifferent to his mounting rage.

"With all due respect, you haven't seen her the way I've seen her, so you don't get to have an opinion on the matter."

"You're right, I didn't see what she was like nine years ago. Then again, when I was thirteen, I got terrifically sick after smoking weed at my first party. Doesn't mean I have my mommy come with me to every event I attend now," she says. "What I do see is a woman in her twenties not engaging in any kind of relationship with the opposite sex because she's too afraid of being let down. That and her overbearing older brother."

The two of them stare at each other, with neither one of them backing down from their opinion of how to best 'look after' my interests. To my surprise, Ben looks away first, but only to glare at me.

"Can I trust her with you?" he asks with a raised brow, meanwhile Callie is pulling a naughty gesture behind his back. I won't go into too much detail, but it does involve both her hand and her tongue. My involuntary giggle has him whipping his head around to look at her, but being the expert she is, she immediately pulls a neutral expression and crosses her arms in response.

"Just go, Ben, and stop interfering with my business, will you? Callie, do you know how to unblock my phone?"

"Fuck, no!" She laughs but takes it from my outstretched hand to pass to Ben. "Unblock her phone, will you?"

My stubborn big brother simply stares at it before defiantly crossing his arms, as if daring her to make him. Callie says nothing for a while, and I can see her silence is beginning to make him feel nervous; it's strangely fascinating to watch.

"Ok, well, Bea and I can go and find someone who can," she eventually says, heading toward the door with the phone still in hand. "Tell me, Bea, do you fancy nipping to Cam's house where I know Nate is currently being chastised for his frightful behavior?"

I cover up my giggling with my hand because I know my brother's purple complexion means he's nearing boiling point. If I look hard enough, I think I can see steam billowing out of his ears.

Muttering obscenities under his breath, Ben swipes the phone from her hand and begins fiddling with it. After shaking his head in disbelief, he hands it back over, just as three text messages ping through. Cutting Ben some slack, I decide not to read them straight away, instead, I reach up on my tiptoes to kiss him on the cheek. I think it softens him a little, even though he's still muttering to himself.

"Watch out for her," he says, jutting his chin out toward Callie, who simply smiles with syrupy sweetness. "And Bea, you call me if you need anything. I'll meet you at Mom and Dad's on Friday."

I give him a nod and one more hug before he finally walks out the door with his bag and jacket. When the door closes, I stare at it for a while, feeling a little guilty for our antics. Ben is only trying to look out for me, but perhaps he needs this as much as I do. We both need to get over that night and maybe it's my turn to save us both from this stasis we've been stuck in for much too long.

"That was too much fun," Callie says, snapping me out of my thoughts. "Now, what do those messages say?"

I press the 'open' button on each one of them:

Bea, don't think I'm giving up on you. N x

Bea, your neighbor appreciated the roses I got for you. I bet you're more of a wildflowers kind of a girl anyway. N x

Please let me know how you're feeling today, Bea. I can't stop thinking about you. N x

"Good, he's stewing, let's leave him to it for a bit. Come, my child, I have much to teach you. Let's do lunch."

I go against the grain and follow her advice by leaving my

phone and all temptation behind.

Chapter 20

Nate

Itchy fingers, a hangover, and a thoroughly bad mood hit me like a ton weight when I wake up. It's not even the weekend, it's Wednesday, and I have three back-to-back meetings today. To be truthful, my mood has been at an all-time low since my epic fuck up on Friday night. Put that together with the stripping down I received from Cam and Dad on Sunday, and you can see why I still feel so lousy three days on.

As for Bea, she's refusing to answer any of my messages. I knew she wouldn't be coming into work, for Cam and I had agreed to her taking some time off. It was also my idea to swap PAs. We can't work together, that's a no-brainer. But it also means I won't lose her completely; she'll still be working at Medina, and on my floor too. More than that though, is the fact that she deserves to keep her job, more so than me. She's right, I have behaved like an entitled prick, only seeing things through my eyes instead of hers.

Before I drag myself to work, I decide to call Callie again, just to make sure Bea is feeling alright, and that things haven't changed since I called last night. God, even I can hear how pathetic I'm being. I've never been the needy party in a relationship before; I can't say I'm enjoying it.

"What's up now, Nate?" she says in a bored tone of voice. "I'm not with her if that's what you're calling for. You know, I'm beginning to feel very used, these days."

"Shut up! You love being the center of attention and you know it. It's like a little fucked up love triangle, just the kind of filth you're into," I laugh, trying to lighten the mood.

"Well, I'm on my own little filth mission, so no need to call me tomorrow because I won't be seeing her tonight. I have a date!"

"So, she'll be alone? Hmmm, interesting," I say to myself, now beginning to fidget with my pen.

"Geez, Nate! No *Who is he*? *How'd you know him*? *Where are you going?* This is becoming such a one-sided relationship!"

Guilt attacks me again and I begin to think I've been infected with something that makes you completely incompetent when talking to women. I let out a long sigh, shake off my self-centered approach, and try again.

"Ok, ok, I'm sorry," I rush out, "I owe you dinner, ok? How about Friday?"

Being Callie, she lets me stew for a little while, remaining silent as if she's considering her options and whether she's going to give me the time of day. I've known her long enough to not attempt first contact when she's in this mood so sit back and wait. Eventually, my strategy works, and she lets out a long sigh of acceptance.

"Ok, fine, but we're going to talk all about me, deal?"

"I wouldn't want it any other way, darling," I tease before hanging up.

Bea

My days have become lazier and lazier as the week has gone on. With each new morning of not getting ready for work, I feel more and more like I'm bunking off school. As such, I don't quite know what to do with myself. I don't deserve this time off so feel like I should stay home, acting as if I'm ill and unable to have any fun. Daytime TV makes me feel depressed, and I've read so many books my eyes have gone fuzzy. Everyone I know is at work and I don't want to face my parents right now, so I've settled for looking at crap on the internet.

Unfortunately, temptation gets the better of me and I end up doing something extremely stupid; I look up my sister's profile. Her small profile picture shows a girl I no longer know. With long, wavy, bleach-blonde hair, and a set of teeth that have been artificially whitened, or filtered, she's become a clone, a trophy wife I never knew Dean was after. But then, I never knew why he had chosen me either. I assumed it was because he wanted someone different, more edgy, a girl who stepped outside the lines to stay true to herself. It turns out I was wrong, so very wrong. I scroll down through her feed so I can see more photographs of her with her friends; she looks happy. She posts daily and there are plenty of pictures to show what an amazing life she is leading. I try not to feel bitter, to not resent her for having a happy life that was built on the back of my pain, but I'm human; I can't help it.

When I eventually come to a picture of her and Dean, I begin to wonder whether I should let it all go. Their happy, smiling faces show they were obviously meant to be together. In fact, they've now been together over three times the amount of time we were a couple. And when I look at his face, with his smug smile that had once brought me to the lowest I've ever been, I realize I'm not jealous or even mad at him anymore. I feel nothing for him. But Emma? She cut me deep, leaving a wound that still feels like it's gaping wide open. She was my best friend, my confidant, as well as my blood, and she took him anyway…and in my own bed!

After staring at their picture for much too long, I eventually glance up to see that her status reads 'engaged'. Funnily enough, I smile, for it honestly doesn't surprise me. Thinking about how my mother has been trying extra hard to get me to talk to her, I'm sure this is what they've been trying to tell me. Slamming my laptop shut, I rub my face with a long sigh. This is why Ben and I have been summoned to a family dinner at my parents' place on Friday. This also means Emma and Dean will be there; I've avoided them for nearly ten years, and Mom and Dad have always respected this, but this time they won't. I'm going to be forced into facing two of the people who brought me to my knees.

Thankfully, my phone rings and it snaps me out of my long list of questions, all whirling about inside of my head. Even better is the name that flashes on the screen, for they are precisely who I need after such a devastating discovery.

"Finn, my hero, please tell me you're free. I'm going out of my mind with boredom."

"It just so happens I was on my way out for a coffee," he says with the sound of a smile coming through the phone. "See you in ten? The usual place?"

"Already got my jacket," I tell him and hang up before rushing to get away from my laptop and the secrets it's just told me.

Bea

Once inside the familiar café, where I had sat with Callie and Lily barely a month ago, I head straight for the same table. Finn, being the friend that he is, has already ordered my usual, which I tuck into almost straight away. Doing nothing all day is actually hard work. I'm sure I'll return home after this to indulge in a long nap.

Finn stares at me with judgment while I eat half my sandwich without even having said hello. I look up and smile at his confused frown, then get straight into filling him in on Nate, my job changes, and Emma's engagement. He listens intently before placing both of his hands on top of his head and mimicking a silent scream.

Having finished my sandwich, I set about shoving cake into my mouth; I don't even feel guilty about it. I'm owning this cake and all its delicious calories right now. Anyone who tries to get between me and this mouth-watering piece of carrot cake is likely to get stabbed with my fork.

"So?" he finally says, gesturing for me to continue. "What's your next move?"

"Besides homicide?" I tease. "I have no idea. But trying to get through Friday at my folks' place is going to be pretty high on the agenda. If only I could get out of it somehow."

"You can't," he says with determination. "You can't let your ex-butthead-boyfriend and conniving little sister cut you off from your parents. If anyone should be hiding away, it should be them. If I wasn't working Friday, I would be coming with you.

I've been waiting to meet ***Emma*** and ***Dean*** for a while now. I am, however, going to be seeing Nate on Friday. He's booked a table for two."

He raises his brow at me in a suggestive manner while I feel a stab of pain and jealousy behind my ribcage. I drop my fork onto the plate in disgust and push the whole thing away from me.

"Damn, Nathaniel Carter, he's even ruined my cake," I grumble, "cake was all I had!"

"Want me to spit in his food?" He smirks at the same time as clutching hold of my hands.

"That goes without saying," I giggle, "but, I'm giving up on him anyway. Besides, he can't have had very deep feelings for me if he can move on this quickly. It was pretty dumb of me to think otherwise."

"Hey," Finn says as he brings my hand to his lips and kisses it. "Bea Summers, you are beautiful, funny, and brilliant. The ass is a fucking nutjob to have let you slip through his fingers, trust me. One day, you'll meet someone worthy of you, and this will be nothing more than an amusing anecdote to tell said someone on your wedding anniversary. You'll both laugh, fuck each other's brains out, all the while thinking of me saying this. It will get awkward, and you'll realize you should have got it on with your best friend, Finn, and then we'll get married…in a castle. It's all very romantic; I'm already phoning around film producers as we speak."

"Yeah, the stuff of fairytales, I'm sure."

"I just gotta work out some kinks but you get the idea." He shrugs before we both burst out laughing. It's just what I needed after the shitty week I've been having. *Remember this moment on*

Friday, Bea.

Bea

Later that evening, while trying to gather the energy or inclination to make something for dinner, my phone pings, pulling me out of my reverie of Nate fucking some Victoria Secret model, Friday night dinners, and awkward wedding days to come. I feel relieved for the distraction, but when I glance over to see it's from Nathaniel, my heart begins thumping wildly about my chest. I'm not sure if it's through fear or excitement, but I know it takes me a good few moments before I can brave it enough to open it.

If I buzzed your door right now, would you let me in? xxx

My hands turn clammy, and rather pathetically, I quickly realize that it's excitement I'm feeling. Though I know I shouldn't, I desperately want to let him in, even if it's just to see if he is sincerely sorry about what happened.

Depends. Are you going to tell me off for anything?

I jump when he messages back virtually straight away.

Let me up and you'll find out. Xxx

I know it's stupid of me to let him in, but for my own sanity, I have to.

Why don't you buzz, and you'll find out.

Ben would be raging if he knew, but this is my life and I need to make my own decisions and my own mistakes. Besides, what happened back then made me stronger in some ways. I know I'm not alone and I'm certainly not the teenage girl I once was. At least, I hope I'm not.

It's not long before he's knocking on the door, prompting me to pause for a moment just to ease my anxiety through a few learned breathing exercises. With my eyes closed, I open up the door, wearing my checked PJs, my comfy bed socks, and with my hair pulled into a messy bun.

"Bea," he says in a low, husky voice. My eyes burst open to see him standing at least a head above me, wearing a pair of dark denim, designer jeans, and a fitted white V-neck. As I begin cursing myself for not changing, he looks me up and down, and grins, just like he did in Helena's kitchen, when we were moments away from giving into one another.

"Come in," I eventually say, pulling the door open to let him through. "Would you like a drink?"

"Sure," he answers before taking a seat on the living room couch. "Whatever you're having is fine by me." He looks around the room, taking in the sight of all the bunches of flowers he's had delivered here. "You have quite the florist going on in here."

"Yeah, funny that." I smile while glancing around at all the pinks, whites, and reds. "Some weirdo keeps sending me flowers. I've tried to ignore him, but they just keep on coming."

"He sounds like a real idiot," he says with a sigh, "you can do better."

"Oh, I don't know," I play along, "if he took his head out of his ass and actually took the time to really get to know me, he might be worth pursuing."

He laughs softly as I hand him a lemonade and sit down on the other end of the couch. We both sip our drinks silently and awkwardly, and I suddenly have no idea what to say. He begins rubbing his hand behind his neck, his tell-tale nervous tick. Being that I don't want to make it so easy this time round, I decide to not help him out with it. Instead, I keep sipping and remain utterly silent.

"Bea," he finally utters, "I fucked up again, I know that. I wasn't really angry with you. I was just angry with the whole situation, but you were there, and so I behaved irrationally. I am beyond sorry."

I smile tightly in his direction, then sip my drink again, to which he smiles, still waiting for me to answer. In my own good time, I finish the drink, then put the empty glass gently on the table.

"I don't know whether to forgive you or not, Nathaniel," I reply with honesty, "you make me feel bad about myself time and time again. Why do you do that?"

"I don't know," he says with a sigh and a shrug, "maybe because I've only felt this way about a girl with you. And Lily, I guess. But Lily was all wrong for me; I was dating her best friend and she was against relationships. She needed a friend; she needed Callie. I wasn't about to screw that up for her, and I wasn't convinced I'd be a better boyfriend than I could be a friend to her. And, as you've seen, she belongs with Cam. They're sickeningly great together. As soon as I saw them getting close, I was happy with the way things had gone. You could say I felt safe in the knowledge that she was no longer an option I could pursue. I could remain single and save anyone the trouble of being with party boy Nathaniel. But then you came along and screwed that plan up for me."

"Gee, sorry," I reply sarcastically, but before he begins to argue, I cut in. "Nathaniel, as much as I'm flattered by your 'falling for me', I can't say I'm convinced. You don't even know me properly, do you. You think I'm a mousey little employee who accepts your shit without argument. That's not the real me, Nathaniel. At least, that's not who I want to be."

"Well, then, let me spend time with you," he suggests with a shrug and hope in his eyes. "Then we can see what we really feel for one another; is there more here than just attraction?"

I look at his sincere expression and silently battle in my head over what to do for the best, for both of us. During which, a rather juvenile idea springs to mind, prompting me to grin mischievously in his direction.

"Lily once told me about how you and Callie got her locked in a room with Cameron. It was a game of 'Truth or Dare', was it not?" Before he can answer, I get up to go and grab a bottle of Jack Daniels from my cupboard. With some shot glasses in hand, I bring everything to where we're sitting. He has a devilish smirk on his face while I open the bottle of whiskey, which actually belongs to Ben, but he owes me after drinking all of Finn's wine. "What better way to get to know someone?"

"Ok, but truth and honesty, right?" he asks, sitting up straight and grabbing the shot glasses to hold them for me as I pour. I nod in agreement and fill them up.

"So, Nathaniel, truth or dare?"

"In the interests of getting to know one another, truth."

"How old were you when you lost your virginity?" I ask casually.

"Wow, really getting straight in there, aren't you?" he laughs but I merely nod with a genuinely curious expression. "Ok, I was seventeen, it was with my best friend's sister, at a party.

Totally pre-planned; she wanted to lose it as much as I did. Both of us drank too much to ease away the nerves and it was totally crap sex. I lasted about two minutes and I think I'm being generous. My best friend found out and gave me a black eye, but then we were fine. I was his best man last year."

"Oh, my God," I laugh, "and the girl?"

"She was dating one of the footballers by the following week," he says with his trademark, cheeky-boy smirk. "She's now divorced with one kid. Offered me a replay at said wedding, which I kind of took her up on. Does that make me wicked?"

"Not if it was consensual. Was it any better though?"

"A lot better," he laughs. "I have a lot of experience now; I never have any complaints in that department."

"You know, that's not as attractive as you think it sounds," I say as I lean in quietly. "Just makes you sound like a player."

"Ok," he says before throwing back the last of his whiskey. "Truth or dare, Miss Summers."

"Well, I guess truth," I reply, turning while bracing myself for the worst.

"Is it true you have thought about me naked?"

"You can't ask that, this early on!" I gasp as I slap him on the arm. "Besides, how is that getting to know me better?"

"Sure, I can," he says with a diabolically serious expression, "I need to know how dirty your mind is. So, fess up!"

"I'm not answering that question," I reply before skulling back the shot, "you can't make me."

"I don't have to, I already know," he smirks. "I can tell you that I have most definitely pictured *you* naked."

"I bet you picture most women naked," I counter, "in fact, I bet you have some kind of app on your phone or something. Truth or dare?"

"Not all women, just those I like," he replies, then waits for a response, one I refuse to give. "Ok, let's go for a dare."

"Hmm, let me think." I take a moment's pause to consider my options, only to turn back as soon as I see his phone resting on the coffee table. "I've got it; I dare you to show me the last text message you sent someone who wasn't me."

"Oh, fuck, I can't do that," he laughs, "no way!"

"Why ever not?" I ask, sounding theatrically indignant over his refusal.

"Because it's about you and it's not particularly gentlemanly!"

"Ooh, I really want to see it now, let me have it!" I try and grab his phone from the coffee table, but he takes hold of my wrist before I can even reach it. His skin on mine causes an electrical sensation that shoots from my wrist all the way down to my stomach. Then he looks at me in such a way, I have to swallow back a nervous gasp. My head already feels fuzzy so my ability to hide what he's doing to me has depleted to nothing. He lifts the corner of his mouth into a smile, one that reveals exactly what kind of desire is whirling around inside of his head. However, to both my surprise and disappointment, he lets go of me while extracting the phone from my hand. He then drinks his shot and moves back into his original position.

"Truth or dare, Beatrice?"

"Truth," I whisper.

"When was the last time you had sex?" he asks with a now serious expression.

I wasn't expecting that question, so take a moment to clear my throat and hide my embarrassment.

"Years ago," I murmur. "After the night with Evan, I decided to stay clear of men altogether."

"Why?" he asks with his brow furrowed in concern.

"I thought I was in love with Dean, but then he betrayed me in the worst possible way. He took my sister and my best friend in one callous move. I was hurt, and angry, and my confidence was shattered, so I took comfort in a bottle of vodka to help numb the pain, but it only led to someone else hurting me. I fell down a slippery slope and only just about managed to pull myself up again, but I came out different. I didn't believe in fairytales anymore. In fact, I always believe in the worst possible situation so I can't be disappointed."

"Is that what you believe of me? That I will hurt you in the worst possible way?"

"No offense, Nathaniel, but you've been pretty hard on me for the past year and a half. You dry humped-me and left me in the middle of a dance floor, then told me you didn't want anything to do with me. That's without the fact that you have a very unscrupulous reputation with women, which you freely admit to. Tell me why I should believe that I am so different from any other woman you've been with?"

He looks at me seriously for a moment before leaning forward to place his glass down on the tabletop. He then shuffles over to where I am sitting but doesn't attempt to touch me.

Instead, he leans his head on his fist, with his elbow resting on the back of the couch and his other hand lying gently on top of his thigh, just a small distance from where mine is sitting on top of my own lap.

"I've never much looked at a woman beyond what most people see in me – their looks. Besides Lily and Callie, when I was much younger, I have always gone for the girl who has about as much emotional depth as I have. Sure, I have female friends, but none that I spend that much time with, not like Lils and Callie. When you came to work for me, day in, and day out, I couldn't help but observe everything about you. At first, I wanted to know why everyone loved you so much, and they do. Everyone thinks you're gorgeous, both inside and out. So, I began watching you from afar."

I look at him as though he's a crazy stalker, to which he laughs.

"Don't worry, Miss Summers, I don't have cameras installed or anything like that. I just took notice when you interacted with other people. For example, I noticed you always apologize, even when someone has bumped into you. I watch how you twirl your hair with your finger when you're thinking about something. You blush when any man says anything to you. You smile when you are speaking to your brother…the whole time. You looked so amazingly excited when Callie came in to see you, as though you were shocked that she actually came. And whenever I speak to you, either in the past or right now, your finger immediately finds your bottom lip and runs across it." He sighs at the same time as he pulls my finger away from my mouth to highlight his point. And just like he said, I instantly blush. "I think you are so damn beautiful I have to stop myself from throwing myself at you because I.Want.You. The thought of you being with anyone else drives me crazy."

His words bring a lump to my throat, and I have to knock back my shot to stop myself from doing something that will make me look foolish, like crying. I've not been called beautiful in a long time, and even then, it was by Dean, who took it all back the moment he got into bed with my sister. I was called a lot of things, none of them nice, so to be called beautiful by Nathaniel Carter, of all people, is a shock.

"Truth or dare, Nate?" I whisper.

"Dare," he says calmly.

"I dare you to kiss me."

I swallow hard, feeling completely terrified about what I have just asked him to do. When he reaches his hand out to hold my cheek, leaning in closer, and with the anticipation building, it sends wild butterflies to my stomach. As our mouths touch, he ever so gently caresses my lips with his, as if being careful not to push me too fast. He pulls away for a moment, looking into my eyes before whispering, "more?" I can only nod, yes. This time he pulls my hand and throws it behind his neck, prompting me to move the other one to meet it. His hands move to my waist, and he tugs me in closer, with his kiss becoming more desperate. He eventually swipes his tongue across my mouth, and I open in acceptance.

It's been a long time since I've kissed someone, and God, I've missed it. The heat, the passion, and the emotion behind it; it's what I had once lived for, especially in the early days of mine and Dean's relationship.

As our tongues collide, he moves closer and I instinctively slide my body down the couch, so he is bracing himself on top of me, moving to lie between my legs. A growing bulge in his jeans presses against my core, and I suddenly pull back in a mild panic.

"Bea," he whispers, pushing a strand of loose hair behind my ear. "Don't worry, we're just kissing, nothing more."

"Sorry," I reply, with a creeping blush spreading over my face and neck. "It's been a while and the last experience was not a good one."

He sighs as he rests his forehead against mine, stroking my hair back in a soothing way, and I feel myself relaxing under his touch.

"I hope you know it wouldn't be like that with me, but more importantly, don't ever apologize for it. I'm throwing a party in my head over having just kissed you."

We both laugh over his ridiculousness before we kiss again. His mouth moves down my jawline and to my neck where he licks and nips at my sensitive skin. I allow myself to close my eyes, to enjoy the intimacy I've not felt in such a long time.

"Shit, I've got to go, Bea," he says, pulling away. "I have a meeting first thing and I think I better leave us on a high. I don't want to push you and fuck it up…*again*!"

"Oh, ok," I reply, trying not to show him how disappointed I am. "I'll show you out."

Before I can shuffle up, he holds my chin between his fingers and kisses me on the lips one more time.

"Have dinner with me tomorrow," he demands, "at my place, I'll cook. You can either come back here or stay in one of the spare bedrooms. No funny business, I promise. Except maybe making out a bit," he says with a wicked grin, "or a lot."

"Ok, what time shall I get a taxi?"

"I'll come and get you after work," he says, standing up and adjusting the bulge in his jeans, causing me to giggle. I then walk him to the door, where he kisses me chastely on the lips. "Until tomorrow then."

Chapter 21

Bea

By Thursday lunchtime, I can't work out if I'm excited or absolutely terrified of going to Nate's house. I've also questioned my sanity several times during the course of the morning. I should be stepping back into the world of dating with someone who doesn't make me feel weak at the knees every time I see him. Case in point, I haven't managed to eat anything beyond half a cookie that was probably ready for the trash. Not that it mattered; I was feeling much too anxious to take note of things like taste.

And now I'm staring at my wardrobe, hoping that some perfect outfit will materialize from out of nowhere. I haven't felt like this since I was a teenager, and it totally sucks. Even with Dean, a boy who I had been friends with since middle school, I hated all this dating crap. The nauseous sensation floating around your stomach, the stress of feeling the need to impress someone, and the pressure of having to dress up to meet someone's approval, are all things I haven't missed during my abstinence from men.

Dean used to love me when I got dressed up, looking like his prize cow to parade around in front of his friends. Short skirts, low tops, heavy makeup, and perfectly coiffed hair. I didn't want to dress like that. Deep down, I knew he was trying to change me into something I wasn't, but I did it anyway, for him, and he still cheated on me. And now, after years of trying to recover from everything, I'm not sure who I am anymore. Who is Beatrice Summers?

After another half an hour of staring at my reflection, all while trying not to freak out, I finally make a decision. Fuck it, I'm going to go for ripped jeans and a tank top. Let's see how much Nate likes me for me. If I don't measure up, then I know he's no better for me than Dean was. I need to start taking charge of who I am and where my life is going. I am not going back to being the girl who gave into peer pressure and ended up trying to kill herself.

However, when the buzzer rings, I must admit, the urge to go and change is strong. Fortunately, Nate is knocking on my door before I have a chance to do a single thing about it.

When I open the door, I wince. Of course, he's in his designer three-piece suit, complete with fuck off expensive shoes. I must look a complete state compared to him.

"Hi," I say with a shy smile.

"Hi," he returns, "are you ready?"

"I think so," I reply, standing up straight to try and look more confident than I really am.

As we walk down the stairs together, I notice him looking me up and down with a devilish grin on his face.

"You look hot, Summers," he says when he catches me looking at him. "You look like you could eat me for breakfast, which I'm totally cool with, by the way."

"Seriously?" I ask in a confused tone of voice. "I thought you'd be used to women dressing up for you."

"Bea, I really don't look at a woman based on what she wears; I'm honestly not that shallow. You look good because you look comfortable. I want you to be yourself with me."

"So, what do you normally wear outside of the office? I think I've only ever seen you once in something other than a suit."

"I mostly walk about in my underwear at home."

"Just like my brother then; he's a lazy ass too," I tease.

"A little bit, but who cares when it's just me?"

"Well, don't let me stop you from doing what you normally do," I say quietly, hoping to sound a little seductive. It's been a while since I've tried to be flirtatious, and I was never an expert.

"As long as you can manage to keep your hands off me," he says with a cheeky-boy smirk on his face. "Actually, *you* can put your hands anywhere on me if you like. In fact, I actively encourage it."

"What happened to getting to know one another properly?" I ask, only being half serious.

"We can still do that with your hands on me," he teases before lifting my hand to his mouth and kissing it. The sensation of his lips on me, together with the way he looks at me, awakens something, a lust I am only just starting to remember having again.

"We'll see," I whisper as we set off inside his Mercedes.

———

Bea

Nate lets me into his place and offers a drink before excusing himself to go and have a shower. I accept a glass from what looks like an expensive bottle of white wine and slope into the living room to see if his couch feels as hard as it looks. I stare at the black screen of his monstrosity of a TV, and half wonder if it would blind me if I managed to work out how to switch it on. So, instead, I turn my attention back to his family portrait and allow my mind to wander for a moment or two. The three siblings look happy together; the shot isn't even posed. It reminds me of a photograph that is no doubt still in pride of place on my parents' mantelpiece. Ben's driving a golf cart with Emma and me in the back, all smiles and missing teeth. I indulge in the memory of him crashing the thing into the club's extravagant water fountain. It was one of the few times I had heard my father swear. However, then I remember the fact that I have to face them all tomorrow, including my cheating ex-boyfriend and my backstabbing little sister.

I know what's coming, can almost hear the grand announcement falling from Emma's deceitful lips, and I also know I will be expected to go to the wedding. Dad will demand it of me, and if I refuse, I'll be seen as petty and stubborn. I can't blame him; he was told the unabridged version of events. As far as my parents are concerned, Dean and I broke up when I decided to move in with Ben. Emma got together shortly afterward, and I became bitter. Even my sudden departure was explained away by my being offered an exciting, once-in-a-lifetime, job opportunity. My mother can't understand my aversion to my sister's relationship - '*After all, you left him so suddenly, Bea. You can't blame them for finding love with one another after you abandoned them both without a proper goodbye.*'

Ben was desperate to give the full story, but I couldn't bear to have it all brought to the surface again. What would be the point other than to cause a whole load of bad feelings? I love my parents too much to do that to them. I convinced Ben to tell the new, 'happy' couple to go along with the fictional version, which they were more than willing to do.

Moments later, trying to block out thoughts of my upcoming family meal, I am brought back to the present with a bang. Walking up to me, wearing nothing but a pair of grey sweatpants and a naughty smile, is none other than my ridiculously handsome host. I'm sorry to say that the sight of his muscular physique, tanned skin, and perfect abs, all put together with that ridiculously cheeky grin of his has me gaping at him with a thoroughly uncool expression on my face. In fact, I can't even begin to try and act nonchalant so give into my girlish giggling without apology.

"Wh…what? What…?" I stutter for the words but can't get them past my fit of giggles, especially when he reaches the bottom of the staircase and does an over-the-top twirl for me.

"You asked me to wear what I would normally wear," he says with a shrug of his shoulders. "I'm just following orders."

"Just how much time do you spend working out?" I walk over to him, taking in his entire physique which doesn't appear to have an ounce of fat. "Jesus Christ, you look like a Roman gladiator."

"I take care of myself," he replies with a smug, theatrical grin. "You like?"

"Well, yeah, show me a woman who wouldn't," I tell him while trying to compose myself again. "But if you start checking yourself out in the mirror or kissing your own biceps, I'm walking home."

"I'll try not to," he laughs, "but I am pretty hot, aren't I?"

"I hope you're not frying anything for dinner?" I ask as he moves around to the kitchen and starts getting out various ingredients from the fridge. "I wouldn't want you to burn yourself."

"Sweetheart, you don't look like this by frying shit," he says as if chastising me for thinking such a thing. "Another drink?" he asks, to which I nod. I need a glass to try and calm my lustful thoughts, especially now that he's flexing his muscles as he moves around the kitchen.

"No wine for you?" I ask when I notice him getting a bottle of water for his own glass.

"Usually, yes, but I need a clear head to drive you home tonight," he explains, still fussing over vegetables and other food stuffs.

"I can get a taxi, it's not a big-"

"Not on my watch, Miss Summers," he says, cutting me off. "I'm not letting you get in a cab late at night. Anyway, I have an unexpected early meeting with Lucius tomorrow. I need a straight head when dealing with him; he won't take any prisoners."

"Nate, I catch Ubers all the time, I'm perfectly safe," I reply with a roll of my eyes. "Regardless of what my brother says, I won't break."

My words have him freezing in his culinary duties before turning to face me with a serious expression that has me feeling uncomfortable. I stare right back at him with my glass poised, ready for something intense to come out of his mouth.

"He, er, told me what happened after Evan," he says

quietly. "Have you ever felt like doing anything like that since?"

I wasn't prepared for this so take a gulp of liquid courage before shaking my head to answer his question. Averting my gaze to the kitchen countertop, I begin fiddling with a stray thread from my top.

"I'm sorry, I didn't mean to pry," he says, making me smile.

"Liar," I whisper, "but it's ok. It's in my past and always will be. I've grown a lot since then and I know how to protect myself."

"By not going near predators such as myself," he teases. I throw a stray bean at him and smile, just as he deflects it with his hand.

"No. I'm just not as naïve or trusting as I was as a teenager, like most people, I guess. I bet even you would say you are more reserved with people than you were at eighteen."

"I suppose, but I never wanted to hurt myself when I was that age either," he says matter of factly. His response makes me feel shameful, but I don't think it was his intention.

"The bullying crept up on me. At first, I didn't notice it, just assumed it was something all kids went through. Then, when I realized I was being targeted, both in the open and online, I had Dean, Emma, and a few guys who I thought were my friends to help me through it, so I brushed it off. I didn't think I needed anyone else, so I leaned on them and pretended it didn't exist. Funnily enough, when it didn't bother me, I rarely went online. But when everything came to a head with Dean and Emma, and I began to let it all get to me, began to believe what they said about me, I found myself looking at it all the time. I don't know if it was self-harming, hoping to see someone standing up for me, or because I felt so utterly alienated, but I couldn't stop myself from looking. It was impossible not to."

"I almost don't want to ask, but what the hell did they find to say about you?" he asks, looking genuinely confused.

"Anything. Absolutely anything. I was ugly, short, fat, a slut, a bitch, smelly, stupid, whatever ugly thing you can think of to say about someone, they said it about me. I don't know why it started, but I do know that choosing to remain one of the boys and ignore what the girls deemed important, really exacerbated things. The final straw was when Dean, our year's answer to God, chose me of all people."

"And then he crapped all over you…for no reason?"

"I thought Dean loved me. I did all the things I thought a girlfriend was supposed to. I dressed how he liked, I was nice to his friends, I let him have his own space, and I was interested in the shit he was interested in. I wore makeup, did my hair the way he liked it, and even slept with him when he wanted to," I admit, feeling ashamed all over again.

"Jesus, Bea!" I barely hear him say as it all floods back in.

"And yet he had sex with my best friend, my sister. There's only about a year between us and we were inseparable. I confided everything in her, especially about Dean, even the really personal stuff. And they both betrayed me in the worst possible way." I pause to gulp back more wine as he stands before me, motionless, as though he wants me to get it all out. "When I found them in my bedroom, in my bed, I stood for about five minutes in shock before they finally realized I was there. It was like a steamy porn film but with a running commentary of dirty talk; things he had never said to me. I just froze, feeling completely sick."

It's only then that I realize Nate's knelt before me and is now holding my hands. His wide brown eyes stare into mine as I feel a well of tears forming on my lower lashes.

"Emma was the first to jump up and ran straight into the bathroom. But he just laid back, looking at me before shrugging his shoulders. The action made it as if what he had just done to me was absolutely nothing. I was nothing more than a throwaway item."

"Beatrice Summers, you are not nothing," he whispers before taking one of my hands to his mouth to kiss, then repeats the action with the other hand. "You are everything and neither of those assholes deserves an ounce of you. I hope your father beat his ass with a baseball bat."

"Actually," I sigh heavily, "Dean and Emma are now engaged and I'm pretty sure I've been asked around to dinner to be told I have to go to the wedding."

"Seriously?! He was allowed to live after that?"

"They weren't told the full story, Nate, I couldn't do it to them or myself," I tell him, which only makes him look all the more horrified. "I needed some form of closure and a new start; you think that would have happened if my parents had found out? That horrendous period of my life would have been argued about for months, if not years. I just wanted to forget about it as much as I could."

"So, why are you going tomorrow? Can't you just blow them off?" he asks, still struggling with my silence over it all.

"I can only blow them off for so long; I've avoided Emma for years," I sigh. "Besides, I don't know, I'm beginning to not care anymore. It didn't actually take me long to get over Dean, but…”

“Your sister?” I simply nod when he correctly guesses the real source of my pain.

“But if she’s truly happy, then maybe I should let bygones be bygones. I don’t think we can ever be like we once were, but if she really loves him, then…”

I shrug my shoulders as my words trail off, for what else can I say about it all?

“I could come with you?” he offers but I shake my head vehemently.

“God, no, you do not want to come into the middle of that shitstorm,” I explain before he can take offense to my response. “Plus, Ben will be there, and I think he may need some warning before I show up with you…*anywhere*.”

“I understand,” he says as he begins prepping food again.

“But thank you for offering, Nate, I mean it.” I smile while reaching out to hold his hand.

“You’re calling me Nate,” he says with a genuine smile, “does that mean I’m forgiven?”

“Let’s say we’re starting again,” I tell him with a firm nod. “You’re no longer my boss; perhaps we can begin on more of an even footing.”

“I’ll take that,” he says as he squeezes my hand in his, “Bea.”

Bea

After a gorgeous, albeit extremely healthy dinner, we go to sit together on the couch, which I can now confirm is as hard as it looks. However, I've drunk enough wine not to care. In fact, I've allowed my usual barriers to lower a little. Soft music is playing, compliments of my smooth host, and I am finally feeling comfortable in his company. Nate Carter has worked his magic and I am finally feeling ready for it. When he sees this, by the expression on my face, he leans toward me and grabs my foot, and places it on his lap.

"I've been told, by my mom, that I give a mean foot massage," he says as he begins to rub my foot. Unfortunately for him, all it does is make me giggle. "Ticklish, I see?"

Being a seasoned playboy, he takes the opportunity to begin tickling me until I end up a laughing mess on top of his seriously uncomfortable couch. Call it cheesy and cliché, but we eventually end up kissing, which feels nice, playful, and genuine. However, I remind myself to not be too trusting of him, he hasn't earned that yet. I'm not even sure any man can.

I push back and awkwardly shuffle up, noticing how he retracts his hands just as quickly. He looks conflicted and I guess I am giving him mixed messages, but it's not something I can control.

"Bea?" he says, turning to face me head-on. "Talk. I get I deserve your cautiousness but you're acting a little more hot and cold than usual. What's bothering you?"

"Date," I blurt out, then instantly shake my head at myself.

"What?" He frowns and tries to reach out for me, but I pull back again.

"I know you have a date tomorrow," I spit out, "Finn told

me. And it's totally fine, I mean I know we're not… But I don't know, I can't fool around with someone who is planning on messing around with someone completely different tomorrow. That's just not how my brain is wired."

"Is that what you're worried about?" He bursts out laughing and it raises my hackles, especially now that he knows what happened. "Bea, I'm seeing Callie tomorrow night. Shit, you thought…" He laughs again so I cross my arms indignantly.

"Well, it's not completely farfetched, is it?" I snap. "I have seen the way you treat women; I've sent the flowers and made the rainchecks for you."

"But that's not what I am going to do to you," he says, reaching out for my hand again, "and if I have to tell you that every day, I will." I look back into his eyes, wanting to believe him, but I think he can see that I'm still holding back. "You will trust me one day, I promise."

Nate places a hand on my cheek and another on my waist before pulling me into him, lowering me gently so that I am completely beneath his body. I soon feel his arousal hardening against my stomach, but it doesn't make me nervous this time. Instead, I reach for the back of his head and run my fingers through his soft, chocolate-colored hair. I open my legs to let him fall between them, which encourages him to move his hand up to my breast where he begins to massage my flesh with a pressure that makes me want to kiss him harder. He moves his kisses down my neck and my eyes fall shut while his mouth and hands work on me. This time, I don't want him to stop.

I move upward so I can lift my tank top over my head, all the while staring into his hooded eyes as he watches me. Once free of my top, his fingers reach out to trace the outline of my bra, making me bite my lip nervously before breaking into a shy smile.

"I haven't done this in a long time," I admit with a glowing blush all over me. "I'm not sure what to do."

"Just kiss me," he says, "besides, we're not going beyond third base tonight."

"We're not?" I ask, confused and disappointed.

"No," he confirms while shaking his head, then carries on kissing down between my clavicle, all while his hand works on unfastening the button of my skinny jeans. "I'm not doing that with you knowing that I have to get up and leave you early in the morning."

He takes my breast out of my bra and begins to kiss and suck slowly while moving a hand inside my matching lace panties. I feel exposed but oh, so good at the same time. Nate runs a finger through me, and I feel a tingle of electricity I have not felt in a long, long time. He begins biting at my nipple as he inserts a finger inside of me, causing me to gasp over the alien feeling.

"Do you want me to stop?" he whispers against my chest, almost having to force himself to pause.

"No, but…" It stings a little, having not had anyone do this to me in years. It wouldn't surprise me if my hymen had grown back, it's been that long.

Nate nods his head as if in understanding and I worry he's going to stop. He sits up, kisses me gently on my lips, then grabs the top of my jeans and pulls them down slowly, looking at me the whole time. I don't tell him to stop, I want him to go further. His mouth finds the inside of my thigh and begins to kiss and nip at my skin before he finds my sensitive spot. Running the tip of his tongue from my opening to my clit, I take in a deep breath of air to try and calm myself. His tongue is a lot softer than his fingers and it helps me to relax. He keeps licking and sucking until lust takes over and I buck my hips to reach him more greedily. Gripping hold of my hips firmly, his movements become harder, quicker, and even offers the odd nip between his teeth. I place my hand to my mouth as a climax begins to build and when I try to push him away to ward off the impending release, he doesn't move. Instead, he holds me in place and keeps going, relentlessly giving me what I need until I orgasm, almost violently.

As I come back down, he moves up to my stomach, which is still clenched up tightly, then kisses me gently before resting his head against mine. I stroke his hair while my breathing begins to even out. His hand clutches hold of my hips again, and he looks down to where he finds my rebellious tattoo, something I got about a year after I tried to end my own life.

"What does this mean?" he asks quietly, now tracing the black outline with his forefinger.

"It's a Viking symbol...for strength," I reply in a tone that mirrors his own. "I got it about a year after I took the overdose. There's a Ben Jonson quote I think of when I look back at it all, *'He knows not his own strength that has not met adversity.'*"

"That's very deep and meaningful, Bea," he softly laughs. "Are you brave enough to trust your heart to me?"

I remain silent, not sure how to answer that yet. Instead, I sigh and continue to play with his hair. Eventually, he moves back to my face and kisses me gently before swiping his tongue into my mouth, though only for a moment.

"As much as it pains me, I best get you home." I must look disappointed and maybe anxious because he then leans in to whisper in my ear, "I want you, Bea Summers, I want you so fucking bad, I need to stop now before I can't."

We both look at one another before he gets up and helps me to my feet, with the both of us practically naked. He looks me up and down, grins darkly, then leans in to kiss my cheek.

"I'm going to go and grab a shirt."

When he returns downstairs, I smile shyly at him, blushing from what just happened between us. He simply grins and shakes his head, obviously sensing my embarrassment.

"You ready?" he calls over and I grab my bag to walk to the front door. Before I walk out, he grabs me by the wrist and pulls me back against him. "Don't be embarrassed, Bea," he says, "sex isn't something dirty."

"I know, but the last time I did have sex, it felt like it was."

"Well, we won't ever be like that," he reassures me before kissing me one last time.

———

Bea

I return home to the lights of the city and notice my own apartment window glowing brightly, meaning Callie must have already returned from her date. I suddenly feel exhausted and hope she doesn't want to dissect every moment of each other's evenings. I know she's missing Lily though, so I won't stop her if that's what she needs to do with me. She's been there for me in the last few weeks and the happiness that brings me feels warm inside. Ben has always been there for me but in a brotherly way. So has Finn, but he's still a guy. It's not the same as having a close girlfriend in which to confide. Plus, the thought of beginning a conversation with either of them that starts with, *'So, Nate went down on me this evening,'* doesn't really appeal.

"Looks like Callie's home early," I comment with a wince on my face. "Her date can't have gone too well."

"She'll be fine," Nate says with a shrug, "she doesn't date men for long. She enjoys the chase and the relationship 'firsts', but then becomes rapidly bored."

"What went on between you two?" I'm not sure I want to hear the answer to this question, but it's fallen from my mouth now.

"Plain old fucking and nothing more," he says like it's no big deal. "We used each other to scratch an itch."

"Not sure if I feel any better about that answer," I reply truthfully, "but I did ask, didn't I?"

"That you did," he answers, "but it was years ago. I can honestly say I am not scratching anyone's itch right now."

"Anyway, I best let you go," I murmur awkwardly, feeling a little odd over his past conquests.

"Ok," he says and kisses me with pent-up lust from our session earlier on. "Good luck tomorrow and call if you need me. If not, I'll call you on Saturday."

After I tease him with a mock salute, I open the door and step out. However, unbeknownst to me, he follows me and before I know it, he's pinned me up against the car door and is kissing me wildly, exploring every corner of my mouth. It's hard and passionate, and his cock is now stiffening between my thighs. I wrap my legs around his waist while he holds me firmly against the warm metal of his car.

When I feel like I could easily come from his grinding against me, he reluctantly withdraws his mouth, but not before biting my bottom lip and pulling.

"I feel like this is the longest foreplay I've ever had," he groans. He squeezes his eyes shut even tighter before pushing off away from me. "Ok, I'm going home to have a cold shower."

He walks over to the driver's door and opens it, waving at me before he slips inside. I return the gesture and head to the door of my building, knowing that I need one of those too.

Chapter 22

Bea

As I approach the front door, the same one that used to bring me comfort, the nostalgic feeling I was hoping for doesn't come. Instead, I am met with a sense of dread, cruel memories, and a need to be violently sick. In fact, when I am halfway down the paved path that still has two chipped tiles from when Emma and I had dropped an antique chest on top of it, I have to take a moment to inhale a deep breath. We were trying to build a den in the yard and what den would be complete without our grandmother's mahogany chest? I took the blame, telling my parents that it had all been my idea. I had to work off the cost of replacing the slabs for the next three weeks. Turns out I was on less than the minimum wage from at least four decades ago, not to mention they never did replace the broken tiles. So, essentially, I had worked for nothing. Not that new tiles would stop this impending evening from being thoroughly awful. I know it will be, but it's got to happen, so I may as well get it over with.

I can see Ben's bike in the driveway, which is another reason to go through with this; he doesn't deserve to face them all alone. Besides, I know he has my back if needed.

In the dusky light of fall, the glow from the windows is warm and inviting. It reminds me of a time when I'd return home from school in the cool night air and feel happy and safe to be returning to see my mom and dad, Emma, and Ben. Now, however, I only feel distant from them, knowing that I'm going to be expected to get over my sister's betrayal and accept the way things turned out. I'm also going to have to accept Dean as my new brother-in-law, which sounds wrong, even inside my head. And then there's Emma herself. Why did she do it to me? Why could she not have done the decent thing and talked to me about her feelings? Was her lust for Dean too much to ignore? And in my bed of all places. Whose fucking idea was that?

I have no idea how long I've managed to put off knocking on my childhood home's door, but now that I'm here, I understand why Dean refused to just walk in; it's not my home anymore. I have a key, but I've not used it since that night. Even when I visit my parents when I know my sister is away, I never use it. I always knock. However, this time, I wish I had, for the person who comes to answer the door is none other than my ex-boyfriend, Dean.

At first, he's not even looking at me, he's too busy laughing over his shoulder to see that it's me, the girl he destroyed nearly ten years ago. When he finally sees me, he freezes, and all humor falls from his face. In fact, I couldn't tell you what expression he's wearing, though I probably look much the same. After all, this is the first time we've laid eyes on each other since he told me hated me, a week or so after he had fucked my sister.

Moments pass, with me trying to understand how I'm feeling. Anger and sadness soon rise to the surface. He's managed to slip himself into my family while I stand here as the outsider. This man destroyed me and alienated me from the only people who were truly mine. And that's what it boils down to; I have felt ostracized my whole life, but I always had my family. His answering the door, keeping me waiting on his say-so, proves that I don't even have that anymore.

"Dean," I eventually utter, trying my best to look as uninterested as I can. He looks me up and down, silently assessing me as the twenty-seven-year-old woman that I am now.

"Bea," he replies, his voice making me bite down on the inside of my cheek.

When he says nothing else, I take it upon myself to step inside and walk past him. I hear him inhale deeply before closing the door, after which, I pace into the kitchen as fast as possible so I can avoid him altogether.

"Bea!" my mother squeals as soon as she sees me. She wraps me up in a mom cuddle, smelling of cooking ingredients and lavender soap. I hold her back just as tightly, feeling like I never want to let her go.

"It's been so long, baby girl. Now, let me look at you, make sure Ben's been taking care of you."

She pulls away from me before looking me up and down, taking me in with her pensive frown and half a smile. Only once her eyes return to mine does she beam at me again, apparently happy with her findings.

"Beautiful Bea, just like when you were a baby," she says, to which I roll my eyes over the story that I know is coming. "Thirty-six hours of labor, a dose of pethidine, and stitches to rival those of Frankenstein's monster, but when you finally arrived with a cry loud enough to wake the entire ward, I knew you had to be called Beatrice, Shakespeare's greatest heroine."

"Mom!" I groan before noticing my now fully grown sister hovering by the doorway over my mother's shoulder. She's wrapped her arms around her waist and is looking at me with a sheepish smile. It's enough to have me step outside of my mother's arms and begin backing away from what I so dearly need.

"Er, where's Dad?"

"Oh, he's in the living room with your brother. He's so excited to have you all here together, all under one roof, just as it should be," she says with warmth in her eyes. She then turns so she is standing to the side of us, her eyes bouncing between Emma and me. "Well, aren't you two girls going to say hello to one another?"

"Course, Mom," Emma says before moving her eyes to stare at me. "Hi, Bea."

"Hello, Emma," I reply, trying but failing to sound anything other than cold.

"It's really good to see you, it's been so long," she says with her foot shuffling around, as though she's considering coming up to me.

"Has it?" I reply with bitterness.

"Beatrice, please," Mother whispers at the same time as Emma drops her eyes to the floor.

"My apologies, you look good, Emma," I reply with a tight-lipped smile, "but then, you always have. Excuse me, I'm going to go and see Dad." I'm already walking away before I can see the disappointment in my mother's eyes.

I'm trying, Mom, I really am, but it's so hard to forgive and forget.

When Dad spies me shuffling through the door, all thoughts of Emma are wiped clean, for his smile is so wide and genuinely pleased to see me, I can't help but fall into his bear-like embrace. Still a handsome man, he's also tall and broad, just like his son.

The man has always been in love with my mother, from the very first day they met at high school; their relationship was once one that I craved for myself. I lost hope of ever having that when I realized their love was the exception to the norm. You can see his absolute adoration for her whenever he looks into her eyes, even when you spy them bickering with fond affection, it's as obvious as the nose on your face. I couldn't be happier for them, though I sometimes think they set me up to have expectations that could never be reached.

"Hey, lil' girl, how's my Bea?" he asks, looking over the top of his spectacles that have seen much better days.

"I'm ok, Dad, but when are you going to replace these things?" I tut as I point to the tape wrapped around one of the arms.

"What do you mean? They're still good," he huffs. "Anything can be fixed, no matter how broken it might seem."

He looks at me pointedly, talking about more than just an ancient pair of glasses. I sigh at the same time as I step back, knowing that it's already started - the guilt trip.

"Dad –"

"Just give them a chance, Bea, that's all your mother and I are asking for," he says before kissing the top of my head. I give him a small smile, conceding to his wishes, but only for his sake. My mother calls for him, so he squeezes my hand and heads for the door, walking out just as Ben saunters in to see me.

We don't hug straight away, our argument before he left for long haul is still fresh in my mind. For the first time ever, we look a little awkward being in each other's company. It's deeply unsettling and painful to be like this with Ben, but after a moment or two, he grabs hold of my shoulders and wraps his big brother arms around me.

"Am I forgiven?" he asks before whispering in my ear, "I've got your back, sis."

"For now," I tell him, soon laughing when his sheepish smile morphs into a wide grin. "Thank God you're here; I wanted to bolt when Dean answered the door. This is harder than I thought it would be, Ben."

"I know, but as I said, I've got you," he whispers as the whole family begin walking into the living room, bringing us all together for the first time in years.

To my surprise and horror, Emma walks over to me, biting her lip before wrapping her skinny arms around my shoulders and burying her head inside the crook of my neck. It shocks me, and for a moment, I stand frozen on the spot. My clueless parents are smiling with far too many teeth to be natural, and they begin nodding as if giving me the gentle push to hug her back. With the pressure becoming too much to bear, I reluctantly wrap my arms around her, to which she makes a sound that's halfway between a squeal and a laugh. She even does a jiggly dance against me, reminding me of how bubbly she always was. For a moment, it makes me smile. Perhaps I can forgive her, but I will never forget what she did.

When she finally lets go, I look straight over at my parents; Mom has tears in her eyes and is wiping them away with the corner of her apron while Dad wanders over to pat my shoulder with pride. Dean, on the other hand, is avoiding the scene altogether by fussing with something on the dining room table, acting the complete contrast to the last time I saw him, acting smug in the middle of this very room.

"Well, dinner is ready everyone!" Mom beams, snapping me out of confusion over Dean's odd behavior. I can see Ben has clocked it, however, so I subtly shake my head, silently telling him to leave it well alone. It's no longer my business what's going on with him, that's all on Emma now.

Besides, when I make my way into the dining room, I begin salivating over my mother's home-cooked offerings that are covering every inch of the table. It's laden with all kinds of food that would scare the hell out of Nate's obsession with everything healthy, but to me, it's like heaven threw up a feast just for me. This is when the nostalgia kicks in; cozy nights in with my family, gossiping and laughing over everything and nothing, just as it should be.

"Mom, this looks like all my Christmases have come at once," I gasp as I take up the space that I always used to sit in. "Cheesy potatoes and glazed carrots?!"

"Just for you, sweety," she says with a wink and a smile. "And from those baggy clothes, you need them. Two helpings for you, Bea."

"You don't need to tell me twice," I tell her as I begin scooping up spoonfuls of fat and carbs without apology. "Ben and I usually survive on rice and pasta because both of us are too lazy to cook. Vegetables, Ben, *vegetables*!"

"Hey, I put peas in the rice…sometimes," he pouts, and everyone laughs, just like we used to once upon a time.

"We always did wonder why you decided to move in with Ben so quickly, the boy has never been able to cook!" Dad teases, but this time, the table falls quiet, especially at Emma and Dean's end.

"So," Mom says with an awkward cough, cutting through the uncomfortable silence, "Ben tells us you're now somebody else's PA. What's that all about?"

"Because the guy she was working for is a total prick," Ben answers for me, which only prompts me to release a frustrated sigh.

"Oh, yes," Mom says, placing her glass back on the table, "bit of a bully, isn't he? I hate to think of someone picking on you, Bea."

Pray you never find out just how much I was picked on, Mom.

"Yeah, well, I sorted it," Ben continues at the same time as I open my mouth to answer for myself. "Turns out he had a thing for her. What a douchebag!" Ben laughs. "Still, gotta hand it to the big boss who came back from honeymoon to sort it. Now, thanks to me, she's up there working for him. Am I a great big brother or what?"

"Well done, Ben," Dad says as he slaps his hand on Ben's back, looking just as smug as my big brother. They look like matching bookends. "I knew we could trust you to look after her."

"Actually," I finally manage to cut in with a sweet smile, "Nate and I are kind of seeing each other."

The whole table stops what they're doing and looks at me in shock while I continue to eat a piece of potato on my plate.

"What the fuck?!" Ben asks with a disgusted expression on his face. I must admit, I take great pleasure in it, seeing as it's wiped his smug smirk away.

"Ben! Language!" my mother snaps. "What do you mean, Beatrice?"

"Yeah," I say casually, "he came over while Ben was away, and we decided to get to know each other properly. It's early days of course, but I think now that I'm not working for him, it will be good. So, yes, big brother, thank you so much for your interference. It's worked out swimmingly!"

I can't help but smile when I see Ben's jaw clenching up in anger. It's all the more amusing when he holds a fist up to his mouth and proceeds to release a long and over-the-top angry breath. He literally looks like a raging bull getting ready to charge at any moment. I hope I look like I don't give a shit.

"Wait," Emma interjects, making me look up at her suddenly, wondering if she's going to have the audacity to try and give me advice. "I thought he was bullying you?"

"He was a jerk of a boss, yes," I reply without pause, all while looking her straight in the eye, "but on a personal level, he makes me feel like the only girl in the world. I can appreciate that after…Well, it's something I value greatly."

I can't help looking right at my sister and Dean after those words have left my mouth. She stares at her plate while moving her food about with her fork, whereas Dean looks as though he wants to run far away from here. I'm beginning to think that he might actually be feeling remorseful. It's weird considering the last time we had been this close he was almost rubbing their betrayal in my face.

"But the guy's a tool!" Ben snaps, breaking my hypnotized stare. "He's probably just using you."

"Thanks for the vote of confidence, brother," I growl, "I'm glad you think so highly of me."

"Now, now," my father says, cutting us off before our tempers can flare up even more. "Before we get all bent out of shape about this, I think everyone knows the real reason we came here tonight." *Oh, great Dad, bring in this band-aid-ripping moment to really make the atmosphere light.* "Emma?"

Emma smiles nervously before getting up to stand behind Dean, who is still trying his best to avoid my gaze. My eyes immediately home in on the rock on her engagement finger while she kisses the top of his head. Dean has turned decidedly pale, whereas Emma appears to have pushed aside her anxiety and is now beaming at us. Ben and I forget our arguing and seemingly reunite by simultaneously crossing our arms on top of the table, just waiting to hear the oh, so happy news.

"Well, Dean and I are getting married, and we wanted to ask you both, personally, to join us in celebrating our special day."

My brow rises as much as Ben's does, for even though I was expecting it, the shock of hearing those words falling from her lips is too much for me not to react. I'm guessing Ben feels much the same way.

"Look, we know things haven't been right between us all, but so much time has passed, and…well…surely we should be able to come together for one day?"

"Er…" I try to articulate my jumbled thoughts but fall short.

"Anyway," she continues when I fail to say anything

beyond random noises from the back of my throat, "we'd really love it if Ben would be a groomsman, and Bea, would be my maid of honor."

Ben and I look at each other from across the table, both completely dumbfounded over not only her request but also the excitement written all over her face. I half wonder if she's managed to talk herself out of all the hurt she caused. I straighten up and lean on the table again, with Ben almost mirroring me by leaning his chin on top of his linked hands.

"Bea, honey," Mom says softly, "I know this might be a little uncomfortable, given yours and Dean's history, but you'd make your father and me so proud if you'd say yes. Let's try to leave the past in the past, shall we?"

"I'll do it, if Bea does," Ben says, breaking our silence and prompting all eyes to fall on me, even Dean's.

"I…I might need to…erm…"

"Beatrice, this is your sister's wedding," Dad says, looking at me like he used to when I'd messed up in some childish way. Now, however, it stings just a little too much. "I think you owe it to your mother and me, after everything. We hardly see you as it is. Surely, you can do this one thing for us?"

I close my eyes and take a deep breath, desperately trying not to throw up my mother's delicious food, but I fear I might fail in that endeavor. After all, it would seem their betrayal has landed on my shoulders, and I'm supposed to be forgiving, even though they took out my heart and stomped all over it.

"Bea," Emma says, to which I open my eyes and look at her with a hint of a grimace, "I know I'm asking a lot, but I…we used to be so close. I can't imagine doing this without you."

We look at each other for a moment, her with sorrow, me with hurt. She's right, we were close, so close, right up until she threw it away on the guy who is still refusing to look me in the eye.

"Can I bring someone?" I finally utter, not daring to look beyond my half-empty plate.

"Sure," Emma beams at the same time as Ben asks, "who?"

"Nate," I reply after a moment's pause.

"Fuck, no, I'll kill him!" Ben shouts, putting us at odds all over again.

"Ben!" my father snaps, giving him a warning stare before turning his attention back to me. "However, I have to agree, Bea. Ben and Nate obviously don't see eye-to-eye, so perhaps not this time, ay?"

"It may have escaped your attention, but I am now a grown woman. Either I get to bring Nate, or I don't come. I think I'm being more than fair, given the circumstances."

"Beatrice, please be reasonable," Mom practically begs, trying to calm the situation by getting me to relent, just like I always had to.

"Wait," Emma blurts out, "it's fine, right, baby?" she says to Dean, to which he sullenly shrugs his shoulders. "And Ben, you don't mind, right?"

We both look at my brother who remains moodily silent for what seems like an age. My parents thankfully remain quiet, seemingly letting us kids battle this one out. Eventually, Ben looks at me and sees the desperation in my eyes, and when I mouth the word, 'please', he finally relinquishes his constipated expression with a long sigh.

"As long as he behaves himself, I'll be cool," he mutters.

"Good, then," Dad says, slapping the table and making a move into the living room. "Em, sweetheart, you best give them all the details. Hailey, let's go and recline in the living room."

"Thanks, Mom, dinner was delicious," I say as I get up to hug her, to which she pats my arm with affection. "Ben and I will clear up, won't we, assface?"

"Sure thing. Mom, go and rest up," he says before getting to his feet to help me.

Once inside the kitchen, Ben runs the water to wash up like he used to do when we were kids, so I grab a tea towel, assuming the role I was always given. However, before I can grab the first glass, he leaves the water and grabs hold of me to give an affectionate and supportive cuddle. We don't say anything, but I can feel tears welling behind my eyes, and I know I've already forgiven him.

"Please let it go with Nate," I practically beg, "I really like him."

"I know, it's what I'm afraid of," he says with a sad sigh. "I'll let it go but if he hurts you again, there'll be no amount of hugging and calling me 'assface' that will stop me from pummeling him into the ground."

"Fair enough," I reply with a soft laugh. "I love you, idiot."

"Love you too, brat."

We eventually break apart to continue washing up, which is when I spy Emma standing in the doorway. She looks as if she's about to burst into tears but remains silent. We've just made her face all of what she gave up on the day she decided to betray me with Dean. She knows she can never have the same relationship that Ben and I share. From the look on her face, I wonder if the sacrifice was worth it.

Chapter 23

Nate

"So, how long has it been, soft cock?" Callie teases. "I'm guessing you haven't yet been with Bea…*intimately*?"

I take a moment to look at her while considering my response to her bluntness, sporting a smirk that answers her question without me having to say a single word. She plays me at my own game, keeping her lips firmly together while twirling her wineglass around with her fingertips. Of course, Miss Stokes has always won our battles of wills, so I eventually accept my defeat.

"We've been intimate," I reply before emptying my glass with one mouthful. "But I'm giving her time."

"Why?" she scoffs. Patience is not a concept that Callie is familiar with.

"It just hasn't been the right time for us," I tell her truthfully, "but trust me, we're getting close…I hope. Her being comfortable with me is more important than rushing into bed with her."

"Well, don't slip into the friend zone, whatever you do," she warns, lifting her brow to accentuate her point.

"Trust me, we don't behave like friends when we're together. Anyway, can we talk about something else? I feel uncomfortable talking about Bea. Especially with you, of all people."

"Why me?" she laughs.

"Because we have a history," I point out. "Plus, the thought of waiting would be like torture for you."

She feigns insult for a moment or two before laughing in agreement with me.

"It would have been for you once upon a time," she says before gulping back a mouthful of wine. "You were once young and foolish like me."

"Well, things change. We grow up…well, some of us do anyway."

"Actually, young Nathaniel, or rather, old and wise Nathaniel," she begins after throwing her napkin at me over my teasing, "I have met someone, but it's a totally scandalous affair!" she adds in a mock British accent that Lily would be proud of.

"Really?" I lean in closer, shocked over this revelation. "Do tell."

At first, she begins to laugh, but when she calms down again, she suddenly looks sad and proceeds to drink more wine.

"Callie Stokes, keeping quiet?" I lift my brow, hoping to get her to elaborate, but when she still appears forlorn, I lean back in my chair to study her more closely. This look doesn't look at all natural on my exuberant friend. "Must be serious."

She seems to shake off her melancholy and grins, attempting to return to her usual animated self.

"Do me a favor and keep it to yourself," she says, and for the first time ever, I fear for her heart. Callie never acts this way about a man.

"Of course," I reassure her, though still frown with concern. "You are ok, aren't you, Cal?"

"More than ok," she lies, "let's talk about the weather."

I decide not to probe further but make a mental note to keep an eye on her. She is, after all, one of my best friends. We were never lovers of any kind. I've never been a lover with anyone, but I do love her as a friend and would hate for her to feel any kind of hurt.

Bea

My phone beeps, waking me from a restless sleep. At first, I feel disorientated and with my hair wrapped around my neck where I've had night sweats. They began after I was put on anti-depressants. I only stayed on them for a few months, but the sweats refuse to go away. It was just another reason not to date. I was voted the most unattractive student at Western, so add profuse sweating to the mix and I can't imagine what would be said about me now. I don't have them every night, just when I'm hormonal or stressed. Being guilted into attending your sister's wedding to your ex-boyfriend will do that to a person, especially knowing that I'll be her head bridesmaid. I half-wonder if that was my mother's idea; I must remember to quiz her on it later.

Reaching for my phone, I end up knocking half the contents off my bedside table. Several curses later and I discover the intruding piece of technology on my bed from where I must have thrown it in a fit of frustration last night. The envelope icon flashes at me, so I open it to find a message from Nate.

How was it? Callie and I missed you last night. Xxx

I half smile, glad to have heard from him but anxious about having to ask him to Emma's wedding. Being that they're so desperate to tie the knot, and the fact that Ben and I have been avoiding them for so long, we only have a few weeks before the big day.

As expected, but I need to ask you something. X

I'm being evasive. I'm feeling a little embarrassed about asking him to a wedding so early on in our undefined relationship. But I really need an ally at this wedding and seeing as I fought my cause to have him there, it would be beyond humiliating for him not to come. If I'm being honest, I *need* him to come with me.

Fire away, Miss Summers. Xxx

I reply almost instantly,

No. Can I see you? X

I cringe over how needy I sound, but time is not on my side, so I can't beat around the bush.

You just stole my next question. I can be at yours in twenty minutes. Xxx

Perfect, but Ben is here so try not to kill each other. X

No worries. Xxx

Feeling equal parts relieved and anxious over seeing him, I slam my body back down onto the bed and release a heavy sigh.

"Bea, you have ten minutes to go and make yourself look halfway reasonable before Nate arrives, who will probably be looking as gorgeous as hell. You then get to ask him to come to a wedding that you would rather stick pins in your eyes than attend, thus looking like a needy, bunny-boiling, baby of a woman," I say out loud to myself.

"Will you stop it?" My brother's voice comes out of nowhere, causing me to jump with a small yelp. "Why do you always sell yourself short?"

"Habit," I reply with a sad shrug. He rolls his eyes and shakes his head before wandering back into the living room. "Where's Leah? Thought I'd hear you humping each other this morning, but it's discernably quiet."

"Er…yeah, we're on a break," he says casually like it's no big deal. I don't react quite so dignified to this news, instead I run into to the living room with my hair still in a sweaty mess and my robe only half tied up around me.

"What?!" I cry. "What do you mean, *on a break*? Why?!"

"Bea, relax, it's just a short break from one another, to reset things," he says with his mouth half full of cereal. "We've been arguing a lot, so she suggested we take some time to reevaluate things. It doesn't mean we're broken up, just means we're having a little freedom to be ourselves."

"Ben, I've not dated for years but I'm pretty sure that is not what she meant when she suggested a break!" I yell. "It means she wants you to get your shit together and move forward with her. Jesus, Ben, you cannot be that stupid."

"God, you sound just like her," he groans at the same time as switching on the TV to try and drown out my logical arguing.

"If Nate wasn't going to be here in…" I pause to check my watch because I know I've just wasted at least ten minutes arguing with the idiot in front of me. "Shit! Five minutes. This isn't over, Ben!"

"Cool," he replies without a care in the world.

Trying not to lose my temper with him and his nonchalance, I rush back to my bedroom to get washed and dressed so I can make myself look at least halfway presentable. As I'm tying my wet hair into a French braid, I hear the buzzer. Ben doesn't bother to talk to the person on the other end, just buzzes them access from the outside door. I frown at myself in the mirror, questioning Ben's sudden change in mood, as well as his laid-back stance over his relationship problems with Leah. I knew they were having problems, it was obvious, but I thought they'd be ok; it's Ben and Leah!

It's not long before I hear Ben opening the door to let Nate in. They mumble an uncomfortable greeting to one another, then shuffle over to the couch where I can hear a sports game playing out through the TV speakers. I try to rush to get dressed but my room is currently in a state of having my entire wardrobe on the floor, so it's not going as quickly as I'd hoped. As for Ben and Nate, I figure they'll either, a) kill each other, b) ignore each other or c) maybe talk to one another. Anything but option a) would be fine with me.

"Hey, there's my girl," Nate says with a beaming smile, "c'mere."

He leaps up from the couch and crosses the distance to grab hold and hug me in a handsy cuddle before kissing me slowly on the lips. At first, I lose myself in his kiss, but I'm soon snapped out of my lust-filled haze when I hear Ben bumbling around in the kitchen. It's nothing he hasn't done with Leah in front of me, but he's never seen *me* with a guy before. Even with Dean, I was always reserved if we were around other people.

"Hey, you ok?" Nate asks when I pull away from his arms.

"Er, well, I need to ask you something," I begin, trying to ignore Ben snorting out a laugh in the background. I glare at him before pulling Nate over to the couch so I can ask him to be my date properly.

"Ok, sounds ominous," he says, "anything for you though, so shoot."

"Ok." I take a moment to let out a long, slow breath of anxiety before I find the right words. "I need you to marry me before next weekend," I tell him with a serious expression. I wink at Ben over Nate's shoulder, to which he smirks and mouths 'wicked' back to me. I then return my attention to Nate who has suddenly lost some of his Californian boy tan. He's staring back at me with his mouth hanging wide open and with a thoroughly shocked look in his eyes.

"Yeah, I've decided no sex before marriage, so the quicker the better, right?" I add, still looking deadly serious.

"Yeah, trouble is, Bea," he finally says, taking hold of my hand in a dramatic fashion, "I'm kinda already married."

"Wait, what?" I pull back from his hands with a thoroughly confused and horrified expression.

Ben tips his head back and laughs manically, prompting Nate to pull the corners of his mouth up into a wicked, teasing grin.

"What do you really need from me, Beatrice?"

"You're no fun!" I pout with a sigh over him winning our little teasing sesh. "It does involve a wedding though, and it's short notice. Ben and I have been railroaded into attending my sister's wedding in a couple of weeks' time."

"Wait, the one who slept with your ex?" he clarifies, looking utterly confused over what I've just said.

"I'm kind of chief bridesmaid," I reply with a wince; our family sounds like it should be on a daytime talk show.

"Yeah, and guess who she's marrying?" Ben chimes in as he takes a seat on the armchair.

Nate looks over at him, then back to me in complete horror.

"And you've gotta be a bridesmaid for them?!" he gasps, to which I nod.

"So…I was wondering if you might come with me?" I end up holding my breath in anticipation of his answer because not one bit of this conversation is at all comfortable.

"Of course," he says straight away, looking actually pleased that I've asked him. "I'm in New York that week, but I can always meet you there."

"Really? You…you'll come with me?"

"Why are you so surprised?" He grabs my hand and kisses it. "I'm here for you, Bea."

"You are?" I whisper, to which he smiles, then kisses me. I melt inside his arms and begin to feel my heart beating again. That is, until Ben emits a fake cough, purposefully prompting us to break apart.

"Let me take you out, Bea," he says when he laughs over my blushing red cheeks.

When Ben finally gets up to put his empty bowl in the sink, Nate takes the opportunity to lean in closer.

"And pack a bag cos you're staying at mine tonight."

Bea

Nate takes me on a long drive to go out for lunch. He told me he wanted to take me to one of his old haunts from his previous, less serious, period of his life. He painted a pretty picture, so I was immediately intrigued. I was also relieved that he wasn't heading to the usual fancy pants restaurants he takes clients to. When we hit the coast, I bask in the sunshine, letting it heat my face and clear all my worries away. No weddings, no Emma, no past, just the sight of the ocean and a handsome guy sitting next to me.

"What on earth made you move away?" I eventually turn to face his wide, carefree smile. I don't think I've ever seen him looking so relaxed; I certainly haven't seen this look on him at work. "This is beautiful…*I* should move here!"

"Dad wouldn't allow me to stay. I only got away with it for as long as I did because I'm the baby of the family," he shouts over the radio playing. "He decided it was time for me to push myself. Cam had been talking about coming to work with him for a long while, so it seemed like the obvious solution."

"Are you happy working with your brother?"

"I love it, no question about it," he begins, but the look on his face is telling me he has more to say.

"But…?"

"I don't know, I just can't shift the idea that I'm only where I am because of Cameron," he says with a shrug.

"Perhaps to begin with," I reply casually. "But nobody thinks that about you now."

"How do you know?"

"PAs are unintentionally privy to a lot of office gossip, overheard phone calls and meetings and such," I admit. "I've only ever heard good things about you. Trust me, people respect you and admire your work, no one more so than your brother."

"Really?" he asks, looking utterly shocked.

"Of course, what made you think otherwise?"

"Besides Cam's teasing remarks? I guess you," he says, keeping his eyes firmly on the road, avoiding my staring at him. "When we first met, you gave off this vibe that I was nothing more than a party boy with a scandalous reputation."

"Well, I hope you know I don't think that way about you," I tell him as I put my hand over his on top of his thigh. He immediately squeezes it before lifting it to his lips to kiss.

"I know that now, Bea, and I also know why you were standoffish," he says. "I cannot apologize enough for getting it all wrong and for being such an ass afterward. I will forever kick myself for behaving the way I did."

"We all make mistakes, at least you've acknowledged yours," I tell him before kissing him on the cheek. "Some things can be forgiven…others not so much."

———

Bea

As lunchtime approaches, we pull into a beach bar parking lot, and I swear I see James moving about through the entrance. The sign overhead reads, ‘El Cid, est. 1978’ and I smile, feeling like I’m on holiday. It’s warm but with a welcome light breeze. The sound of waves crashing in the background makes me want to strip down to a bikini and lie on the beach all afternoon.

Nate grabs hold of my hand so we can walk in together, probably looking like a couple of love-struck teenagers. Today, however, I find myself not caring what other people think. In fact, the only things I’m caring about right now, is feeling happy, and the man I’m currently walking next to. James appears in front of us, confirming my earlier suspicion, with a beautiful smile and a friendly handshake for both of us.

“I see you finally pulled your head out of your ass,” he says with laughter in his voice. “Hey, gorgeous, how are you?” I’m gifted with a kiss on the cheek and a warm hug.

“James, you get to work *and* live here? You’re so lucky!” I grin at him, all the while looking around the place in awe.

A rustic bar stands to my right and a dancefloor is positioned beyond the tables and chairs to the left of us. However, it’s the view that truly takes my breath away. A sandy beach with various sunbeds leads the way to the beautiful blue ocean that is virtually flat calm today. There aren’t many tourists as we’re out of season. Most of the people strolling along the sand are dog owners, throwing stones and sticks in for their furry pets to retrieve just past the break.

“Correction, babe,” James says, bringing me back to the conversation, “I *own* the place. Come and sit over here; I’ll get you some drinks. Are you eating?”

Nate nods before leading me toward the perfect table that overlooks the water.

"I'm glad you asked me to your sister's wedding," Nate says when we've sat down. He then covers my hands with his over the table. "I hope it means that you're beginning to trust me, if only a little bit."

"You say that now," I reply with a smile, "but I should warn you, they only know Ben's rather damning description of you."

"I can win people over; I won you over, didn't I?" he says, to which I giggle. "No, seriously, I'm asking, have I won you over yet?"

"I think so," I reply before frowning while I think about it. "It will take time for me to trust, but I'd be the same with anyone. I need to protect myself, so I never run the risk of going back to that *place* again. But I want to trust you, and that's a pretty big step for me."

"I can give you time," he says before kissing my hand, something I've noticed he likes to do when he's feeling reassured. "So, what was Dean like when he saw you? Was he still a smug asshole?"

"To be honest, I couldn't really tell you. He barely said a word to me, and he avoided eye contact as much as possible."

"Do you think he regrets what happened?" he asks with a thoughtful expression.

"I have no idea, but..."

"What?" he says, leaning in to rub my arm with soothing strokes.

"I don't know what I was expecting, but it wasn't that. There's not a day that hasn't gone by when I haven't thought about what they did or how things would be if I ever had to face them again. I never once thought it would be so…"

"Underwhelming?"

"Does that make me sound crazy?" I ask shyly.

"Not at all," he replies, leaning back when a waitress brings our drinks and some nibbles. "Anyone would want some sort of closure after what happened to you, Bea. It's only natural."

"Perhaps," I reply, thinking about it all, as if in a daze. "Do you think closure is possible after everything?"

"Bea, when you finally move forward and are truly happy, you will find your closure."

"I hope so," I tell him, giving him a knowing smile. Perhaps *he* is my chance for closure.

"I know so," he says before kissing my fingertips again. "Let's eat so I can show you around the old town and then we'll head back to mine if that's ok with you?"

The thought of staying at his place is both exciting and nerve-wracking, so all I can do is nod. Closure could be nearer than I thought.

Chapter 24

Nate

Sitting at my place, in my own territory, I feel a primal need to protect Bea from all that she's got to face with her family. Perhaps my inner caveman is trying to break free, but I know I also care deeply for her. Turns out I can love easily when it's the right girl, and I'm fast learning Bea is the perfect girl for me. She reminds me of the life I led before I was aware of the value of money or what it meant to be the popular boy who earned himself a reputation for partying.

Truth be told, Bea's past has made me think about the horrendous double standards that exist. I was made a god for being a party boy, whereas Bea was hounded simply for dating someone like me. Speaking of which, I can't wait to meet Dean, the very thought makes my hands itchy. I can't imagine what it will be like for her having to watch her parents welcome him into the family after what he did. To betray her the way that he did, followed by exacerbating the torture she had to endure on a daily basis, the guy surely deserves to be begging for forgiveness in the dirt.

"Hey, what are you thinking about?" Bea looks up at me from where she's lying against me on the couch. I must get a new one, one that doesn't feel like a stone bench. In fact, I need to start making this place my own, so it's less show home and more personal.

"Thinking about your bastard of an ex who I can't wait to meet," I tell her with a wicked smile on my face.

"Don't waste time on him, waste time on me," she says as she moves up to kiss me. I wrap my arms around her and deepen our kiss by stroking her lips open with my tongue. She moves up to straddle me, instantly setting my cock hard against her warm body. Her hands cup my face at the same time as I grab hold of her ass to pull against me, all the while we kiss one another with enough lust to make it feel like I'm on fire.

"Nate," she whispers as I move my lips down to caress her soft skin, "will you take me to your room now?"

Her question causes me to pause, to try to hide the excitement running through me for fear of scaring her with how much I need to be inside of her. I've been waiting for this, but I need to make sure she really is truly ready.

"Bea, there's nothing more I'd like to do than to throw you over my shoulder and march you straight to my bed," I admit, "but –"

"Shh," she says, placing her fingers on my lips before I can finish. "I'm not a virgin and I'm ready for you, Nate. I need you to show me that sex can be good."

She doesn't need to say anything else; I grab her ass cheeks and lift her so that her legs wrap around my waist. With her safely in place, right where I want her, I carry her as fast as my feet can possibly walk up the stairs and into my bedroom. She laughs the whole time, reaching up into my hair with one hand while the other one clings onto me.

When I finally reach the foot of my bed that sits in pride of place in the middle of the room, I let us free fall onto the sheets with a soft thud. Her hair spreads out like melted chocolate over the bright white cotton, and with her eyes staring up at me, I take a moment to indulge in the sight of her.

"You are so beautiful," I whisper, making her giggle with embarrassment. She blushes as I begin to stroke her bottom lip with the pad of my thumb. "You still waiting for marriage?"

"I think I messed that one up a long time ago," she says before turning a little serious again. "Just remember, Nate, it's been a few years."

"I won't hurt you," I whisper reassuringly.

Bea

I show Nate a giggly exterior, but in all truthfulness, I'm as nervous as I was when I did this for the very first time with Dean. My experience of sex has been dire to say the least. Dean had always forced his way in while I tried to hide how painful it was, and by the time I came to see Evan on top of me, he had already withdrawn. Besides, I can only remember feeling completely numb to everything that night. I couldn't tell you if I had encouraged him in any way, I was hardly with it. Regardless, when it came to sex, I didn't know what all the fuss was about and although I have had urges, self-love has always been more than enough to satisfy my appetite. Safer too. It wasn't until I started having feelings for Nate that I even contemplated wanting to do anything with a man.

At first, he kisses me slowly, deeply, and as if sensing my fear, keeps his movements gentle. When he feels my muscles relax against the mattress, he begins to push the bottom of my dress up my legs until I move up and let him pull it off completely. He takes a moment to look over my body, his eyes turning darker by the second; it both scares and thrills me. I can tell by his expression that he's been waiting for this a long time. He looks like he wants to eat me alive, however, just when I think he's going to literally ravish me, he rests his forehead against mine and takes in a deep breath.

"I'm sorry this can't be what you're used to," I whisper as I take hold of his cheeks in my hands.

"It's better," he says with a long breath before pulling his t-shirt over his head.

I'm already wet when I finally allow my hands to explore his body, stroking over his shoulders, down his arms, to his stomach, up and over his chest, and back to his shoulders again. He breathes slowly and deeply, all the while they travel over his naked skin, as though he's trying to calm himself. Losing hold of my anxious thoughts, I slide my body under his and begin to plant kisses along his clavicle, his pecs, and all the way down to his happy trail.

As I reach the top of his jeans, his breathing becomes slightly irregular and when I finally undo the buttons to his jeans, he releases an impatient groan. I press my finger gently over the black fabric of his boxers, tracing the outline of his firmness. At first, he helps me to tug down his jeans and boxers, but then he suddenly grips hold of my wrist to stop me.

"Let me," I ask softly. After but a moment's thought, he releases my hand, giving permission to carry on. With one more tug, I set him free, with a smooth, dark, and rather large erection hanging between his legs. With my right hand, I stroke down his length and to his testicles where I gently massage them before kissing the inside of his muscular strong thigh.

"You're teasing," he says with a breathy laugh. I smile, though he can't see it, and lick from the base to his sensitive tip with my tongue. I swirl around the top of his cock, moving around the rim, making him shudder with my slow torment. With one hand holding his base and the other reaching for his hip, I finally put him out of his misery and take all of him into my mouth and start sucking slowly. I flick my tongue against his sensitive tip before taking him faster, harder, until he loses his control and begins thrusting against me.

"Fuck!" he growls through his teeth, with his hand gripping my hair. "You're going to kill me, Bea, you feel so good…shit, stop, stop!"

Grabbing hold of my shoulders, he pulls me away and upward, so I am meeting him face-to-face again.

"You're a dark horse, Miss Summers," he pants before revealing a wicked smile. He then reaches his hand down between the apex of my thighs where he slips his hand inside of my panties, introducing his fingers with a gentle touch. "And so wet already," he whispers before sliding two fingers inside of me. I gasp at the unexpectedness of it, but I must be more relaxed this time because I don't feel the same sting as I did before.

He pumps me slowly while we kiss at a pace that is in no hurry for this to end any time soon. As I get used to the stretch, I thrust my hips up against him, wanting nothing more than for him to be inside of me properly; to wipe away all the other shitty experiences I've had.

Nate eventually pulls out and begins to rub the head of his erection through my soaking lips below. He lingers at my entrance for a moment, all the while he bites and sucks at my nipples through the lace of my bra.

"Are you ready for me, Bea?"

"More than ready," I tell him, and with one gentle thrust he moves inside of me, but I know he's not all the way in. It stings but I'm ok, still ready for this, so I place a soft kiss on his cheek for reassurance. With a deep groan, he moves all the way inside, then rests to kiss me, to hold me, to make sure he's not breaking me.

"You're not hurting me, Nate," I whisper, "fuck me like you want to."

Nate takes me slow at first, and I feel good, if not a little frustrated. But when I wrap my legs around him, he seems to lose his reluctance to take me like I need him to. His thrusts become deeper, and wilder, and I release a moan of pleasure, one I've never felt before.

"Yes…" I pant, "deeper, I want you deeper…"

He curses several times, then leans back to lift one of my legs over his shoulders. It makes me feel so full, so connected to him, that within two or three hard thrusts, I come undone, all while gasping against my arm. My walls clench tightly around his hard muscle, acting as a catalyst for his own climax, which he releases loudly and without apology. When I am finally able to breathe properly again, I notice a heat all over my stomach, so I look up to see that he released all over me.

"Sorry," he says with a sheepish smile. I'm gifted with a small towel before he jumps back into bed and cradles me inside his arms. “Last minute decision. Do you realize we didn’t use anything? I’ve never been that fucking stupid before. I swear I’m clean, Bea, so please don’t worry about that. I told you that you make me crazy. It’s like I forget my brain around you.”

“Me too,” I whisper, grinning stupidly while cupping his face in my hand. “You don’t need to worry about pregnancy either,” I reassure him, “I’ve been on the pill for years.”

“Really?” He frowns. “You’ve been celibate for years, haven’t you? Are you crazy on your period or something?”

“Geez, Nate!” I laugh while slapping his bicep.

“I’m sorry, I didn’t mean to pry” he says and begins kissing me again. “That was…awesome, no other word for it. But, hey, don’t get comfortable because I want to fuck you at least three more times.”

“Ok, dude,” I tease, “and no, I’m not a crazy bitch around my period, so don’t panic.”

“You know you’re mine now, right?” he says, looking strangely serious after our playing. “I’m not fucking this up again; you’re all I want.”

His words make me feel warm, happy, and so much more than I ever felt with Dean. But then I remember what came with Dean, what I haven’t yet shared with Nate - my pain, my shame, my guilt. It is with these heavy thoughts that the realization of what I must tell him hits me. I have no idea what he will think of me afterward, or if he’ll lose his shit with me as he did after finding out about Evan. However, I said I wanted to trust him, and so I must give him the opportunity to earn that trust. Besides, this truth is part of me, and always will be.

I haven’t said anything for a while, and I know he’s

waiting, especially after what he just said. Taking a few moments to psyche myself up, I begin circling around a small freckle on his arm, feeling slightly nauseated over what I'm about to admit to him. But it's me, warts and all, and I need him to still want me despite it.

"What's up, Summers?" he whispers.

"Nate, I've not told you all of my sad little tale," I say so quietly, I can't be sure he actually heard me. However, the frown on his face tells me that he did, so I swallow back my fear and move up to look him in the eye.

"I'm on the pill because when I was with Dean, I fell pregnant." His eyes instantly open up wide with shock, prompting mine to shut so I can hide from them. "We always used protection, but I guess the condom failed. I tried to hide from the fact that my period was late, putting it down to the stress of being bullied day in, and day out, while also trying to hide it from my mom. But when I could no longer sleep through worrying about it, I took a test…three tests. I was too scared to tell Dean, I knew he would be mad, so I hid them away in my room. Another week passed by before I decided I'd have to say something, but before I could tell him, I found him with Emma, so I never did. Shortly after I overdosed, I miscarried."

The emotion hits me tenfold, and I can't help but release a few tears that seem to come out of nowhere. It's the first time I've admitted to what happened since I had therapy with Sonia. I've thought about it plenty, but I've avoided saying it out loud for all this time, and now I'm doing so in front of the one man who has made me feel like I needed to.

"I-I killed my baby, Nate."

Chapter 25

Bea

For a moment or two, Nate says nothing, just sits there looking stunned. The longer he remains silent, the more I psyche myself up for the outburst, the anger, the disgust, and the judgment that I've already given to myself a thousand times over the years.

"I'm not proud of myself and I'm not looking for sympathy, because it's my fault I lost it, but it's something someone needs to know if they want to be with me. I -"

"Bea, I'm so sorry you went through that," he whispers before pulling me straight into his arms and swallowing hard. "Thank you for telling me, Bea, that took a lot of guts. For the record, I don't think it's your fault. I have no qualifications to change your opinion, nor am I arrogant enough to try, but I do know that whatever you did that night was not in your control, Bea."

"But –"

"No buts, baby, you are beautiful and brave, and I have fallen for you…hard."

"God, Nate," I whimper, "I didn't want to like you this much, but you've made me, you jerk."

"I've been called that many times before, but I've never enjoyed it as much as when it fell from your lips just now." He smiles at me, and I end up laughing with relief. "Come here!"

Bea

Would it be bad to admit that Nate and I spent over twenty-four hours straight in his bed? Well, we did. I gave up keeping track of how many times we had one another, it was too mind-numbingly good to worry about such things as keeping count. Nate is not only talented in the bedroom, but he also listens to my needs and what my body is craving from him. I became less and less inhibited and I know I stepped well outside of my comfort zone. Said zone has now grown significantly bigger, thanks to a certain Carter brother who knows how to push someone's boundaries without me even questioning it.

It occurred to me after we finally conceded to needing some sort of sustenance that didn't involve one another, that I have never climaxed with a man before. Sex was always an unpleasant function with Dean, and with Evan, what I do remember was that it was horrible and painful. In the depths of my sex fog, I decided to tell him this nugget of information, which is sure to blow his ego sky-high.

"I've never come with a man before," I tell him after nibbling on some take-out pizza. "In fact, sex was never something I enjoyed."

"So, I'm the first guy who made you climax during sex?" He smiles arrogantly, as could have been expected. Though, to be fair, he deserves to feel good about himself. I've been more than satisfied each and every time; Nathaniel Carter is an incredibly generous lover.

"Lap it up, Mr Sex God," I reply with a shrug.

"Hmmm, Mr Sex God? I like it," he says with a pensive expression. "Yes, that can be what you refer to me at work from now on. Actually, you can call me that whenever - my parents' place, your sister's wedding, with friends..."

"God, you are so full of yourself!" I laugh, nudging him with my foot under the breakfast bar where we're both perched.

"I'm so full of you right now," he says with a dopey grin on his face. "I want you to know that I'm the last guy you're ever going to have sex with again, Bea."

"Oh, so sure of yourself, Mr Sex God?" I tease.

"No, I'm sure of us."

He kisses me so intensely, it makes me believe in everything he's just said.

Bea

The following week passes by quicker than I would have liked, especially as I've spent most of my time at Nate's place. We've been one of those sickly couples who can't stop kissing and staring at one another. Sex has begun to be something I crave, though I am never left waiting long for it. If Nate had his way, he'd not bother going into work and we'd never get dressed. Alas, I can't, with good conscience, let him jeopardize his work. Neither can I keep ignoring phone calls from my family. Mom's constantly phoning to discuss wedding stuff, while Ben keeps checking on me and wanting to know when I'll be back home. With the number of times he's called or messaged, I can only assume he and Leah are still on their 'break'.

But now it's Sunday and I need to be getting back to my apartment so I can get ready for my return to work tomorrow. It's bittersweet; sweet to be starting a new role with Cameron, bitter in that I've loved living with Nate. It's been amazing to be living a life that focuses on moving forward with someone you are fast falling for. Don't get me wrong, I love Ben, and I'll be forever in his debt for everything he's done for me but living with him now feels like an anchor to my past. It's as if I'm still a child, a dependent relying on its parental figure for guidance and survival. We both deserve to move on from that. If only I could convince Ben.

"You know," Nate mutters from behind me on the bed, his arm wrapped firmly around my waist, "you could just stay here. I can take us both into work; you'd be doing your part for the environment by sharing a lift with me."

"That might be true if it weren't for the fact I walk to work," I giggle before turning around to face him again. He merely huffs at me while circling my pert nipple with his finger.

"I want you to stay," he whispers, and with a smile that's half-cheeky, half-sad, for he knows I won't.

"I want to too, but I think we should have this little time apart," I tell him, stroking his stubble with my hand, "if for no other reason than I need a rest."

"No, you don't," he says, pulling me into him at the same time as I emit a giggle, "I've seen your stamina."

"Nate, you're off to New York tomorrow anyway," I whisper as he delivers little kisses along my neck. "Mm…and I'm not ready to announce to the office that I'm sleeping with you."

"Why not?" he murmurs before entering me so suddenly, I gasp. He grins at me when I look at him, pretending to be shocked when in actual fact, I'm totally turned on and ever so close to agreeing to stay. "They're going to find out sooner or later."

"Please, Nate, for me?" I moan as he starts to circle his hips, hitting me at different angles.

"A month, tops," he says, to which I groan with a nod. This man has found my weakness and is going to take full advantage of it whenever he can. What a way to lose an argument though.

Bea

"Er, Bea, I'm going to have to take a couple of days off," Cameron says to me on Wednesday morning, sounding drained. He looks like he hasn't slept, and my concerned features have him flopping back in his office chair. "Family stuff."

"Anything I can do to help?"

"If you can keep me up to date with things here and cancel my meetings for the rest of the week, that will be help enough," he says with a long sigh.

"Will Helena be back soon, or are we going to need a new temp for the reception desk?"

"Er…she should be, but can you check if whoever is on there now is available to cover next week? I'm not sure when

Helena will be back…*if* she'll be back."

"Of course," I reply dutifully before getting to my feet to start my day. When I reach the door, however, I turn back to look at him as a human being, not just his PA. "I don't need to know the details, but can you tell me if she's ok? Helena has always been so lovely to me, and I just want to know she's not hurt."

"Physically, she's fine, thank you for asking, Bea," he says with a tired smile. "I'm sure Nate will fill you in when he gets back from New York."

"So, he's told you about us?" I ask with a bright red heat spreading over my cheeks. "I hope that's not going to cause any problems here?"

"Of course not, I'm glad for you both. He sounded happy, Bea, genuinely happy."

"I am too," I admit, realizing that I truly am. "Thank you for everything, Cameron, and I hope things with Helena sort themselves out soon."

"Hopefully," he says, looking less than convinced.

"I'll pick you up some lunch; your usual?"

"Thank you, that would help me out so much," he says at the same time as rubbing his eyes with the palms of his hands.

Bea

A few hours later and I'm heading down to the exit to go and grab some lunch from my usual deli. Nate just text me a gushy message that turned into something a little X-rated. I'm sure I'm currently sporting a cherry red tomato hue on my face, but I know I'm smiling; I'm stupid happy and it's all thanks to my naughty lover. I'm not even sure how the hell I make it outside without tripping over my feet seeing as my head is looking down at my screen the whole way outside. When I finally look up, however, the sight before me takes my very breath away.

"Dean?" I question my very own eyes as I step closer to the sheepish-looking man before me.

"Bea," he confirms with a nod, then stuffs his hands inside his pockets.

"What are you doing here?"

"Can we talk somewhere?" he asks while looking anxiously around us.

"What about?" I reply bluntly, folding my arms and looking at him like any other stranger. After all, that's all he is now.

"Please?" he says, stepping in closer with a pained expression. "Bea, I know I don't deserve anything from you, but please?"

"You're right, you *don't* deserve anything. You certainly don't deserve to call me Bea anymore," I snap as I begin to shove past him. Before I can get away, he grabs hold of my wrist and pulls me up close to him; the bastard still wears the same cologne. I simply glare at him with an angry grimace.

"Let go or I'll scream," I whisper.

"Please?" he begs, looking utterly desperate and somewhat pathetic. "We loved each other, Bea…Beatrice. I just wanna talk."

"Don't you ever mention *love* to me again, Dean," I growl through my teeth. He merely continues to look at me with desperation in his eyes. Though, it isn't compassion that convinces me to give him my time, more curiosity. "Ten minutes only."

"Thank you, Beatrice, thank you."

I lead Dean to the deli shop I was already heading to; I'll be damned if he's going to mess up my working day. He follows behind like the little doting puppy I used to be to him, but it brings me no satisfaction to see him doing so. I just want to get this over as quickly as possible so he can stop being here and reminding me of all that I lost. I wonder if he ever knew about the baby; the only person I told was Ben. After telling Emma and Dean about my moving in with him, and for them to go along with my story, Ben promised to keep everything else between us. As far as my family are concerned, there was no Evan, no overdose, and no baby. Emma and Dean were more than aware about the bullying, for they ended up being a part of it. However, my parents remain clueless, which is how I wish it to stay. I still don't want any of that being brought to the surface. It is a past I wish to leave there.

After making my food order, I get a cup of tea and head straight to my usual table toward the back. Dean gets his bitter coffee and follows me with a sad slump in his shoulders. I don't care why he's sad, I just want him to say his piece and leave.

"It takes me precisely eight and a half minutes to drink this tea, so be quick," I tell him without expression. He winces over my blunt words.

"I've wondered about you over the years, Bea," he says without looking at me. "I've missed –"

"No," I say before sipping my tea, savoring that first warm caffeine hit.

"*No*?" he repeats, looking genuinely confused.

"No, you don't get to tell me you miss me after you worked so hard to destroy me."

"Bea, please, you have no idea –"

"I have three mouthfuls left, Dean," I level with him, "what the hell is it that you want to say?"

"I need you to not come to the wedding," he says, staring at his lap.

"I would love to bypass your happy day, believe me, but if I don't come, my parents will be even more disappointed in me than they already are. That's thanks to you and Emma, by the way."

"I know and I thank you for keeping parts of our story quiet. Lord knows I don't deserve your discretion."

"I didn't do it for you or Emma," I snap, "I did it for me, for my parents, and for Ben. I did nothing to make it easy for you both."

"Ok, ok, I get it," he flusters.

"Why don't you want me there? Out of interest," I ask him with genuine curiosity in my voice. "You know I'm not going to say anything, I would have done so by now."

"Because I can't stop thinking about you," he says with a whimper in his voice, shocking me to silence and with a pair of gaping wide eyes. "Seeing you the other week has only made it worse. So, you see, I can't have you there when I'm supposed to be marrying your sister."

"Funny, you didn't think fucking my sister when you were

supposed to be with me was such a problem, Dean," I reply with a sad sigh, to which he throws his hands over his face to avoid looking at me. "I'd love to help you out…actually, that's a lie. I don't want to help you, but I also don't want to go to your wedding. Either way, I'm not endangering my relationship with my parents for your sake."

"Beatrice, you have no idea how sorry I am," he sighs through his hands. "I was young and stupid."

"It's too late to apologize, Dean," I tell him truthfully. "Though, you could learn from your mistakes. If another woman is making you feel so uncomfortable, perhaps you should be talking to your fiancée before you marry her."

I pull back from the table and begin walking away, sighing over his need to get at me, even after everything. This shouldn't be any of my business anymore, I walked away and left them pretty much unscathed, so why is he trying to place even more crap on my shoulders?

"I've never stopped loving you, Beatrice, never!"

His words only make me feel a rage I haven't felt since I caught them together. After a moment's pause for thought, I stalk back to the table, lean down so I'm face-to-face, and practically snarl at him.

"*Love*? Don't use big words you don't understand, Dean!"

Chapter 26

Nate

Staring at my cell, I brace myself to make a call I would normally look forward to. However, when you have to deliver bad news that's going to make the recipient feel disappointed in you, it's not exactly a welcome conversation. After everything that's transpired over the last few days, I'm going to have to cancel on Bea. The very last thing I want to do is leave her to attend her sister's wedding alone, but if I go now, I would effectively be turning my back on my family when they need me most.

"Hello, is everything alright?" my girl answers, sounding fully awake and worried. It's past midnight after all.

"Hey, baby, what are you still doing up?" I begin, trying to sound light and cheerful if only to try and set her mind at ease while I procrastinate.

"Nate, it's the day before the wedding from hell, did you really think I'd be sleeping soundly?"

"No, I guess not," I reply sadly.

"Nate, what's wrong?" she asks with concern in her voice.

"God, baby, I don't even know where to begin," I tell her truthfully. "Some stuff has gone down with my family, to do with Helena, and I can't –"

"You're not coming tomorrow, are you?" she says with disappointment thick in her voice. *Shit, I'm the worst!*

"Bea, I would be there in a shot, but I can't leave my sister at the moment. Be honest, how much are you regretting being with me right now?"

"Don't be ridiculous, Nate, of course, you should be there if your family needs you. But…she is ok, isn't she?"

"Not really…but she will be," I try to convince myself as much as her. "We'll make sure of that."

"Nate, please don't worry about me and this stupid wedding," she says softly, "I'll be fine. Some things are more important, and Helena obviously needs you right now."

"But you need me too," I sigh.

"Nate, I've managed this long on my own," she laughs, but her words only make me feel worse. "I'll call you tomorrow when it's all over."

"Ok," I concede with a sorry sigh, "but call me before if you need to. Don't ever worry about calling me, Bea, whenever, I will always answer your call."

"I know," she says with a smile in her voice. "Bye."

"Bye, baby."

"Shit!" I huff while clutching hold of the bridge of my nose between my finger and thumb.

Sitting in Cam's family-style kitchen, staring at my phone, all I can think is what an asshole I am. Feeling torn between supporting my family or supporting Bea, I have no idea what to do for the best. I only ever had the intention of attending that wedding with her this weekend, protecting her from those who brought her to her knees when she was still learning about what love is meant to be, and how it's supposed to feel. But, as it turns out, Bea wasn't the only girl who was brought to her knees when she was barely entering into adulthood.

Helena.

Fuck, my own sister who I've been living alongside my entire life. Cam and I both failed to see beyond the surface, to dig deeper when she was so obviously dying on the inside. We've both had a role to play in what's happened to her over the years. So, yes, I am still an asshole, no doubt about it.

Chucking my cell across the breakfast bar in frustration, I make no attempt to face my big brother when he enters the room, looking as wiped out as I feel. His anger seems to have dissipated a little but he's still on edge. Lily went to bed about an hour ago; she refused to leave him before being convinced that he had calmed down.

"Hey," he lets on a long, sad sigh. He doesn't wait for me to respond before reaching up to the top cupboard to grab a bottle of brandy and two glass tumblers that were part of a wedding gift from our aunt. "What a fucking shit night!"

"Mmm," I mumble, running my finger over my bottom lip in thought. "You think she'll be ok?"

"Who knows?" he replies with a sad shrug before sliding

into the chair next to mine. “The whole situation is fucked up, Nate. I’ve been angry with her all this time, and it turns out I’m the one who’s been the shit brother. How could I not have noticed?”

“You and me both, Cam.”

I give him a sympathetic look to show him we’ve both missed the obvious signs over the years. He merely plays with his glass while shaking his head over it all, after which, we sit in silence, both lost in our thoughts.

“Cam, I have a bit of a situation,” I begin, closing my eyes while bracing myself for his reaction to what I’m about to say. “I gotta be somewhere tomorrow.”

“Perfect timing, Nate, as always,” he mutters sarcastically, his teeth clenching in frustration. “Where have you so desperately gotta be?”

“Bea’s sister’s wedding tomorrow.” I’ve explained the situation to him, so hope to God he understands why I’ve got to be there.

“Oh,” he replies almost straight away, releasing his tension and looking up at me in surprise. “I mean, yeah, course you’ve gotta go.”

“Really?” I laugh at him, pleasantly surprised by his change of heart. “Cos I could have sworn you were about to take a pop at me for merely suggesting such a thing.”

He clears his throat before answering, laughing in such a way that suggests he was clearly thinking about it just now.

“Yeah, but if all this shit has taught me anything, it’s that you don’t let down the ones you love. I know what she means to you, Nate, so don't leave her at the mercy of that situation all alone."

"Do you think Hels will understand? I can't help but feel even worse for waltzing off in her hour of need," I level with him. "You know, 'Hey, sis, sorry you went through years of shit but I'm off to a wedding with my girlfriend'."

"I think her real hour of need passed by a long time ago," he sighs, "we were just too self-absorbed to notice. Plus, no offense Nate, but she won't miss you at the moment. I'm sure she has plenty of other things on her mind."

"And what about you? I kind of feel shitty for leaving you in the middle of all this too."

Cam has always been the head of the family, after my father, that is. However, now Dad is out of the picture, I worry Cameron is going to feel the enormity of the situation weighing down on his shoulders. For the first time in years, he looks... exhausted. He's got his own family to think about; it's time for me to step up, to let him know he has my support no matter what.

"Cam, don't take the burden of everything yourself, let me be a part of this," I tell him, hoping he can hear the sincerity in my voice.

"Hey, I'm ok..." He trails off when I level him with a disbelieving stare. "I'm your big brother, Nate. I've already failed Helena, I won't fail you too."

"I'm a grown man, Cameron, stop treating me like I'm eight years old, hiding secrets about Dad's affair from me because you didn't think I could cope with the truth."

"You knew?" he gasps, looking completely torn up on the inside.

"Course I knew," I tell him with a boyish smirk. "I also knew you had a huge crush on Mrs Fielding, you poor bastard."

"Shit!" he mutters to himself.

"I know, she had a mustache, Cameron."

"Not Mrs Fielding, Dad. I thought Helena and I had managed to keep that from you. Why didn't you tell me?"

"Why didn't *you* tell me?" I argue. When he smiles sheepishly and looks down at the floor, I place my hand on his shoulder and laugh. "Is that why you fought so hard against being with Lily?"

"In part," he replies with a small nod. "You know Lily, though, she's infectious. I never thanked you for bringing her back into my life, Nate, but thank you. I'd hate to think where I'd be without her."

"You're welcome," I mumble.

"It's time you went and got your own girl, brother," he says, patting me on the back with a smug smirk on his face. "I nearly lost Lily, don't lose Bea."

"Thanks, I will," I reply before slipping off my stool to get an early night. However, just before I head out altogether, I turn back to face him. "Hey, Cam, we both failed Helena. Doesn't mean we can't change things though."

He laughs without mirth before tipping back the remains of the liquor into his mouth.

"Night, Nate."

Bea

Oh God, the day is finally here and I'm more nervous than if this was my own wedding. Of course, Ben and I held off leaving for as long as possible, making us horribly late, which consequently had us receiving a stripping down from Mom. We were then torn apart, with Dad pulling Ben away to be with the men and me being pushed into my childhood home to get changed.

The house is a mixture of high-pitched screaming and gossip. I've never seen so much pink and frills anywhere, and with big hair, big makeup, and big shoes. To put it bluntly, the complete opposite of me. It almost makes me question how Dean and Emma have stayed together so long; he couldn't stand any of this either.

"Bea!" Emma squeals, complete with rollers in her hair and a face mask slathered over her skin. "Thank God you're here; hey, everyone, Bea's here!"

I turn to face a room full of familiar faces, faces that still plague my nightmares. These were some of the girls who would spread vile rumors about me, call me names, and generally make me feel cut off from the world. I look at them with the same fake smile they are giving me, and only because my mom is standing next to me. She's grinning at everyone, still completely oblivious to how awful these girls had made my life once upon a time.

"We're all a little tipsy, I'm afraid, but Mom can show you where your dress is hanging up." She hugs me in a manner that I consider overly friendly given our rather frosty relationship. "Oh, Bea, I'm so pleased you showed up. Mom thought you were gonna bail, but I knew you wouldn't let me down."

"Yeah," I murmur. "Nate had some emergency –"

"Tory!" she screams, completely bypassing me in her desperation to get to a tall brunette who had once spray-painted my locker with 'skank'. They meet with air kisses at the same time as Mom begins pulling me down the corridor to where her room is. When I see my old bedroom door, I pause for a moment, for this room always brings back memories of that fateful day. I've only been inside of it a handful of times since, and only to retrieve things that I had left behind in my haste to get the hell out of this town and all the people in it. Before Mom can question me on it, I quickly make my feet continue past.

"Oh, dear God!" I gasp as I look at the bridesmaid's dress that hanging up in the window. It's bright pink. It's short. It has frills. "Mother, everyone is going to see my underwear in that thing!"

"I did try to tell her, sweetheart, but you know what she's like," she replies with a wince when she sees me still gaping in horror over the scrap of ugly material.

"But…but…"

During my inability to articulate a single word with any meaning, my mother leans over and kisses me on the cheek.

"It's just one day, honey," she says calmly, to which I throw my face inside of my hands.

Alas, this isn't the worst of it. An hour later, my hair is pulled back so tightly, I swear I can feel my hair follicles dying. It's then drowned in a ton of hairspray, helping to deplete the ozone layer, before my eyes are coated in black eyeliner and glittery eye shadow. I'm forced to apply fuchsia pink lipstick, as well as layer upon layer of gloss. This delightful ensemble is then topped off with a pair of stilettos that are threatening to kill my feet so they can be buried alongside my scalp.

"I look like a fucking prostitute from the eighties, Mom! There is no way in hell I am going out in public looking like this."

Stepping back from my ridiculous reflection, I stomp past the parade of girls, most of whom are pouting their injected fake lips at each other and taking selfies, and head straight to the bathroom. The first thing I do is take out my hair, practically orgasming over the relief of it. I then pull it into a loose bun to try and at least resemble the rest of the bridesmaids. I scrub off the makeup and replace it with some of my mother's more subtle products. The dress and shoes cannot be helped but at least I don't look like I'm about to begin offering my services on the street.

"Oh, Bea," my sister gasps when she sees me. "You decided to look more…natural?"

I simply nod, then walk past her in such a way that she decides not to push the issue any further. Even my mother decides to keep quiet when she sees the stormy expression on my face. The other bridesmaids, however, whisper in hushed, unimpressed tones.

"No wonder she's single," one says to the other.

"Yeah, I would have chosen Emma too," another responds.

Suck it up, Bea, the day can only last so long.

Nate

Waking up to the sound of someone banging loudly on my door - so much so, I leap up in defensive mode – rarely means anything good. The blinding sun that seeps inside through the open blinds has me cursing and throwing my hands up over my burning eyes. They're as dry as sand after drinking Brandy and only three hours of sleep.

"What the fuck?" I grumble when the asshole outside my door begins banging again.

"Nate, it's eleven o'clock!" Cam yells through the door.

Holy shit! Why the fuck didn't the alarm go off? I must have passed out cold last night; I never sleep in this late.

"Shit!" I shout as I start running around the room trying to dress. Of course, I end up falling spectacularly in my haste to get the hell out of here.

"You fucking idiot, you are so screwed," Cam laughs with a throaty chuckle as he walks in to find me still naked and losing my temper with a pair of jeans that refuse to go on.

"Shut the hell up and help me get my shit together, will you? Damnit, I am so late, there's no way I'm going to make the ceremony!"

"Calm down, Nate, you're only getting yourself nowhere fast," Cam continues laughing but is at least packing my bag while I attempt to move without falling over again.

Chapter 27

Bea

"Don't say a fucking word!" I warn Ben.

The bastard took one look at my ridiculous outfit and burst out laughing. Easy for him, he's been given a suit and a comb and left alone. Not only that, a lot of the bridesmaids have spied him and are now offering him flirtatious smiles and other unsubtle signs of their attraction. Some of them are whispering his name to one another, obviously remembering 'Emma's hot older brother' from when he lived here with us. It's quite the contrast to the reaction they gave me not too long ago.

"You look…er…" He tries to remain straight-faced but fails miserably.

"Like a whore?" I answer for him, complete with a fake smile and a huffy crossing of my arms.

"Er, well, yeah, pretty much," he admits, then glances over at the other bridesmaids for a moment or two. "I'm guessing you toned it down a notch?"

"A notch, or ten, yeah." My response earns me a burst of unapologetic laughter from him. "Look at my boobs, Ben! And my ass! You can see what color panties I'm wearing for Christ's sake!"

"Yeah, perhaps I should pretend to be your date or something," he suggests, now looking serious and full of brotherly concern.

"No way," I reply firmly, "I'm already the sad sap whose boyfriend didn't show, as well as being the groom's ex; I'm certainly not up for being my brother's date."

"Christ!" he says looking at all the bitchiness going on between the other girls. "You might be my sister, but I can honestly say you look a thousand times more appealing than any of these prom queen wannabes."

I laugh and cuddle him, glad that he's here with me, even if he still refuses to tell me what is going on between him and Leah. She was supposed to be here too, but after their 'break', there's been no mention of a reconciliation. I sure hope she's ok, she's been like a sister of sorts over the years, and I'd be devastated if they decided to end things altogether.

"Thankfully, we're walking together, so stick with me, brat."

"Will do, ass face!"

The ceremony is uneventful as far as wedding ceremonies go, apart from the pregnant pause Dean gave before agreeing to take Emma as his wife. The suspense was nerve-wracking and even I felt sorry for my little sister. She might well have hurt me beyond repair, but no one deserves to be left hanging at the altar. Thankfully, he put us all out of our misery by finally giving his confirmation, but not before glancing my way.

Of course, after the ceremony, comes the never-ending list of photographs Emma has requested, most of which involve her bridesmaids. However, after the main ones have been snapped, and I feel like I've lost hours of my life, I decide to sneak off and have a drink of champers with Ben. He wasn't hard to find, sitting strategically at the bar with his back to everyone, so we grabbed a few glasses and went in search of a more secluded hiding spot.

Once I'm sitting with him, I finally begin to relax and stop worrying about all the people of whom I only have bad memories. Alas, I'm still pulling at the top of my dress every few minutes in an attempt to cover my bust, which only causes Ben to laugh at me again.

"Ben!" someone calls from the crowd. "We need the bride's brother, Ben, to have a picture taken with the mother of the bride."

"Fuck!" he mouths to me, which I take great delight in. Finally, it's my turn to laugh at him.

"Don't be long," I whisper when he eventually hauls himself off his chair. "I don't feel like talking to anyone here."

"Believe me, I will be back as soon as I can."

Without any other words, he marches off in the direction of the crowd while I gulp back another mouthful of champagne. It tastes bitter but does the job of taking the edge off, so I keep at it and try to pretend I'm enjoying it.

"Where's your date then, Bea?" a voice full of contempt says from behind me. I turn to see Dean scowling at me as he saunters over to take up Ben's empty chair. His smug edge is back with a bang as soon as he looks right into my eyes with a storm brewing inside of them.

"That seat's taken," I utter, though I can tell he's only going to ignore me.

"It's my fucking wedding; I can sit where I damn well like," he replies with his scowl still firmly in place. "What are you gonna do about it?"

"I'm going to do nothing," I murmur, mostly to myself. "We know you have a problem with me being here, though, so I fail to see why you would want to sit so close to me."

"Maybe I do have a problem with you," he mutters before swigging back his beer from the bottle in his hand. I wait for him to elaborate, but he merely stares at me without words.

"OK then," I mouth and continue to sip my drink, casting my gaze over anything that isn't him.

"So, where is he?" he sneers. "Where's this *date* of yours?"

"He's got a family crisis at the moment," I tell him truthfully, although I'm sure he won't believe me. "Some things are more important than you, Dean."

"Admit it, Bea, there is no date, is there?" he says with a strange expression, one that looks hopeful. "Do you ever think about me, Bea?"

"Sometimes," I whisper, "nothing good. You wiped away any fond memories by making horrible ones."

"We could make new ones…great ones, Bea," he says as he edges closer toward me.

For a moment or three, I just stare at him with nothing but shock and disgust. He, however, does not change his hopeful one.

In fact, he looks at me as though he thinks I'm seriously considering his warped suggestion.

"Are you serious?!" I eventually gasp, now looking around to make sure no one can hear this.

"No one compares to you, Bea," he says, reaching out to cup my cheek, but I'm too stunned to move. It feels like my brain is misfiring all over the place, and I begin to wonder if I'm imagining all this. No one can be this deluded, can they?

"Think about what we could be again, Bea," he says, his hand now making contact with my skin, causing an uncomfortable heat. "We could –"

"Groom! We need the groom!" someone shouts, finally prompting me to pull back and defensively cross my arms.

"Fuck!" he mutters to himself. With one last look at me, which causes me to flinch over its intensity, he stands up and stomps away, swigging his beer as he does so.

"Oh, my God," I gasp as soon as he's left. "Shit!"

———

Bea

It takes me a good ten to twenty minutes to come out of my stunned silence. By the time I force myself into the dining room for the wedding breakfast, everyone is already sitting at their tables, even the lineup. I might be getting a few odd looks from my family, including Ben, but at least I didn't have to get pecked on the cheek by the groom who just suggested we run away together. I head straight to Ben's table, assuming I'm his plus one, as he is to me, however, to my utter horror, my name place is missing. I'm not sitting here. This can only mean one of two things; I'm sitting with the other bridesmaids, most of whom bullied me into that motel room, or I've been placed on the top table.

"Bea, honey," Dad hollers over from the top table, "you're sitting up here, on the end."

My eyes follow the direction of where his finger is pointing, right over to an empty chair that is sitting directly next to the mother of the groom.

For fuck's sake, Emma! Your husband has just asked me to run away with him and you've gone and put me in front of everyone on the top freaking table!

"Oh, God," I whisper, to which Ben grabs my hand and gives it a reassuring squeeze.

I frown at him before plastering on a fake smile for my family and slowly walking over to the table. I'm gifted with a smile from Dean's mother, who was always nice enough, though this doesn't make it any less awkward. Before sitting down, I pick up my little name card just to double-check this is my place. Sure enough, the word 'Bea' is there, written clearly in cursive script.

"Beatrice, dear," Pearl says to me when I reluctantly perch on top of my chair. "I haven't seen you in years, honey, how are you?"

"I'm good, thank you, Mrs Spencer," I reply, giving her a genuine smile, for she strangely makes me feel comforted. There are plenty of worse people I could be sitting with right now. "How are you?"

"Oh, I'm good, dear," she says as she unfolds her napkin to place on top of her lap. "But call me Pearl, Bea," she says with her hand resting on top of my arm, "I always did enjoy seeing you when you were with Dean."

Her words have me shuffling uncomfortably inside my seat, and with flashes of being told about the miscarriage coming to the forefront of my mind to add to my guilt. When I look up at her again, I can see her studying me with a soft smile on her face.

"You know what, Beatrice? I always thought you were very beautiful," she says, causing me to blush with embarrassment. "You never needed any makeup or revealing clothes to catch Dean's eye," she says, gesturing to my ridiculous dress at the same time as I pull it up over my chest again. We giggle for a moment or two before she leans in to whisper to me. "He was an idiot to let you go, my darling girl."

"Thank you, Pearl, that's really sweet of you, but –"

"But we're at your sister's wedding and that kind of talk isn't really appropriate, given the circumstances," she says with a wink.

As the meal continues, Pearl and I fall into neutral topics of conversation, such as my job, Dean's work, and her and Mr Spencer's retirement plans. We don't stop talking until we're silenced by the sound of a spoon chinking against glass, announcing the commencement of the speeches. In other words, my cue to stop listening. Honestly, I couldn't even tell you what was going on while I switched off to everything and everyone around me. I just knew I couldn't bear to listen to Dean spout out a load of lies after he just asked me to run off with him. However, what happens next tells me I probably should have been paying some sort of attention.

"And now we have Bea, Emma's sister," a voice chirrups, interrupting my daydreaming.

Suddenly a microphone is shoved in front of me, and I notice everyone is staring at me as I lazily lean against my hand. I look up with a questioning frown, wondering why the hell all the faces on the top table are looking at me with expectation. When I make no move to take the microphone, Dad performs his own form of sign language in the hopes that I'll take it and give a speech I have in no way prepared for. I look at it like it's a loaded gun before reluctantly clasping my hand around the thing; it feels unnaturally heavy.

"Stand up, Bea," Dad whispers with a hint of urgency.

Grimacing over the thought of public speaking, and with nothing to say, I reluctantly and slowly stand, automatically pulling down the hem of my ridiculous dress. I glance over the sea of faces, all looking at me for words of love and well wishes for the happy couple. A third of them are smiling with pity, a third are whispering to their friends, and the other third is looking at me as though I'm nuts.

"Er…hi," I say as I breathe out nervously, only to hear a couple of people laughing at the back. I notice Ben looking around, trying to see who it is, and with his fists at the ready. "First off, thanks to Emma for not warning me about having to make a speech." More of the crowd laugh, including Emma. "Secondly, I have nothing prepared, so I guess I'm going to have to ramble at you all for a bit."

Again, people laugh over my rather awkward situation.

"So, Emma is my little sister," I begin, even moving forward so I can gormlessly point out the obvious with my finger. "And Dean is…well, the less said about that the better." Thankfully, people laugh about that one, none more so than Ben who is now shaking his head at me. "I thought…I thought I had love once. It was new and exciting, and I was so young and naïve that I thought, yes, this is it; this is what grownups feel when they're in love."

I pause while I try to think of what to say next without upsetting anyone and without letting it slip that Dean is having second thoughts about his new bride.

"But when I think about it, it wasn't real love at all. It wasn't a love that stood the test of time, a love that makes you laugh every single day or even a love that is built on trust and loyalty. But that's ok because it helped me realize what real love should be like. I love my brother for always being there for me, even though he calls me 'brat' and I call him 'ass face'." I pause to look at Ben, to see the smile spread across his face. "I love my parents for trying to keep all of us children in check, even when we've fallen out with each other. And even though we've been through a lot, I love my sister." I turn to see her looking up at me in shock. "I do, Emma. I know we've had a few rough years, but I love you for being brave enough to reach out to me. That really took guts."

Embarrassingly, I realize I now have tears in my eyes, as does she. Within moments, she is out of her chair and grabbing onto me for dear life. Of course, there's a soft chorus of 'ahh' from the crowd but after the initial shock of it, I only hear her quietly crying inside of my ear.

When she finally releases me and returns to her seat, I catch Dean glaring at me with an unreadable expression and a pale complexion. Choosing not to read into his staring, I turn back to face the front so I can finish my little speech.

"I'm also madly, stupidly, and deeply in love with my boyfriend, who unfortunately isn't here right now." I smirk at Ben, who is now rolling his eyes at me. "He makes me laugh all the time, protects me, and is so loyal to everyone he cares about. With him, I've finally learned to trust again." I look at Ben and he smiles, which only makes me beam with pride. "Kind of feels a bit weird telling you all before I've even told him. But I guess what I'm trying to say is that I hope my baby sister feels this way about her new husband, and I hope Dean knows what he's got; he truly is a lucky guy."

Most of the audience clap and shout words of agreement but my focus is on Dean. He knows that last part was more for him than it was for Emma. After a moment of staring back at me, he forces a fake smile on his face, though he still looks like he could throw up at any second.

After I'm convinced that Dean knows where I stand on the issue, I turn away to sip my champagne. It's then that I see the six-foot-three muscular frame of Nate leaning up against the door frame of the dining hall entrance. Butterflies flutter inside of my stomach at the same time as he plasters on a seductive smile and begins to applaud my speech. When my glass begins to slip from my hand, and I end up making a spectacle of myself by trying to catch it, he begins laughing at me. I look so ridiculous, I eventually give up and laugh with him, conceding to my humiliation in front of the guy who now has a small audience of bridesmaids gawping and whispering over the infamous Nathaniel Carter turning up at Emma's wedding.

Thankfully, I was the last person to make their speech, so the dining hall descends into chatting and laughter while the guests finish off their teas and coffees. Some people are beginning to get up and walk outside with their drinks, giving the staff room to change the reception into a dance floor for later.

"That was a lovely speech, honey," Dad leans forward to

tell me. "Especially as it was…er…off the cuff?"

"Completely," I reply honestly. I'm playing with the serviette in front of me, wondering whether to go over to Nate or to pretend the humiliation I've just lived through was entirely imagined.

"Beatrice?" a low, baritone voice says from beside me. His presence forces me to take an extra-long breath before letting it out in a long stream. I've closed my eyes to all the faces now staring at us, which only intensifies the tingling sensation inside of my chest.

"Nathaniel," I return, still with my eyes closed.

"Open your eyes, Summers," he orders, reiterating his words by leaning down and pulling at my hand so my whole body is now facing his. I automatically begin to pull at my dress to try and hide the sluttiness of it. "Stop fidgeting, Beatrice."

I look up to find him smiling and looking smug, but damn, he looks amazing.

"Is there any chance you missed me telling a room full of strangers how I feel about you?" I whisper.

His face turns more serious as he slowly shakes his head. With his intense eyes looking straight into mine, the people around us blur into nothing, and for a few wonderful moments, it's just me and him.

"But I still want to hear you say it to me," he says, stroking my cheek with his fingertips. "Tell me, Beatrice, please."

"Nate," I whisper, breathing out slowly again, "Nate…"

I take another deep breath, then take both of his cheeks

inside of my hands. We stare at each other for a moment or two before I kiss him on his soft lips. He reciprocates and wraps his arms around me, giving me the courage to say what I need to and to trust again.

"I'm stupidly in love with you, Nate." He smiles with his whole face lighting up, and it sends electricity ricocheting up my spine.

"I love you, Miss Summers."

Chapter 28

Bea

Mere moments later, after having declared our love for one another, Nate smuggles me away to a secluded spot. His kiss is intoxicating, his heat addictive, and the way my dress keeps slipping down my boobs and up to my panties, I wouldn't be surprised if we end up going the whole way. The fact that the wedding party is literally around the corner from us, including my brother and parents, doesn't even cross my mind; I'm too turned on to even think about where the hell I am.

"Need…you…" Nate murmurs between kisses. His open mouth travels across my skin, massaging it with his tongue. I emit an excited giggle over his desperation, though it is one that I am sharing with him too.

"Carter," Ben growls from behind us, "molesting my sister, are we?"

Nate and I freeze on the spot, staring into each other's eyes with shock, and a pinch of amusement over being caught out. Eventually, my boyfriend steps back, adjusts himself as discretely as possible, and turns to face the man who has repeatedly threatened his life. He smiles sheepishly while I give Ben a look that warns him to behave himself. Lord knows I've had to see him molesting Leah on countless occasions.

"Not molesting, no, just showing her how much I love her," he says, then pauses for a moment or two. "Her and her body. I believe I've actually heard you showing your love in a similar way."

I hold my breath, waiting for the moment when Ben loses his temper over Nate being so cocky. To my surprise, however, my brother merely quirks up the side of his mouth into a smile, then kicks a chair out opposite to the one he's just occupied. Nate looks at me before taking the offering, as if seeing if I think it's a legitimate olive branch. I shrug my shoulders, not entirely convinced myself. With a heavy sigh, Nate takes hold of my hand and leads us over to the table and chairs and takes a seat with my brother.

"Congrats, Bea, your speech was officially puke-worthy," Ben teases, to which I give him the finger for good measure. "I think it made me feel as uncomfortable as the groom."

"You noticed that?" I sigh.

"What are you not telling us, sis?" he asks, now looking as serious as he did when he first caught Nate and me getting frisky. However, now Nate is also staring at me with a questioning frown. In fact, he looks just as constipated as Ben does.

"I will tell you if you promise not to lose it like an unevolved ape," I level with him, looking at Nate too. They actually glance at one another before nodding. "Dean came to see me in the city, just days before the wedding."

"What?!" Nate gasps, looking like his own inner ape is about to come out.

"Go on," Ben says over him, though his inner ape isn't far behind; I can tell.

"He told me he didn't want me to come, that he still thought about me…still loves me," I admit with a strange feeling of guilt.

"But he's just married your sister?" Nate growls, positively foaming at the mouth.

Ben says nothing, just continues to stare at me with an expression that says he's still thinking about how to react. With each passing second of us looking at one another, with so many words remaining left unsaid, his face turns tenser, harder, angrier. A second or two later, he jumps up from his chair, sending it flying backward, and begins to stomp in the direction of the wedding party.

"Where the hell are you going?" I whisper shout, pulling rather pathetically at his huge arm.

"I'm gonna kill him!" he growls. "Emma and I may not have the relationship that you and I have, but she needs to know her new husband has just married her while still being in love with her sister."

"You can't go in there and blurt it all out in front of everyone!" I argue. "Nate, please talk some sense into him."

"Hey, I'm with him," he unhelpfully replies, getting to his feet and joining Ben in his quest to completely humiliate my family in front of everyone. "You want company kicking his ass?"

Ben merely shrugs, then nods, before leading the way. The

two of them set off like two vigilantes about to go and have a showdown with the local villain.

"Nate!" I shout while trying to grab at him. "What are you doing?"

"The guy hurt you, so I'm more than happy to hurt him," he says like it's a perfectly rational decision to go and beat the groom up. A big old confrontation in the middle of Emma's wedding, in front of my parents, plus the bitches who bullied me for years? No thank you.

"For fuck's sake, stop it, both of you!" I yell angrily, though it doesn't get me any sort of response. "If you don't stop, I will strip right here and parade around the place like I'm on special offer!"

A strange and bold threat, I know, but I have no other ideas right now. I'm sure as hell not going to let them march in there and humiliate Emma and my parents on her wedding day, even if it is based on lies.

To be fair, it does the trick. Both of them swing around to glare at me, probably to question my sanity after suggesting such a thing.

"You wouldn't dare, Summers," Nate smirks, though there's an element of fear in that smile. Ben looks at him as if to say, 'Sort your girlfriend out'.

"Oh yeah?" I challenge him as I begin unzipping my dress from behind. I'll admit, wearing just my underwear instead of this ridiculous outfit is marginally tempting, but I'm doing this for a higher purpose. The stubborn bastard remains standing where he is, as if daring me to go further. The trouble is, I'm just as stubborn, so with my eyes fixed on his, I proceed to wriggle out of my dress to reveal a strapless bra, lace panties, and the most painfully high shoes I've ever worn.

"Fucking hell, Beatrice!" Nate yells at the same time as marching over to try and wrap his suit jacket around my near-naked body. I shove at him, stopping him from getting anywhere near me, which earns me a stern glare. "Beatrice!"

"Holy shit!" a waiter gasps to his friend when they turn the corner to find a scene that looks like it's part of a porno.

"Beatrice, if you don't let me cover you up right now, I will force it on you, and then I will carry you away where no other fucker can set his eyes on you!"

"Are you going to --" I begin to argue, but another waiter soon follows and stops dead in his tracks to stare at me, his eyes almost popping out of his head.

"Right, that's it," Nate growls through clenched teeth, forcing his jacket around me and then throwing me over his shoulder. I yelp and order him to let me go but he ignores my threats and begins marching toward the exit. "We're out, Ben!"

"Ben, don't you dare go in there and destroy Emma in front of everybody!" I shout at him from upside down. To my surprise, he's laughing to himself, taking great delight in my being chastised by a guy who isn't him.

As soon as we reach Nate's Mercedes, he pulls open the door and shoves me inside with a scowl on his face and a look in his eye that tells me I'm in trouble. Without any words, he marches around the car to the driver's seat, gets in, and proceeds to wheel spin down the driveway. Gravel flies up behind us as we speed away.

As he drives, his teeth remain clenched together, his brow

furrowed, and every muscle in his body tensed up with anger. He looks so pissed off, even I'm a little nervous. In fact, we don't talk or look at each other for nearly ten minutes; it's only when his shoulders soften a little that I dare to try and say something.

"Nate?" I venture, but he doesn't move an inch. "Are you gonna say something?"

He remains silent and after a while of being ignored, my anxiety turns into frustration, followed by anger. Ok, so stripping off to my underwear in public might not have been the best idea but diving in to beat up the groom wasn't exactly a top-notch one either. Like two stubborn kids, we continue in this state until he suddenly turns off down a road that appears to be leading into woodland; the type of place you'd bring your dog for a walk. I look at him for some kind of explanation, but still, he says nothing.

Eventually, the road leads to a small clearing where Nate slams on the brakes and forces the car to an abrupt stop. It's not even dark and I know I should be back before the first dance, otherwise, my parents will notice my absence. Worrying about them only makes me want to lose my temper, so I sigh loudly enough to make my anger known. He grips hold of the wheel but still says nothing.

"You don't bring all your victims here, do you?"

"Get out of the car, Summers," he orders, causing my anxiety levels to rise again. *Is he going to leave me here?*

"Take me back, Nate," I whisper, "or at least take me to a train station or something."

Nate ignores me as he gets out of the car and paces around to my side with angry determination. He opens the door and holds out his hand for mine. I stare at it like it's a ticking timebomb, all while remaining frozen in my seat.

"You said you trust me, right?" he asks, sounding a little irritated by my refusal to move.

I look at his hand again before slowly placing mine inside of it. As soon as his fingers have clasped hold of mine, he pulls me out and marches us to the front of the car. I'm left standing with his jacket tightly wrapped around me, all the while he looks me up and down with his arms firmly crossed and his boss-hole stare that used to make me inwardly shiver with nervous anticipation.

"Lose the jacket, Summers," he orders with a jut of his chin. "Place it on the hood."

With fear, or possibly excitement - my head isn't exactly functioning at full capacity right now - I do as he says, leaving me in just my underwear and shoes. I'm so exposed right now, but the look in his eyes is dark, lustful, and a little dangerous.

"Turn around and place your hands on top of the coat, Beatrice," he says, quirking a brow as though daring me to deny him.

I slowly do as he says, all the while breathing out in anticipation. The ground crunches beneath his shoes, and when he is up close behind me, I feel a desperation to have him put his hands on me. Though, when I look down and to the side, I notice his hands are stubbornly remaining inside of his pockets.

"I don't know whether to be raging or turned the fuck on," he whispers inside of my ear, "showing yourself off in front of other men? That was fucked up, Beatrice, but knowing they wanted what was mine? That made me want to fuck you right there and then, if only to make sure they knew that this…that you…" He takes a moment to breathe in deeply, eventually dropping his forehead against my hair, to which I cannot help but arch back to try and make more contact with him. "You are all mine."

His lips begin trailing down my spine and back up again, his fingers still deep inside his pockets. He's teasing me, taking pleasure in his sweet torture.

"You are so fucking perfect, Summers," he declares, sounding like Mr Carter from the boardroom. "I want to fuck you hard and fast."

I lose all breath just waiting for him to do what he wants, for both of us. Long moments pass, with nothing but the sound of nature all around us. Before I scream in frustration, I feel him, all of him. He's running his cock through my wet lips below, all the way to my clit, drawing out his own form of torment and making me want to scream.

"Is this what you want, Summers?" his voice, still sounding authoritative, says before delivering a barely there kiss just below my ear. All I can do is nod, for words seem to have escaped me.

"Say it, Summers," he says in a low growl of a voice, "say you want me to fuck you hard and fast."

"Yes," I reply with a shivering breath, "do it."

But he's not done punishing me yet, for when he pushes himself into the hilt, making me shudder and lower to lie against the hood, he remains still, refusing to move as he grips hold of my shoulders and begins kissing my upper back.

"More?" he eventually asks; I can even hear the smirk in his voice.

"You know I want more," I moan as I clutch the soft fabric of his jacket inside of my fingers.

And still, he only moves at such a pace it's almost cruel. I release a whimper and he laughs, sounding low and taunting.

"I'll put you out of your sweet misery, Beatrice, all you have to do is promise that you will never, *ever*, do something so reckless again," he whispers at the same time as I clench my teeth in frustration.

"And what will you promise me?"

His laugh escapes into the dusky air right before his fingertips find my clit to begin circling and his lips attack my neck.

"Everything," he whispers, "all of me for all of you. No.One.Else."

"Good answer," I gasp as his hands find my shoulders to anchor us, just waiting for me to give him the green light with my submission. "I…promise."

And then it begins. The pace at which he begins fucking me is enough to have me clawing at his jacket. Nathaniel Carter is so much fitter than me, but holy hell, I am ready to return to the gym to get used to this kind of sex with him. This makes up for all the years of having to rely on a machine instead of the real thing. This *is* the real thing…the only thing.

"Oh, God…Nate!" I cry out as I feel my climax begin to rise to an almost painful peak. His hand returns to my clit and begins rubbing with the perfect amount of pressure to make me come before I'm ready to deal with the dizzying feeling of it taking over my entire body.

Soon after, I feel him throb inside of me before he pulls out and releases his hot cum all over my back. He pushes it up and down my skin, as though claiming me as his own. I feel like I should be disgusted, but I'm not; I'm ready for even more of his kind of filthy.

Nate holds my body still for a while before using something to wipe away his semen from my back. He then pulls me up and back against his chest, revealing the fact that he's still in his fancy shirt and suit pants, while I'm completely naked. He looks at me like he's still mad, but then I'm pulled into his embrace where I feel small, but also protected and wanted. *Needed.*

"Christ, you made me so fucking mad back there, Bea." Boss-hole Nate has left; boyfriend Nate is now the one holding me tight.

"I didn't know what else to do, Nate," I whisper, still sounding a little breathless. "No matter what Emma has done to me in the past, no one deserves to be humiliated on their wedding day. You and Ben were about to go in and announce to everyone that her new husband wanted to run away with her sister. I'm not getting stuck in a circle of lies and betrayal again."

"So, you decided to humiliate both of us in the middle of a busy hotel? I hope you don't usually go around taking off your clothes in public places."

"Of course not!" I snap, sounding irritated after having explained myself. "Believe it or not, I don't generally strip off in public, but I knew it was the only way to get your attention."

I pause to calm down and take a breath for a moment or two.

"Look, I've been on my own for years, so I'm used to

defending myself. I don't need Mr Caveman running in to save me, especially from people like Dean." He looks over my shoulder, still brooding, so I continue. "I can understand that what I did pissed you off and I'm sorry. I guess I would be pissed with you too if you stripped off in front of those bridesmaids." He looks back at me with a smile that tells me I'm finally beginning to break through his wall of anger. "I love you and I am yours, just like you are mine, right?"

With a cheesy grin on my face, he breaks into a breathtaking smile that has me reaching up to kiss him. I feel his cock twitch against my naked midriff, making me giggle.

"Can I put on some clothes? It's a little cold."

"Oh yeah, shit," he replies, looking me up and down with a raise of his brow, "kind of like you naked though."

"And I kind of love this suit on you, but we need to get back. The first dance will be soon, and I will be missed if I'm not there. After that, we can escape and get naked again."

"I like that idea," he says, looking like a naughty little devil. "You can put on some of my sweats, shower at the hotel, then…er…" He trails off, picking up my hideous dress which I take back with a grimace.

His clothes are absolutely huge on me, but they smell of him, so I enjoy wrapping them around me. As I'm trying to roll up the sleeves, he suddenly gathers me up bridal style and kisses me on the lips, smiling as he places me inside the car. He then gets into the driver's seat and begins laughing to himself at the same time as switching on the ignition.

"What?"

"Not exactly the 'I love you' kind of sex I was imagining,"

he explains, "but we can remedy that later."

"Oh, I don't know, I've weirdly missed asshole boss, Mr Carter," I tease. "He can come out now and then, can't he?"

"Oh, fuck yeah," he replies with laughter in his voice. "Though, he comes hand in hand with Mr Caveman."

"Well, he's welcome too…but only in the bedroom!" I raise my eyes to accentuate my point.

"Which bedroom would that be now?" He begins to drive down the gravel track and we're soon on the main road again. "Cos you are kind of mine now, so maybe we should think about sharing a room?"

"Hmm...I tell you what," I begin, "what if you clear out a drawer for me and I'll clear out a drawer for you?"

"For now, Summers," he relents, "but I gotta say, I'm not crazy about staying at your place with your brother being just down the hall. I think he'd kick my ass if he heard me doing what we just did."

"Fair enough," I sigh, "but he is a pilot so you can stay whenever he's on long haul. I just need to take this one step at a time, Nate."

"I know, baby," he says reassuringly at the same time as placing his hand on my knee. "But this," he says, pointing between me and him, "is a long-term thing, so don't be surprised if I gradually start moving you into my place."

And that's when I truly start believing that all the crap from my past is exactly that - my past. Nate is my future.

Chapter 29

Bea

We made the first dance by the skin of our teeth and even managed to pretend to gush with the other guests, though only when my parents are looking. After that, the night passes by far less dramatically than before, and I feel like I can manage with Nate by my side. He is finding my ridiculous dress rather amusing, especially when it rides up to my bottom, no doubt revealing the color of my panties. However, he is quick to lend a hand if my modesty is under threat. Several of Emma's bridesmaids eye him up but to my relief, he pays no attention to them. They still look shocked when they realize the great Nathaniel Carter has decided to slum it with Beatrice Summers, the slut who supposedly cheated on Dean.

Halfway through the evening, Emma approaches us with Dean by her side, dampening my good mood once again. I can't look at her without thinking about Dean's words from earlier. I still haven't worked out what to do about it, or *if* I am going to do anything about it.

"Emma, Dean, this is Nate," I announce, and they all nod at

one another.

"Congratulations," Nate says to them both, standing up tall to his full six-foot-three height. "I'm –"

"Please, every girl here knows who you are, Nathaniel Carter," Emma says with a blush and a girlish smile. "You realize every one of them had a mad crush on you back in the day."

"Er, well, nowadays, I'm a one-woman kind of guy," he says, looking at me with a gushy expression.

"I can see why," she says, "that speech was beautiful, Bea, thank you."

"And thank you for the warning."

"Sorry," she giggles, "it was Dean's idea, he only suggested it at the dinner table."

"I bet he did." I glare at him, but he seems too drunk to react in any sort of way.

"So, do you think you two might tie the knot one day?" Emma asks to which Ben almost chokes on his drink.

"Maybe," Nate replies, shocking me to my core. Even Ben raises his brow in surprise. "If she'd have me of course."

"Might I have a dance with the sister of the bride?" Dean asks, only adding to my sudden lightheadedness, particularly when everyone looks at him as though he's gone mad.

"I don't know if –" I begin, but my little sister cuts me off before I can finish my refusal.

"Oh, yes, do, Bea. Let's finally put everything in the past so we can become a happy family again. Nate, you can dance with me. You're not allowed to deny the bride on her wedding day; it's the law."

"Bea?" Nate whispers, looking uncomfortable.

"Er, ok…just one dance though," I finally reply when Emma gives me a hopeful look.

"Perfect," Dean snaps with a grin on his face.

Minutes later and we are taking up our positions on the dancefloor where a slow number just so happens to start playing for this awkward situation. I eye Nate, who looks back at me, nodding his head to tell me he's there if I need him. He gives me the courage to get whatever this is over with as soon as possible.

"Say whatever it is you need to say," I whisper next to Dean's ear, ignoring all the strange looks we're now getting. "But don't even think about asking me to run off with you again."

"What happened to our baby, Beatrice?"

His words cause me to freeze on the spot while a sickness spreads throughout my body. He pulls back to look at me with a quirk of his brow and a questioning expression. I look about me, ensuring no one can hear this. Fortunately, only Nate seems to be watching, but with concern written all over his face.

"Not here," I whisper inside of Dean's ear.

"Then where? I'm not afraid to make a scene, Bea, are you?"

He looks at me with an expression that tells me he's dead serious. I look around once more, realizing I need to keep Emma and my parents well out of this. With nothing else to go on, I walk up to Nate and Emma with a fake smile and an excuse to take Dean away from the dance floor.

"Hey, Em, I've just twisted my ankle," I lie, which Nate more than knows I'm doing.

"Oh no, do you need your man back?" she giggles.

"No, you two carry on. After all, how many nights did you dream about dancing with Nate Carter all those years ago?"

"I'd be embarrassed, I really would, but it's my wedding day so I don't care," she says as she pulls Nate back into dance. "Dean, go and get some ice for Bea's ankle, will you?"

"Sure," he says and begins walking away.

"Bea?" Nate questions, turning away from Emma so I might elaborate on what the hell is going on.

"I need you to keep her busy, please?" I practically beg. "I'll be fine, I promise."

"You have ten minutes tops," he says before kissing me. "Then I'm coming for you."

"Thank you," I reply, then pretend to hobble off, which isn't overly hard in these heels.

By the time I reach the turning circle in front of the hotel, my heart feels as though it's caught in my throat. Seeing Dean pacing around with his hand covering his mouth, waiting for me to come and explain what happened to a pregnancy I didn't think he knew about, only makes me want to throw up even more. My only saving grace is no one is about to see this, besides the odd barman, who all look far too busy to be taking any notice of us.

I slowly approach, the gravel underfoot giving away my presence, causing him to snap up straight and look at me with an expression I cannot read. I automatically wrap my arms around my ridiculous dress, then shiver as the cold suddenly hits me.

"You knew?" I ask quietly, not quite able to look him in the eye as I step toward his intimidating figure, his hands firmly placed on his hips.

"I found the test in your room; I'd been looking for a few photographs to use for a surprise I was making you for graduation," he replies sheepishly. "It was the day…"

"What day?" I ask with a horrible feeling beginning to grow inside of me.

"*That* day, Bea," he says at the same time as closing his eyes with a guilty expression.

"Wait, are you telling me you slept with Emma, in my bed, betraying me in the worst possible way, and made my life a living hell, because I fell pregnant? With *your* child?!" I charge forward and shove at his slumped body, which only confirms what I just said. Angry tears line my lashes and I have to fight the urge to strangle him with my own two hands.

"I freaked out!" he gasps, grabbing hold of my wrists to try and plead his case. "I'd gotten into college, I wanted to see the world, to live life, and there was that one little pregnancy stick threatening to tear it all away from me. I convinced myself that you had done it on purpose, tried to trick me into being yours forever, that the years of shit had made you lose your confidence, to the point where you felt you needed to trap me with the one thing that would keep me connected to you forever."

"Oh, my God!" I cry, feeling my head begin to sway with dizziness.

"Bea, do you not think I wasn't targeted for choosing you?"

he whimpers. "I was constantly being told that I could do better, that you would try and keep me by any means possible. I told them where to go, that you would never do such a thing, and then I found that stick…that *fucking* stick!"

"Oh, boo hoo!" I spit at him. "Must have been tough to be slumming it with little old me when you were constantly being told how great you were. Yeah, Dean, you had it so bad!"

"I'm not saying that, Bea, but in that moment of madness, when all I could feel is frustration over you trying to trap me when I already loved you so much…" He trails off as he steps in closer. "I felt like you had ruined everything; committed one stupid move that threatened to end everything I wanted, even us, and I wanted to hurt you for it."

"Emma?" I sob, now wiping my arm across my nose, not caring one iota about how I look right now.

"I knew you would never forgive me if I slept with Emma, that you'd set me free," he says, only sounding all the more pathetic.

"I thought you were cruel for giving into urges like some sort of dumb animal, but knowing that you were being far more calculated than that…What the fuck is wrong with you?"

"I was an idiot, a pitiful, scared little boy who didn't know what he had until he lost it," he whispers, being so close, I can see the desperation in his eyes. "I know what I did was awful, but I panicked!"

"You made my life hell after that; you joined the very people who made it their mission to bring me down. Why do that, Dean? Why stick the knife in if you had already succeeded in pushing me away?"

"I…I –"

"You didn't want to be the bad guy?" I answer for him at the same time as he begins rubbing at the back of his neck.

"No, yes, in a way," he mumbles from behind his arm. "I thought Emma would be the next best thing; I was still in love with you, Bea!"

"Oh, be still my heart!" I mock, theatrically covering my chest with my hands.

"Saying you had cheated first seemed to be the only way to stop her from panicking and breaking down on me," he splutters, only making the pain in my chest sting that little bit more. "I know how awful I was, how much I owe to you, Bea, but trust me, I know how much I need you now, how much I want you no matter what happens."

"Are you crazy?!" I snap before shoving at his chest, forcing him to fall back.

"Beatrice?" I hear Emma calling out from behind me. "What the hell is going on here?"

Dean and I simultaneously turn around to face my sister and the man walking beside her, Nate. She looks between us with a confused expression before flying over to stand beside Dean, checking him for injury before spinning around to face me again. But I'm not exactly thinking about her right now, I'm too busy trying to process everything, too busy trying not to pass out. I must look awful because Nate comes up in front of me to grab my arms and stop me from falling. Tears are streaming down my face, tears for eighteen-year-old Bea, tears for my lost baby, tears for me. Tears because of all the shit I've been trying to forget, to put behind me, and it's still here, still trying to destroy me.

"Bea? Hey, Bea, it's me," Nate says in a soothing tone of voice, placing his hands on my wet cheeks to try and make me look at him and only him. If only I had met him that night, perhaps things would have been different, and I would never have lost myself. "Tell me, baby, what did he do?"

"I didn't do anything!" Dean shouts from behind me.

"Bea, if you're just here to cause trouble," Emma begins, "then I think it best you go."

"He knew," I whimper to Nate, and he frowns, as if only half understanding what I'm saying.

"Knew what, Bea?" he asks, still keeping his voice low and calm.

"He knew I was pregnant," I gasp, "he knew I was carrying his baby…and he slept with her to get out of it, to make sure I wouldn't want him to step up."

Nate pulls me in against his chest while he looks over my shoulder at Dean, his muscles clenching with anger.

"*Baby*?" I hear Emma gasp. "What baby, Dean?"

"My baby, the one she was pregnant with when I slept with you," Dean replies without any remorse in his voice. "I was asking your sister, here, what happened to it."

"You better back the fuck off –" Nate growls in his direction but I cut him off before he can finish his threat.

"I lost it when I took a lethal concoction of vodka and painkillers," I tell him bluntly when I finally manage to turn around to face them both. "The night I left and never came back was the same night I tried to end my life. My heart stopped three times between a dirty motel and the ER. Two days after they managed to bring me back to life, I was told I'd miscarried. Does that answer your question, Dean?"

"Oh, my God!"

I turn around to the sound of my mother's voice, only to find not just her, but Ben and my father too.

Chapter 30

Nate

The next few minutes appear to happen in slow motion, as though we're wading through glue, just trying to stop a tragedy from playing out before our very eyes. We didn't though. As the blood drains from Bea's face, the horror of having her parents hear everything that happened to her, and the fact that she kept it from them for years, pushes her back into survival mode. Some people fight, some people freeze, but some people, like my girl, flee. I could have foreseen this reaction for it's what she's been doing ever since she attended my party. What I didn't foresee was a car driving through from the parking lot, building up speed as it made its way to the exit of the hotel. Neither did Bea. She stepped back into the road with a desperation to escape; only, she escaped into a place I cannot reach her.

As soon as the car makes impact with her body, she's flung forward. In the brief moment before she hits the ground, my world caves in, and I stop breathing, feeling impotent as I watch on without being able to move. It isn't until she lands with a thump on the road and the car screeches to a halt that any sound returns to my ears.

"Fuck! Bea!" I scream, finally forcing my feet to move so I can run to her side, right alongside Ben who is now yelling for her to wake up, to say something.

"Bea?" I say to her as I gently rub my thumb over the back of her hand. "Say something. Can you move?"

"Oh, my God! Oh, my God!" a woman cries, sounding hysterical. "Is she ok? Please say she's ok. She just stepped out in front of me…Oh, my God!"

"Bea, please say something," I whimper, beginning to reach my own form of hysteria the longer she doesn't answer me. "Please, baby, you have to say something!"

Her eyelashes flutter for but a moment, stilling whatever breath I have left, along with the tiny squeeze she gives my hand.

"Is…is… she ok?" she murmurs, sounding barely audible. "T-t-tell her I'm s-s-sorry…"

"She's fine, babe," I tell her, rubbing her hand reassuringly. "I think you scared the shit out of her though."

I try to laugh, and she smiles but it's soon wiped away to reveal her neutral expression, as if she is simply falling asleep. I don't know much about casualties of head trauma, but I'm pretty sure you're not meant to let them fall asleep, so I start to nudge her, with my panic returning tenfold.

"No, no, no, don't sleep, baby, stay with me!" I cry through grief, panic, and anger.

"Don't move her!" Ben says with warning in his voice. Seemingly having brushed away his relationship to her, he snaps into pilot mode and grabs her wrist, and tries to find her pulse. "It's faint, but it's there."

"B-Ben…Ben, is she going to be ok? Please tell me she's going to be ok!" Her mother is crying beside her father, looking distraught. Dean, the asshole, is standing to the side like a limp dick with his hands over his mouth. Emma, however, is on the phone, jumping into action like her brother.

"I've called an ambulance, should be five minutes," she says with determination. "They said to keep her still and to keep talking to her."

Bea moans again, her eyelids fluttering once more. I'm about to lose it, to give into despair and panic, but when I hear the sirens in the distance, I force myself to be who she needs right now.

"Hear that, baby," I say to her, "they're coming, they're coming; you're going to be fine."

By the time the paramedics arrive, Bea has well and truly lost consciousness and Ben is having to fight me off and away from her. They say things that I don't understand, all the while they rush out medical equipment.

"Who's coming with her?" one of them asks. "I only have space for one and it has to be now."

"I am," Ben and I say in unison. I glare at him and, surprisingly, he backs down, almost straight away. Before I step up onto the back of the ambulance, Emma shoves one of her rings at me.

"Tell them you're her fiancé," she explains, "otherwise, you won't be seen as close family and will have limited access."

I nod and take it before jumping into the back of the ambulance.

"What's your relationship to the patient?" the paramedic asks.

"She's my fiancée," I lie, though, I'll admit, it feels good to say it.

"She's not good, so you will need to back off and let us do our job," he warns me.

"Is she…will she…?" I can't even finish that question.

The other paramedic grabs my shoulder and looks at me as I feel the prickled heat of a tear escaping down my cheek.

"We will do all we can," she says, "she's in the best place." I'm then gifted with a pitying smile that she must have given a thousand other poor bastards in her lifetime.

By the time we reach the hospital, Bea has crashed twice, and each time I've been given a bowl so I can physically throw up. Before we even come to a complete stop, they shove the doors open and there's a small team of doctors and nurses ready to receive her. I follow at the back of them, not being able to comprehend a single thing they're saying. However, I only get so far before a nurse holds me back, telling me I can go no further, to trust them, and to wait for more news. Without anything else to do, to settle my stomach over what is happening to the woman I just declared my love for, I collapse on the floor and watch them wheel her away.

Nate

What feels like hours of pacing later, Ben and his parents arrive, all looking frantic and not at all sure how they got here. None of us can comprehend how we got here, waiting to hear news that will tell us if our girl will live. I shake that thought away as a pang of intense pain hits me in the chest over the thought of them coming out to tell us that she's gone.

Ben nods my way before marching up to the nurses' station where he tries to bark at them. They've no doubt had years of experience of telling people like him to calm down and wait patiently. To me, however, this is all so painfully new and raw. My senses still can't make sense of the smell of anti-bacterial cleaner, the bright white lights, the beeps, and alarms, as well as the tired sound of the nurse who tells Ben to sit down. He growls in protest and continues to pace up and down with aggressive stomping across the waiting area floor. As for me, I continue to sit in shock and complete numbness. I don't even feel Bea's mother as she takes hold of my hand and sits next to me. We've not even been formally introduced, and yet here we are, praying for the same outcome to this awful tragedy.

"She'll be ok," she whimpers, shaking my hand with hers, trying to convince us both of her words. "Bea is strong, she's…"

Her words trail off and a strange look takes over her red and puffy face; she's no longer sure of what Bea is, not after what she heard.

"She ***is*** strong, Mrs Summers," I tell her reassuringly. "I know what you heard but I've also known her for the past two years and I can tell you that she is very strong."

"You promise?" she whimpers, looking at me with extreme fear in her eyes.

"I swear it," I reply, squeezing her hand that little bit tighter. "She sure as hell kicked me into touch," I tell her, looking somewhat ashamed over everything from our past, but when she smiles at me, she makes me feel a little better. "And I'm so very glad she did."

"You look like you haven't aged a day, Nathaniel," she whispers. I laugh softly for I think she's glad of a little meaningless conversation while we await news that I'm not entirely sure I want to hear.

"Thank you, but I fear the laughter lines are already beginning to settle in," I tell her.

"Oh, you should always be thankful for those," she says, "they show you must be happy."

"I am with her," I admit, only to sigh when I realize my answer could soon be something to say in the past tense. She looks the same, so we decide to stay quiet for a moment or two, to try and make some kind of peace with that thought.

Shortly after, Emma and Dean march in, both looking deathly pale, both unable to look at one another.

"Oh, hell no!" I yell as I lunge toward Dean. I grab him by the scruff of his neck and throw him against the nearest wall. "Get the fuck out of here, asshole. You don't get to come and support Bea after everything you've done to her!"

"You've been in her life for five minutes, who the hell do you think you are?" Dean spits at me.

"Hey, asswipe," Ben warns him, "he's Bea's fiancé, so he gets to decide who stays and who goes, so get gone!" His response shocks me a little, and it's then that I realize I've finally gained his trust. Either that or he just hates Dean more.

"I'm not leaving until I know Bea's ok," he growls at me.

"Yes, you are," Bea's father finally speaks up from beside

us. Everyone turns to face this man who looks as though he's lost his entire life in the blink of an eye. Not only that, but he also looks as though the loss is all his fault.

"Charlie?" Dean gasps, to which Bea's father shakes his head and sighs.

"I don't know all of it yet, but from what I heard, you knocked up my daughter, then jumped into bed with my other daughter. It wasn't at all what we were told, but I should have known, should have seen what was happening to my little girl. Instead, I welcomed you into the family, believing that Bea had left you broken-hearted and that you and Emma had sought comfort in one another. I thought I was being a liberal father letting you have both of my daughters because I thought you were a good guy. After all, it wasn't your fault Bea decided to move on, and I know how much it hurt you. But to find out you were the cause of her leaving, that you pushed her to the edge with your lies, your betrayal, your selfishness? No!"

He steps back, shaking his head and clenching up his fists with white knuckle force. I can tell her father is usually a gentle giant, a man who tries to be fair and give everyone a chance. But he isn't that guy right now; right now, he's a father whose daughter has been hurt by the very man standing in front of him.

"Get.Out!" I growl through my teeth, saving him the pain of having to face what's been going on under his very roof for another moment longer.

Looking like he could still become physical with me, Dean eventually turns and leaves, not even waiting for his new wife or seeking her response in any way, shape, or form. She watches him, then glances back at her parents, then back to the door, behind which, her sister is fighting for her life.

"Daddy?" she whimpers with tears spilling over her red cheeks, leaving trails of black mascara in their wake. The old man sighs, glances at his wife, then steps up to her and wraps his arms around her shoulders, into which she collapses.

"I still love you, Emma, but I need you to go too," he says before stepping back to look at her shocked expression. I can see it's killing him to ask this of her, but I can also understand his need to not be with her right now. She betrayed Bea too.

"You're sending me away?" she whispers with pain in her voice, prompting her mother to begin crying again.

"I need you to, honey, just for now," he says, sounding choked up. "What we heard, Emma, I need time to process it, but I can't do that right now. We've always been there for you, Em, but now we need to be here for Bea, like we should have been before."

"We should have been there for her, Emma," her mother adds. "Emma, she thought she had no other option than to try and kill herself. My baby, who was so perfect, so full of life, wanted to end it all. I can't…I mean, we can't delve into all that, all of what happened between you, her, and Dean, not until I know she's going to be ok."

Emma doesn't say anything, she can't, she's too full of tears. Instead, she nods her head, attempts a smile for them, then turns to walk away. You just know she's going to break as soon as she's out of sight, so I turn to Ben, who is also looking conflicted. I jut my chin out toward the exit where Emma has just gone through. He stares at the floor for a few long moments before sighing and pacing after her. There's no denying how much Bea lost after everything, but I know how much it hurts to lose a sibling. Emma's been without hers for so long, I know this is what Bea would want Ben to do.

Chapter 31

Nate

Hours seem to pass by, but no one can move much further than the coffee machine. No one dares to drink the coffee, not since another visitor tried some and immediately spat it out again. I keep staring at my phone, expecting Cam or Callie to message me, even though I've not actually contacted them; I can't bring myself to say what's happened out loud.

"Mr Carter?" A man in green scrubs finally comes out through the double doors, his top showing flecks of blood if you look close enough. I pretend not to notice as I jump up and begin pacing toward him.

"That's me," I tell him, my hands beginning to tremble over what he might be about to tell me. "How is she? Is she--"

"She's in Intensive Care," he explains, holding his hand up to stop me from having to finish that question. I feel a wave of relief pass over me, the same one I see in Ben and his parents. "We nearly lost her a couple of times, but we managed to revive her. However, I must warn you, there was some swelling; the next forty-eight hours are critical, but if she pulls through, I'm hopeful she'll make it."

Bea's mother continues to emit muffled sobs against her husband's jacket, whereas Ben looks like he's pulling lumps of hair away from his scalp.

"Can we see her please?" I practically beg on behalf of everyone.

"You can, though I should warn you to prepare yourselves," the doctor says, "we've tried to stem the bleeding as much as possible, but in these cases, subsequent bleeding may occur." I ball my hands into fists as I listen to him talking about her like she's just meat and bones, which is completely irrational, I know, but I'm surviving on very limited patience here. "We had to remove her spleen but otherwise, everything is intact. Once we've settled her into the ICU, we'll let you know, and you can go and see her."

"Thank you, Doctor," Bea's father gasps as he shakes his hand, to which the doctor nods before heading back behind the doors of doom.

"Fuck!" Ben grits out through his teeth at the same time as running his fingers through his hair.

"Ben, keep it together, for Christ's sake! This is a hospital!" Bea's father snaps.

"Mr Carter? Mr and Mrs Summers?" a woman in uniform says as she seemingly appears out of nowhere. We all turn on her with pensive expressions that probably look angry, though it's only through grief, shock, and exhaustion.

"That's us," Bea's mom finally replies, "can we help you, Officer?"

"Hi, I'm Officer Layton, Harriet Layton," she says with a warm smile. "I just need to ask you a few questions about what happened, if I may?"

She gestures over to the chairs next to the wall, so we all go to sit down, ready to relive the horrifying moment when Bea was sent flying to the ground. She takes out a notepad and pen and begins tracking back over her notes.

"Firstly, I'm so sorry this happened to Miss Summers, my thoughts are with you. I'm here because I need to make sure there was no foul play and to see who was at fault. If we need to do any formal interviews, we'll arrange them for a later date; you must all be frantic with worry."

She pauses to assess our reactions, to which we just nod without much expression.

"I interviewed the driver, and she told me Miss Summers ran out in front of her," she explains, then looks up to face us once again. "Is that what you saw?"

"Yes," Ben voices for us. "There had been an argument and Bea was distressed; she wasn't thinking."

"I see. So, from what you saw, was there any fault on the driver's part?"

"No," I reply at the same time as I hear Bea's mother emit a muffled sob.

"We've looked at Miss Summer's history and it would seem she was brought into hospital when she was eighteen," she states, her neutral expression now turning into a frown of curiosity. "An overdose, suspected attempt at suicide?"

"Yes," Ben replies with a ghost of a voice, and I notice her father shaking his head toward the floor.

"I just wondered if this recent incident may have been another attempt to end her life."

"No, absolutely not," I reply with conviction. "This was different, and we can each give you statements that confirm this, but right now, we have other matters to deal with."

"Sure," she says with a forced smile, "here's my card. Please call when you feel able to." She hands over a card, then gets to her feet. "I hope she pulls through, and I wish you all the best."

She shuffles away with a sad smile, and I close my eyes to her retreating figure. However, they soon burst open when I hear Bea's father jump to his feet with a sigh that tells me he is getting ready to lose his shit with someone. That person appears to be his son from the way he's now glaring at Ben.

"Start talking now!"

Bea's father has always looked so placid whenever I've seen him, but right now, he looks like he could rip the entire hospital apart. He grabs hold of his son's shirt and hauls him to his feet. Ben, now taller and broader than his father, remains slack in his father's grip, but eyes him back with the same anger.

"Stop it! Stop it!" Bea's mother cries out, and in a ridiculous twist of fate, it's left to me to calm everyone down.

"Can we all just settle the hell down? The only person I give a shit about right now is fighting for her life in a hospital bed...again! Now sit down and take a damn chill pill!"

Thankfully, Ben's father releases him, and they both sit down, though it doesn't look like the subject is about to be dropped by either of them.

"This isn't my story to tell," Ben states with conviction, "and I won't betray Bea's confidence. I've kept it thus far, I refuse to talk about her behind her back."

"Don't be so childish," his father snaps, "this is serious!"

"Oh, is it now? Well, fuck me, I thought it was just a casual conversation about what the hell's been going on with your child for the last decade. How could I, the man who's been looking after her for all these years, possibly understand how serious this all is."

"Well, I'll be damned, you've been hiding huge secrets from us, and your mad with me?!"

"*Mad*? Yeah, I'm pretty fucked off, Dad. I've been taking care of that girl for years, too afraid to let myself move on in case I missed the signs all over again. Because that's what happened, Dad, we all missed the fact that she was dying on the inside."

"You should have talked to us, Ben," his mother says more softly, though it only seems to rile him up even more.

"You mean like you calling her to force her into talking to her sister who's been sleeping with the dude who knocked her up and cheated on her? Or perhaps guilt her into attending their wedding with all the bitches who bullied her in attendance? I wonder if they shared makeup tips or talked about the good ol' days."

"We didn't know what had happened, all we knew is what you all told us," Mr Summers argues, now sounding less angry and more contrite.

"Perhaps, but you still accepted a guy who had slept with both of your daughters into the family, even when Bea made it quite clear she was against it. Perhaps you should have dug a little deeper into why that was."

"We didn't know, Ben!" Mrs Summer snaps.

"Whatever, point is, this isn't my story, my fight, or my fault, so back the hell off. I'm here for Bea, no one else, like I've always been. Ask Leah, my ex, if you don't believe me."

"You and Leah broke up?" his mother gasps.

"She dumped me because I refused to move out with her," he admits sadly. "Can't blame her."

"Ben, if you had just talked to us –"

"That's it, I'm done," he huffs, getting to his feet and marching away before they can question him anymore on it. We all sit back in awkward silence, leaving him to stew on his own. After his epic bombshell, it's the least we can do for him.

"Excuse me, but are you waiting for Miss Beatrice Summers?" A young nurse comes out of the double doors to greet us. The poor guy looks tired but still manages to put on a soft smile when we all turn and nod. "She's settled into her room upstairs and if you want to, you can come and see her. Two at a time, maximum, I'm afraid."

He walks to the nurse's station, presumably giving us time to decide who's going to go up first.

"Nathaniel," her father barely whispers, "I know she's your fiancée, which is something else we didn't know about, but would you mind if her mother and I go and see her first?"

"Actually, she's not my fiancée," I clarify. I can't let him sit there thinking Bea has kept something else monumental from him. "I'm a traditional guy; I wouldn't dream of asking her without your permission first."

"My permission?" he says with a soft laugh, but the merriment doesn't reach his eyes. "It would seem I don't deserve to call myself her father right now."

Before I can attempt to reassure him with words I don't have, the nurse rescues me by coming back to ask who is going up to the ICU first.

"Her parents," I reply before anyone can say anything. Even though I am ready to kill in order to see her, I have to let them have this one. They both silently thank me as they get up to follow the nurse.

As soon as they've left, almost to the very second, Ben strolls back into the waiting area with a couple of cups of coffee from one of the chain stores from up the road. My face must give away how desperate I've been for something wet and full of caffeine because he laughs as he sits down, then offers some packets of sugar. The first mouthful hits me with the perfect hit to fool my senses into believing I'm not as exhausted as I feel. From the gasp of appreciation that leaves Ben's lips, it's fair to say he must be feeling the same way.

"She'll pull through, you know; she's done so before, she'll do it again," Ben says with determination, though all I can manage is a nod, which is more for his benefit than mine. I'm not ready to face the possibility of her not being fine; I just don't want to talk about it.

"You and Leah really broken up?" I ask to change the subject.

"We did, yeah," he says with a sad sigh, "can't blame her."

"I'm sorry," I tell him. "Not that I don't think Bea could totally take care of herself, but I asked her to move in with me. Would that not change things?"

"Really?" He looks surprised, but in a good way.

"I never believed Cameron when he told me you instantly know when you've found 'the one'. Always told him to keep his cheesy crap to himself, but now I'll have to concede that he was right. I'm ready for it with Bea, all of it."

"Well, then, if you're being sincere, you have my blessing," he says, sounding like the father figure he's been to her. "But in answer to your question, I don't think it would change things with Leah."

"Firstly, thank you, and secondly, why not?"

"Because the being 'ready for it', as you so eloquently put it, I've never felt that way with Leah. Neither has she, she recently admitted. We got together not long before Bea ran away from home. We both became honorary parents to her, or at least a big sister on her part. She's stayed with me for the same reason I've refused to move out – Bea. We both love that girl, sadly, more than we love each other."

"She is lovable, no matter how hard you try to fight it," I laugh, thinking back to my behavior when I was her boss, and how stupid I was. "You gonna stay friends?"

"I don't know," he replies with a grimace. "Surely, being friends with an ex can't be anything other than a recipe for disaster."

"Oh, I wouldn't say that. Callie is one of my best friends," I admit, "couldn't imagine her not being in my life. And I can honestly say, there's not a hint of sexual tension between us, no matter how much she likes to joke about it."

"You dated?"

"Many years ago, before I went to work at Medina," I tell him, deciding to be totally transparent about my past. "Been friends ever since."

"I bet that was fun," he says before swigging back his coffee. "She seeing anyone?"

"Why?"

"Future reference," he replies with a smirk. "Perhaps when you and Bea are living together. That's if Bea agrees to it of course. Because her turning you down is the only reason she won't, not because of any of this. Trust me, Bea's a fighter and a winner, even if she doesn't know it."

"Yeah, you're right," I tell him before settling back in my chair to await the moment I can finally go and see her.

Chapter 32

Nate

When Bea's parents finally return, all bleary-eyed and puffy cheeks, I brace myself for what I'm going to find when I finally go and face the love of my life lying in a hospital bed. Her father walks up to me and smiles sadly before patting me on the shoulder, as if silently wishing me luck. He then walks up to his son and offers him a hug, which I'm pleased to say, Ben reciprocates. I sigh heavily and begin walking toward the elevator where the same nurse from before smiles and shows me inside.

For the most part, we stand in silence, just watching the numbers light up one by one as we move up toward the upper levels of the building. They seem to move at a snail's pace, so much so, I'm overcome with a sudden urge to get to her. My feet begin to rock back and forth at the same time as I fist my hands. Panic descends on me; the confines of this metal box making me sweat and lose my breath. I'm about to freak out when the doors open to finally let us out. I make a hasty exit before emitting a long-held breath.

"You ok?" the nurse asks as he places a hand over my

shoulder. "She'll just look like she's sleeping."

Being grateful for his reassurance, I nod and straighten myself up, putting on a show of confidence, even though I feel anything but. He smiles with sympathy, and we begin walking down the long corridor of machines that are hooked up to patients in their private rooms. Loved ones are huddled over their sleeping bodies; some with tears, some with long sighs, some passed out through sheer exhaustion. The fact that I'm here to see Bea seems surreal; it's like I'm watching this on a TV screen.

"She's in here," the nurse declares as he gestures into a room in front of us.

I follow his arm into the room to see her hooked up to breathing apparatus, tubes, and beeping machines. A whole load of stuff of which I have zero understanding. It smells clinical and is so overpowering, I can no longer smell her usual scent of coconut shampoo. Her skin looks sallow, devoid of any color, apart from the deep purple bruising and crimson cuts from her superficial wounds. I take special note of her chest rising up and down in exaggerated movements because the machines are doing it for her. It's only when I look at her small, delicate hands, that I know it's really her. I reach for one and curl my warm fingers around her cold ones. There's no reciprocation, no pressure, and it's the final thing to force tears to fall down my cheeks.

Kneeling before her bed, I rest my forehead against her soft skin. I half expect her to run her fingers through my hair, but I feel nothing. When I finally force myself to stand and find the chair next to the bed, I notice the nurse has already left us to be alone.

"Hey," I say out loud, and it feels underwhelming, but it's all I can give her right now. "Summers, I'm so mad at you right now. We should be back at my place." I swallow hard, trying to stop myself from breaking, even though I know the moment when I lose hold of myself is coming soon. "We'd be naked." I laugh softly, but I'm not feeling it at all. "I'd have my wicked way with you and then chew your ear off about moving in with me." No answer. Just the beeping of the machines next to us. "Which you will be, by the way. No arguments," I tell her firmly as I grasp hold of her hand a little harder. "Please talk to me, Bea," I beg her in a whisper, "I've never loved anyone like you, no one. You can't leave me now, you just can't." I finally give into my grief and let the tears fall without restraint. "If you go, you have to take me with you."

A heavy hand falls over my shoulder and I instantly know who it belongs to. I'm not sure how he talked his way up here, but ever the businessman, he must have done some clever dealing or flirting with whoever was behind the desk. I stand and face him like a little boy seeking comfort after he's hurt himself, but I don't care, because right now, I'll take my big brother's affection with my pride intact. He holds me close as I release gut-wrenching sobs over his shoulder.

"Don't let me hear you talking like that, Nate," he lectures me when we finally part. "You'll both get through this, so stop with the whole 'taking me with you' crap!"

I sigh, flopping back into the chair next to my girl. I then clutch hold of my eyes between my fingers, grateful for the sting of my tips pressing into my sockets.

"I can't lose her, Cam," I say determinedly. "I don't want to be without her anymore, to go back to being someone without her. I wasted so much time being a dick, and now that I've got her, I might lose her again. Is this my punishment?"

"Fuck, no! Drop the heavy shit, Nate, we've already had

more than enough of that over the last week or so, and Bea doesn't need it either." He scrapes over a spare chair from the hallway and sits next to me. He also looks exhausted after the emotional hell ride this week has been.

"We both look like crap," I tell him, even managing a soft chuckle, only to feel guilty for it.

"Lily's pregnant," he says with a smile he can't help emitting. "But you don't know that, right?"

"Sure," I reply with almost as big a grin as his before shaking his hand with genuine happiness for them both. "How far along?"

"A couple of months. She's not showing or anything yet, but we've heard the heartbeat," he says with a cheesy grin all over his face. "It was amazing!"

I look at the bed while contemplating what it would be like to have that with Bea, but then I realize there's a real possibility that we might not get the chance to have that happy ever after. Cam tucks something into my hand, a small ring box that looks slightly battered from years of wear and tear.

"Mom told me to give this to you," he says with a knowing smile, "for when you guys are ready."

When I open it, I see Mom's sapphire ring sparkling up at me. It brings a mixture of emotions to the surface, and I find myself crying like a baby again. Cam chuckles softly beside me, so I flip him the bird and try to ignore him by placing the ring on Bea's finger.

"It fits," I whisper to her sleeping body.

"Yeah, best to ask a girl when she's conscious though,"

Cam murmurs in the background.

"That's *if* she wakes up," I reply with a sigh and a stabbing pain running all the way through me.

"*When* she wakes up," he corrects me as he clasps his hand over my shoulder again.

Feeling hopeful for the first time since seeing her in this state, I stare fondly at Bea's finger, still sporting the ring I've just placed on it.

Nate

Over the next day or two, I practically move into Bea's room. I'm on first-name terms with all the nurses and have made it my mission to bring in sweet treats on a daily basis. Bea's out of the forty-eight-hour critical zone, but there has been no change in her condition. I talk to her all the time and only ever leave her side to sleep or to allow others in to see her. Ben is often here with me, but he's still got to work. I'm only working if I can do so remotely, which is another perk of working for my big brother.

On the Monday following the accident, I'm making my way down the familiar path to her room, where I find a sorry-looking brunette sitting beside her. Almost a carbon copy of her sister, but with curlier hair. Of course, I know who she is, and I'm glad she's left her piece of shit husband behind, but I can't help wondering what to say to her. Apart from dancing with her at the wedding, we've never spoken.

After a while of silent contemplation, I purposefully cough from the doorway, prompting her to jump and turn around to face me. From the worried look on her face, I think she's expecting me to throw her out, so I offer her a small smile of reassurance. Her shoulders slump, as if feeling relieved.

"Hi," she says awkwardly, "do you mind me being here?"

"She's your sister; you probably have more right to be here than I do," I tell her at the same time as taking the seat on the other side of Bea's bed.

"I'm not her sister, not after what I did to her," she says sadly, and we fall into a few moments of quiet reflection.

"Can I ask you something?" I venture. "You can tell me to mind my own business."

"Why did I do what I did?" She blushes as she takes hold of her sister's hand. "It will always be the biggest regret of my life. I didn't know the full facts when I went to bed with Dean. I was so in love with him, I just went along with the lies he told me." I lean in closer, hoping she'll elaborate. "He told me she had been sleeping with his best friend; that he had caught her in the act when he went to see her a few hours earlier. He then said he was surprised when he had felt nothing when he saw them, that he had always been in love with me."

"But you must have had your doubts. You knew Bea better than anyone, surely it sounded out of character for her."

"I was young and naïve and had been pining for my sister's boyfriend for the past year. I had been swimming in guilt, hurt, and obsession, for what felt like forever. When he began kissing me, it was like a surreal situation, seemingly my dream coming true and, regrettably, I didn't take the time to think about it. I didn't think about how my actions were a complete betrayal to my sister. Kissing led to touching, touching led to…well, you know. It didn't even register with me that we were in Bea's bedroom. I had just heard him rummaging around in there so had gone in to see who it was." She lets out a long, painful groan before releasing a tear down her face, which she angrily swipes away. "I swear I didn't know about her pregnancy or attempted suicide. I just thought she had decided to get away from it all and move in with Ben. Had I known, I would never have stayed with him."

"You sure about that?" I ask, probably sounding judgmental, but how can I not be?

"I deserve that," she says with a shy smile and nod of her head. "I'm not trying to pretend I was anything but selfish back then, a truly terrible sister, however, I want you to know that as soon as we got back home on Saturday, I told him it was over. I've already sought legal advice. For all that I threw away for him, he didn't even try to fight me on it."

"I'm sorry," I tell her, trying to sound sincere because I am. No matter what happened in the past, she's been screwed over by him too.

"It's no less than I deserve," she admits as she strokes back a lock of her sister's hair. "I have so much to make up for, so many changes to make."

"Well, I'm glad you know the truth," I offer, "it sucks now, but it sounds like you are so much better off without him. Imagine learning about all this with kids. And, if it helps, I get how crazy being in love with someone can be, especially when you don't allow yourself to be with them. *Believe* me."

"And I'm glad she found you," she says with a genuine smile. "The whole world and his dog wanted to be with Nathaniel Carter, the popular boy with a heart, and he chose my big sister. Lucky you."

"Hmm…" Bea releases the sweetest sound, making us both

jump up with expectation and excitement. She doesn't make any other sound, but Emma is already running out to get someone who knows what they're doing.

"Say it again, baby," I plead as I grip hold of her hand, "please…for me?"

The nurse rushes in with a doctor quickly following behind her. She gets out a long needle-looking object and begins to poke at various patches of skin on her body. Meanwhile, the nurse is checking all her vitals. They keep looking for a response but it's not until he reaches her toe that she twitches against it. At the slightest movement, we all immediately look up at the doctor with desperation and held breaths.

"Good news," she finally says to us, "she's beginning to come out of her coma. We'll keep monitoring her, but hopefully, it won't be long before she shows us more signs of waking up."

I pepper Bea with kisses over her forehead while Emma begins to sob from the other side of the bed. I've never felt such relief, such hope, that everything will be ok.

"Well done, baby," I say as I lean into her, "keep waking up for me."

Chapter 33

Bea

My senses are dulled but I can hear the muffled sound of voices all around me, accompanied by a shock of bright light stinging at my eyes. I keep dreaming that I'm up and ready for work but then I find myself back in bed again. It's exhausting and I'm going to be late. After a while of this happening on repeat, I can't work out if I'm awake or not. Whatever is happening, the sensation is not pleasant, and I wish I could just get up and stay up.

After what feels like such a long time, a face suddenly looms in front of me, but I'm not sure who it is. In my head I think it must be Cameron because I'm at work…or am I?

"Mr Carter?" I mumble but I can't be sure if the words have come out right. "Do you need coffee?"

The figure makes a muffling sound that could be laughter, but again, I'm not sure. I try to get up, but blackness begins to consume me, and I soon fall under it.

Nate

"NATE!" Cam hollers down the hall for me after I've literally just escaped to go to the bathroom. "Quick! Get in here!"

I run as fast as I can, ignoring the angry stares of hospital staff and visitors. I offer apologies but still pelt it down the linoleum floor to get to my brother.

"Nate, she just said something; something about getting me a coffee," he all but yells, beaming as I lean over her, trying to get her to respond to me.

"Bea, baby, say something to me, anything," I beg, but she says nothing. I try in vain for a little while longer, but end up slumping in my chair, vowing not to go to the bathroom until she wakes up.

"Don't look so disheartened, Nate," Tamara, one of the nurses, says with a grin, "these are all good signs, be patient."

I let out a groan like a frustrated little toddler, but she just laughs at me.

"I hate you," I pout at Cam, all the while he smiles smugly in my direction.

"Hey, I've always been the one to have an effect on the ladies," he says with a casual shrug. "Some of us are born with it; some of us aren't!"

"Oh, you're a bad man." Tamara grins at him. "Cute, but so bad!"

"Don't tell my wife that," he chuckles, "she's pregnant and oh, so hormonal. Why do you think I'm here with this miserable bastard?"

She lets out a loud laugh before sauntering off down the corridor.

"Ass," I retort, then return my attention to Bea, who

continues to sleep soundly.

Nate

I don't remember falling asleep, but I do know it's one of the most peaceful ones I've had since all of this happened. I dream I'm at work, all routine, all normal, and Bea is sitting at the desk with me. I'm rambling on and on about God knows what while she writes it all down on her tablet, only stopping to look at me every now and then. After what feels like a long time, she looks up and beams at me, literally taking my breath away. I stare at her, not realizing that she's reaching out to take hold of my hand.

"Nate?"

I wake with a start, feeling disorientated and confused. I stare at the woman who is now stirring in front of me, though it takes me a while to realize that this is actually happening; this is real. Her delicate features pinch together when she tries to speak, as though she has a sore throat, the type that burns.

"Nate?"

When my senses finally return, and I believe this is reality, not my dream, I rush to her side and grip hold of her hand with everything I've got. I place my lips on her forehead and hold the back of her head as softly as I can. When I finally pull back, she reaches up and weakly places her hand on my cheek. It's got to be about the best feeling I've ever had.

"Hey, baby," I whisper, noticing her poor eyes wincing against the light. "Oh, thank God, you're here, you're really here!"

She looks at me like I'm insane, especially with tears spilling down my cheeks. I take in her consciousness, feeling so overcome with emotion that she's finally coming back to life.

"Mm," she moans, closing her eyes as she tries to talk, but it must be difficult for her.

The nurse comes in after I've pressed the 'call' button and does the usual checks, all the while grinning between Bea and me.

"Can she have a drink?" I ask.

"Is that what you want, honey?" the nurse asks her, to which Bea nods at the same time as clutching hold of her throat. "Just sip it…here, use the straw."

Bea sips at the water gratefully, before leaning back onto her pillow. She appears to be a little disorientated but then turns to look at me with the most beautiful smile I've ever seen. I beam as I grip hold of her hand, feeling beyond excited by the pressure of her fingers as she gifts me with a gentle squeeze.

"I'm sorry," she whispers to me with a crackly voice, "I guess I flipped a little."

"You remember what happened?" I smile at her, and she nods, only to find the movement too much to bear. She closes her eyes and winces through the pain.

"How long have I been out of it?" she asks with her eyes still shut tightly.

"Four days," I tell her. "Bea, I was so frightened I'd lost you. I love you so much, please don't scare me like that, ever again."

I bring her hand to my lips and begin kissing it over and over.

"Four days? Wow," she says with her voice beginning to

slur. "I love you…"

She passes out and I begin having heart palpitations; the steady beeping noise of the machine is the only thing keeping me vaguely calm.

"Relax, Mr Carter," the doctor says as she enters the room, "she's going to find these episodes pretty tiring, so be prepared for her to fall back to sleep. Her waking should get longer, but for now, be thankful she's waking at all."

"Jeez, you're going to have to set up a bed for me because my heart's going to give out after all of this." With relief washing over me, I slam my face inside my hands. The nurse and doctor laugh at my inability to play it cool. "I'm going to update her parents, excuse me."

Nate

It's been over a week since Bea woke up and her episodes of being awake are getting longer and longer. There doesn't seem to be any lasting damage to her, besides her missing spleen, and they've even started talking about her getting out of here. I've already told her she's coming home with me, but I think I need to drive the point home. She says she doesn't want to put me out and begins rambling on about having to take care of an invalid.

"I've only just started going to the bathroom by myself," Bea argues, "I can't sit at your house all day doing nothing. Especially as you'll be returning to work. I can't expect you to then come home and cook and whatnot."

"Oh, baby, I have someone for all that," I tell her, which doesn't seem to be a good argument, for she merely rolls her pretty blue eyes at me.

"Look, Nate, I love that you want to take care of me, but I can't ask that of you." She smiles before taking hold of my hand and bringing it up to her cheek, which will always feel warm after having felt it when she was stone cold. "I'm an awful patient."

Don't I know it! She's incredibly impatient and often ends up arguing with everything and everyone. Then she feels guilty and becomes emotional.

"I know that," I tell her truthfully, earning me a hard stare. "But you're mine, and I want to take care of you. Who do you think has been by your side each day and night?"

"That's different," she mutters.

"How so?"

"Because I had no control over that," she huffs.

"Well, I guess you have no control over this either," I argue. She opens her mouth to argue, but when no words come out, I simply plant a quick kiss on her lips, a kiss that soon turns a bit too passionate for a hospital. She grips hold of the back of my head and leans further and further into me, so much so, I have to chuckle into her mouth. "Frustrated, babe?"

"Having you here fussing over me, showing me how much I mean to you; I'm sooo frustrated," she whispers with eyes that tell me how hungry she is. My cock involuntarily shifts inside my pants. As much as we want this, it makes me nervous because I don't know how safe it is to engage in any of that stuff, so I force myself out of her grip. She groans with irritation as I back away. It's a good thing too because right at that moment, Cam walks in with the doctor following behind him.

"So, the good news is we can let you get out of here," the doctor beams and I hear Bea clapping her hands with excitement from beside me. “Have you decided where you’ll be going?”

“My place, I’ll leave the address-”

“Wait up,” Bea interrupts, “Doctor, how soon can my boyfriend and I…you know?” She then actually winks at her!

“Holy shit, Beatrice!” I gasp with complete embarrassment; all the while, Cameron begins belly laughing. The bastard then walks over and holds his fist out for her to bump.

“Well, I can’t really answer that, you need to let your body guide you, Beatrice. You’ve been through a massive trauma, but you’ll know when you’re ready. So long as you begin gently and don’t push things,” she replies matter of factly. “Your stitches come out tomorrow so you should be fine.”

“Really?” I ask, suddenly sounding much more interested in the conversation. She nods at me like I’m an idiot for asking her to repeat herself.

“I’ll be at his place then,” Bea replies, and we high five-each other. “So, when can I get out?”

“How does tomorrow sound?” The doctor smiles and I literally fist-bump the air.

Bea

Nate drives me back to his place, the whole time fussing and treating me as though I’m a newborn baby or something as equally as precious and fragile. He flusters over me as I exit the car by myself, but I’m after one thing and one thing only. I don’t know what’s come over me, but I need him right now. As soon as I enter the house, I’m heading straight for the staircase with him in tow. I can't say my sexy walk is anything to write home about but seeing as I recently got hit by a car, I'm not exactly up to much more than what I'm giving him.

"Bea, babe, can I get you a drink?" Nate begins asking as I lead him by the hand and up the stairs.

"Nope!"

"Don't you want to unpack first?" he asks, laughing at my less-than-subtle behavior.

"Nope!"

"Is there anything I can get you?"

"Nope!"

I march him right into the bedroom where I spin around and wrap my arms around his neck, practically slamming my lips against his. I guess he's finally given in too, for he drops my handbag where he is and wraps his hands around the small of my back. His tongue is soon swiping through my lips to make our kiss more intimate, stroking and caressing me as he gently picks me up to carry my fragile, recovering body the rest of the way to the bed.

"God, I've missed you," he says against my lips while I continue kissing him, "I can't wait to be inside of you."

He moans against me as I grind against his hips, being careful not to upset my bandaged wound. I immediately begin unbuttoning his shirt, after which I quickly move onto his jeans where I literally tear the fly apart. I grab hold of his firm heat and begin kissing down the side of his neck while he enjoys the sensation of me rubbing up and down his length. I don't bother removing his shirt or my clothes, I simply release his cock, hitch up my skirt, and move my panties to one side so he can enter me without upsetting any of my injuries. Doctor's orders.

"Fuck, Bea, what the hell has gotten into you?" he gasps, sounding like he is more than enjoying whatever it is that has got into me.

"You, hopefully," I reply with a long breath, feeling desperate for him. "I'd straddle you right now, but I'm not sure that's the 'gentle' the doctor recommended."

My words seem to push away any reluctance he might have had, as he quickly crawls between my legs and begins to slide in deep. We both moan when he enters me, and I'm soon thrusting my hips up for more. He moves gently, as though I'm a virgin again, so I wrap my legs around his waist and use my feet to push him into me. He laughs and takes the hint to move harder, faster, all the while gripping hold of my hands above my head. I writhe underneath him as the building crescendo of an orgasm mounts up within me, the whole time holding eye contact with one another. He flinches and I can tell he's getting close.

"I love you so much, baby," he whispers, his eyes turning even more intense than before. "Marry me."

We both release together and it's beyond words. I've never felt this way about someone before, and I don't believe I ever will again…but marriage? He slowly lowers his body down to the side of me and buries his face into the crook of my neck, kissing me gently while stroking my skin with softness.

"Well?"

"Wait, what?!" I gasp, still trying to process what he's just asked me.

"I meant to do it more romantically, but I guess the mood took over me." He smiles softly, cupping my face gently as he does so. "It can be a long engagement, we can live for a while first, but please, wear my ring, Bea."

"C-can I think about it?" I ask nervously. I don't want to upset him or think that I'm turning him down, but I don't want to rush into this, not after everything. "I'm not saying no, honestly, I just –"

"Bea, I expected this answer," he says with his grin still shining through, looking wide and genuine. "So long as you say yes in the end, then I'll be happy. So, so happy."

"I'm not moving back to Ben's place, am I?" I ask with a soft laugh while he plays with my fingers.

"Doesn't look that way," he replies. "But at least we can make this place ours. It's a little generic, don't you think?"

"Well, I didn't want to say anything," I admit with a teasing smile. "And you, Nathaniel Carter, are anything but generic. I love you, you one of a kind."

"And I will always love you, Beatrice, one-day-to-be, Carter."

Chapter 34

Bea

It takes me a while to have the courage to acknowledge the fact that we've arrived. I've been putting this off for nearly ten years, but I can no longer do that. I can't pretend it never happened. Emma and Dean have separated, Mom and Dad are frantic with worry over their family, and Ben has lost his long-term girlfriend. He might try to ease my guilt by saying I kept them together for longer if anything, but I can no longer ignore a past that has affected each of our lives. Our family is at the point of being broken beyond repair. This meeting will either set us on the road to fixing things, or it might destroy us completely.

"Bea," Nate eventually says, placing his hand over my knee, "you sure you're up to this?"

"No," I reply bluntly, "but I need to do it anyway."

"I will not leave your side and if I think we need to have a break, I'll tell everyone, including you," he says with a telling look. I guess he's learning just how stubborn I can be.

"Ok," I reply before taking a deep inhale. "Listen, I need

to grab something from my old room; you think you could get them all to sit down together?"

"Sure," he says with a reassuring smile that has me wanting to say yes to marriage, even though I have promised myself that we'll get this over and done with before I seriously consider his proposal. That and I've told him he needs to survive living with me for at least three months before I say yes.

"Ok," I tell him with a sigh, knowing I can't put this off any longer. "Let's get this over with."

Nate grips hold of my hand the whole time it takes to walk up my old home's garden path, still with the chipped paving slab that always catches my attention. Last time, the sight of it had brought me comfort, a momentary pause to put off seeing Dean playing house with my sister. Now, it only makes me feel anxious over how my family is going to react to hearing the truth of everything that happened all those years ago. Nate seems to sense my trepidation and delivers a quick kiss to the top of my head, after which he whispers, "You've got this".

For the first time in nearly a decade, I use my key and walk inside, not because it feels like home, but because I want to walk in on my own terms. Almost as soon as Nate closes the door behind him, Ben walks through the living room with a solemn expression. I nod in greeting before turning to Nate, silently asking him to give me the time I had asked for only moments ago.

"Do what you need to," he says after kissing my temple, "everyone else can wait."

"It won't take me long," I tell him truthfully, then turn to head up to my room.

As always, I pause at the door, bracing myself to see what I always see when I walk inside of my old room. Dean's muscular back moving back and forth as he braces himself over my little sister. The positive pregnancy test hidden behind a photo frame on my dressing table. The computer that held such terrible secrets, I couldn't resist looking, even if what it said pushed me further and further inside of myself.

"That's it, baby, feel me inside of you, feel all of me..."

"I love you, Dean, I've always loved you, but Bea –"

"Is not half as good as you, Em, not half as beautiful, not half as sexy..."

As I flinch over the image of them, I make my way over to the bottom drawer of my old desk. My computer still sits on top, looking practically antique, who knows if it even works anymore. I doubt my parents have ever tried to switch it on since I left. No matter, I was so obsessed with torturing myself after what happened, I had printed it all off and kept it in a file. A little bedtime reading to remind me of how much I was hated, how little I meant to everyone other than Ben and my mom and dad.

After one last look around the room that was my own prison once upon a time, a torture chamber, I make my way down to the living room where everyone is waiting for me. There's no talk, no laughter, nothing that reminds me of the happy childhood that I once had. After I give them this, tell all to those who I care about the most, I hope to remember that childhood once more.

"Bea, honey, it's so good to see you walking around again," Mom smiles at me, even though she's anxious, I can tell. She moves to stand, but I put my hand up to stop her. I need this to be done; I can't drag it out a moment longer.

"Bea?" Dad questions me with a frown across his

exhausted face.

"This is going to happen once, now, then I never want to speak about it again," I explain, trying to sound authoritative, even though I'm just as scared as they are. "I thought I could hide it forever, take it all to my grave, apart from Ben and Nate. And it's not because I don't trust you, or don't love you, it's because I didn't want to see the hurt that I can already see on your faces. I wanted to forget it all, move on, and reinvent myself. But after nearly a decade of holding everything in, I've finally realized that it's a part of me. It helped shape the person I am today."

"Bea, I wish –" Mom tries to cut in, but I stop her once more.

"If I'm going to live through it all again, to admit to things I really wish I didn't have to, as well as make all of you feel uncomfortable, you need to let me just get it out, Mom."

"Ok," she mouths, pretending to lock her lips shut, to which I try to smile in thanks.

"This is how it started," I finally admit, even to Nate and Ben, who have never seen the extent of what was being said about me. Emma saw some of it, but the worst of what was said was through private messaging or chatrooms that someone had added me to. I hand out sheets of paper with reams of insults, threats, and vile lies about me. I say nothing, just let them read, take it all in, just like I had to once upon a time.

For a while, I sit on the edge of my seat, with my eyes remaining shut, even when I hear my mother beginning to cry, my father muttering curses under his breath, and Nate clutching hold of my hand in support.

"I had no idea it was this bad, Bea," Emma whimpers.

“Me neither,” Ben mutters angrily.

“Why didn’t you tell anyone?” Mom asks the obvious.

“Beatrice, we could have gone to the principal, had this sorted out, and held these horrible, vile sons of bitches to account!” Dad snaps with frustration.

“It didn’t start out this badly,” I try to explain, “and I thought it didn’t bother me; I actually took pride in the fact that I could brush it all off. Dean said to ignore it, that it was just girls being mean. I felt silly and dramatic, so I pretended it didn’t bother me as much as it did. It built up gradually over the years. By the time I realized it was as bad as it was, I already felt isolated, and part of me…part of me started to believe them.”

“*Believe them*?! Bea, one bitch says you once cornered her in the bathroom and started stripping and playing with yourself. Another one says you had chlamydia when you were only thirteen years old. And then a guy, who I’d happily like to dismember, claims you had let him and his friends have ‘every hole, in every position.’ What the fuck, Bea?!” Ben cries in outrage, and I realize I’m already crying.

“It’s hard to explain,” I tell him truthfully and with Nate now wrapping his arm around my shoulders. “But that’s how I felt all the same.”

“Why did you keep looking, Bea? Why didn’t you just switch it all off? And why did you keep records of it?” Dad asks with curiosity.

“To begin with, I thought I’d rather know,” I explain, “I’d rather know why they were whispering about me, why I was being pointed at, so I could prepare myself. But then it became ‘addictive’, for want of a better word. Sonia, my therapist, told me that it was 'age-appropriate', that it's natural for teenagers to seek out whatever acceptance they can find, be it in real life or online. Unfortunately, after what happened between Dean and Emma, I felt more alone than ever."

I look at Emma, who physically curls into herself, trying to look small and inconspicuous. I can see how much guilt she feels, and how much she is also hurting, and it's not pleasant to watch.

"Emma, I promise I'm not saying any of this to get at you. I know how bad you feel, and I've learned to forgive you after everything because life's too short. It's one of the many reasons why I don't want to ever bring this up again. I want us to move forward."

"How can you possibly forgive me, Bea?" she cries, and just as I used to when we were kids, I rush over to hold onto her shuddering body. It feels nostalgic, like all the times she used to crawl into bed with me when there was a storm outside. "I will never forgive myself for what I did to you."

"I can only offer you mine, Emma," I tell her with soothing strokes of her hair. "You must learn to find your own forgiveness."

"I swear I didn't know you were pregnant, Bea," she whispers as she looks up at me, and I realize everyone is now looking at me to elaborate on the next part of my sad story.

"Dean and I were always careful, but I suppose accidents happen," I murmur with shame. "I can't have been too far gone. When I finally plucked up the courage to tell him, I walked in to see…"

"Oh, God," Emma whimpers, covering her face with her hands while she shudders against me.

"What I didn't realize was Dean had found the test, freaked

out, and orchestrated the whole betrayal to try and get out of his responsibilities. Told me that if he couldn't have me, he would have Emma instead."

"I'm gonna kill him!" Dad shocks us all by getting to his feet in outrage, his normal calm persona gone within an instant.

"Charlie, please, sit down!" Mom snaps, chastising him like a little boy. "Let Bea finish, this is hard enough for her as it is, and we did agree to listen before doing or saying anything."

"Can't believe I let him in this house or gave him my blessing…"

He trails off while I brace myself to admit what happened with Evan, a married man.

"He made up shit about me to keep everyone on his side, meaning our mutual friends, such as they were, and Emma."

"I should never have believed him, Bea, I shall forever regret it," Emma rushes out, but I simply smile and take a breath to go on.

"Things became significantly worse after that. On the day of Nate's party, I came home to find you both kissing, as if me and him had never been anything. I was going out of my mind with worry, being pregnant and all, so I took Ben's car and drove. I didn't know where I was going, but I knew I was getting away from it all…or so I thought. I stopped at a convenience store, saw some kids from Nate's school, and heard he was having a party. All you needed was a bottle of booze and you'd be in. It seemed like the perfect getaway from it all, so I grabbed three bottles of vodka, and some packets of painkillers for the morning after, and made my way over. I was already slurring my words and wobbling all over the place when I got there. I remember talking to some guy in a suit, his appearance seemed surreal, like a dream. He was nice, charming, and comforting. He took me to a room upstairs, and I let him. But then he started kissing me and it felt wrong. I thought I was fighting him off, but I couldn't tell you for certain. I became exhausted from fighting him, so I passed out. When I eventually came to, he was on top of me…pushing inside of me…releasing himself inside of me."

"Oh, Bea," my mother whimpers at the same time as Nate comes over to wrap his arms around me.

"After he was finished, he told me he was married and had to get home to his family. I remember feeling so sick, so ashamed, that I ran from that room, half-dressed and with tears streaming down my face. Of course, kids from our school were there and took to messaging straight away. After that, the beeping of notifications coming through became deafening. I drove, knowing that I shouldn't have, I was way over the limit and feeling completely irrational, but at this point, I no longer cared. The gas got low so I pulled over to the nearest, sleaziest motel I could find, for I knew I didn't deserve anything better and rented a room. The beeping continued and I ended up reading all of it, all of the hateful words, all of the rumors, all of the sleaze, to the point where I became dizzy with it. I couldn't even focus for the fog of all the words, the bad memories, and the desperation I felt. But then someone posted something, a simple instruction, something that could end it all. It simply said, 'Bea Summers, you should just kill yourself.'"

My mother falls against my father while Ben jumps up to begin pacing around angrily. He's heard all this before, but it still riles him up.

"It felt like such a relief, to have someone make a decision for me, to have a way out of everything. I'm ashamed to say the fact that I was pregnant was no longer a part of my muddled thoughts. After a few hours of drinking vodka and taking painkillers, I felt almost out of it - death would soon come to take me away. So, I decided to phone Ben to say goodbye, to wish him well in life, and to let everyone know I was ok with dying because I'd finally be free."

"Why didn't you call us, Ben?" Dad asks, though he doesn't sound angry this time, he sounds more curious than anything else.

"Bea's phone call was very disjointed, so I knew she'd done something stupid. When I asked her what she'd done, she broke down into floods of tears, begging me not to call anyone. She'd only tell me where she was if I swore not to tell you or Emma. I called the emergency services, and tried your phone once or twice, but I guess you guys were asleep. When Bea eventually came around, and the doctor explained about the baby, she told me everything. Mom, she trusted me to bear all. After what she'd tried to do to herself, I felt like I couldn't risk losing that trust. I had to be her everything, even if meant keeping things from the rest of you."

He sighs sadly, looking suddenly exhausted. The guilt's hitting all of us hard, none more so than me.

Mom says nothing, just stares at him with an unreadable expression; she could easily lose her temper or take him into her arms like she did when he was a small boy.

"I owe Ben my life, Mom," I tell her with conviction, making him sink even further in his seat.

"We're proud of you, Ben," she says with a smile that's soon going to turn into a sob. "I'm so proud of everything...***everything*** you've done to keep Bea going, thriving, and making it through what she did. If it wasn't for you then she wouldn't..."

She trails off as Ben crosses the room with two giant strides and takes her into his arms, the both of them crying and offering the other unconditional love. My father soon joins them, and I take the moment to watch Ben getting what he's so desperately needed since that awful night.

"You ok?" Nate whispers to me, kissing the back of my hand with what feels like reassurance. I nod with only a semblance of a smile, for I'm not sure I'm being entirely honest.

"I'd miscarried, killed my baby, slept with another woman's husband, and condemned Ben to be forever scarred by what he saw and heard that night."

"Beatrice, don't ever say that," Ben says as he wipes tears away from his face, "we're family, and you needed me. I will always be there for you, no questions asked. I love you, Bea."

"I love you," I cry as I go to him and wrap my arms around him so tightly, it reminds me of how much I had leaned on him in those first few months afterward.

"So, where do you want to go from here, baby girl?" Mom asks as she too wipes away her tears.

"I want it all to end, once and for all," I tell them determinedly. "No more anger, no more guilt, no more blame. I want us to be a family again; I want to forgive everything," I admit, turning to face Emma with a genuine smile. "That's if you can all forgive me," I continue, now looking at Ben.

"Sounds like a plan, baby girl," Mom smiles with relief.

"Agreed," Dad says softly before bringing me in for one of

his warm, papa bear hugs, the type I always craved as a child.

Ben simply nods with a smile and a kiss on the top of my head. However, when I turn to face Emma, she doesn't look so sure.

"I'm scared, Bea," she says with a whimper, "I'm scared of never being able to forgive myself. I hurt all of you. I was so desperate to be noticed, to be accepted, to have this great romance, I hurt the most important person in my life."

"You did hurt me, Emma," I tell her bluntly, breaking away as I go to where she's huddled over with fresh tears in her eyes, "but I forgive the Emma from nearly ten years ago. As for the Emma who is sitting before me now, I really want to get to know her again."

"Really?" she asks with a smile creeping through her tears.

"Really," I reply. "You were my sister and my best friend once, before Dean. Let's not let him win, not after everything."

"Then I want that too," she says, all the while clinging onto me as if her life depends on it.

Bea

A few hours later, Nate and I are sitting in his car getting ready to go. The emotions of today have virtually wiped me out and I am more than ready to curl up on our new couch with a glass of wine and a half-naked boyfriend. Things will take a while to return to what we once were, but at least my family is on the road to recovery. With that thought in mind, I take hold of Nate's hand to stop him from starting the car. He turns to face me fully and smiles with warmth and affection.

"Thank you," I tell him, which only causes him to frown at me, seeking further explanation. "You've made me happy again, and if it wasn't for that, I wouldn't have been able to forgive Emma, or myself."

"Bea, you're not the only one who finally feels happy," he says, brushing away the hair from my face. "I can't imagine being with anyone else."

"Me neither," I tell him as I cover his hand with mine. "Which is why I'm going to blow caution to the wind that has always stopped me from taking any kind of risk."

"You are?"

"I am," I giggle with nervous anticipation. "Nate Carter, I'm finally ready to answer your proposal; my answer is yes."

"Yes?" he gasps with pure excitement pumping through his entire body. "*Yes?!*"

"Yes," I laugh as he takes hold of my cheeks and begins kissing me all over.

"Shit, I don't have the ring," he flusters. "I have a ring, I promise."

"Nate, I just want you," I tell him. "Rings can wait."

"When can we get…"

His voice trails off when something catches his eye from out the front windscreen. He takes hold of my hand, looking concerned all of a sudden. When I follow his line of sight, I find myself staring at the boy who I once loved with childlike innocence and naivety. He looks destroyed, and although he caused me so much pain, I know I need to end this once and for all.

"You want me to sort this?" Nate asks, looking at him with both anger and pity.

"Not this time, Nate," I tell him, still staring at Dean's dejected expression. "I need to do this…alone."

"How did I know you were going to say that?" he says before sighing heavily. "I will be right here, ok?"

"Ok," I whisper, bracing myself to tie up all of my loose ends.

Dean physically braces himself when I finally step outside the car, all the while Nate glares at him from behind the windscreen. I know he would dearly love to go and give him a piece of his mind, but I respect him for letting me do this. Ultimately, this all began with him and me, and now I need to end it with just us two.

As I slowly pace up toward him, he stuffs his hands inside his jeans' pockets and sinks his head down, with his shoulders naturally rising as he does so. He's back to being a teenager after we had had a fight, for which he is trying to apologize. Unfortunately for him, it won't work this time. There is no resolution, just an ending.

"Dean," I finally utter, causing him to flinch. "Why are you here?"

"I dunno," he laughs without mirth as he runs his hand over his hair. "My wife's inside, but the woman I'm in love with is right in front of me; I guess I just felt like I needed to be here."

"You hurt both of us, Dean," I tell him plainly. "Hurt you can't come back from. There is no you and me, not since you made the decision to take my sister to bed with you."

"I was scared, Bea, a scared little boy," he tries to argue. "I'm not that guy anymore."

"You're a guy who stayed with my sister and married her, even though you claim to be in love with me," I state with incredulity in my voice. "You are exactly the same guy. Scared of what you might not have. Screwing someone over to get the best possible outcome for yourself. How could you possibly think I would forgive you after what you did to me?"

"Truthfully, I didn't," he replies sheepishly, "but if I didn't try, I'd always regret it."

"Dean, you have an awful lot of things to be regretful of," I level with him, "not asking me to run off with you when you're engaged to my sister shouldn't be one of them."

"You really happy with that guy?" he asks, jutting his chin in the direction of Nate with a sneer on his face. "Doesn't seem like your type at all."

"What would you know about my type after all these years? I learned very quickly that my 'type' wasn't someone who was going to be good for me. My 'type' brought me to my knees, to the point whereby I could only see vodka and packets of painkillers as a way out of the hell he had helped to put me through."

"So, you're blaming me for trying to commit suicide? Come on, Bea, that's not fair; you made that choice yourself."

I ignore the knot of anger in my gut, for this proves Dean still only thinks about himself. There's no arguing with him, for he can only see what happened to me as something he's now having to work through. He has no empathy for me, it's still all about him.

"No, Dean, I'm not blaming you," I tell him with a smile. "But being around you, and letting you into my life, is not what's good for me, Dean. Whether I blame you or not, the fact remains, the way I let you make me feel was extremely dangerous for me. You can think as you wish, blame me if you like, but as far as I'm concerned, you no longer exist in my world, and you never will. So, go, live in your world, and I will live in mine. Our paths no longer need to cross, and that can only be a good thing. I wish you well."

"Emma might take me back," he calls out when I turn to leave. I freeze for a moment or two before turning back to face him, still with a genuine smile.

"She might," I agree with a shrug, "but I wouldn't count on it. And in answer to your question, I am more than happy with 'that guy'. He's got what you so callously threw away – all of me. I hope you find that with someone one day, though I honestly don't think it will be with Emma. You can only be as happy as I am when you truly love that person. I hope, for her sake, you don't try and convince her that you do. Let her find someone who really deserves her. Goodbye, Dean."

He doesn't say anything else, just turns and slumps away, still with his shoulders hunched up to his ears. I watch for less than a minute before returning to my new world and the man who brought me back to life.

"You ok, baby?" he asks with a smile that makes me feel warm inside.

"More than ok," I reply. "My past is finally behind me."

"Good, because I've got plans for our very near future," he says before kissing me gently on my lips. "It involves me worshiping you."

"I like the sound of that. Take me home, Mr Carter."

Epilogue

Bea

6 months later

"I don't know if I want the big, white wedding," I tell the girls who are sitting around the table. "I loved the idea of what you and Cam did," I say to Lily, who is now heavily pregnant. "It was so romantic!"

"It really was," she daydreams. "And now I have a huge belly, swollen feet, and trouble going to the bathroom. It's such a magical time!"

"You've gotta have a white wedding," Emma pouts at me. We're slowly getting back to being sisters again, but we've still got a way to go. Most of her so-called friends dropped her after she and Dean broke up. She was sad for a while but found clearing everything out and starting again was somewhat refreshing; cathartic you might say. She's taken over my apartment and has found a job as a finance assistant for some up-and-coming clothing boutique.

"I really want to be your bridesmaid," she says in a daydreamy voice. I could bring up my awful experience of being a bridesmaid at her wedding, but I choose not to. No one wants to bring up anything that might remind her of Dean.

"Plus, we all like a free bar," Callie weighs in, "you can't deny your friends. Not even Lily took away the free bar experience."

"*You* could always get married," I tease. "When are you going to tell us about this mystery guy of yours, anyway? He sounds like he has marriage potential."

"And I'm still waiting for *my* free bar," Lily joins in.

"Maybe I will marry him," she says like it's a simple, everyday decision. "But not until Lily can drink again. Drunk Lily is so much fun!"

"Yeah, might be a while," Lily sighs as she pats her pregnant belly.

"What's lover boy think?" Callie juts her chin out toward Nate, who is currently walking over to us, looking totally edible in his low-slung jeans, fitted tee, and ridiculously expensive aviators. I bite my lip while giving him a naughty smile, to which he chuckles before slipping his arms around me.

"What's that?" he asks Callie.

"Bea's wondering about the whole white wedding thing, what are your thoughts?"

"As long as there's a wedding night, I'm cool either way," he says before planting kisses down the column of my neck.

"We can have a wedding night right now if you want," I whisper, for the feeling of his lips on my naked skin is too much for me to ignore.

"In my brother's house?" he asks with a cheeky grin on his face.

He's gifted with a seductive nod of my head, to which he drops his glasses slightly down his nose so he can look into my eyes. When I stare right back, he simply holds out his hand for mine, then pulls me to my feet.

"Bea and I are going to go and discuss the options inside," he declares, gesturing over to the house while pulling me along with him.

We barely make it into the house before he grips hold of me and invades my mouth with his own. We then hightail it into the nearest private room, which happens to be Cameron's personal gym. Figures, it's Nate's favorite place after the bedroom. He rips off his shirt as I fall to my knees, where I begin releasing him from the confines of his pants. Then I'm on him, nipping and sucking as he thrusts his hips into me. He grabs hold of the weightlifting bars, so I take him more urgently, pushing him to release not long after. He growls appreciatively and whips me up before he's even fully recovered. I lean back into the chair of the weightlifting bench as he rips my panties away, the flimsy fabric practically disintegrating inside of his hands.

"Nate!" I cry out, pretending to sound mad. "What am I supposed to wear after we're done?"

He simply grins as he slips between my thighs, wiping any concerns I had away with one swipe of his tongue. And when his fingers join in by thrusting inside of me, I can't even remember what I was worrying about.

"Oh, God, Nate…" I moan as I grip hold of his hair.

"What were you saying?" he teases.

"No fucking idea, but don't stop, please!" I beg as he brings me closer to the edge. Though before he lets me, he stops and pulls me up to straddle him. I would shout at him for stopping at such a torturous moment, however, the feeling of him inside of me is too heavenly for me to care. As I move on top of him, he lifts away my top, releasing my breasts so he can suck and massage my flesh.

"Bea?"

"God, yes?" I moan as multiple sensations overload my ability to talk.

"Let's do it; let's set a date and tell everyone now," he pants as I slam down on top of him.

"Babe, you've gotta stop asking me serious questions like this," I gasp.

"Why? I usually get what I want this way," he says with a cheeky boy smile on his face.

"Yes!" I shout as I reach climax.

"I love getting my own way," he laughs, then lifts me onto the floor and really lets me have it. After a groan of euphoria, he begins kissing me, though I have to roll my eyes over his tactics to get what he wants from me. "May third," he whispers, "May third is when you become Mrs Carter."

"Who says I'm taking your last name?" I tease.

"We can discuss it tonight," he replies with a smirk, "when I take you to bed. It's usually when you come around to my way of thinking."

"Ass," I mutter.

As I lie back, watching him pull on his jeans and throwing on his t-shirt over his tanned shoulders, I bite my lip to stop myself from moaning over the image. When he catches me gawking, he laughs before leaning down to kiss me on the cheek.

"Again?" he asks with a happy expression.

"I would, yeah," I reply bluntly. He begins kissing me with his expert tongue, but before I can pull him back on top of me, he jumps away, then lifts me up to get dressed.

"This kind of behavior won't cut it when we're married, you know," I huff.

"Babe, when we're married, we won't be leaving the bedroom for I don't know how long," he says as we walk out hand in hand.

"May third," Nate announces to everyone. To my horror, Cam, aka my boss, bursts out laughing and high-fives his little brother. He then offers me a kiss on the cheek while I feel myself turning a deep shade of red.

"Congratulations," he says to me, "my brother's a lucky guy."

"Nate!" I whisper-shout with humiliation. "He's my boss too, you know!"

"Relax, Bea," Cam says as he cuddles Lily into his side, "I'm not letting my best assistant go anywhere. I have big plans for you. Especially after you proved yourself under your last boss. He was a total A-hole!"

"Let's hope I make a better husband," Nate says, flipping the bird at his brother.

"You better," Lily says sternly. "Though, judging by the blushing glow on Bea's face, I'm guessing you're an expert in one area at least."

"Oh, my God!" I gasp while she laughs.

"Oh, screw it," I finally say, giving into it, "Nate *is* an expert in that department."

"Thank you, baby," he says before kissing me on the cheek, "but only with you."

My past is finally behind me, and I've found my happiness with a guy who I know truly loves me.

"To Bea and Nate!" Cam toasts while raising his glass.

"To Bea and Nate!"

'The Knight', Cameron's book, is now available on Amazon KU

'The Devil', Helena's book, will be released onto Amazon KU on July 8th. For a cheeky excerpt, please see below

You can also check out Ellie's story, 'Willows and Waterlilies' (aka 'The Gentleman') on Amazon KU as part of the Wild Bloom's Series.

Find all links below.

Thank you for reading!

Let's connect!

Facebook Taylor K Scott | Facebook

Instagram: Taylor K Scott (@taylorkscott.author) • Instagram photos and videos

Website (including my blog) www.taylorkscottauthor.com

Author Dashboard | Goodreads

Sign up to my monthly newsletter through my author website or through the link below:

Taylor K Scott Author (list-manage.com)

Other works by Taylor K. Scott:

Learning Italian

A romantic, enemies to lovers, comedy

The Darkness Within

An enemies to lovers romantic suspense.

Claire's Lobster

An age-gap, romantic comedy novella

My Best Friend

A Friends-to-Lovers contemporary romance

Mayfield Trilogy

A dark, suspense romance.

A Marriage of His Convenience

A historical romance

Coming this year:

Willows and Waterlilies (The Gentleman)

Ellie's story from the 'Carter' series and in connection with the Wild Bloom's Series.

The Knight

Cameron's Story

Coming later this year:

The Devil

Helena's Story

A Marriage of His Choosing

Elsie's Story from my historical romance series (see A Marriage of His Convenience)

Here is an excerpt from Helena's story, 'The Devil':

The Devil

Prologue

Let us begin with a party.

An innocent night of care-free fun amongst teenagers.

Nate Carter, the popular boy with a heart, was throwing one of his infamous bashes that aimed to let the kids of Western High let down their hair and give into their urges within the safe confines of the Carter household.

Everyone knew who the Carters were, but none more so than me. After all, I grew up with them, lived with them day in, day out, right up until just over a year ago. I was their big sister, their little sister, and their best friend. ***Was*** being the operative word. Now, we barely talk.

I never attended Nate's party. In fact, I wasn't anywhere near my parents' house that night. I was lying on the kitchen floor of my two-bedroom cottage, far away from anyone, knocked out cold. While I lay there, oblivious to the world around me, together with the mess of another dinner thrown across the floor in a fit of rage, my daughter was sleeping soundly upstairs. And for that, I am thankful. My Jessica is everything to me.

Conversely, my husband, Evan, was nowhere to be seen. But he would return; he always does. I might not have been at that party, but I felt the repercussions of what happened that night. I lost a little bit more of myself, brushed away another few bruises for another day, and pushed back more bad memories for my future self to deal with. So long as Jessica needs me, I will absorb the pain, become that little bit more numb, and plaster on my fake smile for all of them.

And it works; no one sees and no one asks. So long as I am what they expect me to be, they are happy with me tied up inside of their little, neat box. My brothers have always been forgiven for stepping outside the boundaries, but as the girl, I was destined to fulfill a role of subservience, obedience, and a contentedness to be what I essentially am – a function. A wife, a mother, and a daughter who always does as she's told, and who never steps outside the lines, never answers back, and never complains. And perhaps I could have lived in this role without question or the need for more. But then I met ***him***.

To tell my story, I have to go back much further in time. In fact, I need to start with someone else's history. Someone who is as damaged as I am. Someone who is feared. Someone who has a reputation so bad, I was warned by my entire family to keep away from him. Someone who demanded that I be his. Someone who won my heart. Someone I lost.

This is not just my story, it's also his. This is the story of how the little mouse fell in love with *The Devil*.

Chapter 1

Past

Lucius

Have you ever wondered what it feels like to have

everything you thought you knew wither away and die in a matter of moments? Alas, the day my mother died was not the first time I was forced into feeling like this. Being only thirteen when she passed, you would think this was my first introduction to heartbreak, especially when I tell you she killed herself with a piece of rope and an old tree in the backyard. To be fair to her, she had at least chosen to wait until I was at school before carrying out her task that day; I suppose I should be grateful for that small mercy.

Magda, my nanny and the housekeeper, was the first to discover her lifeless body, however, it had taken both the gardener and her husband to cut her down. Everything was nicely cleaned up before I returned home from school and with my tea already waiting for me – spaghetti meatballs; it was Tuesday, after all. Meatballs were always served up on a Tuesday, even when your mother decides to take a premature exit from the world. I still refuse to touch my once-upon-a-time favorite meal.

I had already had a thoroughly frustrating day, all because Tommy Slater had decided to start a fight with my best friend, Eric. Being the brains of the friendship, I had to get involved, if only to prevent them from killing one another. Of course, all the thuggery got the better of me, resulting in Eric and I having to participate in a week's worth of after-school detention. The truly sad part of all this was the fact that it was all over hurt pride during a football match, but I couldn't stand by and let Tommy-the-gorilla-Slater pummel Eric into a bloody mess. Our counterattack was extremely simple and not at all sophisticated; I held the lump of a boy from behind while Eric kicked him in an area that would be sure to keep him hobbling along for the next few days.

Had I simply returned home to normality, I might have brushed aside my anger and seen the funny side. However, this wasn't ever going to happen after my father sat me down to inform me that the woman who had given birth to me had decided to end her own life. No, after that little chat, I had had about enough of this particular Tuesday. Life was, forgive my crassness, a shitshow, and you only had yourself to rely on.

"Lucius," Paul had begun, sounding suitably grave as he sat down next to me, depressing the sofa cushions under his large frame. "I guess now is a pretty God-awful time to tell you the truth, but after what's happened today, I think this conversation is long overdue."

He then paused for breath while I waited with a disinterested expression on my pubescent face. Do not judge my obnoxious reaction just yet, for truth be known, I already knew what he was going to tell me. His 'big reveal' was going to be thoroughly anticlimactic, for me at least.

"Now, this doesn't change anything between us," he reassured me before he'd even ventured to tell me the actual bad news, "but I'm not your biological father, son."

I remember smirking over his choice of words. You see, the bitterness of it had begun to seep in years ago, when I had first found this out.

"But in every other sense of the word, I am still your dad."

Looking pale and grief-stricken, he finally sat back and sighed with a hint of relief. He remained staring at me, as if he was giving me the time and space to let that revelation sink in.

"Ok," I replied with an arrogant shrug of my shoulders. My cold reaction to such news had caused him to lurch forward with a look of shock and hurt written all over his puffy, red face. I don't remember feeling angry at Paul, just knew that I was angry. I had already been an angry child for so long, I had forgotten what it felt like to not feel such an emotion in my everyday life. I knew he loved me, and I knew he had loved her, but it still didn't make up for the fact that *she* hadn't loved me. My.Mother.Did.Not.Love.Me.

"*Ok*?! Is that all?" he eventually gasped, to which I merely nodded before asking if I could go outside and kick the ball around. My laidback reaction to everything that had come to pass that day was enough to silence him for a good five minutes or so, all the while I stared back at him with an expression that only spoke of my desire to go outside and play.

"Lucius, you've just lost your mom, I'm not the man you thought I was, have you nothing to say? Nothing to ask me?"

I pretended, for his sake, to at least think about it, but eventually settled on a shake of my head.

"Ok, son, yeah, go ahead."

What my poor father didn't know was that when I was nine, I had blown up in an almighty tantrum that was all aimed at my mother. She wouldn't let me go to Eric's birthday party because she didn't approve of him. So, I kicked and screamed and threw things all over the place.

When I had eventually expelled all of my energy, I was, quite rightly, sent to my room and told to keep my ass there until I could show her more respect. I remained brooding up in my room until I heard Paul return home from work, because I was just that stubborn; I still am. In fact, it was another two hours before I ventured out, being finally ready to apologize for my deplorable behavior.

On my very first step outside of my room, it was as though I had walked inside of a Stephen King novel. The house had been eerily quiet, dark, and atmospheric. I recall sensing the presence of something nightmarish, an intangible fog that's only purpose was to suck the living soul out of unsuspecting pre-teen boys. In the back of my mind, I knew I was being foolish, allowing my immature fears to take over the rational part of my brain. However, the back of my mind was wrong, for something was about to reveal itself to me, something that would diminish my soul into something lost and dark.

My mother sounded exasperated when I finally heard her tired, somewhat frantic voice. Paul and Mom always took to the living room after dinner, so I came to the logical conclusion that I had missed the evening meal in my attempts to punish her through sulkily remaining inside of my room for hours. Though, that didn't bother me nearly as much as the obvious disdain lacing every word that was coming out through my mother's lips. Lips that smiled at me, lips that uttered placations - 'I love you baby', 'I'm proud of you, son', and 'whatever you want, honey' – lips that kissed me goodnight. However, the words escaping through those lips now were anything but affectionate or reaffirming. Now, I got to hear what she really thought of her 'baby'.

"Oh, come on, Elenore, you love Lucius," I heard Paul practically begging her. "He's a nine-year-old boy being a nine-year-old boy. That's all!"

"Do I, Paul? Do I love him?" Her words hit me like a sledgehammer covered in torturous spikes that were ready to pierce through every crevice of my heart. "How can I love someone that reminds me of *him*? He has those same eyes, that same smirk, even that same cruel laugh. He is an exact replica of his biological father!"

"You can't think like that, Elenore." Paul's shoes shuffled across the room before coming to a dead-end stop, presumably closing the gap between him and the woman who can't even bear to look at me. "He knows nothing of his birth father, and besides, it's not Lucius' fault. That boy idolizes you, adores you, how can you say these things?"

"I can't help it; I see the same evil in him," she replied, sounding desperate, as though a monster was about to unleash itself from her son's human casing any day now. "I didn't at first, he was just a little kid, but today, I saw it. I can't ignore it anymore, Paul. How can I love someone who has that in him? My poor boy is going to end up alone. No one can love him, he's the product of a monster, can't you see that?" Her words began to spill out in a jumbled mess of contradictions before she finally cried out the words that could never be taken back, could never be forgiven, and would never allow me to trust another woman again. "I should have terminated him!"

"I don't know how you can talk like this! Have you been drinking?" Paul gasped at the same time as his shoes took a few steps back over the parquet flooring. "Elenore, darling, I love you, but I'm worried about you. Lucius can never hear you talking like this."

"Maybe," she mumbled, more to herself than to anyone else. "Maybe you're right; maybe I need to go to bed."

Her rational brain might well have been beginning to take over at this moment, however, my head was anything but rational. Paul was not my blood, and my mother, my unconditional love and protector, had just wished I never existed. She'd condemned me to loneliness and a lifetime of therapy I would stubbornly refuse to go to. So, ask yourself, what would a nine-year-old boy do in my position? I cannot speak for any other kid who has found himself questioning everything in a life that had been built on lies, but as for me, I got the hell out of there and enclosed my heart in an icy case, vowing to never let anyone near it again. Self-preservation turned me into the devil of an asshole I would become.

Years on and now with a dead mother, my mind is clearer, harder, and lacks the capacity to suffer fools like Tommy Slater. The imbecile shouldn't have tried to jump me on the day after my mother had ended her life. He should have left me well alone. But being one brain cell away from an inanimate object, he ignored my warning and tried to attack me anyway. I was forced to teach Tommy a hard lesson by gifting him with a broken nose and a black eye. It was worth it to see his pain, and to also show the gathered crowd what would happen if they tried to replicate Tommy's blunt course of action. People soon came to realize that I had absolutely no qualms about beating someone to a bloody pulp if I so chose to. I had no qualms about telling anyone exactly what I thought of them, even when it led to a parent teacher meeting that would have Paul reaching for the top shelf whiskey bottle afterward. I had no qualms about destroying anything or anyone if I felt it was necessary for my own amusement.

I don't want their pity or their understanding, I want them to realize that if you come after me, I will destroy you. If you try and get close to me, I will burn you. If you try and hurt me, I will not break, I will make you crumble instead.

Fortunately for most, if they leave me well alone, I usually lack the inclination to bother with them. Unfortunately, for my little mouse, she ignited a passion for more, emotions I had wished to repress. She never intentionally set out to cross me, but cross me she did, and in the cruelest way possible. She brought my heart back to life; she made me fall in love with her.

THE FOOL

Printed in Great Britain
by Amazon

45512260R00245